SUNLIGHT PEOPLE UNDERGROUND

A novel

by

Samuel J. Thompson

Sunlight People Underground
by Samuel J. Thompson

ISBN: 979-8-9985036-0-3

Sunlight People Underground

"Ye are all the children of light, and the children of the day: we are not of the night, nor of darkness."

\- 1st Thessalonians 5:5, KJV

BOOK I

'Z-Bloc'

ONE

There were 11,480 apartments in Z-Bloc. Mine was on the thirty-eighth floor, a Deluxury Singles box - roomier than the regular Single units, yet smaller than the Family ones. Levels thirty-seven through forty-one were all Deluxury Singles; sixty at each point of the compass, two-forty per floor. The residences went from the seventh level up to the forty-seventh, with a floor/ceiling dividing each quintet of the fifty-story megastructure into its ten Subsections. Overpopulation was thoroughgoing, save for the three penthouse floors, which were dead and Sunscorched.

Unit 3211 was on the fifteenth level; a Standard Family unit. Here Buddy lived, in the unit he had inherited from his mother, who was a de-facto dignitary of the Bloc. She wasn't around much. If she was, I would never visit, yet she was indeed present on that day, passing through to retrieve some bejeweled adornment-trinket too valuable to be kept unhidden.

I listened to Buddy in the other room, mired deep in argument with the other preeminent female in his life to whom he was inextricably bound: the girl of his impotent dreams and mother of his offspring, an irascible double-wide woman whose lips slapped together infuriatingly as she whinged, similar to the manner in which her thighs slapped together as she strode. Buddy's impregnation of her had not interrupted the cyclical nature of their liaison; it merely interchanged it. Prior to the birth of their boy, their quarrels would result in the impermanent extinguishment of their confederation, whereas now these served as mere interval-markers sundering the periods of strife and reconciliation, between which they alternated hourly, as if they had some private wager to see how badly they could impair their child's evolving conception of conjugality. Buddy was a fool, yet he was my friend still-

and-all. I always felt conjoined to him by some inexplicable type of kinship. Regardless, I wondered what the ruddy fuck I was doing there...

Buddy's mother entered in her evening finery; a top of silky fabric and a skirt that could be mistaken for a belt. I marveled (as I always did upon the sight of her) at how Buddy had come out unsightly. Her form was lithe and jiggled only in pleasing places, unlike her son, who jiggled everywhere. The lines fluting out beside her eyes were the only indicators of her advancing age, and even those were barely noticeable past her facepaint. She asked me if everything was okay, and I nodded and said I was fine. I didn't need anything. I didn't want any trouble. She sat beside me on the daybed and her teeth shone clean and straight and bright as she bit the corner of her lip. Ivory against burgundy - oh yeah, she was a singular beauty in the Bloc and well-known as such by many names: the impious Queen Cleopatra of the Bronco, Czarina of the Mechanical Bull, She Who Gapes For One-Thousand... or something like that - I don't speak the Old Tongue very well, and it doesn't ring the same in the New. A more befitting moniker would be She Who Gets Men Killed By Other Men, but that wouldn't sound so sensational in either language.

Buddy came into the room, spotted us, rolled his eyes, and told his mother to get lost. The manner in which he spoke to Cleopatra was all his own, inimitable by anyone else in the Bloc. He wanted her gone before the kid awoke from his nap. I imagined that if the child had slept through his parents' argument, he was probably lost to that strain of sleep from which one never wakes. Baby Mama appeared on Buddy's heels, and I perceived that he was hoping to use me as a buffer to quell the abundant discontent. Better be on my way. I didn't want to get caught up. I didn't want any trouble. Buddy wanted me to stay, but Cleopatra bade me walk with her to the lift and ride down to the Bazaar. Another day in the Bloc, another onerous decision to be made. Between these two evils, there was no lesser.

***

Cleo took my arm as we made the hundred-or-so yard walk to the nearest Main Lift. The mezzanine on fifteen was crowded, as it always was at the conclusion of the day. Couples walked arm-in-arm, mothers and kidsitters herded children, men in their employment accouterments hurried back to their homes. The music of a thousand voices echoed through the Subsection.

From what I heard, Z-Bloc was better than most, yet was still far from the utopia initially envisioned by the Corporation. Here was crime, Gunbosses, gangs (The Sons of the Sun being the foremost of these) and, of course, the Zealots of Horsche, those religious fanatics, with their leaflets and speeches and loudspeakers, calling for all to be reborn into Holy Wisdom, for baptism in the Eternal Light of Gordyume. We had murders, Sudokus, and ideological supremacists of all types... and we had Lawmaker. No one had seen him in years, but I was certain he still presided over us.

When the South Lift arrived, several-dozen of us piled in before the steel doors ground shut. Earthward we went. The Main Lifts crawled, but fifteen down to the floor was a brief ride. When the door reopened, the smog and stink hit me and I breathed it deeply. Cleo removed her arm from the crook of mine and disappeared into the mess of bodies in the Bazaar. She moved fast, I moved slow. She had an objective, an intention, purpose clearly-cut, whereas I had none of those.

The Bazaar was swarming and alive, hazy with dust and smoke and heat of humanity. The cacophony was deafening. Here, forever contained by the Great Gates, lay the epicenter of our civilization - ramshackle shanties built up one-upon-the-other, brick-and-clay-and-aluminum storefronts and markets, with the Burghal under the center dome, and above that, the residences; all concrete and steel untouched by Sunlight, and by now, none living who could remember it...

A line stretched out of the door of Ringo's Barbershop and went down the mainstreet, past the various vendors. The Burghal had semi-authentic physicians, but in the Bazaar, the barbers had long-since assumed the role of surgeons. The water had been worse than usual lately. It was rarely good, but the current quarter-season had bred an aggressive smatter of novel afflictions. Many were wanting bad for bloodletting. Above the line of patients, a Prophet of Horsche called out the Sermon of the Day from atop an upset wheelbarrow.

I walked lackadaisical past a few shops selling rat-and-dogmeat. Men slouched on rugs and smoked hookah or drug-dust as merchants hocked handcrafted wares of every sort; clothes, pottery, vases, tools. A group of kids rushed by pushing a wire quasimodo. Across the street, an old woman upended a shitbucket into a drain.

***

The Blanco Bronco was on a corner where three alleys converged, its large vertical cold-cathode sign illuminating the intersection green and purple, and music spilled out with the neon light into the viscid air. The bouncer was named Jobe. I knew him well and hailed him on my approach.

"Quiet night?"

"Not so. The Sons are in numbers, pissing up the walls to see who can get the highest."

"What's the band?"

"Call 'em Flayed Fetus."

"Sons band?"

"If not directly, the fandom crosses right over."

"Take it easy."

I went inside. The mechanical bull rocked every night without exception - five nicks to ride for men, three for ladies, save during the midweek happy-hours when it was free for them. The joint was crowded. The Sons of the Sun wore tight black leather and jewelry; rings, chains, piercings in every spare lobe and flap and convexity of the flesh, both their adornments and they themselves grotesque in appearance and excessive in quantity. One of them got in my face and sneered. There was a scar on his exposed chest, permanently-discolored from grafts and stitches; a war-wound worn with pride. He grooved cool and glimmered slick with perspiration. Lining the bar was a bite-sized slice of all the walks of Bloc life; an assortment of gangsters, smokers, warfighters, gay Cowboys, regular Cowboys, Millworkers, Hammerjacks, oldboys, john-boys, and, of course, whores all frilly and preening. The number-one-and-two commodities of the Bazaar: whores and druk. I had come for the latter.

I ordered a shot of swill too, because my pay was on its way. I had an enviable schedule with HydroElectric; five nine-hour shifts and two consecutive off-days. There were only fourteen other jobs like that, all held by oldboys. I wasn't even up for promotion to the spot, but I did the supe a good favor by figuring out when Inspections made their random visits. My connection in Inspections had told me, because I did him the ongoing favor of ratting on those of my neighbors who ran rackets - harboring Unregisturds, building bombs, keeping guns or harvesting organs... Residents like me were referred to as Stoolies. This was not a term of endearment, but to some extent, almost everyone did it. The Bloc demanded coopera-tion.

***

Druk and firewater-swill - gonna shit liquid tomorrow, like. The drink made the world move a little slower. The band was rowdy, the singer a tremendous blob of androgynous meat vociferating out lyrics regarding blood and Sunlight that bore thematic resemblance to the sermon called by the Proph-et outside Ringo's, except that the delivery was more akin to the nocturnal screaming heard on the Favela-levels. I thought that if Sunlight made a sound, that would be it... and that's all anyone ever talked about, sang about, dreamt about. I've seen the pictures in the books, and I don't get what the big deal is.

Kassie Pink. A paradigmatic streetborn gutter-urchin, a frazzled Unregisturd grown up into sex incarnate; the best ass of our generation - and there she was, standing up on a table, tits out, fuschia pixie-cut, ripped fishnets under her dunga-rees, hips gyrating, hands above her head. She's a nasty one, boy. She'll take your goddamn heart out your chest. I've seen many a fullish foolhardy schmuck lay hands on her and get his throat opened a moment later, carried out by the Sons to die bleeding in an alley. Kassie was protected by the Sons, but she wasn't their girl. She was nobody's girl, beholden to none but the Bloc itself. Such wasn't much, but neither were we. This was our world - it belonged to Kassie and I, and all the other urchins who never knew our folk. She spotted me and came to say hi and said my name as she sat in my lap. I politely requested that she get off.

"I don't want any trouble."

"Don't lie, stringbean. You're bad at it."

She winked at her boys across the bar, who were looking at me side-eyed. Fucking sickly goth-boy ratfuckers. She reassured me that they wouldn't bother us none.

"Like. Still hop off, will you?"

Out rolled her abnormally-long tongue, pierced through the middle with a shiny pin, but she got off and we got to talking. Kassie always had a lot to say about things; the gangs, the music, all the different schools-of-thought that came up around here and grew like head-mold. According to her, there would be another Uprising soon.

"Here?"

She nodded gravely. I snorted out a laugh.

"Who? The Sons?"

"The Zealots, baby."

I supposed that was the most plausible scenario, but far-fetched nonetheless. I told Kassie that anyone who spoke of Uprising was living in the old days, caught up in the fantasies of our forefathers, stuck in the bygone times when the tram-lines still connected the Blocs.

"They're going to open the Great Gates."

"Come on."

"It's true, I'll betcha anything."

Kassie was sharp - or used to be. Maybe druk really does fuck up your head like they say. She perceived my skepticism and tried in earnest to convince me.

"Visit Monogatari. Ask him."

"I hate the Favelas."

"He's staying in the Burghal. Three days, now."

"Monogatari is in the city?"

If that was true, I would go to see him. I asked Kassie to

accompany me, but she declined and screamed loud and lustily at me, licked the whole right side of my face, and ran back to her entourage of Sons, who hoisted her above their heads and bore her towards the stage as she screeched like a beast possessed, thrashing and laughing and burning up the oxygen the way a fire does.

The Corporation built twenty-six Blocs on this tram-network, megastructures initially intended to house ninety-thousand each. Kassie and I were born after the Third Uprising. Many say it was the Second that finally broke the chains of Corporation authority, but I say otherwise. What was Lawmaker, if not the last remaining remnant?

One fact stands indisputable: the Second Uprising broke the tramways, and now only those brave enough to traverse the tunnels move between the Blocs - those millions of feet of pipes and hallways, utter blackness through-and-through, with the constant danger of being swept away by an unspeakable river of filth. Still, people attempt it, and some succeed, which is part of the reason for our overpopulation. Most blame the Unregisturds, (actually, everyone blames them, because even those that don't still refer to them by that sobriquet) but it wasn't entirely our fault - we were simply an acceleration of a problem that worsened with each new generation. People like Buddy and his woman push out kids, and in-turn push all of us ever-closer to the breaking-point. What is to be done? We love to fuck. The Histories claim we always have, and this assertion is authenticated by our very existence.

The Administrative City sat under the floor-level dome, six stories tall, surrounded on all sides by the Bazaar. In the early days, there were gardens and farms on the floor level, but as the sunlamp-bulbs became more precious, these were dug-up and paved-over and converted to the Bazaar marketplaces. The Burghal (as the complex was called) was made of steel. It is said to have glimmered brilliantly when the Bloc was first erected; a sprawling mall of polyvinyl flooring and fluorescent lights in which everything was clean; a deliberate layout of Administrative Offices, shops, cafes, fitness-centers, conservatories, libraries, common-areas - all warm and bright under the artificial sunlight. Now it was just as grimey as the rest of the Bloc.

Through consummate necessity, all the Departments were headquartered in the Burghal. Here was a degree of safety that couldn't be guaranteed anywhere else. Everyone was a Stoolie, so you wouldn't be stabbed for your shoes or teeth. It was a nest of informants, all servicing society in some way or another. Department workers toiled around the clock to keep the water flowing, the lights shining, the waste-incinerators hot - we were a gang unto ourselves, more important than anyone else, because to do away with us would be the end of all things.

I found Monogatari waiting in the water-line for Station 112. In the Favelas, all the dispensation-stations were either deactivated or destroyed, so most of those residents came down to the lower levels for water. I took advantage of his position in the queue, cutting in beside him. Solo, such an act would have been opening the door for trouble, but nobody was going to challenge Monogatari.

I said hello. He grunted. We didn't travel or spend time together, but I knew he liked me, owing to the history we shared. Laying that aside, however, Monogatari was impossible to read. You could be his greatest enemy and you wouldn't know it one second before he wanted you to, and one second after that, you'd be dead.

"Best-tasting water comes from one-one-two." I said.

"Hm. Fresher."

"Worlds. Talked to Kassie lately?"

His frown deepened. "Get along, doggie."

"She told me the Prophets of Horsche are going to open the Great Gates."

"Her mouth gotta be big, to house that tongue."

"Talk to me. A grain of salt will make me thirsty."

The lessening of his frown was equivalent to boisterous laughter from Monogatari. I got a good feeling and knew I was in the clear - not overstepping, not bothering him. No trouble.

"You ain't around the rumblings-and-grumblings, and

that's respectable."

"I'm around, I just ain't no truster."

Monagatari looked at me and sighed - it was clear my curiosity would not be rebuffed by a few casual vagaries. He cast a hesitant glance at the others in the line, and then leaned close to my ear, keeping his voice low as regaled me with a particularly-outlandish tidbit of Bloc-gossip.

"They say a couple Gadabout Unregisturds found a creature in the sewers - say it been residing down there for a long time, feeding on rats and cockbugs, eyes melted out by sanitation chemicals, skin all burnt, yet residing nonetheless. Say it knows every inch of the tunnels. Take it one route, it'll remember the turns forever, no matter their number. Some ratfuck been feeding it, got it trained, had it leading him between the Blocs - say he made a hundred trips in as many days! He claimed he found a place down there, a control-override, and he boasted to every tommy-dick that would listen that he's got the power of the Undersun itself in his hands. What does power like that mean around here, you think? A Gunboss got ahold of him, beat him, broke his legs, worked him over but good... Now, here comes the joke: it turnt out the creature only answers to our friendo, so the Boss had to fix him up, put him up nicely in a good suite, all that. Man is in a wheelchair, tended by the creamiest whores, fed the best food, sipping fine swill, got a Boss waiting on him hand-and-foot, all so that he might talk to his pet and assuage it. Supposedly it got real upset when its master was so badly mistreated."

"That doesn't sound an ounce like truth."

"Like."

"Who's the Boss?"

"What's it to you?"

"Curious is all."

"Poppa Daddy."

I knew that Monogatari knew Poppa. They went back.

"You've seen this thing? The creature?"

"Not myself. Once word got out, some other ratfucker came creepin' and purloined it."

"It was stolen?"

Monogatari nodded. "Carried off in a dog-crate."

We got our water and continued our walk through the Burghal, up the walkway towards the North Lift. There were four main liftshafts that ran the entire height of the Bloc tirelessly throughout the days, carrying residents and Unregisturds alike between the floors. The carriages themselves were large enough to fit fifty people - a capacity that could be doubled by squeezing in junk-to-trunk - and on the wall beside the control-panels, the Corporation left us with directories depicting their initial vision for life in the megastructures.

Floor Level: *Gates, Agricultural and Livestock Environs*

By-far the largest single room of the Bloc; a massive space lit by sunlamps and organized meticulously to provide food for the population. It was on the lowest level owing to its proximity to the labyrinthine entanglement of sewers and powerlines buried beneath our feet; that lifegiving complex upon which we depended for light and water. In a vain effort to combat overpopulation, the Livestock Enclosures were the first to be converted to shanties, and, as myriad unforeseen problems piled one atop the next, the Agricultural Environs were also overhauled, and the Bazaar took form - the forum of our civilization, where we bartered and traded and consorted amongst ourselves.

Central Floor/Levels 2-6: *The Grand Plaza, Conservatory, Administrative Offices and Divisions, Resident Services, Bloc Security and Armory, Medical Center, Historical Archives, Fitness Club*

In the dead-center of ground level, under the six-story dome, sat the defunct home of the Corporation. The Administrative Offices formed a conurbation of steel buildings that could only be entered via turnstiles on the main footpaths, at which there were Security checkpoints. As the Corporation gave way to our current structure of feudal government, the Burghal became the property of the Gunbosses. After the last Uprising, however, it was bequeathed back to the Department laborers, whose expertise only became more valuable as the various lifegiving systems began to deteriorate.

Levels 4-6: *Corporation Family Housing*

These dome-adjacent residences were initially reserved for the families of Administrative and Departmental workers, as they enjoyed ease-of-access to the additional service-lifts that ran to the Burghal. By now, these units had been modified and expanded, their walls knocked down to create the super-suite domiciles of the ringleaders of our world.

Levels 7-11: *Subsection A, Singles Units #601 - #2600*

'Here is where dreams come true! Safe, affordable housing in the company of those you can trust! An idyllic community founded upon the values of~'

The lettering of the North Lift plaque was worn-off at this point. Doesn't matter - that was all bullshit. Owing to their location directly above the Burghal dome, these levels became our main foodfarms. The upkeep of the large sun-lamp-arrays on the ceiling of the eleventh level was amongst the most critical duties of the Department laborers.

Levels 12-16: *Subsection B, Family Units #2601 - #3600*

The residential levels were prorated every sixth floor with a ceiling and courtyard for the levels respectively above and below it. These divided the Bloc Subsections, which alternated between the Singles and Family units. There was an old joke that the Corporation designed it this way so that nobody could throw themselves down all fifty levels in a Sudoku. While structural integrity may have been the chief concern, I would not discount this consideration as a factor in the blueprinting.

Levels 17-21: *Subsection C, Singles Units #3601 - #5600*

The Favelas were an ever-worsening stain upon this place. The Third Uprising brought out the picks and jackhammers, and ten floors of units were hollowed-out, ceilings caved-in, ladders stuck up; everything interconnected into an involute anthill of sin; a thousand alleys and alcoves for murderers to lurk through, for the druk-sick and dopers to doze and die in.

Levels 22-26: *Subsection D, Family Units #5601 - #6600*
More Favela shanties. As aforementioned, the courtyard floor on twenty-two had been breached to conjoin the whole mess together. As if the burrows and crosscuts through the units themselves were not enough, they built skyward as well, so that now a vertical cluster of shacks and huts extended up from the seventeenth floor to the twenty-sixth.

Levels 27-31: *Subsection E, Singles Units #6601 - #8600*
Singles residences and the secondary foodfarms.

Levels 32-36: *Subsection F, Family Units #8601 - #9600*
Family residences.

Levels 37-41: *Subsection G, Deluxury Singles Units #9601 - #10,800*
The cleanest and quietest of the Subsections, and the one I proudly called home.

Levels 42-47: *Subsection H, Deluxury Family Units #10,801 - #11,300*
Deluxury Family residences, larger and more ostentatious than the regular ones.

Floors 48-50: *Penthouse Units*
In the Second Uprising, a bomb was utilized on the forty-ninth floor to kill the penthouse aristocracy. The propellant was an unstable mixture of sewage-treatment chemicals that proved far stronger than intended. The ceiling of the Bloc was blown open and the Sun came pouring in. The Histories tell us that Sunlight is like liquid - it can gush and pour and flow...

Such was life in Z-Bloc - my home, and home to every person I've ever known. The Gadabouts claim it as the end-of-the-line, the last megastructure in the network, with nothing beyond. I cannot say for certain if this is true, but I put stock in it. The stone and steel of this place feel perennial in this manner.

TWO

I hate the Favelas, as do all who are unaffiliated with the gangs and syndicates that control them. There stood no reason for any Lawmaker-fearing resident to go there, lest one sought pain or trouble. Monogatari lived smack in the center of level twenty-two, but he was Monogatari - he fit into the Favelas like a cock into a condom; he could ball the whole mess up and stuff it into his pocket, if he so desired.

He told me he intended to see for himself if the creature was real, but I knew better. Monogatari never did anything for nothing. This fact, coupled with his longstanding familiarity with Poppa Daddy, give me cause to suspect that he had been contracted to hunt down the filcher who had abducted the prize. If the creature truly did exist, and had been lifted from the care of the most feared Gunboss in the Bloc, it would be somewhere in the Favelas - the only place where it could be concealed, the only place where the Stoolies don't go. There was no indiscreet information in this gangland maze; only secrets; occasionally traded, but mostly but guarded fast.

The stench was terrible and the people were bony and shuddering. Most of them flinched when looked in the eye. The dour music of intertwined pain-screaming and pleasure-moaning echoed through the untold hallways, amplified and transformed like wind through organ-pipes. Here was fear and anguish and psychopathy and the climaxes of sex and death. This was hell.

It was dim and dingy, and our footfalls did not have the comfortable thud I was used to, as the places where the mezzanine concrete had survived were few. Instead, we walked on wooden planks that rattled and flexed under our weight. If one were to split, we would fall who-knows-how-far. We went up a ramp to a higher floor, but the aggregate of shacks pro-

vided no notion of what level it was. We crossed a chain-sus-
pended bridge out towards the center of the provisional complex, which was catacombs and alleyways all one, and down
a narrow corridor, past some tarpaulin curtains, then a lad-
der-climb up into a black hole in the ceiling which became the
floor. I followed Monogatari's directions unquestioningly until
we arrived at some furtive place tucked away beyond the eye
of Lawmaker, and God, if indeed he existed. It appeared as
a shopfront of sorts, where what was retailed was never put
into words; more spiritual transactions than literal ones, and
Monogatari went to the back and knocked on an iron door.

A slot in the door slid to reveal a choleric visage. Monogatari whispered something and the door opened, its hinges
protesting noisily. The both of us went inside, and it became
somehow darker and the smell of shit became somehow
worse. The minutes we spent in that candlelit backroom felt
like hours. The exchange was in the Old Tongue, garbled, reminiscent of the sermons of the Zealot Prophets, yet I knew
these rag-clad figures were not Prophets, nor were they bound
to any ethical code or constitution whatsoever.

I could not breathe until we left, and when we finally did,
Monogatari's pace quickened and grew more deliberate. We
moved through gutted units; ingresses smashed through solid
stone with sledgehammers, hallways and circumscribed aisles,
up stairs and ladders. I didn't bother to ask where we were
going. Why had I come? What was I seeking?

I figured us to be on the twenty-fourth floor, but it was
impossible to keep track. All the markers that made the Bloc
familiar and navigable had been long-since vandalized or destroyed. We were in the heart of the maze, a place into which
I would never venture alone. All those we passed were dregs
and lepers, and we stepped over their unmoving bodies, dead
or deep asleep. Firelight cast minatory shadows out of open
doors; the shaking silhouettes of players engaged in carnali-
ties not offered by the Bazaar brothels. Around every corner
we were propositioned aggressively by dealers of debasement,
but they drew back when Monogatari's hulking shadow fell
across them. I was glad of his presence. From crevices and

slits between boards we were watched by sullen eyes - below, above, all around us - sourpusses waiting for us to stumble or stop, so that those eyes might grow hands with which to steal from us and molest our beings.

Finally, we arrived at an apparent destination - an authentic concrete unit with a number still on the door. 6313. Monogatari knocked brazenly, pounding with a balled fist.

A scrawny Son opened the door and beckoned us inside. The unit still had its four walls and ceiling intact; one of the few in the Favelas left as such. The walls were covered in graffiti and Sons posters - black banners with a yellow-gold circle in the middle, which took on a brighter gleam in the flickering lamplight. There were others in the unit, and they stood upon the sight of us, as if our arrival was expected. They were all Sons of the Sun, and lifers of the clique, judging by their tattoos. The scrawny kid who greeted us introduced himself in a high-pitched carp as Skudd. Initially, I thought he was doused in blood or oil, but upon closer examination in the half-light, I realized that entire sections of his flesh had been tattooed pure onyx black. He was slight and wiry, limping, his eyes full of that dull look of the mushroom-dustsmokers, but his black hair was long and thick and full. A scabbed excrescence on his face marked the spot where a knife had once gone through his cheek.

Skudd led us down a hallway to a bedroom where several much larger men awaited us. They held hatchets and blades, and one of them had a gun. Few words were spoken. For my fear, I remained silent, unsure if I could speak even if I wanted to. Monogatari took stock of the room and postured himself in such a way that communicated to the Sonsguards that if his demands failed to be met, this room would become their tomb. There existed a wordless understanding amongst these Favela-dwellers to which I could not relate; a supposition that some prior arrangement would be honored. Affirmatory nods were passed around, and the eldest Son opened the washroom door.

The creature was brought out in a large dog-crate, hissing in great displeasure and thrashing its tail against the metal crisscross of its confinement. Its warbling grew louder as it was placed in the light. I looked at it and figured it was just-as-well that it didn't have eyes, because to look into them would surely render one's spirit permanently unclean. Monogatari examined the wretched thing for a moment before grunting in satisfaction and dragging the wheeled crate and its hissing occupant out of the room with me fast on his heels. Several of the Sons accompanied us, to ensure our safe passage back down to the Burghal.

***

We couldn't take the Main Lift. Gossip traveled posthaste through the Bloc, and we toted precious cargo. Instead, we took a slapdash Favela-lift down to the level seventeen - a rickety cage of our own, made of welded reinforcement-bars and hand-lowered by a chain on a winchcrank. The Sons then guided us to a service-access lift that they regulated the us-age of, as evidenced by the gold symbol painted on the door. There were many such service-access lifts in the Bloc. Most only went the distance of a single Subsection, and more than half were decommissioned, although on E, all ten of the ser-vice-lifts still worked, which made it a desirable place to live.

I often wondered how many hours of my life had been spent ascending or descending the staircases between the lev-els. Whenever I contemplated this, it became even more fas-cinating to me that Buddy and his Baby Mama both stood so thickset. How does one become fat on a diet of beans and ratmeat, treading a billion steps per year? Maybe they only took the lifts? But then I wondered how many hours of life we all wasted waiting for the lifts? Whatever the number, it was too high...

The service-lift ride was endured in silence, save for the hissing of the creature. When we were let out on twelve, one of the Sons put a heavy black cloth over the crate. We walked amongst the people and received side-eyed examinations as we did. I had presumed we were going to Poppa's suite on six, but no - Poppa wasn't taking any chances. He wanted the creature brought to the Department of Security and put in the old Corporation Armory. Here, my own purpose in this endeavor became clear: they needed my Department badge, which would permit us entry into the Burghal through one of the lesser-utilized personnel inlets.

We arrived at the Burghal barricade, a turnstile-station housed by a concrete enclosure, the top of which was peppered with broken glass and razor shards. After my badge was swiped, Monogatari ordered us in no uncertain terms to get gone. The Songuards dispersed, but Skudd elected to walk with me back through the Bazaar, to the Bronco, which never closed. As we went, he told me about the fights they'd been having in the Favelas; how a family of Unregisturds had been flayed and hung off the mezzanine of twenty-one, a gangrape he participated in, and other inelegant detailings of the daily happenings to which he was privy.

The musicians at the Bronco had stowed their instruments, yet remained tarrying about to chat up the Sons-girls. Ass-grabbers, the lot of them. I scanned the scene for Kassie, but she was gone. Buddy's mother was riding the mechanical bull, set on slow-mode, swaying erotically in the saddle; her skirt riding way up so that I (and everyone) could lay our randy imaginations to rest. She moved to no music save the rhythm of the collective heartbeat of the Bloc. I watched her and wondered how the world must look through her eyes, thinking that she was indeed the queen of this place. She would not save us, but might yet redeem all our spirits by finalizing their disintegration...

Skudd asked me if I knew my folks - a trick question, code for 'are you registered.' That was a big deal to the Sons of the Sun. It was unfortunate that so many Unregisturds ended up in the Favelas, as the Sons were merciless in their persecution of them. Oh well. I suppose the same Sun shines on all of us, even if we can't see it. Yes, I lied. I told him I knew my folks.

"Department man?"

I didn't have to lie for that one, as Skudd already had the proof of my attestation. Yes, I said, I worked for Hydro-Electric. Skudd loosened up. There were many Unregisturds working Department jobs, but the function of HydroElectric was so imperative that, in his mind, (and the uninformed minds of many) only a card-carrying resident could possibly be trusted to hold such a position. It was a good job of which I was proud - good pay, extra water-and-produce rations, and a measure of sway with the other Departments. In truth, all Department people were part of a family akin to the Sons or the Zealots. We had each other's backs, regardless of registration-status. The gangs were merely tolerated, whereas we were essential. This place belonged to us more than anyone else, as all breathed and ate and drank because the water flowed and the sunlamps shone tirelessly, all owing to the diligence of our efforts. We were the circulatory system of the Bloc, which was one body with a million watching eyes and listening ears and mouths all whispering and loquacious; a living beast able to restructure itself, unable to cease restructuring itself, becoming constantly bigger and stronger and smaller and weaker and contained forever, like everything else, in this great tower of stone and steel.

"So... uh, whaddya think?"

I assumed without asking for clarification that Skudd was referring to the creature. I told him I didn't think it was a good thing. He nodded gravely in agreement, and had a lot more to say about it than I did. He wanted to discuss why it looked the way it did and trade theories about how it had survived down in the sewers, and how it had mutated into that abomination that was now being passed between the most prolific and dangerous residents of Z-Bloc.

***

I was home. Level thirty-eight, unit 9805, with my little stove, my little fridge, my loftcot, my small patch-repaired daybed, and my leisure nook where I rolled tobacco. Four-hundred square feet of livable space, complete with a functioning sunlamp and shower-stall - ah, the benefits of being a Department man. Thirty-eight was nice. The fountains on the Subsection floor (one level below mine) no longer ran, but it wasn't so bad. It kept things peaceful. Every part of the Bloc was crowded; the lifts, the Subsection gardens, every mezzanine and stairwell and residence, but the Deluxury Singles levels didn't see much trouble. The Zealots were the controlling faction here, but they had the good sense to turn off their sermon loudspeakers in the late-evening hours. I suppose you don't win many converts by irritating them.

Up the stepladder and into my bed. Sleep didn't come. I thought about going back down to the Bazaar for more druk. How many dimmies did I have left? I didn't want to check. I wanted to check out, permanent-like. There hadn't been a good Sudoku in a long while, at least outside of the Favelas. It had been nearly a year since someone jumped from the top of a Subsection and splattered, legs through their head, insides out. I figured we must be due for another one soon. There were always fallers. The rumor-rags and bulletins loved to tell of them: 'Faller! Hit on twelve! Kaboosh! Splat!'

The Sanitation Department would get the call within the hour. Clean it up, boys.

***

The next day was average. I woke late, as I often did on my off-days, and wandered down to twenty-seven. Like the lifts, all the sunlamps on Subsection E still worked, so we grew beans and tobacco in the courtyards where the fountains had been retrofitted to serve as irrigators. I strolled in the aisles between the plantbeds. The leaves of the smokeplant-ferns were starting to show those yellow splotches that signified ripening. They'd be ready for harvest soon, and the Bazaar merchants would haggle viciously for first-bid rights.

Jobe was selling coffee out of his cart by the East Lift, as he always did in the morning hours, prior to clock-punching at the Bronco. Good old Jobe; a hardworking true-bluer if one there ever was - not that he had much choice, as he had nine children and two wives; an even dozen mouths to feed, including his own. They all lived in two broken-together units on twenty-nine. One of his kiddos, whose name I couldn't recall, was helping him with the java cart. They appeared to be packing up, so I hurried to catch him while the pot was still hot.

"Almost missed me today."

"Almost."

Jobe, to his young daughter: "Run over to them folks and see if they want a cup."

The little brown-haired girl moseyed away happily, having not yet learnt the difference between work and play. Part of me envied her, as she'd grown up nursefed and had a daddy, which were much better circumstances than those of Bazaar urchins like myself.

"Saw ya with a Son last night."

I grunted. Jobe continued: "Looked stern. They don't let greenhorns have the black pools like he was sporting. Didn't think you were chummy with that type..."

"He's just another asshole in a sea of them."

"Still. I smelt something."

"With me?"

"No, just generally."

"The Sons are low. Always have been. It'll be a better crowd tonight."

Jobe shook his head. He was driving at something, but I couldn't rightly pick up the hint. Kassie's theory rolled through my head again, but I didn't think that Jobe was sociable with her, as his nighttime profession demanded that he never get too cool with known rabble-rousers.

"Zealots? They're crazy. Lots of followers, which probably gives them the best chance of causing wrong, but they clamor for peace, eh? Not a killing yet can be traced to them."

"I'm not worried about any explicit set - I'm talking wholesale."

I nodded and sipped my coffee. It was hot and bitter and stung my tongue as it went down. I liked Jobe, so why was I getting an uneasy feeling? There was a pause, then a question.

"You heard about the Lizard?"

"The Lizard?"

"That's what folks have been calling it. All over the Bloc."

"The Lizard?"

"That's what it is, idnit?"

Jobe was looking at me suspiciously, and once I realized that this was no innocent Bloc gossip, I recoiled instinctually upon ascertaining his true intentions in the conversation.

"Why don't you get along, doggie?"

And he asked me outright, point-blank: "You seen it?"

That was the beginning of my day - the first conversation of three, all of which served to keep me awake another night. Job asked me about the Lizard, and what do you think I told him? I lied, of course. I couldn't have told him the truth, not only for fear of Poppa's wrath, but because the knowledge of it was so grody that I didn't want him to have to live with it as I was. From the day's first waking moment, I felt down-as-dirt and wrestled with the wonder of if the previous night had been a bad dream. Had I really gone to the Favelas with Monogatari and seen what I had?

After Jobe, I went to fifteen, to drop in on Buddy. When his door opened, he looked relieved to see me. He came out onto the mezzanine and we went to lean on the railing. I wanted to go down to the courtyard floor and buy us some sweet-smoke from the hookah vendor, but Buddy started talking before I could voice the suggestion.

"I don't think I can deal with that woman!"

His mother, or the mother of his child? Could flip a nick, equal likelihood either way...

"The complaining! The quarrels! I could jump and fall if I keep having to–"

"Will you please be quiet? You've made this clear plenty-much before."

"Oh, but I ain't yet! She's been acting up worse than usual, say I! Talking the strangest games, talking this whole mess, like what the Prophets do!"

It was clear to me by this point that he was talking about Baby Mama. "What games?" I asked.

"About what's on the other side of the Great Gates and such! Stuff about Sunlight!"

"That's crazy talk."

"Like! I don't know what's to be done! She's been listening to our neighbors on fourteen, and they been filling her head with proclamations of another Uprising! They say the Zealots have bombs, and that they're going to open the Gates and let the Sun come rushing in like a flood!'"

At this point, I decided it was my duty to put a stop to this. Buddy was my friend, and, more importantly, he was another heartbeat amongst us; a resident, and therefore not immune to the paranoia that seemed to be sweeping through us all. There was something in the water. It had been getting worse lately, and I told him so. He told me that Baby Mama had already had her blood let three times this month, once when she was on a cycle, and she had almost bled to death in Ringo's chair and had not been well since. He was quite distressed. I was worried too, but I didn't make it obvious. We need more stoics - more men willing to behave as if nothing is amiss in the face of indomitable evil. There are altogether too many causes and credos these days; too many people taking up arms and marching off to battlefields of their own creation. I did my best to reassure Buddy and get him thinking of something else. I told him that the Department had a plan to improve the water, that the chemists had identified a new bacteria and would soon find a way to exterminate it. None of that was true, but it seemed to make him feel better. At any rate, it made *me* feel better. Maybe if enough of us spoke sanguine, our reveries would harden into fact and all our problems would be resolved without us having to do anything. Dick in hand, head in the sand. That was my credo.

With this second disquieting conversation under my belt, I found myself with a fresh preoccupation to agglutinate with all my other ones. I was thirsty, too. I passed a water station on twelve, but I didn't stop. Although I worked alongside them, I was no tester or chemist. I didn't know how bad the water truly was, but I knew that it hadn't been tasting right. I ambled all the way across the Bloc, to the North Lift, so that I could go through the Burghal and stop at one of the first-rate stations on my way to the Bronco.

The noise and dust and smell of the Bazzar bewildered my senses as it always did. This megalopolis, this great hive, home to thousands upon themselves all rash and bedraggled and impoverished, most hoping they don't get killed tomorrow, or that they might win some dimmies gambling or happen to find some stashed in the cracks of the eternal cement. I moved invisible over the puddles and past the shacks and boutique-tents, treading the same ground I had a million times before, with the same stinking air recycling through me - the air of my shit and the shit of all the other residents, both registered and not. Shit-air and shit-water, mostly, depending on which station you got it from. I could see why some people converted to Zealotry and worshiped Horsche. It was impossible not to hold out hope that someone would save us from all this...

Past a man selling ratmeat seared on a flat piece of metal. He hollered for me to buy, and I was hungry, so I did. Why not? We could all die very soon. I had had two conversations so far, so anything was liable to happen. My thoughts wandered like flecks of dust in the sunlamp rays.

No authentic Sunlight. Never seen it before, and even those who told me about it never saw it themselves. That's the way for all of us now. We speculate on what it must have looked like, felt like, and we make contrivances for how we might recapture a bit of that glory for our own generation. We are contemporaries obsessed with nostalgia, all agreeing that the Sun must have been soft and warm and beautiful beyond compare, and the people who built these structures must have been grand and gentle giants, inspired, intrepid, comely and wise, and inured with an orphic purity of both body and soul by that ultimate power which none of us had never beheld.

Fuck all that in the dirt. I've seen the paintings. They're nothing special - just a lot of yellow light. We have light, but I suppose that isn't the point. The Sun shone without our striving; a light above-and-beyond us, exalted past our lowliness, until it became cross and decided to scorch us to ashes for the sins of our predecessors. A cruel and unforgiving tutelary.

There was a Prophet outside the Bronco, calling out the Sermon of the Day. He talked about the Sun, the Great Gates breaking, the sewers flooding. He talked about it all falling down. He claimed that Lawmaker had abandoned us. He fed our fears and fools harkened and nodded in hypnotized agreement. I listened until I grew bored. It made no difference. To seek relief from pain or fear is a fruitless grinding of the mill. People used to die outside in the Sun, whereas now they die in the shade after spending a lifetime in it.

***

Inside the Bronco, I watched Buddy's mother cross the room in my direction and felt nervous; a sensation that had plagued me all day and only worsened as the hours passed. She sat on a barstool beside me and tossed her hair, all sex and opiates, glittering and looking at me with those sapphire eyes... ohh, like. I felt myself turn over in my pants like a rat awakening, but I've always been too hip to wind up dead in a hole or thrown down a decommissioned liftshaft. I can't deny that I liked looking at her, but when she spoke to me, I shuddered at her words.

"Lawmaker is going to kill Poppa Daddy tonight."

"Liar."

"Wait and see."

"How do you know?"

"Such is being said."

"Why?"

"You know why."

"No, I don't."

"Scared he might come after you as well?"

Mustering up my best impersonation of Buddy, I told Cleopatra to go fuck herself, and I took my beaker of druk to-go. I walked out of that place, all-the-while wondering why I persisted in returning night-after-night. What was it about those familiar faces that made me feel better about myself? In fact, why did I do anything? What was the fucking point?

That was my third conversation of the day, and I didn't like it any more than the prior two. Perhaps my luck was running out, as Poppa's had...

If that was even true...

It couldn't be.

THREE

To be jarred from fitful slumber by the stentorian Bloc fire-alarms is what I imagine it's like to pass from this world to the next. As all the amenities in my unit still functioned, the squall was accompanied by the activation of the alarm-light above my door. The rotating shell threw black shadow across my unit and chased it with refulgent crimson in a strobing alternation. I made myself ready for impending and certain death. It had come - was I ready? I didn't feel ready in the slightest. Terror, sheer and inestimably-epic in its profundity, gripped me. The molecules of my being were cleansed of the rust that had tarnished them, and a steely will to live brimmed to a spilling point. I didn't want to die. I wanted to persist.

There were blazes in the night on Subsection B; levels twelve, thirteen, and fourteen, and the retrofitted sprinklers had dumped our entire reserve of clean water before they could be rerouted. Bad. The fires incinerated nearly two-hundred units; melted possessions and made the air so terrible that the filtration-systems were failing. All over the Bloc, people were coughing past piss-wet rags and scarves knotted behind their heads. Babies wailed as their parents looked fearful, wondering if we had finally arrived at the world's end. I'm certain that amidst the flames and smoke and fluttering embers stood a Prophet of Horsche, calling out the Will of Gordyume...

Fire was our great fear. The suppression-systems were once more sophisticated, boasting potassium-carbonate-and-citrate sprinklers in every hall and unit, yet the Corporation (in their magnanimous brilliance) failed to account for the fact that these were effectual conductors of electricity. In the Third Uprising, when the fighting was at its worst, walls were blown open, wiring exposed, and the resulting electrical fires killed thousands. The suppressants spread the currents, and those who didn't suffocate were covered in voltaic gel and seared to black bones. This was before my time, but men longer in the teeth than I, who had borne witness to this spectacle, always assumed a harrowed stare when asked to recount it. In the times of this Uprising, it was estimated that only one-in-five adult residents of Z-Bloc survived. Those rates rose to one-in-ten for children and the elderly. Fire was the cause of over half of these deaths, either directly, or via asphyxiation. Of the many systems rendered inoperative by the Uprisings, or by neglect or decomposition, the fire-suppression sprinkler-matrixes were perhaps the most sorely-missed. Now, the danger posed by fire extended far beyond mere heat and smoke. Fire, if not immediately contained and extinguished, stole our food and water...

Once the wailing alarms ceased, all Department workers were called to report to their respective Administrative Offices in the Burghal immediately. Compelled by morbid curiosity, or perhaps seeking further proof of my own mortality, I detoured through the afflicted Subsection. The scene was one of Gehennic suffering unimaginable. If the Bloc had been overdue for Sudokus, we'd filled the fucking quota tonight, boy. More residents on the burning levels had survived than those on fifteen and sixteen. As the heat rose, those units had become kilns, and many had evidently preferred to throw themselves off the mezzanines rather than cook alive. The stench could have brought even Monogatari to tears - it could have made Horsche himself start spewing out of both ends and soil his white vestments. A man in Department coveralls and a particle-mask walked on the ashen sludge, toting a splitting-maul with which he put the irreparably-wounded out of their squealing, begging misery.

***

The Burghal was mobbed. The Security Department had enlisted Poppa Daddy's gunmen to help maintain order, and Department laborers moved in all directions like scattering roaches. The loudspeaker announcements were barely-audible over the clamor, but for the most part, we didn't need instruction. Procedures had been established and practiced in drills for this and other calamities. I found my group and we were counted off by our foreman and charged with our assignments. HydroElectric would bear the brunt of the burden. We may have strutted proud under usual circumstances, as our Department was the one upon which all others depended for light, but our self-righteousness demanded dividends in times like these.

Down to the Basement levels. My group had to go deep, past the main turbines and into the Greater Sewer Network itself, to get the backup purifiers working. The access-lifts let us out into the Hydromills and we moved past them quickly, each man with a hand on the shoulder of the one in front of him, the beams of battery headlamps and flashlights jumping around in a discombobulated fashion, like how string-fire-crackers go off. We crossed the threshold of a yawning cave-mouth and entered the first level of sewer access tunnels - a hive interior black and musty. Vermin scurried past our rubber thigh-highs, fleeing from our lambency and noise. Alpha Team had journeyed through the slime already, and had left snaplight flares every hundred feet. Some were submerged underwater; glowing clouds of glitzy yellow-green that rippled strangely as we passed them.

The final snaplight marked a dichotomization in the tunnel. Above it stood a radio-relay man - an indispensable part of any subterranean operation, as our signals couldn't travel through the infinite concrete of the sewers. He was bathed in eerie color, illuminated insalubrious, with his shadow cast above-and-behind him on the low ceiling of the tube. He informed us that Alpha Team had checked-in with a report that the auxiliary turbines directly beneath the Powermill were up-and-running, but that didn't help us on this side of the Bloc. No team had yet been down the way we were headed. We were on our own.

We followed the tunnel until we came to a door marked with red paint. The team leader double-checked the laminated diagram of the basement levels and confirmed that this was the door leading to the south egress of the main sewage output channel, meaning that we had passed the waste-processing engines and were at the end of charted territory. The door opened into a small room with only three walls, and where the fourth wall should have been were railings and a steel cat-walk extending out into totalitarian blackness. The air in this small chamber had a sense of spaciousness and stank like the wide-gaping asshole of an unmentionable devil. Beyond the railing was a much larger room of pipes and enclosed aque-ducts which rose and ran on both sides of the catwalk verti-cally and horizontally. These carried the waste of the Bloc to the mainlines, down which it was flushed to the lower levels of the sewers through umpteen miles of pipes, until it reached its destination; the Undersun Engines, buried far, far within the earth. The pipes were wet and rusting at their fittings and conduits, and liquid fell in droplets from the ceiling. We ven-tured in single-file onto the catwalk, gripping the wet railings and shining our lights down to the floor, fighting the vertigo induced by the height, until we came to a platform-grate built around a large perpendicular pipe with a rust-roughed lad-der bolted to its convexing surface. We made the climb down, reaffixing the safety ropes every few rungs with spring-snap carabiners.

The soles of my galoshes sank into the slush which cov-ered the entire floor of the output channel maintenance-room. It was by no small effort that we kept up our trudge; every step a battle, heaving to unstick our feet from the rancid muck. The team leader told us to spread out and find the pipe numbered 2421-C, which supposedly had an electrical-override box to control the valves. Buddy-system was the axiom; never wan-der out of sight of your nearest companion's headlamp, and in this manner we proliferated through that rainy forest of rusted iron and filth like a breed of vermin ourselves.

The oppressive stink was alleviated ever-so-slightly by a breeze - not truly a breeze, of course - more that distinct fluctuating atmosphere of hugeness and distance. I paused to catch my breath, turning in the direction of this better air. The Main Line - leading forever away, cavernous and unhal-lowed. The escape from Z-Bloc; the dark from whence occasionally came the Gadabouts. With my gaze, the beam of my headlamp disappeared to infinity down this tube; naught but a diminutive pinprick subsumed by eternal night.

Years ago, when the majority of the systems still functioned, lookouts were posted on the catwalks above. In those times, it was patently illegal to enter the deeper levels of the sewers... and yet, possessed by an irreconcilable longing for freedom or death, some people still did so. I couldn't help but think of that shriveled reptile, and of its profane emergence from thence, and I shuddered at the thought.

Someone found the maintenance-box and called out the sought number loudly. We used a crowbar to breach the encrustation of rust on the hatch and open it, exposing the multiplicity of wires and switches within. The team leader, a Department oldboy, went about the work of getting the waste-treatment lines rerouted. The pipelines, old and long-dormant, shuddered and creaked as they were reutilized. The system would have to run for hours before the muck was flushed-out of the backup reserves. Huddled around the box, we made attempts at doddering conversation, necessitated by our desire for distraction from the rumbling within the pipes and the omnipresent dripping all around us.

"What set the fires, you think?"

"Fuckin' Sons."

"Not on twelve! My mam comes from there, it's good people on twelve. It was likely a cookfire."

"Ain't no fucking cookfire!"

"Like. Notta chance. Seen the levels? Cookfire don't melt stone."

"Course I seen the levels. I said my mam comes from there, ain't I?"

"She... uh, all in-order?"

"She lives with me now, on four-five. We sold her old unit years ago, thanks be."

"Probably a gas accumulation in a dead liftshaft."

"Or Lawmaker."

"Lawmaker ain't been to the Bloc in decemvirate, at least."

"It was he, I'm certain!"

"Stow that talk. Hand me the chain-wrench."

"Ugh... I'm gonna reek like shit for a month."

"Reckon the Department showers still run?"

"Fuckin' better..."

We concluded our task and found the ladder. Back up to the catwalk, gripping the cold coarseness of the rungs. Somebody said they hoped this would work. We all hoped so, and we wondered about the fire, and we wanted to get topside and never come back down here again...

***

Despite the late hour, thousands of people swarmed in the Bazaar streets, displaced from their homes by the fire, or else taking duplicitous advantage of the pandemonium. Groups of neighbors huddled together clutching to their chests boxes of possessions, homemade weapons, crying children, all united as one in their ragged angst.

We went to the HydroElectric Monitoring Office to get ourselves cleaned up. The lines at all the Burghal water-stations were long; several-hundred bodies each. I doubted they would be getting anything for at least a full day. Security was everywhere; the underlings toughing-out the disgruntlement of the Magistrates, but HydroElectric was spared. We stank so badly that the crowds parted before us, and I caught glimmers of pride in the eyes of my companions. Despite our repugnancy, we were still the shit-caked saviors of the general Bloc populace.

Down the long fluorescent-lit hallway to the Department lockers and communal showers, of which only one head-arrey still sprayed. As I waited in line behind maybe two-dozen other HydroElectric men and women, two Security flatfoots came in, talking about how they planned to seek out the culprit behind the fires and beat them and throw them down a sewage line - give them a personal escort right to the afterlife, those Unregisturd fucks. These harsh bluffs were recapitulated by many of us standing in the naked queue. Futile words of violence and cruelty rang in accompaniment with humorless laughter. Each of us was allotted a half-minute under the showerhead. The water was steaming and ran off of us brown and spiraled down the drain. I tried to poach a few extra seconds, but someone shoved me out from under the flow.

***

Home in my loftcot, smoking a handrolled. I couldn't focus past the buzzing of my unit sunlamp. Time passed a tick-tick-tick at a time as I traced my finger along a crack in the cold wall. The Bloc would bleed if it could.

All doors and entryways were kept wide ajar, to improve air circulation and filter out the smoke more efficiently. Down on the thirty-seventh floor, in the center of the courtyard, a woman sang in the Old Tongue an ancient hymn, the lyrics of which made reference to the 'Windows of the Soul,' which was also a passible translation of the song's title. According to the words, these 'windows' were beautiful... yet there was no such thing as windows. I had never seen one before - not a real one. Ash fell from the end of my roll and got in the bed. I swiped at it and it smeared gray across the linens. My knees and ankles hurt. My eyes itched. My blood wasn't running right - I should go to Ringo tomorrow for a letting. Something in the water. It had not tasted clean in months. There was a madness in this place that we were too afraid-of to point out to one-another - we hadn't yet chosen a name for it, and our refusal to acknowledge it increased its power, but for all we knew, a name might give it a physical form with which it could overpower us entirely.

What came next? What happens when the cracks in this antediluvian stone run too deep and let in the Sun? Or will the Great Gates open? Regardless of how, it *will* happen. Someday, it will all come down around our ears. Would there be any progenies left to remember us? Will they sing songs about our eyes?

***

In my childhood years, an old softhearted vendor-woman gave us breadcrusts and boiled gristle, and as we gnawed, she would tell us about the great and monstrous beings that walked the face of the earth outside.

"This one has six heads, with hungry mouths on all sides of each..."

I used to hang onto every word for dear life, as if memorizing her descriptions of all these prehistoric creatures would give me the tools to survive, should I ever meet one. As I grew older, I realized she had fabricated every word for our entertainment. Adolescence is abjured in Z-Bloc. We are children for years and then suddenly and in our own ways we are struck by the realization that we will never leave this tower - our fathers and grandfathers died here, and so will we. The ovens of the Crematorium are fitted with no portholes, because the flames burn too bright to look at. Corpse-disposals take twenty seconds, or so I've been told. They clean out the filters every forty-or-so bodies, and the refuse amounts to about three cups of flakey gray ash...

"Scales for skin, big curved horns on its spine..."

Memoriam-trinkets are sold in the Bazaar - mostly urns, solely symbolic in function, as they sit empty on the shelves that uphold them. They are personalized with etchings and constructed with clay that was made from grinding up bits of the stone that shelters us and mixing it with water. In this way, we truly become one with this place after our deaths. The walls grow ever-thinner as we dig out of them nuggets with which to immortalize ourselves...

"Walks on twenty legs, with steel pincers and ten-thousand teeth..."

In those days, my favorite daydream was imagining what the old breed of us used to be - how they lived and spoke and carried themselves. They were godlike in my mind, seven feet tall, the women beautiful and the men handsome, all rippling muscle bronzed and slick with sweet-tasting sweat. Nude and magnificent they stood on mountaintops, their long tresses blowing in the True Wind and the edges of them fading into the True Sky. By night, their huts were lit by cookfires that, from a distance, made little dots of orange on the vast horizon, and I imagined the fertile landscape bespeckled with a great number of these dots, visible only from a lofty vantage at twilight, as the Sun sank into the deep waters. They were the potentates of empyrean civilization; eternal and liberated from all woe and heartache...

"Breathes flames and bleeds acid, tongue twelve feet long..."

By night they were warm in their humble dwellings, in furs and nestled beside hotrocks, with their archaic weapons close at-hand. They made love noisily and often, and sprung alert at the smallest sound or smell unfamiliar...

"Feathered wings, eight arms, dangling talons, whiplike tails..."

Pale and skinny and squatting in the dust to eat my crust and fat - my first meal in three days, washed down with water from a runoff puddle after the vegetation-sprinklers cycled. Months-old bloomers unchanged, unwashed, and so sublimely filthy that the fabric had lost all pliability. Twelve years old, Kassie ten, and there were other children too, and none of us had yet wondered if we were the final generation...

"A mouth within a mouth, and another one within that…"

I'd grown up and surmised that monsters were not real, yet maybe they are... maybe they had already devoured us and we were stranded in some arcane gastrointestinal circumvolution. I had never heard the Prophets speak of such. A novel theory. I could garner a following with that...

***

The smell of the fire, permeated by the filtration systems, lingered in the Bloc for days. It took a week for the water to come back, by which time the thirst had become life-threatening. It would take far longer for the reserve tanks to return to acceptable levels, so we could not risk another incident anytime soon. The auxiliary purifiers were kept running to hasten the process, which leeched power from the backup generators. Even in the best of times, the purification systems were a slapdash mess of technical improvisations patched one-over-the-other, and it often functioned erroneously. The quality of the water worsened - when contained in a transparent receptacle, one could see microbes wriggling in it without even holding it to a light. Yet despite this, and its metallurgic taste, it was consumed rabidly.

There were no hydro-allotments for the in-unit showers. That meant the residents who desired to bathe (an unfortunately-scant percentage) had to enroll in daily raffles for the communal showers in the Burghal Department Offices. The groups of each day were sorted by gender, to forestall rapes. Power from all over the Bloc was rerouted to keep the agricultural sunlamps on, forcing entire Subsections to make-do without light. The Favelas were obviously the first levels to be cut-off, and the detrimental effects of this were evidenced by the influx of corpses brought down to the Crematoriums each day. For every body delivered for proper disposal, there were others simply tossed down the inactive liftshafts - so the fetor worsened, as did the air-quality. The Security Department posted notices on all the lobby-level bulletins that any resident caught burning unapproved combustibles would be exiled into the sewers and thereby condemned to death. Regardless, fires were everywhere, and not half of them were jelly-alcohol or anthracitic ashwax. Thus, the symbiotic Departmental dance with the Bloc continued and complexified. There was never enough to go around. Water rations had to be proper, lest the reserves run dry. No reserves, no water for the agricultural irrigation-systems, nor steam for the Hydro-Electric turbines. No turbines, no light, and if the light went, so did the crops, and we would starve in darkness. Famine and filth and disease. Z-Bloc needed us to keep it breathing just as much as we needed it.

***

As of late, I have not been sleeping well. Ever since the fire, I suffered from a recurring nightmare. The visceral nature of the dream was disturbing. Sometimes after waking, I couldn't tell what was real - as if my senses were restituting false perceptual currency back unto me.

I'm in the Bazaar. The smell of roasting corncobs and dogmeat mingles with the general tangy pungence of sweat and smoke and sewage. In a narrow alley, the paper accordion-lanterns project their hues in the puddles and on the slanting galvanized-steel roofing of the shacks and shopfronts. There is a collection of teepee-tents, into which customers are taken for privacy as they are tended-to by whores and gigolos, and the candlelight in these tents makes them glow and makes visible the silhouettes of those inside. I wonder why I am here - I don't get massages, nor do I pay for fornication, as the risk of disease is too high. I prefer the pleasures of good druk and swill, which are self-sterilizing and reliable in effect, if not in flavor. I walk amongst the tents. The opera of the Bazaar is hypnotic; the loudness of it is reassurance enough that I'm not all alone in the world. Yet, I'm on the East Side, far from my usual haunts - from Ringo's, the Bronco, the reliable vendors to whom I give my patronage... I don't know why I'm here...

I round bends and move like a mist through the teeming life, and as I do, I become aware of a pursuer: a woman with no face. Besides this, there is nothing inordinate about her - her appearance and accouterments blend in with all the others of the Bazaar crowd... yet she has no face - not featureless skin over her skull, but rather a distortion where her face should be, like the way ripples in liquid warp a reflection. A trick of the eyes; an effect like that of good mushroom-dustsmoke. I am taken-in by the blanket folds of an insoluble uneasiness, and I sink deeper into the sensation with every glance thrown over my shoulder. The woman draws nearer...

I find an auction-block where a large crowd has gathered to gander at the valuables being lotted. Into this mess of noise and bodies I venture, in hopes of losing she who trails me, but to no avail. I push and elbow people aside, yet behind me, they move out of her path unprompted. She has no face, and this malconformation to reality becomes all-the-more disturbing as she gains on me. I think I know who she is, or is supposed to represent...

Like most of the Bazaar urchin-children, I never knew my mother. She could have been a migrant Unregistered without a unit to sleep in, or a fully-fledged card-carrying generational resident. She could have been a whore made pregnant by any one of an innumerable string of john-boys, or she could have been a willing parent with a steadfast husband. I have no way of knowing, and one of the first conclusions I, like all my urchin-kin, came to was that it is better not to dwell on such conjectures. For all I know, she's still living. Perhaps I've passed her in the Bazaar, or on the Subsection mezzanines, a million times - locking eyes for only a second before turning away or nodding a polite acknowledgement. It's possible, but more likely is that she is long-deceased. Perhaps she had other children, and my anonymous brothers or sisters pass me by unknowingly on a regular basis at the water-stations, or at the Bronco, or perhaps they vend me hookah or druk or patch the holes that wear in the bottoms of my shoes. There exists no way to be certain, and in Z-Bloc, the cardinal rule of survival is to fixate only on that of which you have concrete proof. Those who seek investment in something beyond our walls are easy marks for the Zealots, who preach that our suffering is righteous and deserved.

I always wake before the Faceless Woman reaches me. Because she has no mouth, she cannot speak, but there is nothing in her posture indicative of warmth or compassion. I have no reason to suspect that she is my mother, yet I cannot shake the notion. Perhaps this is the hollow faith I cling to - my own personal Zealotry - borne of suspicion and paranoia, and perhaps a longing to be touched, loved, beside and inside and entwined with another soul...

***

There was a Sudoku from level forty-one - a headfirst nosedive to eternity, and after Sanitation mopped up the stain, there was much ado and speculation about the fact that it had been a Zealot Prophet. The Prophets never jump; there had not been a single similar instance in all the time since the Uprisings, when the first evangelistic processions had come up out of the darkness of the sewers. In-need of distraction from the backbreaking days at the HydroElectric mills, (and the exhaustion exacerbated by my sleepless nights) I elected to utilize the advantages of my Departmental employment-badge, and my reputation with Security as an upstanding and trustworthy Stoolie, to discern what had occurred.

The Security Department Magistrate to whom I usually passed information was not his quotidian self. The man usually stood as all Magistrates do; with a lofty air of condescending superiority. I'd never seen him smile or laugh or look anything other than magisterial. He was always eager to take information from Stoolies, but was stingy in dispensing reciprocation of any sort. However, when I went to his Burghal quarters on the fifth floor of the Security building, the disarray I found him in caused me concern. If he knew anything about the Zealot Sudoku, he either didn't care, or else regarded it as too sensitive to acknowledge. What he did tell me was that, at the moment, the chief objective of the Security Department was to locate Poppa Daddy, who had seemingly disappeared. It was hypothesized that the fires on Subsection B had been set by Poppa's gunmen to facilitate his escape from the Bloc, and Poppa himself was now down in the tunnels with his lieutenants and the Lizard.

I asked if Poppa was hunted by Lawmaker. This seemed to confuse my source, who went on to tell me that Lawmaker had not been to Z-Bloc in many years. The Gadabout reports of him denoted that he was old and moving slowly, not nearly as dangerous as he once was. At this, I scoffed. Lawmaker could age a thousand years and still be quick as quicksilver.

"Have you ever seen him with your own eyes?"

"Years ago, as a child."

"It is said he rusts. His iron bones creak when he moves. His back is hunched. He limps. His talons are dulling and his eyes are going gray. There is a whistling as he draws breath. I tell you, he slows, and will eventually cease to move at all." Here came a pause. Then: "I don't think he can even fly anymore..."

FOUR

I had been dreaming of the Faceless Woman when it began. Gunshots; crisp earsplitting pops duplicating and abounding, indisputably on my level. I snapped out of sleep and flew to my feet to rush undressed to the door, which I opened to find the Subsection transformed into a dogmeat smoker-barrel. The shots rang deafening off the walls and pillars and there was a galling stink that watered my eyes and made my tongue puffy. Crowd-suppressant gas. I caught a fat whiff and started coughing. Through the clouds appeared a mannish form dashing for his life. He was felled by a shot. I slammed shut the door and threw the bolt-lock, hyperventilating, thinking of nothing besides this man; the sight filled my cognizance as I watched him fall on a loop, over and over, and I didn't tire of watching it - my mind's eye replayed the sight as I looked on with a detached fascination.

The teargas crept under my door, reaching in gray tendrils for my vent-fan. It would have filled my unit by now, but the air-circulation system had been cut-off, presumably to the entire Subsection, if not to the entire Bloc. My mini-sunlamp flickered and died. They meant to blind and starve us. I had to make a run for it...

I dressed fast in my sturdiest threads, grabbed my satchel, and wet a rag to tie across my face. With the disengagement of the bolt-lock I was off-and-running across the mezzanine with my head low, stepping over debris and bloodpools. I nearly tripped over the dead man as panicked figures came rushing out of the haze from all angles to collide with one-another. Muzzle-flashes winked on the upper-level balconies, and the cacophony was such that I wished I had been born deaf, or else belonging to a species with no concept of sound, if such a thing existed.

By a stroke of superlative luck, the West Lift was stopped on my level. Packed around it was a swelling crowd of hundreds pushing to get inside, their clothes bloodstained, their faces panicked. Those underfoot cried for mercy as young and old alike were trampled in the stampede. I balled my fists, windmilled, struck a woman, and took her place as she fell, fully-invalided in the transcendent dolor. The carriage was full well-beyond capacity, and I was amongst the last few across the threshold. A mess of hands grasped at the narrowing entrance, trying to drag out those on board, and an older man was caught between the sliding doors as they met. He was crushed and halved, and we took the upper part of him along for the ride, us pushing backwards as he crawled, sputtering, leaving a trail of entrails behind him.

There was no lull in which to breathe or gain composure before the blast. It must have been a bomb - I'd never felt the Bloc shake like that before. It came from above, and there was a great lurch as the lift-cables broke. We fell. The failsafe-brakes engaged, yet did little to slow our descent. At the bottom of the Bloc we crashed; the slew of us thrown together, filthy, choking, hands and feet and elbows and knees everywhere, mixed and kneaded with steel and stone in that screaming cistern. The doors broke open upon impact and light promised us a bogus salvation. As I dragged myself over the hill of bodies, the jagged edge of a fractured bone cut across my flank. My blood flowed freely as I emerged from the lift-carriage released of all humanity save that empyrean and all-consuming desire to survive.

The Bazaar was burning and the sprinklers were not working. The smoke was so thick that I could see neither the ceiling nor the arching dome of the Burghal. If there was shooting down here, it was inaudible past the din. Firelight pierced the smothering fumes, illuminating silhouettes black and writhing in a horrid ballet against the backdrop of the enkindled shacks and shops. Usual navigation was impossible - the streets and alleys were destroyed and the rubble was scattered by great crowds of those who, like myself, had become feral in their desperation to hold onto life.

Get to the Department Complexes. Get to HydroElectric, where you will be known and admitted. Flee this perdition. Fight for breath. Fight against the smothering heat. You are cooking alive. Run. Run to the center of this. How far was it? A thousand steps? Close to it. I was shoved and knocked in the dirt. The industrial sunlamps above flickered. Half of them were gone and the other half naught but sickly yellow holes in the black brume. The spice-planters were ablaze, all of them, and people ran out of the flames with boiling flesh. Run, trip, fall, get back up and keep going...

Five hundred steps. A child clung to my leg. I shook him (or her - I didn't pause to look) off. No pause or rest. People everywhere; residents and Unregisturds, never more united in spirit than they currently were, yet never more willing to harm and kill one-another. I climbed a pile of debris and got to the top of a devastated galleria of interconnected trinket-shops and lounges. The Bazaar was an roily ocean of heads bobbing amidst the flames and toppled structures. Z-Bloc was burning, like it was said to have done during the Uprisings. Who could save us from this?

Three hundred steps - back on the ground, as the galleria ended before the seamstress-and-cobbler districts. Pushing, bleeding, coughing, feeling the damp flesh of bodies against myriad others compressed. I formed a spearhead with my hands to wedge myself through the putrid humanity, the screaming horde, with the percussive hits of gunfire and explosions and chaos both near and far; such an uproar that it all could only be fit for the end of the world.

How close? One hundred? I had neglected my count. The Burghal turnstiles were a dam to the crowd - floodgates cracking and springing hairline leaks. The Security Magistrates were striving in vain to keep it all together. Where were the Gunbosses now, with their conscripted numbers? It was only the Department lackeys that were maintaining any semblance of order. The ghosts of the Corporation would be proud. I thanked my stars for all the years as a good Stoolie that had gotten me my Department Badge, and all the hours spent cleaning Hydro-filters, as these had afforded me better odds in the out-and-out apocalypse.

In ten steps, I would be through the turnstiles. Security had shot those without badges who had come over the ingresses or climbed the barricades. Bodies littered the floor. The Burghal was on total lockdown, yet the loudspeaker announcement called for all Department laborers to report for immediate duty. I waved my badge and heard a Magistrate call off the shooters.

Inside. Like cool water after years of fructose-syrup was the less-polluted air cycled by the Burghal filtration-system. I gulped emphysematous lungfuls. Twisting black tentacles swirled above us as the huge fans in the domed ceiling sucked up the smoke. I went to my knees and vomited and wiped my mouth, scanning for a medic, or anyone with bandages. I was bleeding. The soles of my feet were burned. Death felt like a certitude, but I knew I had to get to the East Wing, to Hydro-Electric. It was paramount that we get the water flowing again, get the auxiliary pumps rerouted to the waste-lines, so that our shit might smother the fires...

Then, I noticed them: dozens of them, standing about in their robes and reciting verse in the Old Tongue. Why? The Prophets never visited the Burghal in droves... The sight of them filled me with an alien repulsion. Their white robes shone clean against the grime and graffiti, and they were calm; no crying Sermon, no rites of warning or reproach. *Why?*

A hand found my shoulder and I was spun and pulled afoot by an iron grip. Monogatari looked down at me from his towering height, a billhook-blade held fast in his bloody right hand. He told me to lead him to the service-shafts that ran up to Subsection B. I coughed out that they were, in all probability, not functional. He didn't care. We moved. In the hallways of the Security Department Tower, we strode past the scurrying Magistrates unquestioned and untouched. They dispersed before us, flattening against the walls, and then recommenced their racing in our wake. As we went, I considered asking my friend if he was afraid to die, but then I thought better of it. He had never lied to me before, and I didn't want to hear him do so now.

The service lift still functioned and was unguarded. We got up to level sixteen, where the air was noxious, yet there was no shooting. Those on Subsection A had all fled to these levels to escape the heat of the floor-level fires. Ironic, how just a week ago, these levels were the ones to be escaped. We found a stairwell and ascended, coughing past our masks. Halfway up to the seventeenth-floor landing, Monogatari paused to give me a fresh rag, dampened by water from his dog-stomach gutjug. Before I tied it behind my ears, I asked him for a drink. He denied me.

***

For once in Bloc-history, the Favelas were preferable to the levels below. As everything here was made of wood and tarpaulin, uncontrolled fires were a fatal and ever-present danger. The structural integrity of the shack-compounds would be compromised by even a moderate blaze, so these reusers made their own fire-suppressant from sewage. It smelt appalling, yet was so effective that commodities-merchants in the Bazaar hocked it as a means for extinguishing grease cookfires. Regardless, the panic of the Bloc had not abated on these levels. The electricity had failed and the darkness of this place, ubiquitous even on an average day, was now far worse. Monogatari pushed on unflinchingly, with me trailing him through the passageways. I was quite afraid, but I tried to act as brave as he.

At a tight intersection of two alleys close to the heart of the compound and (best I could judge) roughly halfway-up, we were ambushed by a foursome. They emanated from the shadows in an instant and seized us, and I saw in the feeble lantern-light the glint of filed teeth and jagged shivs. I was caught by surprise and yelped a syllable, but before I could form words with which to protest or implore, Monogatari's billhook swooshed through the air. I felt a hot splash against my chest and was released as the arm of my assailant dropped severed to the ground. Its owner fell to his knees to retrieve it, but he and his cohorts were all felled-and-portioned by my guardian, who carried out the killings with the nonchalance of a rat-skinner. They screamed something dreadful as they died.

We left red footprints as we continued, moving straight through the intersection and down the alley, which narrowed until it could hardly accommodate the width of a normal man, much less one the size of Monogatari, and then we arrived at a vertical shaft made from an old water mainline, inside of which hung a knotted rope. Monogatari scaled the twenty-foot distance in a few seconds, but I had to stop halfway and call out beseechingly for his assistance. Unbearable pain was fructifying through my body, originating from my wrist, which had most-likely broken when the West Lift crashed. Monogatari seized the rope and hauled me skyward.

I was bleeding continually from my side and felt faint from oxygen-deprivation, and the burn-blisters on my feet and ankles had burst. The new concern of contracting a bloodborne disease from the gore of our ambushers supplemented my thoroughgoing perturbation. My eyes stung from the teargas; I was coughing unmanageably, and the pain and disorientation cut my knees from under me. I fell against Monogatari, who half-dragged-half-carried me onwards. Such was his breed of pity; the most merciful gesture his nature could accommodate. He told me we couldn't stop or rest. We were going to rendezvous with Kassie.

***

Monogatari harbored a sort of older-brother complex for Kassie, and perhaps one for me too. He just happened to be that streetrat who was older than the rest of us and got stuck with a younger crowd that had no one else to take care of them. He was our collective mentor growing up in the Bazaar. I looked up to him - even idolized him, in fact. In my memory, it seemed to me that he had always been the exact same in appearance - huge and muscled, six-and-half feet tall, bulging veins in his neck, an almost-perfectly round bald head with a mandala tattoo of the Sun inked deep and perfectly-centered at the top of his cranial vault. He kept his entire face shaved, eyebrows and all, and had good straight teeth. Even in youth, he carried himself with the confidence of a Gunboss, yet with none of the ostentatious vanity. When he spoke, his voice always commanded attention and respect. As a boy, I envied him a great deal once I realized I would never grow up to be as big and strong and unflappable as he was, but, as the dogmas of childhood often do, this envy subsided as I matured. So many of us, that gang of orphaned scions who (in our minds) ran the Bazaar, had grown up to become useless dustsmokers, whores, or had indeed not grown up at all. Only Ringo and myself had possessed the wherewithal to climb above our allotted stations in life. Ringo had taken an apprenticeship from the barber who had previously run the shop, and I had found that my pedestrian invisibility enabled me to do precisely what Monogatari could never hope to: blend into crowds unseen. My observant eye and unimposing manner molded me into a valuable Stoolie for the Department Magistrates, and Monogatari had taught me how to barter for my own interests. Before long, I had a Badge, and not long after that, a unit of my own, and I was an Unregisturd only in spirit from then-on.

Yet, Monogatari's protective inclinations always seemed at their strongest for Kassie. He had a real soft-spot for her. I'd never pressed him about it, (he'd never answer if I did) but I think that a part of him loved her deeply. She was the only one in the Bloc with his same capacity for violence - the same raging spirit, the same ability to bend the edges of reality to her whims. The nature of that love (which positively existed, even if it was buried beneath layers of obdurate callousness) was surely so complex that I don't expect even Monogatari fully understood it. He was an atypical father taken by incestuous desire and struggling with the resulting guilt, and so profound was this struggle that it was only via means of cloistering it deep inside himself that he could continue to draw breath.

***

We came to what appeared to be a family corner-unit. The door had been replaced with a sheet of galvanized steel, which had been reinforced and fitted with a bolt-lock system much sturdier than the ones on the regular residence doors. A combination-padlock was linked onto the bolt mechanism, preventing it from sliding free. Monogatari tried the combo once, muttered in frustration, and tried it again. Click. We walked into the unit, divided into several chambers by curtains. What was once the sitting-room now stood quite empty, save for a trio of chairs and a felt-topped table, like those used for playing cards in the Bazaar staking-places. Monogatari closed the door. The inside of the unit was dark, until he struck a match and lit the wick of a candle on the table. The sunlamps and fluorescent bars had been smashed-out long-ago, and the room felt lonesome and forgotten. Inhabiting it, I was filled with the same sensation. Here, even the anguished howling and staccato pops of gunfire seemed to be far away. Although I expected her to emerge from behind the curtain that veiled the rugged hammer-made doorway to the other room, Kassie was not to be encountered. This upset Monogatari, but not beyond the brink of what he could accept. I asked him where we were, what was this place?

"This is the place. Kassie knows if she's in trouble, we meet here."

"Maybe she's not in trouble?"

"We're all in trouble."

Like. No fucking shitting. Still, I felt a compulsion to try and make things better with my words. I said: "Kassie is a tough chick. She's bound to rough it out. "

"Like."

"So she might not be in trouble. Maybe she, uh, she could have, um…" and I trailed off, unsure of what I was trying to say. Unbearable silence settled until I broke it again. "Will we be safe here?"

"None are safe."

"What do we do?"

"We wait for Kassie."

"What if she doesn't show?"

"She will."

"What if she doesn't?"

"If you want to leave, you're welcome to it."

That was unthinkable - I didn't trust myself to find my way out of the Favelas, let alone survive the chaos on my own.

Monogatari's feet were already up. He leaned back in one of the chairs, which was strained to its absolute limit supporting his hulking frame, and his eyes closed. He folded his arms tight across his chest, still gripping the billhook, and this resolutely signaled the end of our conversation. One of two things would happen: Kassie would show, or we would wait until we perished. Monogatari sat so still and breathed so steadily that I wondered if he had fallen asleep. I could not rest. Pain and fear consumed me...

I shed my shoes and what was left of my jacket, which I tore to strips to dress my wound and wrap my feet. Then I took up the metal chamberstick and held the flame to another candle which had previously melted into the felt of the table. The minikin light in the room doubled, but only momentarily, as I moved by the fluttering glow across the unit to draw aside the curtain-divider and commence an exploration that led me into an even further-removed and pitch-black chamber - what had once surely been the main bedroom of this repurposed residence.

Here were painted carvings on the wall - not capricious splattered vandalisms, but willful, carefully-considered illustrations of the Old World and the Old Times; stick-figures etched into the stone, primitive-yet-elaborate scenes of war, death, and of the hunting of long-ago-extinct horned beasts, with the Sun blazing above it all, rays falling in wedges across mountains and hills and cities. The placement and spacing of the artwork was quite dissimilar to the typical markings that covered the stone surfaces of the Bloc; there was no dripped ink, no messy lines, save where such was intentional. While at first glance the paintings seemed layered haphazardly over one-another, it became clear as I held the candle nearer that everything was in its proper spot; the overlaps melded consummately to form a single artwork stretched across the walls and floor and ceiling of the chamber. As I examined the designs, I became enamored with their beauty and the vast sadness of their anonymity in this sequestered place. They should have adorned the halls of the Burghal Departments! It seemed like a sort of spiritual scurrility that they should remain unseen in the darkness. I reached out to touch, now feeling a bit calmer, despite the world crashing down around me.

As I moved deeper into the domicile, I became aware of another presence in the room, evidenced by strained breathing, and a faint cough that sounded like dice rattling in a cup. As I moved with the light towards the corner of the room, (and the corner of the megastructure itself) I found a cot occupied by a frail, emaciated form under a rent and rough and utterly threadbare blanket. As I approached, the figure turned and I was filled with shock at the wrinkled infirmity of the man. Unexplainable guilt filled my heart - as if it was somehow my fault that this poor and sickly citizen had been excommunicated from the rest of us in this forlorn closet. I moved closer still, and the man stirred and spoke. His voice, gravelly and croupy, could barely be qualified as a whisper, so I had to draw very close to make out his words.

"Take... away... the light..."

"What? Sorry, I didn't–"

"Cover... the... light..."

I adjusted myself in such a manner that my shadow fell across the cot.

"Hurts... my skin..."

"The light hurts your skin?"

"Yes..."

With a colossal effort, the Ancient Man turned away from me to face the wall, and I was left only to imagine the leathery coarseness of his flesh. I tried to preserve in my memory the single glimpse I had been afforded. He must have lived for nearly a century...

"What is this place?"

"A cave... within a cave..."

"And these artworks? Did you make them?"

"All we can do... is paint... on the walls..."

"Why?"

"It is... all... we have ever done..."

I asked another worthless question, but there was only quiet wheezing in reply. I edged closer still to the cot. I wanted to see his eyes...

When Monogatari called me, I had to pull myself out of the room. Kassie had arrived. I asked the both of them about the identity of the other party, expecting some answer because this was 'their spot.' Neither of them knew him. They told me that he had been there for years, and that nobody bothered him, and that this was his spot long before it had become theirs. I saw the Ancient Man many times in dreamscapes following, but never again in the flesh.

As we departed the unit, another explosion shook the stone walls around us. The Favela amalgamations began to splinter apart - fires were breaking out on these levels, and rubble was falling from the ceiling, smashing through the frameworks of the shanties. We, like all the others here and everywhere I knew, fled for our lives.

Z-Bloc had met its end.

BOOK II

'The Tunnels'

FIVE

Before me flickered a tiny flame, blue until the very tip, hissing in anger as grease dripped into it - a small light, yet to me it may as well have been the Sun. It was my whole life; all I could see, all I could assimilate. All was pitch-dark, save those few feet of space illuminated by the flame and the skewer of meat held above it, rotated by Monagatari. The sizzling of the grease and our ragged breathing were the only sounds, yet these were enough to let us know we were alive. The scent of the cooking meat caught in my nostrils between gulps of rancid air. That little burning can of jelly-alcohol and that strip of meat comprised the entirety of our world; all we had was what we could see by the light of that oblong orange-tipped oval.

Kassie squeezed my shaking shoulder and asked me in a timid tone if I was okay. I could not reply nor pull my eyes from the flame. Kassie said some other words, but they faded fast and I couldn't make them out. An emptiness I had never felt before enveloped me, and I sank into it as if it was mud. Our world had burned.

Monogatari took the meat back from the flame, sniffed it, and took a small bite from the corner, hissing away a mouthful of steam between his teeth. He passed the skewer to Kassie, who made an 'O' with her lips and blew air onto it before tasting it. There were few words exchanged between us as the food made a rotation. I said I wasn't hungry and was rebuked into taking a rubbery bite, flavorless save for the salt. I couldn't tell what had died so that I might live. I took a second bite only because I needed something to force down the first. Starved by exhaustion, we ate quickly. Monogatari pulled a tin flask from his bag and unscrewed the top, and we passed the flask and drank good swill soured metallic by its container. The flask went around twice before Monogatari used the last drops to wet some rags he had wrapped around a piece of re-bar. The torch was put to the canned flame and the rags went up apricot and crimson, and the light expanded to the walls of the tramshaft. We could see each other fully then; matted hair, skin encrusted with cracking filth, faces grave, wide eyes sunken back in our skulls, and we were shaking; vibrating in a manner that made the air around us pulsate with the labor of restraining us to our physical forms.

We got up, packed up, and walked into the darkness. The distance was unperceivable. All around us was black, and our torchlight formed a weak globe, like an orange fishbowl, and we swam in this bowl and had no awareness of anything outside of it. The stench of the sewers was preeminent. Our feet splashed in scattered puddles until eventually the hard ground gave way entirely to wet slush. I didn't look down. The noise of our steps in the wastewater echoed in the corridor. Occasionally, I heard vermin skittering; rats or insects or abominations unimaginable.

I knew that I should have been fearful, and perhaps I was, but the sensation was externalized - it was out there in the darkness, not settled in my interior. My bodily aches had become my subconscious median; I felt no pain nor fear, but I knew they lurked about, waiting predatorily in that eternal underground night. It would have been prudent to try to devise methods of survival - some measurable course-of-action to take towards our conservancy - but instead, the memories of my entire life played all-at-once, with me reexperiencing them from an overhead perspective, outside myself. The sum of my days made no impression on me. I kept waiting to witness my own demise at the end of the pageant, yet it never came...

We had fled our world as it burned. Those who lived above were dead, and now all that remained were those below; half-human creatures mutated and evolved a thousand years in five minutes. Anew and impaired we continued our aimless plod through the tunnels.

***

We had escaped Z-Bloc via the plumbing-networks. The

mainlines, those claustrophobic pipes slick with feculence, were large enough for a human to crawl through bent-double, or sometimes fully procumbent. There was no light and we knew not where we were going. When we came upon dead-ends and blockages, we had to retreat and find other routes; alternative pipes shooting off from the primary ones, most hardly more than three feet in diameter and filled at least half-way with sludge. Shit covered every inch of us. We breathed it and swallowed it and retched our stomachs dry. Monogatari led us, his blade between his teeth, and when he became stuck, we all crawled backwards to rearrange ourselves. We slid down vertical drops and rounded U-bends, listening to faint faraway roaring and feeling the pipes rattling, certain we would soon be swept away by sewage and drowned; a fate to which burning alive seemed almost-preferable by comparison. With every breath gasped with my head above the squalid muck, I cursed myself and my companions for our willing departure from the semi-literal frying pan in favor of a far-worse fate... yet we eventually slithered out of the pipes and found ourselves in a deserted tramway tunnel.

The tunnel was rounded and couldn't have been more than twenty feet in width, yet it felt massive to us after our prior ordeal. The wastewater was up to my hips, but there was more air through which the stink could disperse, and the way was straight, so that the pitch-darkness extended eternally both before-and-behind us. We held hands and chose a direction in which to walk, and as we went, the water-level sank to our knees, then ankles, and eventually we came upon dry ground. It was here that Monogatari sat on the tramway-rail and opened his shoulder-bag, and we crouched by the flickering light of the canned flame and cooked a bit of meat, drank a bit of swill, made the torch, and rested for maybe twenty minutes before continuing onward.

***

Upon standing, I felt pain in my feet, dulled by shock, yet so intense that I realized that if I sat down again, it would likely be forever. We found a door leading off from the tramshaft and followed a narrow maintenance-corridor, sloshing through sewage, until it opened up to a larger chamber. Monogatari spoke for the first time since our break. His voice sounded deafening as it bounced off the stone. He asked me if I knew where we were. How would I know? The fact that it fell within the circle of reasonable expectation that I could give a valid answer boggled my mind.

By the torchlight, we came upon another door. Monogatari crashed himself against it and the lock broke after several tries. The rusty squealing of the hinges made me shudder, as did the blackness of the corridor that extended before us. It could have run for several yards or several hundred miles. With no way of knowing and only one way to find out, we ventured forward. After five-hundred steps, we found this new shaft obstructed by rubble and discovered amongst those stones a novel sense of hopelessness. Back we tracked. There was an offshooting hallway which led to an enclosed U-shaped stairwell that only went down, so down we went, four or five stories, until we found another door. This door was ajar, and, from the scent of the air and the sound of our footfalls, I knew immediately that it opened into a very large room. As we crossed the threshold, I was proved correct.

We emerged from an alcove cut into the side of a concrete pipe, and the torchlight could not find the ceiling nor the wall opposite us. Monogatari whistled, to get a sense of the space by means of the echo, and the shrill noise did not return properly - it rushed away into the black and was swallowed by hugeness. We descended the moderate curvature of the tube until we lost sight of the alcove, and our fishbowl became smaller as we walked into the gargantuan dark; blackness thick and inky and pregnant, the sensation of which was thoroughly unsettling. Indeed, it might have been utterly terrifying, if the acumen of our collective consciousness could still process such an emotion. The walls and ceiling and everything outside of our fishbowl ceased to exist.

"What... the..." Kassie sounded very scared; a way I'd never heard her sound before.

"We keep moving."

Monogatari's voice, so loud previously, now sounded miniscule in this great tunnel. He asked me if I had ever been down this far before. Of course I hadn't - even the Main Line with which I was familiar was not half as big as this duct. We were now very far underground, below even the HydroElectric millrooms. We walked to the bottom of the tube, where the curvature of the floor planed for maybe two-hundred feet before sloping back upwards again, and we began to trek longways, rather than across, our sense of direction informed only by the evenness of the ground - walking upwards meant you were moving sideways, walking flat meant forward.

Kassie: "It's a huge tunnel..."

"Like."

"Have you ever been here before?"

"I already said I haven't."

"We must be so deep..."

Monogatari: "Keep moving."

We kept walking, going nowhere...

Then, something interrupted the blackness: a pinprick of light in the distance, off to one side and above us, that grew larger as we approached. It shone out from another alcove cut into the curve of the wall, which half-obstructed the glow. As we neared it, fervent with expectancy, someone called to us. The voice was familiar to me. My hands began to tremble and I began to weep piteously at the relief brought on by human noise cutting through the vast silence.

Skudd came rushing out of the alcove to hug Kassie, and behind him, more lights came; flashlight-beams and lanterns, and hope was rekindled. In ones-and-twos, several dozen people emerged from the alcove, all in various states of dismay and distress.

The majority were Sons, but there were also several Department people, as well as a collection of run-of-the-millers. Some were badly injured - one man couldn't walk, another was missing an eye, arms were cradled in makeshift slings and soaked bandages appeared black and shiny in the poor light. As all were bloody and caked with sewage, there were no defining features on any of us; we were all alike, distinguished only by height and our frame-shapes, and this uncharacteristic uniformity resultant of our desolation made us all equivalent. We hugged one-another and cried in harmony, simultaneously jubilant and sorrowful. The leader of this pack was a Son, but Monogatari took over command immediately, as he was better-suited for it. There were no complaints amongst any of us at this adjustment. As my big friend took footing on the curved wall, we all fell silent to hear his words.

"Everyone sit, take a rest. Who's got water? Hold it up so I can see..."

A few raised jars and stomach-gutjugs. Monogatari squinted, his eyes whipping over us, searching out those tightfisted few who sought to withhold their supply.

"Alright, who's got swill?"

Someone had a large jar that had remained miraculously unbroken. His eyes dropped parsimoniously to the floor as Monogatari ordered me to wrench it from his unwilling grasp.

"Any provisions you carry, lay them out. I'll come around and take inventory, and we'll rest and have a drink. We can't stay here long. We got only what we carry, which ain't much; hardly no food or water, and very little swill, damn it. We will die here if we don't move to find more. Anyone have experience with the sewer-labyrinths? Any Gadabouts here?"

There was silence. Then, a timid voice: "My father came over from F-Bloc. He told me stories of the big tunnel. He said never to sleep in it, or walk it for long. He told me never to come down here. Better to die above, he said..."

There was murmuring and fresh tears all around.

"Way I see it, for the good ol' daddy Corp to construct something like this, it must lead somewhere, to someplace. Am I wrong? I'm happier without shit up to my dick. When my time comes, and it sure-as-Sunlight ain't come yet, I'd prefer to die on dry stone. Anyone else here feel differently? No? Good! So we got no choice but to push on, agreed?"

It was clear that few were comfortable with the prospect, but Monogatari had boxed us all in with his rationale. Indeed, we had no other choice.

We passed the swilljar around until it was empty. I felt

much better now that there was more light and other voices to break up the silence. On Monogatari's command, we helped each other stand, and those able-to carried children, packs, and half-full gutjugs. Someone's wife had been crushed before his eyes by falling rubble, and the man was crying. A Son went to embrace him, and that gesture of humanity imbued me with fresh strength. I held a position at the front of the group, at Monogatari's right hand, and I felt like a Gunboss lieutenant. Maybe we would be okay...

We walked and walked. Time stopped, yet we persisted nonetheless. I counted my steps past ten-thousand before I lost my numerical bearing, and I started over and got to ten-thousand again, but stopped there. I considered starting over again, but couldn't bring myself to realize the point of it. If the constructs of time and distance still held any relevance by which we could assess our progress, we would have found that our sojourn covered miles, with half-a-day passing as we plodded down that vast shaft that never bent or shrank.

***

Eventually we came to a halt the way a cart does when its axle breaks. There were no alcove-doors to be located, so the warning against sleeping in the 'big tunnel' was disregarded. We made a fire out of rags to keep warm in the cold blackness; puny flames that sputtered and tossed writhing bits of themselves onto the nearby stone. As we had nothing to burn save our clothing, (and some of us didn't even have that) the fire was short-lived. Broken and filthy and greatly harmed we huddled together and traded stories to make ourselves feel more real.

The man who had claimed his father came from F-Bloc said his name was Abraham. He was an agriculturalist who had lived on thirteen, and he had been in the Bazaar-gardens when it happened. As he recounted the fall of Z-Bloc from his perspective, his voice would often falter in sadness or disbelief, and big tears would slip down his cheeks and leave glistening aisles through the grime thereon. At these moments, we would all lean in further, breath bated, urging him with our eyes to continue. He had a very honest quality about him, and it was for that reason that he was deemed most-adequate to represent our collective suffering, and was elected in a voiceless balloting as our impromptu poster-child; the figurehead of the newly-orphaned Z-Bloc children.

However, when Abraham laid the blame for the uprising on the Zealots, anxious chatter and argumentative defiances traveled through our huddle.

"Why would they do that? The Zealots were the most peaceable among us!"

"They're crazy! We've all heard them!"

"Did the Great Gates open?"

"Don't be fullish, those old doors can't never be opened!"

"Maybe they found a way! I heard a tremendous noise - it shook the whole Bloc!"

"That was a bomb. I saw the West Liftshaft blow open like a bursting pipe."

"Surely it was the Zealots! Had to have been, what with all their talk! Damned detestable ratfuckers, the lot of them! Striding about in those silly vestments! Fucking fanatics!"

These and other statements were made, and as people argued, they gained confidence in their opinions. Contradictions and accusations abounded as our noise grew louder, reaching out further in the dark and echoing back in a way that reminded us of the sheer size of the tube, and of our insignificance in comparison to those who came before us. Surely they were titans; terraforming giants with ambitions grand, to have constructed this conduit and laid it so deep within the earth. Lost in these fascinations, I was startled when someone nudged me in the ribs, and I winced painfully as a demand was made for my thoughts.

"Where are you from? Your face looks familiar..."

"Thirty-eight."

"You frequent the Bronco?"

"On occasion."

"That's it, then. What do *you* think?"

I pointed up into the crepuscularity above. "Incredible, is it not? How do we even know if any ceiling exists? We just have to take it on faith..."

"Of course there's a ceiling, of some sort. If there wasn't, we'd see the Day, huh? I mean what do you think about the Zealots? Think they opened the Gates?"

Another face pushed in close, melding out of the shadows, angry eyes reflecting the firelight.

"Why don't you shut up, like? The Prophets had nothing to do with it, they've never done anything of the sort! Must have been one of the Gunbosses, or those–" he pointed to the huddle of Sons, further up the slope, brooding together "–gangsters over there!"

"Who are you?" the first man demanded. "I don't recognize you! What's your level?"

"What you asking me for? I don't know your face either!"

Before any real altercation could transpire, Monogatari stepped over us and growled for silence, saying we all ought to get some sleep, because we'd be moving again in a few hours. I had nothing with which to cover myself, so I laid as close to the coals as I could. The stone was cold against my back. There was groaning and small noises all around me, and I tried to make out the whispered words. Many people were hugging, spooned against one-another for warmth, but no-one wanted to spoon with me, and I didn't want to ask for it. I gazed up at the darkness and felt my fear more internally - it no longer seemed so far away. The fire burned low and the darkness came closer, until it was right on top of me - I could reach out in any direction and touch its milky slickness. It was like industrial grease. I rolled on my side and shut my eyes. The man from earlier, the defender of the Zealots, was lying beside me. I wondered if he was asleep, and, as if he could read my thoughts, he spoke quietly: "You believe me, right? About the Zealots?"

"I don't know."

"You gotta believe me. Please..."

***

In the depth of the night, (or what could be called 'night' simply because it was the time we had chosen to rest) I was shaken by Monogatari. I had been sleeping the way an old dog does towards the end of its days, but the expression on the face of my friend, which I could see only by the light of the lit match he held, roused me at once. He looked crazed; his bloodshot eyes desperately searching the impossible blackness for any sign of life, no matter how remote...

"Do you hear that?" he demanded, seizing hold of my shoulder. "Hear it? Listen!"

I listened. The silence was so complete that I could hear the blood rushing in my veins and the sound of my neurons sparking. Monogatari put his starving eyes on my face, willing me to hear whatever it was that he suspected was out there. I held my breath and strained my ears. There was something... it could have been a chorus of many distant voices, all singing in the Old Tongue; thousands, or even millions, vocalizing together in anguish as they burned alive nailed to crosses dotting a Sunlit hillside... or it could have been (and most-likely was) nothing. Somebody coughed in their sleep and Monogatari hissed and cursed and resumed scanning the darkness. His balled fist tightened as he turned back towards me, gripping me vicelike, urging me to give him something, although I wasn't sure what...

"You hear it, yeah?"

"Yeah... Um, yeah, I hear it..."

I couldn't hear a thing. I hoped that none of the decumbent bundles around us, who were surely awake and listening, could make out the specifics of our conversation. My false answer seemed to placate Monogatari, who nodded and muttered under his breath and stalked off back to where he had been lying with Kassie, a little ways off from the rest of us...

**

We walked onwards through the big tube without firelight because there was nothing left to burn. Flashlight-beams cut through the black, yet not even the strongest of these could find the ceiling. We joined hands, so that none might be separated from the pack and lost. I walked with Abraham holding my right hand, Skudd holding my left, the lot of us silent. It was sobering. We had all by this point come to the individual conclusions that we might have perished in the chaos above and were now damned.

When the first flashlight died, someone started crying. It was discussed and agreed-upon that we should take the next corridor leading out of the main tunnel; the logic being that because none of us had accessed it directly from Z, it wouldn't stand to assume that this cavernous and seemingly-endless shaft would lead undeviatingly to another Bloc. This line-of-thinking held up amongst the entire group, so Monogatari conceded that we should find a door. We passed several with their alcoves set low, near the bottom of the pipe, and Monogatari and the largest Son used a crowbar to prise them open, despite insistence from the former that it was a waste of energy, because the alcoves that led to hallways and maintenance-corridors were set further up the slope. The lower ones were electrical closets, hardly bigger than those in the Bloc. We walked for several miles before finding a door, stripped from its hinges, lying at the bottom of the pipe. The alcove from which it had come was further up the tube, and, as Monogatari had predicted, this one led to a narrow hallway. As we entered this tunnel one-by-one, another flashlight gave out.

Before stepping over the threshold, I took a long last look down the massive main tunnel. All I could think of was how, if I shut my eyes and opened them again, there was not a lick of perceptible difference...

SIX

We wandered hopeless and thirsting, lost in the infinite laby-rinth; that infernal maze of tunnels, corridors, and shafts of varying sizes and degree-of-degradation. At first, we did our best to vote on which turns to take, but this democratic prac-tice became counterproductive and dysfunctional. Nonethe-less, when Monogatari assumed full authority, his decisions were called into question at every turn, and we commenced to complaining and arguing, all-the-while with the batteries of the flashlights and headlamps dying. Progress, if we were in fact making any whatsoever, slowed greatly as paranoia flour-ished and abounded. If we were not so weak from hunger and the stingy water-rations, violence would have ensured.

I made my way to the front of the pack, where Monoga-tari and Skudd were leading, and suggested that we take a rest.

"We keep moving while we still have light."

"People are demoralized. There is dissent. Could become a problem if left unchecked."

"Fuck 'em." Skudd said.

I frowned. Monogatari brought the group to a halt.

"Twenty-minute rest. Kill all the lights but one."

"Where are we going?!" a voice called from the rear of the pack. There was further chatter as we took off our loads and splayed out. Abraham sat beside me, and I could tell from the look on his face that he was going to make an attempt to to speak with me privately about something that couldn't be good. I wished he wouldn't, but I had come to accept that my role within the group was to keep tabs on how everybody was getting along, so that I might make reports to Monogatari, and problems could be headed-off before they arose.

"I don't trust Kaide."

"Who?"

"Kaide. That guy. *Him*. Remember? He was talking about the Zealots, defending them, and I heard him earlier... sounded like he was praying..."

"So what?"

"Who is he? Who knows him? Seems to me that everyone has their people, save him!"

"Who are *your* people?"

Abraham turned up his face in indignation and made an act of huffing offendedly as he got up and walked away.

Then Kassie came over with two of the Sons. It hadn't taken her long to integrate herself into their cohort. She took a flashlight from one of them and then dismissed them both, and they ambled off pointlessly, as if attending her was the sole function of their existence. She switched on the light as she sat beside me. I thought about telling her to keep it off, as Monogatari had ordered, but I knew he would not rebuke Kassie; their distinctive relationship gave her full operating autonomy. She reached out and squeezed my hand. With reluctance, I looked her in the face. The light and the sight of her hurt my eyes - she looked rattled and timid in a way that I had never seen her look before.

In Z-Bloc, Kassie always had the ability to appear aloofly disheveled, as if she had just come out of a dirty fight or rough fuck - ripped clothes, smeared facepaint, tousled hair, but always weirdly, dangerously beautiful. You never saw a girl who could be so pretty with both her eyes blacked. Looking at her made you want to find out if you were man enough to be with her. I'll readily admit that, despite our intemerate friendship, I often hypothesized as to what such would be like. She used her untarnishable vitality to charm, similar to the way Monogatari used his size and strength to kill, and even I was not immune to her wiles. Yet now, with her face half-defined by the blade of the electric light, she simply looked poor. I took stock of her and thought to myself that it was likely she would die quickly after all the lights went out, which was a certainty - not a matter of if, but when - and it was bound to happen at any point. I surprised myself with this speculation, because I had never before imagined that Kassie would die sooner than the rest of anybody in the Bloc. She was two years younger than I, yet I felt like I was her elder by a century. Still-and-all, she, just like the rest of us, had been aged by the darkness. I squeezed her hand back and put my arm around her shoulders. In a voice barely above a whisper, she said my name and laid her head against my chest.

"Do you think everything will be okay?" she asked.

"I don't know."

"Remember when we were kids?"

"Yes."

"You tried to teach me to read, with those old copies of the annals."

"You never learned."

"I didn't need to read them myself. I liked hearing you read them."

I didn't have anything to say to this. There was a pause. Then: "You told me you loved me once. When we were kids."

"I do love you."

"Good."

Another pause, somehow more weighty than the last.

"Do you think we are going to die?"

"Everybody dies eventually."

"I just wish something would happen. It's bad that we're stuck down here. The dark is so awful, it's like the only thing that's real is what is in our heads... We're turning on each other. I wish something would happen..."

I nodded in agreement. The silence and the stillness and the uncertainty were far worse than any commotion. We were starving and going dry and blind. Yet, although the esoteric power of Kassie Pink might have been dulled by the tunnels, its bandwidth diminished by those untold miles of concrete, it remained very much astir. The proof of this lay in the fact that, only seconds after she said she wished something would happen, something did...

✳✳✳

There was a sudden turbulent lurch all about us. The walls of the corridor grumbled and dust sprinkled from the cracks in the ceiling above, falling to the quavering floor upon which the intermittent puddles rippled. We had felt no disturbance of even half this magnitude since our descent from the Bloc. In an instant, we were all on our feet, shouting, reunited in disposition by fear, breathing as one body again, and thinking as one mind with a singular focus: survive.

The deep rumbling moved down the corridor, away from us, and the shaking diminished. I went to the wall to lay my ear against it. The noise was faraway, yet still cause for concern. It was rushing; aqueous, to be certain, water or sewage in pipes running adjacent to the access-shaft we occupied. Others listened also, and made comments, mostly hopeful, because it seemed like the flow was departing us... yet, what gave me pause was the sheer volume of the sound. As a HydroElectric man, I was well-familiar with the sounds of various quantities of surging liquid, and this sounded like a lot - millions of gallons, easily - to be able to vibrate the concrete against my cheek in such a manner. Although the actual rush seemed to be receding, the vibration was intensifying, becoming nearly unbearable, putting my teeth at-risk of rattling out of my mandible. I moved back from the wall.

Monogatari found me in the small crowd and asked me what I thought it was. I hastily explained that I wasn't sure, but I didn't think it was good. It sounded like a magnified version of the telltale warning that came just before a hydro-pipe burst. To explain the specifics of how the HydroElectric systems functioned would have taken forever-and-a-day, and my understanding was admittedly limited, but I felt that we were in very grave danger... and I was proven right straightaway.

In the darkness up ahead came a sudden, deafening crash. The entire corridor shook again, far worse than before, and was filled with a roar that was definitely and undeniably drawing towards us at a breakneck pace. The noise was so loud that I would venture to claim it was the loudest thing I'd ever heard, and growing steadily louder; already so cacophonous that it drowned out our screaming...

We all broke and ran in the direction opposite the approaching thunder. Ahead of me was a lanky Son, his long strides keeping him in the foremost position, the beam of his flashlight hacking wildly in the black. I was on his heels with a few other young and able-bodied men; the fastest runners. We rounded a corner where the straight hallway branched off to the left-and-right at a cross-intersection. After making the turn, I hazarded a glance over my shoulder.

The scattered eyes of the flashlights blew out like snuffed candles as the water-wall swept down the corridor. All those who had not taken the turn with us were taken away forever, if they survived the force of the wave (which filled the hall entirely) crashing down upon them. The water smashed against the corner-edge of the intersection and chased the remainder of us with impossible speed and rampancy. We were swept off our feet and forwarded as the branching shaft was filled almost-instantly by the indomitable current. I became weightless, bone-soaked and thrashing, with my up-as-down and vise-as-versa; sputtering and struggling as the darkness reclaimed the autonomic rights it had lent to me and all of us. It affianced me as its own and was all around me, inside me, making me one with it...

My head broke above the surface and I gasped for air, filling my lungs to retain buoyancy. Even in the jet-blackness, the sensation of pace was astounding. I was struck by the fact that I had never moved, or, more rightly, been moved at such a rate. I stopped my flailing and laid back, sucking in air and dirty liquid, until my stomach jumped into my throat the same way it had when the West Lift fell. The corridor gave way and I lurched into a plummet, falling an unimaginable distance - miles, perhaps - for a long time; a full minute or more, disoriented by the pinwheeling volutions until the fall stopped and the water crushed down around me, forcing the air from my lungs and thrusting me deeper beneath the impalpable surface. I choked and reached and grabbed for anything besides the water by which I was hopelessly enveloped, but there was nothing besides it. As I suffocated, I felt myself slipping away, losing discernment between myself and the water, which was darkness made manifest and incarnate, a physical embodiment of all its qualities; infinite, cold, all-consuming, and not angry with, but simply indifferent to all save itself. As my desperation subsided and was replaced with a lymphatic acceptance, I snagged against something solid - a steely grapnel lodged into my armpit - and by this I was dragged out of the darkness and up, up, up into the stinging dry air and roaring noise.

***

Before we fell, Monogatari had bear-hugged Kassie, and even the tumult of our tilting, headlong pitch had not separated them. As if this was not evidence enough of his dynamism, he had also managed to seize with one hand the rung of a ladder that hung down from a catwalk above. Kassie kept a death-grip on him, and Skudd had caught her leg, and he in-turn had caught the wrist of Abraham, who grabbed Kaide, who took me under the arm, and the six of us formed a human chain in that swelling river. By the virtue of his herculean strength, Monogatari climbed hand-over-hand up the ladder, dragging the rest of us within reach of it, and we pulled ourselves one-at-a-time out of the raging current. Gasping for air and climbing precariously with wet hands and feet we hauled our waterlogged carcasses up to the catwalk and collapsed on its iron-grate flooring, limp limbs dangling off the edges, feeble, blind, and utterly spent.

"It's so dark! I can't see anything... oh, help! Help, please! I can't see! I can't see!"

"Who's there?! Sound yourselves off!"

"Listen! Is the water rising—"

I could hear the water surging below, rising indeed, but slowly. I rolled onto my hands and knees, clinging to the metal grate, my fingers slipped through the slots. It was so dark... until suddenly there came light - blinding, definitive, an explosion of substantiality, and we came together in it, embracing and sobbing. Our forms cut shadows between where the light played, us making noises and feeling one-another, to be sure of reality and reminded of its finite boundaries, and we began laughing, and the shrieking of our laughter echoed back to us from the unfeeling stone walls by which we were surrounded. Below us, the water rose steadily.

Monogatari, our savior and our shepherd, had kept hold of his bag and had withdrawn from it a flashlight that still worked, its metal casing waterproofed by putty and electrical tape. We found our feet and moved down the catwalk, out of that 'main' room, to another hallway; bleak vanilla concrete spiderwebbed by cracks, extending off to nowhere, and we took hold of one another and walked. No words were spoken regarding the certain demise of the rest of our party. They had been washed tracelessly away, and we enacted a tacit resolution between us that it was best to forget that they had ever existed. All that was real was what we could see and touch, as such is all that has ever been. We walked.

"How long do you think that light will last?"

"We'll be sparing." Monogatari said.

"I swallowed a lot of that water... you think it was dirty? Will I be sick?"

"We'll find out."

We continued walking.

Continued walking.

Walking.

Perhaps more impressive than the architectural accomplishment of constructing this maze of tunnels and hallways would have been the topographical achievement of mapping them out. I wondered if the Corporation had actually managed to do so, and if they had, if any of those master blueprints still survived. It was doubtful. This network exceeded human comprehension. It must have been a multi-generational endeavor, with new levels and passages adjoined to the old continually. They dug deep, and kept digging because it was all they knew, venturing forever deeper, until the entanglement surely grew far beyond what was initially needed or intended.

Abraham: "Do you smell that?"

"Shit?"

"No, I smell it too..." I said.

"Smells fresher? Or, um, *bigger*. Yeah, like in the big tube, back... um, was it two or three days ago?"

"Fucking years ago..."

"Bigger air, definitely... and fresher, too." Skudd stated in a wimpish voice. He seemed to be taking up any excuse to feel hopeful about something.

As we went, the air took on a definite quality of being cleaner. It was difficult to construe, but perceptible nonetheless. We came to an intersection and went one way, until it became clear that we were moving away from the better air, so we doubled back. Our wetness had dried, as we had been wandering the corridors for several hours by this point, yet I could have sworn I felt something like a draft against my skin. This stirring sensation in the air became more salient with every step, until Monogatari stopped suddenly and jumped and shouted: "Everyone stop!"

We came to a halt and gathered around his shoulders to look out at... nothing. A yard before us, the floor and walls and ceiling of the corridor simply broke off in jagged edges and gave way to enormous gaping blackness, like that of the big tube, yet even bigger, if possible. The weak beam of the light once again raced off into eternity and failed to find anything.

"Put out the light." Kassie said.

"Why?"

"I want to *see* it."

Something about the way she said this made us all understand and concur. Monogatari switched off the flashlight, and we breathed and gazed, trying to imagine how far-and-deep that astronomical expanse extended...

***

All fear, when reduced to its most fundamental essence, is the fear of the unknown. Full understanding of fear cannot be derivatively comprehended secondhand - it comes on its own terms to a person only upon their firsthand experience of it. Authentic fear, sublimely primal and intrinsic, originates from, and is manufactured by, darkness and silence, and only those who have gained acquaintance with True Darkness unadulterated by light, or True Silence unpolluted by sound, can reach an agreement with themselves - or, more rightly, enact a transcendental denial of the self, through which true fear can be disseminated. The absence of light and sound reveals to us ourselves, annihilating the illusions of sovereignty that we so audaciously attribute to our senses. We are not what we can see and hear; we simply *are*, and when confronted with ourselves, we yearn for something, anything, dissimilar to the innocent helplessness of our innermost piths, with a longing less-specific, yet far greater than those we hold for food or water or air. We desire the taintless freedom of unbeing, because nothing, no matter how vile, that could emerge from the abyss would be worse than the emptiness of the abyss itself, and that quintessential reflection of our spirits gleaned therefrom.

***

That great pit bestowed an impression beyond immensity. Unlike the big tube, it seemed wholly void. Even in the largest of those halls and chambers through which we had come thus far, there had always been that sense of enclosure, of entombment... but this cavern was altogether different. It might have been the end of the earth! I felt an urge to fling myself over the edge... No. It wasn't time yet, because for all its grandiosity, this darkness still lacked something - some esoteric touch of absolute cosmic purity...

I squinted, searching in the dark, and I thought that I might have spotted something. I couldn't be certain, but the others saw it too. It was Kassie who spoke of it first.

"Up there! Look! Is... is that... light?"

"Where?"

"There, way above! Little twinkling dots, you see?"

"I see!" Skudd cried delightedly. "I see! Little lights! Oh... oh, they're beautiful!"

"A long way away..."

"Or just very small lights. Hard to tell."

Kassie: "No... Kaide is right. They're really far. I don't think we'll ever get up that high..."

I felt Skudd deflate beside me. Of all people, it was Monogatari that took pity on him in the best way he could, dropping a heavy hand on his shoulder and saying in a low voice: "We won't know until we try. Let's go."

The flashlight came back on, and we all took hold of each

other in our manner, once again forming a chain and resuming our roam through the subterranean maze that played some obscure role in keeping us alive, or keeping our ancestors alive, but had now become so chillingly empty that we felt at once large and small, our footsteps and grunts and coughs rushing out so fast into the silence and space and returning so distorted that we could hardly recognize them as our own... yet, they were our own. We were the world down here; the only thing by which to define ourselves, the only spectrum of comparison, eternity personified... at least while we survived and continued to plod endlessly over the cracked stone, drinking from puddles, carrying naught but our hides. Ten-thousand steps ten-thousand times... until we found a stairwell.

We were quite happy, because we'd all wanted to find skyward stairs so badly back when the group was larger, yet they had eluded us, so to find them now felt all-the-more significant, because it made us think of the others, and then shy away from thinking of them and imagining what their final moments in that torrent must have been. Were they still alive somewhere, as we were? Could they too be crouched in some remote corridor around a single light, starving, thirsting, dreading being lost forever?

The stairwell was almost identical to the ones in Z-Bloc: U-shaped, enclosed in cement, boxed-in, so there was no way of knowing how many flights went in either direction. I hoped it would be a long distance, and that we were near the bottom, so that all the height would be above us. On the first landing, Monogatari proposed that we take a rest before beginning the climb. There were no complaints against this. We settled and the light was killed. In the dark, I felt hands touching me. It was Kassie. She cuddled up under my arm, and I wondered why me and not Monogatari, but then I realized she was crying - from fright or pain, I couldn't tell - but she must have been embarrassed and wished to hide it from him. I hadn't seen her cry since we were kids. Even now, I couldn't see her, but I could feel her spasming with the effort of containing her sobs. Eventually, this tension quelled and she went limp into sleep, for which I was thankful.

SEVEN

We awoke stiff and broken-ended in utter bedragglement. In the beam of Monogatari's flashlight, Kassie, Kaide, and Skudd all looked as though they had wept through the night, and the light reminded us all that we had more suffering to endure before our deaths, which would likely not come fast nor painless. Our thirst was tremendous - our lips were cracked and our joints aching, and upon standing, we found ourselves lightheaded. My stomach burned, as if the digestive acid was chewing through the lining. I could taste only sodium and iron in my parched throat.

We commenced our climb up the stairs. To our initial delight, they (like everything else in those infernal sewers) seemed endless. At least we were going upwards, skyward-like. I probably should have voiced that reflection, yet didn't. There was no telling how long of a climb we had ahead of us. The water had swept us down unimaginably low...

I counted as we climbed, but the going was slow. The stairs sapped what little energy we had, and there was no food or water save for the occasional puddles. We ascended ninety floors. A dozen steps, then hang a louie to a fresh dozen. Occasionally we found landing-doorways that led out to halls and corridors. At one point, Monogatari said that we should go looking for water, yet we failed to find any after walking several hundred feet, all-the-while growing concerned that we might lose our way. The stairs were more arduous then the tunnels, but fuck tunnels - fuck them in the dirt.

Shortly after climbing the hundredth flight, we found both hope and fear exemplified in the dark. Dusty human bones sat long-undisturbed on a landing, and, in our gazing silence, we heard noise coming from the narrow shaft beyond the doorframe. It sounded like liquid trickling. We pursued the sound to a place where the wall had been busted open to expose a cracked pipe from which water was dripping. We rushed and pushed to taste it and found it sweet and clean. Avidly we cupped our lips to the crack and tried to suck the water out, but it was transuded to us only a few droplets at a time. Monogatari filled his gutjug and told us to rest as he did. Still, the water would not save us from starvation or madness. Bones and water... we could not stay in this place, or more bones would soon litter the floor. We drank and slept and drank more when we awoke.

***

The next 'day' was worse than the previous one. We climbed a hundred-and-fifty flights and sucked through the water fast. Then, the light died. That was terrible. It was an eventuality that we had all been bracing ourselves against, but no amount of anxious anticipation could have prepared us for the fear that took hold once it actually occurred. The blackout became eternal and levied against us a peerless epistemic despondency. Although I couldn't see him, I could tell Monogatari was especially affected - his fortitude succumbing to that insurmountable question of 'what would happen now' - yet he urged us onward, saying that it was simple enough for us to keep going; we had only to keep one hand on the inner-wall of the stairwell and the other upon the shoulder of the person in front of us. We had been going for long enough that we were all well-familiar with the dimensions of the stairs and could easily climb them blind.

That was only partially true. It didn't take long before Skudd stumbled over some loose rubble and fell and crashed into Kaide, whose ankle sprained. His shouting filled the stairwell. It seemed louder and was indisputably far more unsettling to the spirit in the consummate darkness. Bad vibrations. Although he was hardly at-fault, Skudd apologized profusely, and with the help of Abraham, he assisted Kaide up the next flights, until Abraham, winded, advocated for taking a few hours rest and 'figuring out what to do next.'

Over the course of recent events, a friendship had budded between Abraham and Kaide, (perhaps because the former had saved the latter from the river) and this developing comity gave me courage; a belief in our inherent altruism, that all that was within us was righteous and good. Nonetheless, we were washed-up and burnt-out. We settled on the landing, dropping in the very spots where we stood, wretched, pained, forfeiting the mental preoccupation of the climb and the physical distresses of our diversified injuries. Yet, without these, things got real. Even the most rugged amongst us couldn't bear to face the claustrophobic dusk and the questions it tendered. Would starvation end us? Would we eat the first to expire? Who would it be? Who would be last, and how would they bear the loneliness? Would the stairs ever end, and even if they did, would it matter? Would we lose our minds in these tunnels?

I heard speech choked out between Kassie's stifled sobs, although I couldn't ascertain the words. Then, Monogatari, in reply: "No, don't say that... don't..."

Skudd was also crying, and making little-or-no effort to conceal it. "We're going to die down here!" he shrieked.

"Stow that talk!"

"We're going to die... we're already dead..."

"I am not going to die in this place." I said, surprising myself with the conviction that I managed to muster. I didn't fully believe the proclamation, but I repeated it. I would not die.

***

I waited for what felt like hours, but could have been only a few minutes - no way to tell, as time had long-since become meaningless - and then I stood and picked my way silently across the landing until I reached the wall. Up twelve stairs, left to the next twelve, and the next, and the next... until I could no longer hear the breathing or crying of my companions. I kept going up, figuring there wasn't any harm in it - I could always turn around and descend until I returned to them. I kept track of how many flights I climbed. Twelve, round a left, twelve; that was one. I climbed nine total, until I found something to shatter the unmitigated night...

On the ninth landing was a door, the frame of which I could make out because there was light in the hallway beyond. Not a lot of light, but in the blackness to which I had acclimated, even a wee small amount made all the difference. I moved down the hallway towards the light, and as it brightened, I could make out an assemblage of paintings on the walls, mostly in black and red inks. The style of them was familiar to me. For the first time since I had fled Z-Bloc, I thought of the Ancient Man, and his antechamber decorated with similar depictions of bygone humanity constructing their own enslavements. Spirals, pyramids, stick-figure crowds amassed before an elevated figure with flames (or perhaps wings) sprouting from his back... I touched the cold adorned stone, half-expecting it to feel like something other than stone, as if the illustrations might be blood-warm with life. A long line had been drawn unbroken down the hallway, and I assumed this to be the horizon, as it was dotted with obelisks that surely represented the Blocs, and there was the True Sun above this line and the Undersun below it, and writing and symbols in the Old Tongue, most of which I could not decipher...

The light was coming from a man-sized aperture in the wall where the cement had been mined - a jagged adit adorned with thousands of primitive delineations layered one-over-the-other in schizophrenic fashion, though not altogether at random. The shaft had been cut through ten solid feet of stone, and as I ventured into this hole, the light grew very bright as I neared the source of it, stinging my eyes like teargas.

Squinting and with a racing heart I came into a shabby chamber lit by a single oblong bulb overhead. The light was warm and yellow, and I realized that it was cast by a mini-sun-lamp (like the one I had in my old unit) hung by a hook wedged into a crack in the ceiling. The cable that powered the lamp bowed to a slitted steel locker-door in the wall across from me. This was closed, its surface painted-over, like every other surface in the room, with that disorganized skein that was possibly a hopelessly-attempted schematic of the tunnels themselves. Besides the handmade passage by which I had entered, there was only one other point-of-access to this closet, and this was obstructed by the debris of a cave-in that formed a rubble-hill that spilled halfway into the room and went up to the top of the blocked doorway.

On the floor opposite this gravel incline sat human remains; the skeletons of a man and two children. Hair still clung in patches to their dusty skulls. The distinct odor of very old death abounded, and there were putrefied black stains on the wall against which the corpses rested. The bullet-holes in the skulls and the angle of the rifle resting between the man's legs suggested Sudoku. Slung over his ribcage was a fabric satchel. I picked up the rifle and used the barrel to remove the bag from his arm without disturbing the bones. The sling was rotted to naught, and as it came apart, its fibers twirled and danced in the yellow light.

Within the satchel, I discovered sweet deliverance: an oil-lantern and a half-full container of fuel, a dented can of jellied alcohol, a cracked gutjug, a knife, and some loose ammunition for the rifle. The gutjug was as badly-withered as the bag itself, and was so dried-out that I could crack it to pieces in my hands. I did so, and used a strip of it as a wick for the lantern, and then I opened one of the rifle-cartridges and poured the powder in a neat pile on the floor and used a piece of stone against the knifeblade to spark it. After several tries, it ignited and hissed violently and burned bright. I lit the oil-wet wick and had light, subdued by the grime on the chimney, yet light nonetheless. I cursed in relief and stared at the flame for several seconds, not daring to hope that it would persist, but it seemed to be feeding well-enough and not burning too fast. Such luck was enough to make me utter aloud praises to Horsche and Gordyume, and whatever other gods the Zealots believed in.

Nothing else in the room remained to be searched save for the closed locker, which bore resemblance to the electrical-access boxes in the Bloc HydroElectric control-rooms. I wondered if this was a room constructed for a similar purpose, or one even more critical, as it would have taken tremendous effort to excavate the stone between this place and the hallway adjacent to it. The hinges of the locker-door were decrepit and caked with dust, but I pulled it with all my strength and it creaked-and-grinded open to reveal a miscellany of wires; hundreds of them, knotted snaking tangles, with half of them clipped or ripped out of their ports, their brass-and-copper innards splaying out like the anthers and filaments of exotic flowers. From this roost of vipers a single cable emerged prominent, thicker than the others, intact, and with my eyes I traced it until it ended at a conduit-attachment to which was affixed a small oblong cylinder.

A battery of some sort? I examined the rest of the nest and could find no other explicable source of the power. I knelt and held the lantern close to see better. The object was three inches long, rounded at one end, no more than an inch in diameter, and the brushed steel had a strange luster to it. Housed by the external shell was a glass core, visible through a narrow window in the side of the metal. This was half-full of liquid - not cloudy or nubilous, but shiny, almost glowing, and extremely dark vantablack. Gently, I flicked the window with my finger. The liquid jumped and swirled and settled without smearing or leaving any bedaubulations on the glass. I found the coupling-mechanism to be uncomplicated; a simple counterclockwise twist, and it detached with a click. The connector capped immediately - the cylinder sealed itself, now rounded at both ends, an ingenious feature that functioned by either magnetism or magic, which prevented any damage from being inflicted on the plug that might set free the swirling sticky darkness within. The lamp above died and the room darkened instantaneously upon the detachment of the Battery. The low glow of the lantern was insufficient to adequately illuminate the paintings on the stone, but I knew they were watching me nonetheless. I held fast my prize and hung the lantern from the rifle-barrel, so that it might illuminate my retreat.

***

When triumphant I returned to my companions in the stairwell, I attained my place amongst the Immortal Saints of Horsche. There was incredulous joy and laughter, and Monogatari pulled me into a tight hug and kept saying 'you son of a flea-bitten dog!' in a strange voice.

By the glow of the lantern we could see each other once again, and were reminded that we were human after all, under all the dust and grime and shit, and although we lived like rats, we were not rats, as once again we wielded promethean fire with which we could wage war against the subterranean gloom. This brought us all such rejuvenation that we agreed to continue onward up those indomitable stairs, and as we did, we congratulated ourselves on the progress we had made thus-far. We must be getting close to the top now; it would surely be only another day before the stairs came to an end - after all, they couldn't go on forever - so we climbed, light on our feet for the first time since the Bloc plumbing had shat us out into these demeaning catacombs.

I quite enjoyed the new status and admiration I had gained in the eyes of the others. I was our new savior, the bold one who had ventured out into the maze and returned victorious, bearing that most-precious of resources in our time of great need. Kassie stayed at my right and held my hand, Monoga-tari on my left, holding the rifle, with I in the middle with my prize: the lantern, held proudly above my head. The others kept close, eager to stay within the crowded dim-orange fish-bowl. I was the custodian of all our hope, our new fearless leader. What I had accomplished was beyond the imagination of these people; an act of titan bravery. With me, they could not lose nor become lost, and their hope fueled my own con-fidence, which in-turn compelled me to act in a manner be-fitting of their faith. We pressed on. Up and up and up. I for-got to count the floors, but it must have been nearly another hundred. Eventually, it was I who issued the command to halt and rest, which was received with unanimous agreement. We settled and bedded-down on the hard cold stone. With care, I opened the slot-door of the lantern and snuffed out the flame, plunging us back into the inky sea, but it wasn't so oppressive any longer. We could all breathe and sleep easier.

**

Halfway through the next uphill day, the stairs finally

came to an end, concluding in a moderately-large room with doors on opposite sides, each leading nowhere, and a tunnel opposite the stairs that stretched further than we could see. Beside the stairwell-access door was an iron plaque; a Corporation remnant similar to those in the the main Bloc Lifts, that identified the stairwell as one of twenty-five Unabridged Access Stairwells. Five-hundred floors! With the assumption that each flight covered a fourteen-foot height, that meant that the total distance to the bottom was nearly a mile and a half - and this did not account for that pit we had encountered close to the bottom, which ran far, *far* deeper...

Before we entered the tunnel, we backtracked down the stairs to a place where we had previously found another steady water-drip, and we drank and rested while Monogatari refilled his gutjug, which again took several hours. Then we climbed back up to the top and started down the tunnel. It went straight for a distance before veering off to the right, and as we walked, we found that it had a downhill angle. This disheartened us, but nobody said anything until we came to a fork where the tunnel branched off into three separate paths. Everyone looked to me for the decision, and I was ill-prepared for the responsibility. Until this point, my position as our new leader had been a mostly-symbolic one. On the stairs, there was nowhere to go but up. Now, a definite and possibly-irrevocable judgment was required - one that I knew would inevitably be called into question shortly after being put into action. I didn't feel so bold or confident anymore, but I tried not to show it. We took the tunnel furthest to the right. Right is right, right? That's what I said to them, and there were no objections.

***

The maze continued. Tunnels and pipes, some squared, some rounded, some bare, some with cable-housing running their lengths; iron or polyvinyl tubes bolted into the walls or ceiling. Morale languished. We had not eaten in over a week, and hunger had rendered us emaciated and sickly. We were naked, the few shreds of clothing some of us had were reduced to stiffened rags, and these had been surrendered to Kassie, as she was the only woman amongst us. Our eyes were bloodshot and black, reflecting only the dusky lantern-light. The darkness had crept inside of us, and our edges mixed and mingled with its essence. If someone spoke, the words were naught but ghostly echoes. All other physical discomforts were dwarfed by the pain in our feet and knees. The winding tunnels were monotonous, and with every turn we took, we all wondered if we were getting closer or further-away... to what? We didn't know, and had given-up trying to imagine. Death would have been a relief. I was so hungry that I was contemplating using the knifeblade to section off a bit of my own flesh...

We continued until the tedium was broken by noise - an insectoid skittering in the tunnel behind us, on the floor, the wall, and then the ceiling, getting rapidly closer. Panic broke out. I held the lantern high, but the fishbowl was not spacious enough to fill the corridor we occupied. The noise passed speedily over our heads and receded beyond us.

"The fuck was that?!"

"I could barely see it! It... it looked like a dog!"

"That ain't no dog, like!"

"Be silent!"

We quieted and listened to the sound of the slithering in the shadows...

"It's still there!"

"Nobody move!"

In an instant, Monogatari was in command again. He held the rifle against his shoulder, scanning the dark, his eyes narrowed to slits. There was silence for a moment, and then the noise resumed, moving back in our direction, unseen, yet magnified into something horrendous by the unbridled phantasms rampaging in our half-crazed heads.

"It's coming back! It's—"

Abraham's exclamation was cut off as he tripped over some rubble and fell. We got him back to his feet posthaste. My knuckles were white on the knife-handle, my every muscle tensed. I felt weak and cursed myself for it - I had been reduced to impuissance by famishment.

"If it tries to touch me, I'm gonna fuckin' *bust* it, just let full-loose on the whore!" Skudd said. His tone was that of a man not ready to let loose anything save the contents of his bowels.

"Quiet!"

"I... I don't hear it anymore..."

"It's still out there–"

"Let me listen, you dogs! Shut up!"

We drew close together and gawked into the blackness, straining our senses for any sign of anything. The skittering grew louder. Whatever it was, it was quite nearby... I could make out its labored breathing and the wet dripping of its saliva, and I realized with a jolt that I had made its acquaintance before! I glanced at Monogatari, to see if he remembered, yet he looked empty.

"Shh! Listen... there's something else!"

There was something else, another sound, faint, yet certainly intentional. Human speech? Confused looks were passed around the group - was it one of us, ventriloquizing their voice to a far-off spot? It must have been, because nothing else human existed in these tunnels... Yet, the calling persisted and became more resonant. It was not one of us! It was indeed someone else; a new voice hailing us, gruff and panting. We strained to make out the words, and, for the first time in my life, I began to pray.

"Someone is calling to us!"

"Run! They're telling us to run!"

Skudd broke into a panicked sprint, which ended after a few yards when he tripped over more rubble and spilled. Monogatari did not budge.

"Get him back here!"

"We need to go!"

"We're not moving. Set down the light."

I placed the lantern on the floor and we moved back from it, out of the fishbowl, so that whatever stalked us could (hopefully) not see us. Monogatari kept the rifle fixed on the furthest point touched by the light. We could hear shuffling and movement and indiscriminate speech mingling with the noises of the creature... and then came a dazzling explosion of luminescence - blinding incandescent crimson filled the hallway, sparking and hissing, and so bright at its center that it could not be looked-at directly. I could feel it on my skin as it fell on me. We all let loose shocked exclamations, and I shielded my face, squinting out between my fingers. It was an emergency flare, held high by the figure of a man fifty feet down the corridor and moving towards us. As he came near, he hailed us and tossed the flare on the ground between us and himself. We were drenched in the red and our shadows rushed back away from our forms. The man stared dumbfounded, as the sight of us appalled his soul. We stood pauperized and zombified, seeped head-to-toe in innumerable layers of sordid sludge, hardly more than disembodied eyes suspended by frayed veins in gaunt sockets, starting out of naked, fading, caliginous forms that shivered in the incarnadine bath.

Straightaway he muttered something in the Old Tongue that sounded like an orison, and then he said: "I found you."

He had indeed.

***

His name was Halbert. He had a surname in the Old Tongue that I could not pronounce properly, and he was attired in sturdy fabric and outfitted with Gadabout equipment: lots of rope, a sharp blade, flares, multiple gutjugs, and a large supply-ruckpack. On his head was an electric headlamp and there were spare battery-cartridges on a bandolier slung across his chest. He was from Z-Bloc. Monogatari knew him, as he was one of Poppa Daddy's lieutenants.

Hal took up the flare and led us back down the hallway in the direction opposite the one we had been going. As he walked, he coiled the rope around his elbow. This was in-keeping with a technique used by the Gadabouts; the laying of rope or string when exploring the sewers. At the end of the length, the specifics of the distance and the turns taken were denoted on a bit of parchment before the process was repeated, so that the pathfinder might find their way back to the starting-point if such was necessitated. Hal explained that he had been in the tunnels for three days and had run into some exceedingly-nasty things on this level, and the one above it.

"Damned thing... It knows where to go, but some of the routes are bad - foul places with all manner of vermin sneaking about in the dark... don't bother it none, of course, but it don't know those types fix to make a meal of us... or maybe it does know, and that's why it chooses those stretches. Damned, accursed thing..."

One of us inquired in a small voice which 'thing' he was referring to, and he told us. My suspicions were confirmed. Monogatari and I exchanged glances. The noise of the creature was still present in the hallway to our rear - it was following us, and we all felt riskily exposed.

"Yep, likes the dark, it does - dark and the wet. It don't come out where we can see it too often... just goes off by itself, but it gives those little chirps, to let you know where it is and which direction to go."

"How does it know?"

"I don't know, but it knows. Got an acute sense about it. Never gets lost. It's real useful, I'll say that. Might be a damn fuckin' stark unsightly thing, but it's useful. Doubt I would've ever found you otherwise. Sniffed you out, it did..."

Hal proceeded to inform us that Poppa Daddy had sent men into the low sewers with the mission of seeking out any survivors from Z-Bloc. They had set up a Gadabout camp and took turns making expeditions into the deeper maze, with the Lizard as their guide, yet they had found no-one besides us in nine days of searching. We didn't question the specific reasons for our deliverance. In truth, I don't think any of us could believe that rescue had actually come. In our minds, we were still lost in those countless, endless, fathomless tunnels...

***

We traveled with Hal and the Lizard for the better part of a day. In that time, we only saw the latter once, and the former wouldn't meet our eyes or look at us directly, as he was made uncomfortable by our skeletal esurience and the way we seemed to suck up the air around us. We were roguishly-offensive to any human sensibility; an effect amplified by the nonchalance with which we carried our naked selves; without shame or abashment of any sort, as such concerns were derived from the procedures of civilization, and fell fast-away once civilization itself ceased to exist as ours had. We didn't attempt to make conversation with our guide; we simply followed him until we came to another boxed-in stairwell where the stairs had crumbled and a ladder had been set up to reach the landing above. At the top of this, Kassie asked where we were going. Hal said that we would see soon enough, but that it would be prudent to rest before continuing on, as we still had a good distance to cover. We reclined and drank from Hal's gutjug as the white cone of his headlamp cut the darkness like a rapier. When the light fell on us, I and my cohorts winced and shirked back, unable to relax until we were once-again cloaked in familiar sable.

After a few hours of sleep, we continued. Hal would occasionally bring us to a halt and examine his map to ensure we were on the correct path. Only once did he make an error, coming to a place where the way was caved-in. We backtracked (thankfully not far) and found a hole in the wall that led to an adjacent corridor, and, in time, we came out of a door and found ourselves back in that huge tube; so incredibly spacious that neither the walls nor ceiling could be touched by Hal's headlamp. We descended the slope to the lowest part of the floor and walked for an hour before we could make out lights in the distance - many lights, a whole assemblage of them, unmistakable twinkling specks of firelight and artificial sun...

As we approached civilization, I expected to hear whoops or crying or jubilations from my companions, yet I didn't. We marched into Undercamp in a dead, traumatized silence, seedy and inhuman, casting out black auras far before us that stank of sickness and bode nothing good.

BOOK III

'Undercamp'

EIGHT

Undercamp was built in the Great Hall, (the inhabitants' name for the big tube) up a gigantic rubble-hill where a collapse had blocked the way and filled the Hall to the top. Residences and boutiques had been dug into this hill, and as the population of this underground roadstead increased, supplementary construction had erected a structure resembling the Favela shack-tree in Z-Bloc; a multileveled garrison of catwalks, terraces and interlocking joists-and-columns rigged to support one-another, these quite slapdash and altogether contradistinctive to the edges and right-angles of Corporation construction, yet well-built nonetheless; an absorbing execution of craftsmanship and ingenuity, especially when one considered that the wealth of the materials had been carried here from far-flung places. Collectively it was an improvisational amalgamate of the repurposed ruins of old Blocs, all alight with an apricot dapple of oil-lanterns and anthracite-ashwax torches.

On our approach, our walk inclined where the bare concrete of the Hall had been filled with a great amount of soil, the odor of which indicated composting. We trod this gradual incline for maybe two-hundred yards until the ground leveled out again. There was no fence or barrier at the perimeter of Undercamp; it was open to all, a sanctuary - the first and only of its sort to be established in the sewer networks. The dirt underfoot was damp, and wooden planks had been laid end-to-end to form footpaths between the planter-enclosures. We came into the warmth of large sunlamps fixed atop posts amidst the agricultural plottage at which we marveled. The crops were green and healthy and sweet-smelling, and nearby laborers tended them diligently with spades and pruners.

As we moved through this agrarian spread, I lifted my eyes and found that I could see for the first time the dimensions of that colossal tunnel that housed us. It had to be nearly fifteen stories high and an equivalent distance wide, and the sheer size of it made even the Undercamp structure look meager.

The narrow board-footpaths led us to a cobbled court-yard, the stones of which formed a mosaic of assorted col-ors and shapes that bestrewed the base of Undercamp. This seemed to be the common-area where business was conduct-ed amongst the residents. At the center, a well had been dug and was bordered by a circular stone wall three feet high. A child was drawing water up from it, hauling a chain hand-over-hand, and we could hear the sloshing echo coming up from the hole as we approached the outskirts of the emporium. The scent of frying meat hit our noses and our mouths be-came wet with this painful reminder of our hunger. A nearby vendor was cooking dogmeat and corncobs on an iron grate, and we rushed him, and he became terrified at the sight of us and fled, abandoning his cart and wares for us to plunder. All throughout the camp was an increase of movement and ac-tivity; women shepherding their children into the huts, shop-keepers drawing closed their shutters, people moving along the catwalks, crowding to the outer balconies of the shacktree, to lay eyes upon us and pass their judgments.

We huddled around the ebbing coals of the cookfire, gro-tesque and naked and gnawing. The food-vendor's stock was sacked and consumed without care. Hal stood by, watching us uneasily, shuffling his feet in a self-conscious manner. In the light cast down from the Undercamp belfries I beheld our ugliness in full. We ate ravenously, staring at one-another with-out emotion, troubled speechless, trying to not look up at the camp and its many surveilling citizens. The humanity of this place felt alien - we were set apart from it; a different breed of animal altogether, as the resignations to death we had made in the sewers had metamorphosed our souls, or perhaps replaced them altogether with some jet-black venom like that within the little cylinder I had discovered in the depths...

***

Armed guardsmen accosted us, corralled us, and rinsed us

off with hoses connected to a pressure-pump that was usually reserved for watering the crops. They gave us clothes that smelt of lye-soap and assigned us vacant dwellings in the tree, all up close to the top, where they could keep us under close observation, no doubt. My new neighbors all had that Stoolie mannerism of trying too hard not to appear as though they were watching us. Poppa Daddy also came down to receive us, and to hear news from Z-Bloc. He did not seem surprised to learn of the circumstances from which we had absconded. He took Monogatari up to the Mayoral Palace, which overlooked the shacktree and all of Undercamp, and, despite Poppa's objections, Kassie went with them.

The hut assigned to Skudd and I was bare save for two floormats, two rough blankets, and a water-basin and oil-lantern sitting atop a small table. The glass of the lantern was clean and the light from it plastered our shadows against the sheet-metal walls of that ignoble room. We hated the light and our shadows. Skudd snuffed out the flame and we laid on our floormats in opposite corners and said nothing to one-another in those first twenty-four hours.

Here, the coming of night was denoted by the shutoff of the agricultural sunlamps on the ground below. The bustle of the camp stilled and quieted, and it seemed that these people fought to ward off the encroaching blackness of the Great Hall by keeping lamps and candles burning always. (I later ascertained that lamplighters made nightly rounds through the structure to renew the oil and wicks.) However, the darkness was a comfort to me, and I wished there was more of it. The smooth cleanliness of my skin was an irritant. The linen smock they had clad me in itched, so I shed it. Sleep did not come at all that first evening. I took up my floormat and hung it over the small window of our hut to block out the light. In the dark, Skudd came over to me and I felt that he was naked as well. He hugged me and began sobbing bitterly and touching me. I told him to fuck off, but he kept on. I could feel his warmth and his heartbeat, and I began crying too, and we cried and held each other all through the night. The next morning, he receded back to his corner and didn't look up as

I dressed and walked out.

Such were all the nights of our first week in Undercamp. When sleep did come, it was filled with nightmares of fire and light and a great river of filth washing us down an infinite hole.

***

Days passed. I learned how to navigate the camp; the ladders and catwalks and stairs, and I discovered that the lamps below derived their power from a single source: a transformer-room several levels down. It was discovered flooded, but an effort had been made to excavate a nearby shaft to allow the electrified water to flow out, and new lengths of cable were gathered from the sewers and patched into the boxes, which still siphoned power from the Undersun - which I now knew to be well-over five-hundred stories down, and likely far further. There was no plumbing in Undercamp; only intermittent outhouses, the pipes of which led to holes dug into the rubble-hill. The waste was accumulated and used to fertilize the dirt in which they farmed. There were hydro-reserve tanks at several junctions, yet the water was not rationed as it had been in Z-Bloc; it flowed freely to all. The digging of the aforementioned main well had been the most laborious project in the history of the camp, as it ran a great length down to a make-shift reservoir-chamber purposefully-situated to fill up whenever the circumjacent tunnels flooded, which happened often.

Many of the residents of Undercamp had Gadabout experience - they came from Blocs far-and-wide, and while in its early days this place served as a temporary bivouac for travelers and exploratory expeditions, now almost all of the population took permanent lodging here. I heard stories of Bloc uprisings, of terror and violence, and I came to know that my experiences were shared by many others. An old man told me that the age of the Blocs was over, and that Z-Bloc was likely the final one to fall, and all those who still endured did so deep underground. While plausible, I later learned this to be false...

I also gained from those retired Gadabout explorers a more definite understanding of the sewers. There were ten levels above the Great Hall: the tramway lines, (which were the surest means of moving between the Blocs, back when it was still worth attempting to do such) the HydroElectric mills, plumbing networks, waste incinerators, and other facilities that, for decades, had kept the Blocs alive. The Great Hall was the dividing-line between what belonged to us and what did not, and though the exact function of the Hall itself was a mystery, there was rampant speculation on the topic. All that was known for certain was that everything below, that endless labyrinth of passages and rooms and corridors and pipelines in which I had wandered for days, were largely uncharted and exceptionally dangerous. The same old-timer who told me that the Blocs had fallen also told me that few had ever been lost in these lower levels for as long as we had and lived to tell of it.

Aside from this codger, (who I should mention was blind) the residents of Undercamp avoided me as if I was Lawmaker himself. On the footways and catwalks they steered a wide berth and refused to hold my gaze, afraid of me; fearful of what I might do or what bleak enlightenment I might impart. I tried to confederate myself with them, but they couldn't stand the sound of my voice or the look of my face. Perhaps it was my rapacious air that put them off, as I drank mightily every day following our arrival and was often reeling fullish. As I staggered on my aimless way and passed groups of them, I could feel their eyes and hear their whispers: *'Z-Bloc... Sewers... Lizard...'* - all words that had lost significance to me. The only social contact I had was with Skudd, and occasionally Abraham and Kaide, who roomed together two levels down. I had not seen Kassie or Monogatari since our arrival.

***

The seventh evening was the first to afford me more than a few hours of fitful rest, and I awoke on the eighth day and left Skudd in the hut (he never left it, except to visit the shit-shack) and walked along an outer terrace that overlooked the Great Hall and the cropfields. I neared a vendor who ran a shop out of his home, a multi-room two-leveled hut. He and his wife lived on the upper level and he retailed his merchandise out of the lower one - leaf-tea and swill made from fermented berries. As I approached, he wordlessly put out his hand to receive my gutjug and he filled it without looking at me. I had found that vendors would give me whatever I asked for. In fact, I could even forgo asking and simply point, and they would hand whatever over without charge. I retrieved the now-full vessel and screwed the nozzle-sipper back into place.

At the ledge of the terrace-catwalk was a railing made of rebar bent and twisted into form. I leaned against it and drank deeply, unconcerned by the fact that the vendor was likely hoping I would pitch over the side and fall. Let him keep hoping. The view from this spot was good - the crops below shimmered green under the sunlamps, and the whole arrangement formed a dappled yellow pool that thinned in a gradient until it gave way to the crepuscularity of the Great Hall above-and-around it. I admired the sight and drank until I was drunk, and then I ambled over the narrow platforms and came to the stairs that had been built into the rubble-hill. These stairs ran the entire height of the camp, from the plaza-patio to the Mayoral Palace, and they passed under the shacktree as they went up the hill. The stonework of these steps, which were long and wide, also doubled as a foundation for the main support-columns of the tree itself.

I descended to the base of the stairs and walked through the plaza emporium. The sparse crowd fled from my path as I swaggered to the verge of the cobblestones, to a place where the tanning-tents and smokehouses were set out from under the obscuration of the camp structure. Here I could fully assimilate the vast sense of openness in the Hall. The Under-campers moved around me like water around a rock, stabbing me when I wasn't looking with supercilious eyes. I drank and dropped my gutjug in the dirt and no-one helped me - they merely watched with both hatred and pity in their faces as I wobbled to pick it up and clean off the sipper with the sleeve of my smock. I felt orphaned and thought of Z-Bloc. It was a long way away...

My thoughts were interrupted by a hand on my shoulder.

The delicacy of the touch told me it was a woman, and I figured it must be Kassie. I was glad at the prospect of talking to her, but when I turned, I got a real jolt. It was Cleopatra, smiling in all her airs. Startled, I spoke her name aloud - her real name.

"You're not looking well."

"You? Y-you're... here?"

"Here I am."

"How?"

"I came with Poppa, of course."

"Of course."

I felt like an idiot for not piecing this together on my own. Maybe I was too drunk. Cleo touched my arm sympathetically and led me back towards the emporium. I couldn't believe how utterly casual and unaffected she looked - as if nothing had happened! She looked exactly how she always did in Z-Bloc - or better, even; well-dressed and clean and racy as always, preening and tossing her hair, and she seemed unbothered by the fact that her son was surely dead. She didn't even bother to ask about him.

"You really should get yourself back together. People are depending on you. Things are happening. A groundswell is coming. Since Poppa came to Undercamp, he has been ruminating and fixing to stage a revolt, but the Mayor's guardsmen have weaponry... oh, have you met him yet? The Mayor?"

I shook my head.

"He's a lecherous old squeezer. He's got eyes for your friend Kassie, and it looks like that might have something to do with things. Kassie can't be bothered, of course... she's fuzzy with your other friend, the big strong one–"

"Will you get to the point? My word, how can you act like nothing has happened?!"

"I'm unconcerned by what *has* happened, only interested in what will happen hereafter. Aren't you listening? Things are happening currently! Your friend is not well, and of course I can see that you yourself are not well at all either, but you must be better than he, if you're able to stride about and drink like you used to do back home!"

"You don't know... If you knew..."

She rolled her eyes in that way of hers and spoke more gently as she took the gutjug from me. I grasped for it, but she was already walking away, so I pursued her up the stone steps.

***

The Mayoral Palace was constructed of cobblestones that had been individually painted and laid together in a polychromic assortment similar to the composition of the plaza-patio. It sat atop the rubble-hill under the wide-rounded toppoint of the Great Hall and overlooked the entire camp. I had been informed earlier that the Mayor had instituted a law that not the shacktree, nor any other structure on the hillside, could be built to a height above that of his Palace, which was by-far the largest single residence of the entire camp, and the only one made entirely of stone.

Inside the guarded gates was a courtyard of the same mosaic of flagstones, mismatched in both size and color, and there were ashwax torches in steel holders that formed two lines leading up to the double-doored entrance. Across the yard to the left was a guesthouse, also of cyclopean masonry, and of finer luxury than the huts in the tree. There were oil-lanterns hung at each corner of the roof, and all throughout the courtyard, and more torches lining the pathway leading to the guesthouse and a brick shitshack. To me, the whole site seemed boisterously vain.

Cleo led me past the guards, who eyed us, yet did not hinder us as we went into the foyer of the Palace, which had a high angled ceiling. From the main beam, a large iron bowl had been suspended by chains and filled with a great quantity of ashwax coals and what smelled like resin-incense. Affixed to the rim of the bowl with rebar and wire was a circle of mirror-glass, which reflected the firelight in a concentrated beam that cut through the hazy air and hit the circular window above the entry. This window was fascinating - admittedly one of the most beautiful things I had ever seen; comprised of many shards of multicolored glass all fused together, which reflected the aimed firelight and twinkled a chimerical kaleidoscope of color that filled the room.

Kassie came into the foyer, dressed in a smock similar to mine, except she had cut slits from the hem to the waistline to show her legs. When she saw me, she shouted and rushed to me and leapt into my arms, trying very hard to act like she was back to her old self. Fullish as I may have been, I could tell that she, like I, was yet different, and would never be quite the same. Still, I appreciated her effort, forced a smile, and we shared trivial greetings. Cleopatra hovered at my shoulder and Kassie offered to fix us both a drink. Kassie, fixing people drinks - imagine that. Cleo declined, saying that she had better go let Poppa and the Mayor know she was back. With Cleo's exit, Kassie's entire demeanor changed in an instant. She took me aside, deeper into the foyer, and spoke in a serious tone.

"I'm so glad you've come. I've been thinking of you constantly, but they won't let me leave the Palace grounds! You saw the guards at the gates? There are more of them throughout the house, and when I sleep, there is a man posted outside my door!"

"Where is Monogatari?"

"In the guesthouse - he has hardly left it since we arrived here. He is... not the same."

I didn't say anything at first, as we both lingered in the memory for a protracted moment... the darkness, the endless stairs, the days spent trudging, the dank air and the smell and the whole of it...

"Do you think any of us will ever be the same, Kassie?"

"Please don't ask me that. I can't think of it. You must speak to him, because I cannot rouse him or get him up to do anything. Come, please."

"Why me?"

"Because you will know what to do and say."

Kassie took my arm and led me out of the Palace and across the courtyard.

***

The interior of the guesthouse was forebodingly stygian, as the curtains were all pulled. The reception-room was furnished with upholstered daybeds and chairs, all of fine quality, but the darkness cast the whole place in a bleak guise. Kassie led me down a hallway, into the living space, in the corner of which sat a dormant stone fireplace. The cold and the dark of this lodging was eerily-reminiscent of the sewers, which aggrandized my blossoming uncomfortability, as I had managed to reaccustom myself to the comfort of light in the past days.

There was a corridor to the left, offshooting from the living room, and Kassie gestured encouragingly for me to proceed on alone. I felt a sense of dread, because I didn't want to see Monogatari in poor condition, yet still I ventured down the corridor and came into a bedroom.

Monogatari sat in a chair in the corner, nude and motionless, staring across the room with blank eyes that gave me no acknowledgement as I approached him. I spoke softly and waved my arm, the shadow of my hand moving across his face. He didn't blink. I took a chair from nearby and put it across from him and sat directly before him. He stared through me. I felt ill and was afraid to reach out and touch him, thinking he might turn to dust and crumble, or else seize me and snap my neck... yet I overcame this fear and laid a hand on his knee in a soft, comforting manner. I felt a jolt go through him, like an electrical current; lots of ends buzzing all together suddenly. He blinked and his eyes focused on me. I swallowed past the lump in my throat and spoke with my voice low, acutely aware of Kassie watching us from around the hallway corner, creating a vacuum in the air as she strained to listen.

"My friend... I'm here. I need you. We are disconcerted at a time when it is inopportune to be so. There are things happening, I guess. Rest and get well, but you must know that we are unwelcome, and circumstances are already taking form to dragoon us from this place. Forces are conspiring, as they always are. Cleopatra is here, and Poppa Daddy and his men are crooked and scheming, and I heard tell of some business between Kassie and the Mayor? I hear many things... The people in the place do not know how loudly they talk. You should know that things are happening, like? I'm going to leave here, and Kassie is going to hit me with a hundred questions, and

I'm going to have to say things, you know? Because you won't say anything, I shall be forced to. That's why I'm saying so much right now, and I'll tell you, I don't like it one bit..."

There was a long and terrible pause, but I saw a bit of the darkness recede from his eyes. He looked at me, his face twisted into an expression I had never seen on him before...

Softly, he said: "You brought the light to us."

"Yes. I brought the light."

"Where did you find it?"

"Don't worry about that anymore. It's done. Put it out of your mind."

"*How* did you find it?"

"I... I went off and stumbled upon it."

"In the dark?"

"Yes."

"You went out in the dark... alone?"

"I didn't go far."

"Must have gone a ways... alone... in the dark..."

"It's not something I wish to dwell on."

Monogatari's face hardened and his eyes went black again. He looked off to the corner of the room, as if looking at me was bringing him physical agony. I squeezed his knee and stood up and kissed him on the cheek. He sighed softly and I think he felt a bit easier. As I turned to leave, he said my name to halt me.

"Bring them the light."

I wanted to ask if this was some sort of metaphor, but instead I just said 'like' and walked out to where I felt like I could breathe again. Kassie was awaiting me, looking befuddled. I took her back to the reception-room and spoke before she could assault me with a barrage of questions for which I had no answers.

"Firstly, let us go back to the Palace, to see about the Mayor and Poppa and whatever is brewing between them. We must get a sense of the dynamics here. Cleopatra will Stoolie for us, but we should not trust her–"

"I don't like that you call her that."

"What? I thought you didn't like her?"

"I don't, but it's a gross name regardless."

"I didn't assign it to her. Many people called her that."

"It's unpleasant. Do you call me 'The Pink Bitch' when you're not in my face?"

"No."

"Why not?"

"Because to me, you're just Kassie. And I call Cleo by that name to her face directly."

"I just don't like it."

"Take me to the Mayor. I wish to meet him."

"Ohh, must I? He's a horrid boor!"

"We can't sit around gabbing! It's our heads on the block. We must act a certain way, talk a certain way, or else things might get very bad for us. We must move with purpose!"

My raised tone seemed to impress upon Kassie the criticality of our present situation. She took a moment to fix her hair and apply some crimson candelilla-wax to her lips (her own genre of armor-and-weaponry) and then she took me back across the courtyard and we reentered the Palace of the Mayor of Undercamp.

NINE

Every room in the Mayoral Palace was extravagant and bright-ly-colored, and very hot, due to the abundance of torches. The air smelled sweet, yet seemed to be of poor quality. There was also an abundance of guards, as Kassie had said. We were free to move about unaccompanied, yet we were always watched, and there were locked doors through which we could not pass. Kassie led me to a big drawing-room with carved stone col-umns around a sunken floor. The ceiling above the sitting-area was open, the walls and floor variegated red-and-orange by the glare of mirrored firebowls hung between the pillars. In the center of this communion-pit stood a sculpture; a human-oid figure fabricated with plaited rebar, contorted and androg-ynous. Cushions of assorted sizes and materials were scat-tered all about, and there were tables; concrete circles several inches thick, set low enough that they could be accessed from a reclined position. The room smelt strongly of resin-incense and perfume, and the contours of the light and shadow gave one a heady impression.

Cleopatra floated over to greet us, smiling saccharine, now dressed in a lacy babydoll tunic that showed a lot of her. The others in the room, all men, were reclined lazily on cush-ions. They met us with artificial smiles and hollow eyes. Poppa Daddy was amongst them, and indeed he looked out-of-place. Poppa was old - at least seventy, but he was strong and his gray beard was thick. War-scars covered his arms and face, and one of his eyes was permanently-discolored from a shrap-nel wound. His gnarled hands betokened his violent nature and his ugly features were sharp - I am quite certain he was a handsome man in his younger years, before he had person-ally murdered hundreds and beheld the deaths of thousands more to boot. Attending him were several of his lieutenants that I recognized from Z-Bloc, who in their ultra-casual wraps and togas seemed like peevishly-reformed thugs - or not even 'seemed like' but in actuality, that is what they all were. Poppa rose to greet us. I had never personally made the man's acquaintance, yet he treated me like an old friend, pulling me into an embrace and bestowing upon me an ovation of familiarity loud enough for the benefit of the others in the room. I didn't mind. It was wise to show unity, because the Mayoral cabinet were all glowering at us omnivorous and vulturine.

Poppa ushered us over to his table and laid next to Cleo, who slouched aside him in a feline manner and purred. I took a seat on the edge of the pit, but Kassie pulled me down onto a pillow and sat on my lap. All this touching made me uncomfortable. Cleo perceived my agitation and seemed to relish it. I shifted my hips in such a way that adumbrated my discomfort to Kassie, and she moved off and relined with her head in my lap, which was only a slight improvement.

Although I had no idea what the Mayor of Undercamp looked like, it was plain to see that he was not present, as there was a total lack of groveling amongst the gathered sycophants. A power-vacuum existed in the room, longing to be filled. In as confident a tone as I could muster, I posed a question as to the Mayor's whereabouts.

"He's probably off porkin' one of his whores!"

Poppa said this loudly and laughed. Nobody else seemed to think it was funny, but Poppa pushed on nonetheless: "I sure hope he finishes soon, because I'm damned hungry!"

One of the diplomats across from us sneered disapprovingly and began whispering to his companion. I took this as an invitation to follow suit, and leaned over to speak to Poppa in an equally-clandestine manner. This wasn't a good time to go against the flow. A side had already been chosen for me, and it would be best to stick to it.

Poppa told me the Mayor had fifty gunmen, and ammunition enough for each. He kept Monogatari and Kassie in the Palace guesthouse, as he mistrusted them, and Poppa and Cleo in the Palace itself, because he trusted them even less. The rest of us were considered peasants, but we had spies on us and were kept under constant observation. Poppa also requested my aid in getting Monogatari back to his typical condition, but before I could ask why, (or what was in it for me) the Mayor of Undercamp came through the columns with a procession of housegirls.

He was ornamented in gold jewelry - chains around his neck, hololith bracelets and cuffs, rings on every finger, and he was garbed in flowing red drapery that was kept off the floor by the girls. Despite his crooked, rotting teeth, he smiled wide and simpered pompously. The ground itself shook as he walked - he must have weighed five-hundred pounds! Rotund flabs of him spilled over other flabs, with purple veins spread taut under his near-translucent skin. He had a booming voice appropriate for a parliamentary orator, and his hands moved animatedly as he spoke and welcomed us. He liked to touch, this one. He took me close to him and I could smell his salt, and then he discarded me and pulled Kassie up off the floor. I didn't like the way he hugged her.

The Mayor, to Kassie: "Come here my dear yes just like that yes yes sit on my other side so I might see you better oh my you dishy little thing you look shabby in that smock, we must find you something nicer to wear, yes?"

I wasn't having that. "Sit here, Kassie." I said.

The Mayor gave me an appraising look. I could tell that he was wondering if perhaps he had misjudged me. The authority in my tone, coupled with Kassie's immediate adherence to my instruction, showed that I was not merely the Bloc-peasant he had initially pegged me for.

"Ah yes yes you are another Blocboy, yes? Zee? A traveler from a great distance yes you must tell me how things were out so far. I have heard a great deal about the dread endeavor you all undertook to come here yes I must say it is quite impressive yes a week in the great below is far too long yes it is doubtful you would have ever found your way to us if not for that creature mister Poppa keeps oh what a sinful frightful shameful thing it is but I suppose it has its uses does it not? In my years I have found that to be the case in-general yes oftentimes even the most lowly and unassuming things have their uses and prove themselves to be linchpins... but ah... of course I do not have to tell you this, do I? You seem to have an understanding of it personally!"

The Mayor was overly-friendly towards me, and I could tell Poppa did not like it, nor did any of the Mayor's advisors. I made nice back the best I could, mainly to keep his eyes off Kassie. For the first time in my life, I could relate to Monogatari's feelings for her. We spoke for a while, just the two of us, with the others listening in. I expounded upon the conditions in Z-Bloc and about the upbringing Kassie and I had received, while the Mayor listened intently, appearing to take great interest in what I had to say.

"I was an orphan-child myself yes I was born here on this hill and I plan to die on it too. Back then it was only a few tents but you've seen what I have built in the time since... we are a municipality unto ourselves persisting in our own ways yes a humble settlement and a beacon of civility in this great quiet underworld... in sixty long years so many have come up from the depths and stayed with us and while they may have passed through or moved on Gadabouting or else lived out the remainder of their days here you see plainly that I still remain alive and presiding over all!"

As the Mayor spoke, his housegirls brought out food on platters alongside potted pitchers of fruitswill, and I encouraged the Mayor to continue by taking the liberty of refilling our goblets whenever they ran dry. As he grew fullish he draped his arm limp and fleshy over my shoulders and drew me closer to him, and as his tumescent fingers spun in my hair, he launched into a grandiloquent harangue regarding the 'Histories of the Humanities,' or so he called it...

***

In erstwhile days long gone, we lived under the Sun and were nourished by Him, our god and our True Father, revered and worshiped by all cultures since time immemorial. Such was His majesty that He outshined all other heavenly bodies; they could not even be seen in the face of His light, and His authority over all corporeality was total. He was the epicenter from which the spiral-of-life originated, and daily all that lived turned to Him to be microcosmically-inseminated by His glory. It was through this benevolent sowing of His golden seed that the spiral remained unbroken, forever-gyrating outwards in a continual manifestation of His sacred altruism. He was the almsgiver of sustenance and vitality; the supreme symbol of divinity, royalty, wealth, with all other lesser forms of power encompassed by His quintessence.

Because we were unworthy of His benevolence, we could not even look at Him, lest His radiance blind our eyes and scorch our skin, and when this opulence, relied-upon by the planet itself, became unendurable after prolonged exposure, we, in our apostate impiety, sought refuge from it... and so it came to be that we would toil under Him and find our rest in shadow, wherein we drank and loved and rollicked... until our appetites grew heretical. We sought dominion over the Sun, and in seeking such, moved permanently into the shade, where our toils assumed a darker intention, as we no longer dug for food or water; we did so for shade itself; fuller shade, which we strove to make unfluctuating and interrupted only by light manageable and agreeable. Our labor became the means by which we aspired to establish asylum for ourselves from labor itself, fleeing from Sunlight just as we flee from the travails of spiritual revelation, the heartbreak of exclusion, the aching smart of contrition... we sought the shade, not for earned respite, but for everlasting abeyancy, privacy, clandestinity, and the emancipation so mendaciously promised by these. In the dark, there exists no shame in nakedness nor sex.

So we mined the soil and from it ripped that with which we forged machines for the sole end of inflicting greater scarifications upon our True Mother, and with these, we dug ever deeper, until we reached the Undersun beneath our feet; deep in the earth, entombed by miles of stone, yet resplendent nonetheless, and full of energy which we harnessed and bastardized to service those colossal apparatuses and the infrastructures that sustained them. These creations, epic in proportion and terrible in purpose, became monolithic idols, and we felicitated ourselves for our own ingenuity by the light of the Undersun, which had been shackled and contained so that we might dispense it as we saw fit... until finally, we divorced ourselves from He by whose hand our dust was animated, creating distinction between the Sun and the shade, and between ourselves and God.

***

With that note of pride that I had heard many times before, the Mayor told me his parents had come from A-Bloc. They fled during a Bloc-war, which he claimed to be vicious, as A was the flagship superstructure of the Corporation. His mother had given birth in the tunnels to the monstrosity that now sat before me, stuffing his face with grilled corn, swill dribbling down his many chins. He told me of the early days of the camp, when his Gadabout coterie settled against the hill simply because they could go no further, and of the dramas that arose as new settlers came, and giddily he reminisced of how he had come to 'make his name' by cutting a sleeping man's throat; a statement which he followed-up by saying "you know how it is like."

Then, his eyes fell on Kassie once again.

"So now... your sister..."

"What about her?"

"She is your sister yes?"

"She is under my protection."

The Mayor took a long moment to regard me, serious-like.

"That is all right yes that is good because your friend over there would cut her up and sell her to me packaged piecemeal for some guns so you see it is good that she has a brother to watch out for her. I must apologize for keeping the two of you apart you see I was uncertain of who amongst you I could trust and honestly I still am."

I was watching Cleo, who was laughing hard at something Kassie had said and fondling her. This made me nervous. I was more concerned about *her* than the Mayor, as whenever shit was being stirred, Cleo always had two hands on the ladle.

"I want you to trust me." the Mayor continued. "I like you and you like me yes?"

"I think you are pretty okay."

"That is all right yes that is good see you know that I covet and indeed hanker for her but I will not do anything that might provoke your disapproval. I am a friend of Zee."

"Thank you."

"I will give orders to my guard that she is henceforth free to move about the camp as you are... but first please please tell me more things about Zee! Mister Poppa was your king?"

"One of them. We had many kings, but we didn't call them such."

"And you? Were you a king?"

He said this without the good faith of curiosity - he was appraising my honesty.

"No." I answered, unpretentious and foursquare. "I was nobody."

By the conclusion of our dinner, the Mayor was quite fullish. He thanked and hugged me and again whispered into my ear that he was a friend of Zee. Poppa Daddy led us back to the courtyard, and we walked to the gates, so that we might look out over Undercamp. The Sunlamps below were dead, but the many lamps and torches of the tree still sparkled against the darkness of the Great Hall. When the ladies went off by themselves, Poppa spoke to me.

"So? How ya standing? Seemed to be getting real chummy with the old fat fuck..."

"What do you want the guns for?"

"For me to know and you not to worry about."

"Well, he's right not to trust you. Is he supposed to simply hand you over the means to overthrow him?"

"If I don't, someone else will. It's a wild wonder it ain't been done already."

"We are not in Z-Bloc anymore. Things are different here. He's got a firm handle on this place, and you would do well to remember that he's smarter than he looks. He's cunning, like? Keeping us separated, under watch... Now isn't the time to go against him. We just got here."

"*You* just got here. I been here. It's a shithole akin to the Bloc, and I'll tell you I plan to fuck it deep-and-wide. I won't sit stewing in the dark my whole life - I'm getting out, boy. I'm going up!"

I caught Kassie's eye from across the courtyard and waved her over as Poppa repeated that last sentence resolutely. The women walked over arm-in-arm, taking their time as Poppa hovered over me. I could smell the meal on his breath mingling with the stench of his psyche.

"Just relax. Bide your time, wait for him to make a mistake. Don't go rushing in now, because he'll kill you and might probably kill us too."

"Bide my time. Wait."

"Yes."

"Like what you've been doing all your life?"

Me, to Kassie: "Come on, let's be going. The Mayor said you're free to leave."

"Oh, but it's still early! I might stay a bit, won't you? There is food and drink inside!"

I told Kassie I was leaving. She urged me again to stay, but I didn't want Poppa talking in my ear and Cleo leering at me the way she did. She had worms in her smile. I asked Kassie if she felt okay and she said: "Whatever, you know." I tried to give her a smile, and I kissed her on both cheeks and told her to take care.

***

I went halfway down the grand staircase, to where the shacks were piled atop one another three and sometimes four-high, and I sat on the steps in a place that had a good view of the Great Hall and its beckoning gloom. The Mayor smoked rolled tobacco and had gifted me a cigarillo, which I lit by a lantern-flame and smoked as I sat. A few of the Mayoral Guards, in their leather coats and worn boots, came up the stairs and eyed me all-the-while. I sucked the smoke deep and held it, and at that moment I decided that the shacktree structure, with its many columns and catwalks and the interconnected entanglement of its rigging, was quite beautiful...

I sat for half the smoke, then found a wide walkway suspended from the level above, and followed this to the base of a main column, and took winding circular stairs up two levels, to a place where there were people. Here it was mostly single-room shacks, all attached, save for the places where narrow alleys divided them. Night-people crouched in doorways or moved silently between the levels via boards and ladders. It was dark here, and I walked incognito. None looked at me and I didn't look at them either.

I considered what the Mayor had told me; his claim that his citizens were the purest of humanity because they had established a self-sustaining civilization lower than anyone else had before. I thought of our ancestors, who knew only the Sun and the shade, and had no cognizance of true darkness. I wondered what they must think of us, their children, who now lived so deep beneath their buried bones...

I ventured into an impromptu bordello district where piquant mushroom-powder smoke was thick in the air. My head started to hurt. I became dizzy, but kept walking. An auctioneer had a few bodies up on blocks aside a sign advertising the hourly rates. Of the four bare-skinned forms, only one was even halfway-alluring.

Past this, I entered a fiendish establishment with a bar going the length of one wall and curtained booths set into the other. The drugsmoke was thick and soupy here. A short fat girl wearing only a loincloth came over and served me stale druk and asked if I would like to be released. Her tits were long, wide-set and bell-shaped, and her skin was spotty and very brown. Altogether she was not belligerently unattractive, and something undefinable about her did indeed stoke my fancy, yet I told her I was fine. She went back behind the bar, until a disgusting-looking man paid her with a sack of cornmeal to go into one of the booths with him. When the curtain was moved aside, I saw that, contrary to my assumption, this booth was not a booth at all, but the entry to another room; a lounge for dustsmoking, with pillows and mats on the floor, and candles shaded by pink glass. I had already constructed in my mind speculations of the faces the girl would make during love, and I desired to know how close to the money I was.

I followed the duo back into the den, where the air was

laden and anesthetized. Most of the inhabitants were passed-out, or else staring into the flickering candles as if they were searching statically for their very souls. With some surprise, I found that I recognized one amongst them. Skudd was in the far corner, a distance between him and all the others, crouched and hiding his face, looking supremely alone. In the rosy lamplight I could make out his ribs showing through his back, his scars and black tattoos, and the white places on his scalp where he had pulled out his hair. It was apparent that the others were made uncomfortable by his presence, and on my entrance they all looked to me in hopes that I had come to collect him. I figured I would grant their wish.

When I touched Skudd, he jumped and yelped the way a dog does just before it's killed, but he recognized my face and simmered down and allowed me to lead him out of there.

The secondhand exposure to the dustsmoke had gotten me high, plus I was still fullish from dinner, and therefore lost and reckless in my wandering. I could have taken Skudd back to the main stairs, but instead I elected to explore. We walked through several levels, across narrow catwalks lit only by treacherous and scant light, and failed to find our way back to our room, but I found us lodging for the night anyway, as there were many unoccupied stalls in Undercamp; places left vacant by the deaths of their previous occupants.

We went inside and found a dry basin and a single bed with a patchy quilt. The room was completely dark. I un-dressed Skudd and put him into the bed before going back out to find a lamp by the flame of which I could relight my smoker. Back in the room, I sat on the bed-edge and pulled hits, the glowing orange tip calling to memory the fishbowl in which we swam down in the tunnels, and I felt dreadful vibrations coming up from my core with the recollection. Skudd said my name softly several times, and I could tell that he too was suffering from the same anamnesis. I pitied him. Though I didn't return his lachrymose whispers, I put out the cigarillo between licked fingers and undressed and got into the bed and pulled him close. His shuddering stilled as I held him fast, so that our bodies and warmth were together, and neither of us were so alone. I fell asleep quickly and did not wake until late the next morning.

***

I spent the next days in the company of the Mayor and Kassie at their respective houses on the hilltop. Kassie only wanted to drink and talk fullish, and the Mayor only wanted to eat and lounge about and go on-and-on forever about himself and his domain. This was palatable to me, as I learned a great deal from him. I learned that the Great Hall went for miles, yet the full distance of it was uncharted, as after four days' journey, one came upon an uncrossable pool of noxious sludge. He claimed to have led an expedition in his youth down the Hall for weeks, in a time prior to the development of the sludge-pool, and told me that the way never forked or bent. I believed him. I asked about the cave-in against which Undercamp was built, and he told me that the cause of it must have been a seismic event cataclysmic beyond reckoning, and this, he said confidently, was surely what made the Deep.

"The Deep?"

"Yes yes you know that great deep dark void where the tunnels end but you think you can see lights far up at the top and you are made to dream."

"Ah. I know the place. What are those lights?"

"You don't know?" The Mayor seemed surprised by my ignorance. "You shall soon learn. The Festival is coming in three nights' time."

My requests for clarification regarding this were met only with condescending vagaries. I developed an itch behind my ear that needed scratching. This damn place was like the Bloc: hot and confusing and chock-full of assholes who only spoke in riddles.

After this conversation with the Mayor, I visited the Palace guesthouse and looked in on Kassie and Monogatari. The latter still sat nude and motionless in his shadowed corner. Again I kissed him on the cheek and spoke some words to him and left him sitting there. Kassie told me she thought he had been looking better lately. I feigned agreement and didn't let on that I was wondering if his days were soon to end.

Kassie and I sat in the reception-room and drank swill and talked for a while. She spoke about Poppa and Cleopatra and the Mayor, who had not put forth any advances since he had met me. She was impressed by this, but I didn't let this go to my head. I disliked the way she seemed to be relying on me, because she had never done so before. In the past, Kassie could always take care of herself much better than I, but the days spent in the sewers had warped her as they had Monoga-tari and Skudd and all of us. She tried to hide it, but she had that same fucked-like look in her face; a distrust of everything and everyone. I invited her to come down into camp with me, but she didn't want to. I told her it wasn't like her to turn down a good old scrap in an alley, and the air soured after I said that. I departed shortly thereafter.

***

I didn't feel like going back up the hill the next day, so I spent the morning on the floor with Skudd. We didn't talk. He was a hopeless worthless mindless pile of flesh. My pity for him came and went depending on my mood, and at present I felt it going, so I arose and strode to the balcony-overlook, which was vacant save for the usual drinkseller, as most of the dwellers on our level descended to the cropfields to work and took their daytime meals under the sunlamp-posts. I downed some water before I started in again on the swill, and as I did, I spoke for the first time to the vendor, who suggested that I dress myself finer for tomorrow night.

"For the Festival?"

He nodded, contemptuous lines carved across his cineral face.

"Just what is the Festival? I've heard tell, yet no details."

"The Festival of the Zealot Pilgrimage."

Ah. The Zealots. I figured they would crop up again...

I talked to the old man about the Festival for some time, and gleaned further illumination on the topic. The Zealots passed through Undercamp annually, making the final stop before the Treacherous Accent to their High City. Their journey was arduous, yet necessary for converts who had served for a decade in the Light of Gordyume. The Pilgrimage took these from their homes and led them through the sewers on their way to the mecca of their faith: a city of stone carved underneath H-Bloc, or so it was said. The drinkseller gave me swill free-of-charge (as always) and made an excuse to flee my presence. I half-considered another exploratory stroll, but the prospect seemed altogether pointless. I returned to the hut, wondering if the Mayor would have Poppa and Cleo beheaded before the Festival. Such would be prudent.

I missed the Bloc; my old life, the way the water tasted fresh when it came from the good dispensation-stations. Here it was bucketed-up from the well, so it tasted wooden. I missed the Blanco Bronco, with its shitty bands, and I decided to tell Skudd how I missed it. I sat beside him and told him, and I think it made him feel a little better. I tried to prompt him to say something, but it was fruitless - he hadn't uttered a syllable since we had come up from the tunnels.

TEN

The Zealot Pilgrimage came to Undercamp as a column of torchlight; a shimmering crack that cleft the dark of the Great Hall and looked, for a time, as if it extended back forever. I brought Kassie down to the foremost terraces of the shack-tree to watch the procession approach from a good vantage, snug amongst the crowds seated with their legs dangling over the ledges.

As they came into the light of the Undercamp sunlamps, we beheld the Zealots all clad in their familiar white robes, but with the hems stained brown-and-black. Their fabric moccasins were worn-through and some even went barefoot, yet the white hoods shone clean and none went without these. Every one of them carried a torch and the men bore supply-packs and coiled ropes, and several carried rifles. I had never seen Zealot guardsmen before. They marched into Undercamp and were greeted on its outskirts by an eager crowd, the shacktree all alight in its ramshackle splendor to welcome them.

The Festival Grounds were erected in a barley-field that had been scythed-and-harvested the day prior, and tents were pitched, made of multicolored tarpaulins all stitched together, and within these, vendors of all sorts gathered to hock their wares. The Prophets and Pilgrims put up tents of their own, of white fabric kept unbesmirched in plastic, and they set a great number of iron torch-poles in the earth, each seven feet long and sharpened at one end, with wrought fire-holders at the other. The shorter wooden torches were piled up in a bonfire in the middle of the field, and the Festival commenced.

The music of the Zealots was percussion-based; made with hollow drums and steel drums and timpanis and tambourines and animal-leather-headed goblet-drums. The beat started slow and hypnotically-rhythmic, yet swelled in both tempo and intricacy as bodies began to flail. Dancing soon filled the Festival Grounds; the residents of Undercamp intermingling with the Zealot Pilgrims. Kassie and I fell in with the crowds moving down the tree, cocooned in the excited chatter all around us. For the first time, I felt like I was one of the Undercampers, and I realized that, to the Zealots, there was nothing to distinguish me from them. As we neared the sun-lamps, the light of which was turbulent with smoke, the Pilgrim Choir took up a song to accompany the drums, and their dozens of voices coalesced with beautiful congruity to uplift foreboding lyrics in the Old Tongue. The sound was rich and the hymn filled me with emotion. I took Kassie by the hand and pushed through the crowd to the circle of torches where the dancers spun, and we watched in astonishment, having never seen such abandon exhibited by the Zealots before. A ways to our right, a Prophet stood on a box and began calling out a Sermon above the sea of heads. I looked out over the crowd and saw other Prophets following suit - one every fifty yards or so, all calling out the Sermon of the Day. The Old Tongue words mixed with those of the hymn and fostered in all of us a sort of rabid spiritual lust as we were conjugated into the impassioned mesh. Undercampers were pushed-and-pulled into the cotillion, forming conjoined circles of bodies all clasping hands and nimble on their feet as these rings went through-and-around one-another in perfervid spirals.

Kassie and I joined and danced for a while, and the drums pounded on long after we grew tired. Then we found a sitting-area and ordered druk and cooked peppers, and these we ate in the midst of the indefatigably-continuing celebration.

The Mayor came down from the Palace to formally receive the Zealots, and I spotted Poppa Daddy and Cleo amongst his cavalcade of diplomats and servants. The crowds parted to make space for the High Prophets to meet the Mayor. I had never seen High Prophets before, or even heard of their existence. They were distinguished by age and wore crimson amices about their shoulders and had braided cinctures tied about their waists. Only one of them touched the Mayor, accepting his extended hand and giving it a limp shake, and immediately afterwards, a lesser Prophet (in white) gave him a cloth with which he wiped his fingers. The Mayor didn't seem offended by this. He dismissed a number of his diplomats to go join the festival, including Poppa, and moved with the High Prophets to a grandstand-platform where comfortable seating had been arranged. I got close to the platform and caught the Mayor's eye, but he ignored me and continued schmoozing with the white-and-red-robed High Ones. Feeling moderately jilted, I led Kassie back to the center of the field, where she danced with some young Pilgrims who had their hoods down; fetching pretty-boys who I could tell liked Kassie, and she liked them too...

The Festival continued through the night without any lull or break, but I possessed not the stamina to keep up. The smoke and the blazing sunlamp-light began to water my eyes, so I went up the tree, finding its platforms and catwalks to be vacant, which they never were under regular circumstances. The solitude was comforting. I was exceedingly sober and in no mood to sit in the dark with Skudd, so I found a secluded nook and rested my head against one of the support-poles of the walkway above me.

On their own accord, my fingers felt in my smock-pocket and found the cylindrical Battery. I held it in my hand for a long time, enjoying the cold of that steel which never seemed to warm, no matter how long or tightly I clasped it...

***

I awoke in the same place I had left myself. The noise of the festival was still roaring down below - if anything, it had grown louder. I went down and rejoined the merrymaking and Kassie, who had a glow in her face that I had not seen since the downfall of Z-Bloc. To see her flushed and slick and breathless gave me hope that the old Kassie might yet return, and if it was possible for her to recuperate, perhaps it was possible for all of us. It made sense that she would be the first, and that we would follow in our own time.

The music and dancing continued until the twenty-fifth hour of the Festival, at which time the jubilee was brought to a halt as the Zealot Choir sustained a high, sharp note. Swelling anticipation went through the crowd as the Pilgrims used the long torchpoles to hector us back off the by-now well-trod dirt, around which the Undercampers formed a circular perimeter. The torch-poles were then reset, and all around me was audible the burble and hubbub of enthusiasm; people saying 'it' was about to happen...

They called it the Holy Disrobing, and it was exactly that. The drums rolled frenetically as a group of Pilgrims gathered in the center of the circle and cast off their robes, revealing pristine nudity. Cheers went up from the crowd as the number of these Disrobed grew steadily, all of them shapely and strong, and they beckoned us (the generally-filthy Undercampers) to join them in the circle. A petite girl with messily-chopped hair and an absolutely perfect figure looked me dead in the face and smiled, gesturing for me to approach her. Oh, this was an inimical stratagem of some breed, I was certain of it. I didn't take the bait, and nobody else did for a while, until one young buck plucked up the courage. A wild and tremendous roar ripped through the onlookers as he stepped into the circle, and four Pilgrim girls fell upon him like starving dogs and ripped off his tunic and pulled him down into the dirt. An electric current sparked through the rank-and-file of the residents, who indeed seemed to be thrilled by something beyond the sight of sex - yes, this was an esoteric arousal that permeated deeper, activated not simply by base carnality, but an instinct more sinister and asomatous...

Others joined the circle until there were nearly sixty people all rolling free and fucking wanton in the field. Before I could caution her against it, Kassie ventured forth and let her smock fall even before the Pilgrim-boys had their hands on her. It was at this point that the electricity in the air put a brackish taste on the roof of my mouth, so I decided not to watch any more. My spot in the throng was assumed instantly upon my leaving it, and I had to push against these surging, virulent gawkers to find a swill-vendor to fill my gutjug. I went beneath the Mayoral grandstand and sat and drank and listened to the calamitous noise, until She Who Gapes approached me, appearing as she always did: out of the fucking troposphere at the fringe of my vision. I was moody and in no mood for her, and I could tell she knew that, and it was for this reason that she had selected the present moment to accost me.

"What do you want?"

"What do you want, Zee? That's what they have been calling you, huh? Got yourself a new name? Cheer up. Gordyume shines his light even on the smallest amongst us."

She said that last sentence in the language preferred by the Zealots, but with ironic spite.

"I can't speak the Old Tongue."

"None your age can. A shame, how our history doesn't persist anymore."

I agreed with her, yet didn't say so. I wished she would get along and ask me whatever it was that she was going to, and this wish was forthwith granted.

"We need you to talk to your friend."

"Monogatari? I've tried. He'll get back to himself when he's ready."

"Not him. The Mayor. Tell him Poppa could bring the Lizard to him in a cage, to trade with the High Prophets."

"What does he seek from the Prophets in return?"

"I don't know, but they could surely offer him something."

They probably could. I was polite as I could be in telling Cleo to go away and leave me to my swill. I finished the jug fast and got inordinately fullish to the point that I couldn't stand, so I laid down right there on the earth under the grandstand. Many Undercampers slept in the fields during the Festival nights; their scads of tents lit by lanterns and the shadows of those within dancing as they pleasured themselves and others. The air in the Great Hall was hazy and of exceedingly-poor breathing-quality, but all felt good... All save me, that is. I slept with my arm crooked under my head.

***

I awoke to find the Festival diminished. The Holy Disrobing had taken the gas out of the communal Undercamp tank, but people were still roving, some still fullish, unable to let the party die entirely. A Prophet was calling out his Sermon, and this made me think of home. I got up and climbed the staircase to the Mayoral Palace, which was now under Zealot guard, as the High Prophets were presently communing with the Mayor. I was admitted by the Mayor's soldiers, but informed that I had to wait in the courtyard until the Zealot leadership departed.

After the coterie of High Prophets in red-and-white exited the house and pulled up their hoods, I was shown inside. The Mayor received me happily. His fleshy purple lids hung halfway over his eyes, edifying to me that he had been awake for most of the night, most-likely enjoying the spectacle of the Disrobing. I was worried that he might ask me about Kassie, yet he didn't. We had lunch, just the two of us, unaccompanied by any of his diplomats, and afterwards he lit a smoker and offered one to me as well. The tobacco was sweet and its aroma induced a pleasant somnolency. I brought up Poppa's offer as casually as I could.

"Hmm I see yes I see but I must ask what is in all this for you, Zee?"

"I wish to go with Zealots. They do not take uninitiated strangers on the Pilgrimage, but I believe they would make an exception, if they believed it to be necessary for the creature's keeping."

"I will freely admit surprise Zee yes I thought you were happy here after all I have shown you every kindness and you have enjoyed the best of our way of life. Why would you possibly wish to return to the tunnels and to the darkness after what you endured?"

"It is precisely because of what I endured that I wish to return. I am restless."

"You wish to see the Lights of the Deep?"

"Very much."

The Mayor waved a dismissive hand. "Ah those lights those damned lights there is nothing special about them save the fact they're not bright enough for the space they are lighting you see no light is bright enough but the Sun itself! Harken now to what I tell you about the Zealots and their light see they think there awaits other things in the depths which right there tells you the problem with them because for something or anything at all to be down there be it Gordyume or what-have-your-mum that is assuming that there must be a bottom to that pit and that is fullish talk. There is no bottom to the Deep. If there was which I assure you there is not then no man nor creature could find its way down so far sewer-lizard or not I don't care."

"I don't care if there is a bottom. I want to see the top."

"Yes yes yes you are still a strapping young man and you want to see the world and find yourself within it and you think you will find something anywhere but where you stand. You are dumb but I can't blame you for being dumb because I was young once myself and dumb as they come but I was smart enough to get smart! I got all I love right here and I don't need to trade up for anything because I am at the top, Zee. Look on me and look on the best that exists for any living thing under the earth!"

"Like."

I didn't press the topic, but we talked for another hour about the Zealots and the Deep. The Mayor loved to talk about the Deep. In spite of his pronouncement that it was nothing and contained nothing, he loved to speculate about the nature of that nothing. As we spoke, nothing became something indeed - a complex and multilayered thing to be examined through different lenses and approached from various philosophical angles. I could not understand his dismissal of my desire to see with my own eyes the Holy Lights shining into that infinite emptiness.

It was shortly after we finished our smokers that the Zealot High Prophets returned and joined us in the sunken lounge, hoods down, only three of them now, not the full company who had departed earlier. It was two men and a woman. One man had a slate beard and very severe eyes staring out from under bushy white eyebrows, and the other man was clean-shaved and had a stern nose and a thin face, yet both of them may as well have been invisible beside the woman who accompanied them. She was young, yet she did not show it in her manner or gait, which was balletic and timeless. Her hair was light-blonde, pinned behind her head like a halo, and her red lips were full and contrasted brilliantly against her pure skin, which was white as bleached linen and beautiful as the Sun. Her eyes were blue, like it was said the True Sky was, and she cut a stark portrait of superlative and blemishless perfection, save for a tiny mole on her left cheek; an almost-imperceptible brown dot against her blushing pale, and the sight of her struck me dumb to such a degree that I almost fell from my cushion and became a believer right there-and-then.

The Mayor snapped his fingers and a servant-girl brought him a towel with which he mopped the parts of himself that he could reach, and one of the male High Prophets requested our attendance on the walk down to the Festival Grounds. The Mayor donned an orange robe and fastened it at his neck with a brooch, and as he pulled it about himself I took his arm and stood on my toes to speak into his ear, requesting leave, so that I might visit Monogatari. The Mayor said 'yes of course' and told me to reconvene with him later, because he did not want me to miss any of the forthcoming pageant. He said this with an air of derision that unsettled me. I asked him why, and he answered the question with one of his own.

"Did you enjoy last night's proceedings? It seemed that your sister did..."

"She has always been licentious."

"Funny yes I may have expected such behavior from Poppa's woman but not her... and your big friend hmm is he faring any better as of late?"

"Difficult to say, really. I'm going to drag him out of that damned dark room and bring him down to the Festival tonight. I'm hoping that might bring him back."

"Surely it must yes it is a good Festival this year and if tonight does not put life back in him then I'm sorry to say that I don't believe anything ever will."

I departed, feeling hot under the collar of my tunic.

In the courtyard of the Mayoral Palace, I could hear the Zealot music and the noise of the resuming Festival filling the Hall. I paused to listen. The echo of the drums and multitudinous voices ringing in so large a space was hypnagogic. Very little seemed to matter all of the sudden, yet I forced myself to care, because doing so made me human.

***

Monogatari was no better, but all my fear of touching him had faded. I spoke gently and helped him up out of his chair and found him a decent shirt and britches that would fit him. He scratched dumbly at the fabric and squinted in the light as I brought him out of the guesthouse. I felt morose as the light fell on him, because I remembered how awesome he used to be. We went down the big stairs slowly, me reassuring him that the drums were fun and the food was good. Halfway down, he stopped to urinate in a trashbin, and afterwards just stood there with his pisser out.

"Come on, now - I'm not putting that away for you."

He said nothing, and I became angry. I stood close and without looking felt around and tucked him back properly into place and wiped my hand on his face.

"You're a fucking disgrace, like? A disgrace that should be fucking ashamed of himself..."

After that, I was vexed. I pulled him along into the festival crowds and didn't care that he was shaking. A druk-vendor with whom I had become familiar was selling special stuff that he claimed was brewed using an old Bloc recipe. I got two tankards and encouraged Monogatari to drink, and he did so only at my goading, taking small sips and quick swallows. I started to hate him. Earlier, on the stairs, I had decided that if the festival didn't cure him, I was going to escort him out beyond the fields and open his head with a spade - such would be what he wanted - he would instruct me to do it himself, if his old clay could behold this new constitution. He watched the crowds from miles inside his head, away, alone, with that fucked-like face and stricken eyes like Skudd. Fucked Skudd, with his fucked mouth and fucked butt and all of him: fucked. No way to bargain with the barber on that one.

***

I looked around for the Mayor but could not find him until he emerged from the High Prophet's tent and moved like a
wrecking-ball rolling unchained, parting the crowd with no effort whatsoever. The Prophets walked beside him, twenty of
them or so, and I searched the group for the woman-Prophet
I had seen earlier in the Palace. I spotted her, and to my surprise she broke off and cut a beeline towards me and without
a word almost-telepathically communicated for me to follow
her. I fell into her wake, dragging Monogatari along. She did
not walk, but floated, and her robes swished around her like
vapor as she came to a halt under the grandstand. When she
turned to me, I caught a flashing glimpse of her face under
her low hood. It was not only possible, but altogether doubt-
less that she was the most beautiful person I had ever laid eyes
upon. She was so pretty that it hurt to look at her; she burned
through my retinas like Sunlight and scarred herself into my
psyche like a hot blade cutting through the curdled margarine
of my consciousness. I introduced myself formally, bending
at the knees and making myself smaller, so that I might get
another look under her hood, but she dropped her chin low.
When she spoke, it was to the dirt at my feet.

"You are the keeper of the finder-creature?"

"Oh, no, not at all. What have you been told?"

"It was you who made the offer."

"I could procure it for you, yes, but I am not its keeper."

"Who is?"

"You'll meet him soon enough, like?"

She paused, and I was gripped by fear that I had estranged
her with my vagary. I hadn't meant to speak to her like that,
but because it was how everyone spoke to me, it was simply
all I knew.

"We are interested." She said tersely.

"For you, I'll see what I can do."

"Keep the interest close to your chest, as what we speak of
is sensitive. There are those amongst the Brothers and Sisters
who do not believe that the creature can do what is claimed
it can... Yet, we have heard stories that cannot be disregarded.
The reptile is of significance. Lawmaker himself may seek it."

"The man who could be called the keeper is up there. Shall I introduce you?"

"I cannot meet nor engage with him. I am a High Priest-ess and a Vestal-Elect."

"How does one get high, priestess?"

She raised her chin and I saw a tiny part of her that wanted to laugh sparkling in those beryl eyes. Meanwhile, the drums started pounding a fast beat, dirty and building...

"There are myriad rites one must undergo, a gauntlet of spiritual assessments. Only a few Sisters ever have the hope, and those who distinguish themselves as truly worthy become Vestals. We lead the Pilgrimage, and then ascend to the High Temple to be with the everlasting Horsche and his council of kin. Tonight, I shall select those to be Redeemed from the Sinners." Her dainty hand came out of the folds of her robe and she opened her fist to show me a small silver awl, sterilized and glinting needlelike, and she continued: "I shall pierce the ears of my selections."

"The Sinners?"

"What is wrong with your friend?"

"Oh, he is unwell. We were down in the sewers for a long time - days and days and days, and I think it may have broken him. It broke all of us, most beyond repair. Do you have anything you could do to help him? Seeing as you're a Redeemer and all? He is my dear friend and I hate to see him in such poor condition. You should have seen him before - he was magnificent!"

"He is still lost in the darkness. Have faith. The light of Gordyume will find his eyes, and he may yet be renewed..."

With those words, she left me. I liked her a lot. A High Priestess, a Zealot Princess. Light of my life, apple of my eye. I wished the world around us would burn, so that only we two would be left, and I took heart in thinking that it likely would...

The drums built to a crescendo. I went up onto the grand-stand and saw that the High Prophets were not present as they had been on the previous two nights. The Mayor was calling down to the Undercampers to join him and fill the vacancies on the platform. I picked my way over to him, working against a crowd that was flocking in all directions, and he bade me sit down on a cushion by his feet. I obliged. Monogatari sat beside me, staring absently at the ring of fire in the field before us, which was clearly prepped for something, although I didn't know what. The Mayor leaned over and spoke in my ear, his tone disdainful, his words tipped with a callous amusement.

"You have a good view do you not Zee? Surrounded on all sides by my people yes yes neither you nor your friend can run off tonight... you will behold the whole thing right up until its conclusion!"

I had a bad feeling. A group of whiterobes had set up two large worn wooden beams in the dead-center of the circle, where holes had been dug in the earth to support them, and they used a cord to bind the beams together where they met, so that an X was formed, and at the top-and-bottom of these posts were hinged iron cuffs that could be locked shut, presumably around wrists and ankles...

Behind me, I heard the Mayor chuckling hideously. I did not turn back to look at him, and I didn't turn to look at Monogatari either. I simply kept my eyes fixed forward.

The Whipping of the Sinners commenced.

ELEVEN

Ten High Prophets came into the circle with lashes, each with ten tails of rope woven tight and knotted over broken shards of flint and glass. I didn't need to be informed of the identity of the Sinners to be whipped; I knew automatically and beyond any shadow of question that they were those from the prior night who had ventured into the circle. Sure enough, those same overeager miscreants were brought out of the whiterobed crowd, all bound at the wrists and restrained by two Zealots each, who showed no gentility in their handling, and dragged forth those 'Sinners,' who had participated so willingly the prior evening, yet who now shouted and struggled and resisted in a futility from which their persecutors seemed to glean amusement. Indeed, if the robed Pilgrims had been enthusiastic last night, they were now positively rapt at the prospect of inflicting pain upon those whom they had previously pleasured. The poetic irony of this was not lost on me. I probably would have cherished it, had it not been for the fact that Kassie was amongst the condemned. If Monogatari (still sitting to my left and staring) didn't knock up at the coming sight, then it was done - to slay him would simply be the discarding of an empty vessel, a dried and cracking gutjug long past its useful days.

The cardinal Sinner to be whipped was the young man who had been the first to break the circle. I figured it made sense to start with him. As he was dragged to X, he realized that, as the first, he was to be made an example-of. He fought good; kicking and howling and cursing with bitter fury the Zealot gods, disparaging their women, and love him, he nearly got one hand around the neck of one of the whiterobes before they pulled the ropes and gave him a swift kick between the legs. We as a crowd didn't like that - we liked this boy and wanted to see him win, and our liking imbued him with an extra measure of ferocity, yet the kick sank him to his knees all the same. We booed as they put him on the X with his chest at the cross-junction of the beams and fastened the cuffs to his wrists and ankles. In the struggle, his smock had been so ripped that it didn't matter to remove it from him.

Then I saw her; that very beautiful High One. She stood out even amongst the other High Prophets because her alb and amice and chasuble and cincture were all gold, (not red) and she was the only one amongst the Zealots adorned as such. The gold fabric was coruscant - not of a material I had ever beheld before, which seemed to glow in the dancing torch-light. Then, out of the white lake, more like her appeared in identical garb; all women, and in these gold robes they moved across the trodden dirt like specters. The High Priestesses, of which there were five, took their positions out of spitting-distance from the restrained Sinners and faced the boy on the X. On the opposite side, the High Prophets stood waiting to begin. The foremost red-and-white-clad man dropped his hood and called out in a very loud voice what sounded like an excerpt from the Gospels of Horsche. Although I could not speak the Old Tongue, the full intention of this leg of the Festival was by now clear as glass to me.

The Sinner was asked to confess his transgressions to the Vestal-Elects, who stood by listening and waiting to pass judgment. Our frantic and beleaguered friend did not want to confess, and he made this abundantly-known with the curses he heaped upon his harassers.

It is a great spectacle to see a man whipped publicly in an ecclesiastical demonstration. It began with a swooping motion of the chief High Prophet's arm; very slow, craning far back and up, up, up, and then suddenly it happened - to blink would be to miss it - a noise and a jolt through the body like electricity; every muscle squeezing in a subito contortion, and the look on the boy's face; the grimace against the pain... It was mesmeric. Our boy tried not to cry, but after the fifth lash, it all spilled forth at once in tempestuous anguish, a noise solitary above the din. The way beads of moisture on a tarpaulin hover in the air for an instant when the canvas is struck with a rod - that is how the blood looked as it came off of him. They whipped him until he became keen to confess, and he was made to call out his sins at the top of his voice, sobbing and begging as he divulged his darkest secrets to us all, rattling-off whatever came to mind, no matter how trivial, in an effort to make it stop... yet, it did not.

The High Prophets dragged things out with the first boy, for both our entertainment and the sake of gristly showmanship, yet by this point we were bored with him - our attention had shifted to the others, whose violent resistance had given way to pathetic bargaining, as they now perceived the fate that awaited them. I felt short-of-breath as I looked down from the grandstand at all those dismayed faces. The first Sinner was whipped to tatters and left tied to the crossbeams. I was positive that he would die from the flagellation.

Then the other Sinners were hauled in groups of five-and-six into the ring and kicked to their knees and stretched-out via the cords at their wrists. Most began confessing even before the first stroke of the whips fell. As the High Prophets moved amongst the bound, the Vestal-Elects stood by to hear their sins. Occasionally, one of them would raise a hand, and the whipping of a select Sinner would cease momentarily as they pierced the ear of the whipee. Now, with multiple people being concurrently flogged, the Hall was filled with the cracking of the lashes and those terrific cries of lamentation, the confessions; an overlapping chorus delineating all the misconducts committed by these Undercampers in their mostly-young lives; stomach-turning things that together formed a canticle so unlike that of the previous night that it made my skin stand up in little bumps.

I glanced over my shoulder and saw that the Mayor had accomplished a feat of dexterity: getting one hand over his gut and into his pants, and he was hunchbacked and sweating profusely and drooling from the mouth, eyes alight. He caught my gaze and looked at me good.

"Should have let your sister come to me boy oh yes oh yes I would have kept her pretty but you thought you knew better

eh? You make me laugh you filthy little tunnel-mongrel you–"
and he said something in the Old Tongue with lots of 'chsk'
and 'rch' syllables that I recognized as a curse - a literal curse,
a hex, bad luck type-like shit.

"I was your friend yes your only friend worth a warm fart
and I desired her!"

"She didn't desire you. You are fat and ugly and the Pilgrim boys are young and pretty. It really is that simple, and I
don't see why you insist on making it more complex than it
needs to be."

"Such a shame such a blasted bloody fucking shame to let
beauty like hers be wasted. I would have kept her beautiful."

"You would have kept her nothing, like."

"They will flog her to shreds."

"They whip all the Sinners? Even those with the stitch?"

The Mayor nodded. "Them especially."

I turned away to watch more whipping, unable to bring
myself to glance at Monogatari. The Zealots left the Whipped
Sinners lying in the torchlit dirt, resembling piles of red rags.
Some tried to crawl, smearing their puddles like rough brush-
strokes across the earth. I had lost track of who had been
stitched and who had not. The Prophets, fagged and panting, hurried things along as best as they could - to flog thirty
people right to the doorstep of death is a lot of work for old
men, but they got it done proper regardless. There was only
one group left, and Kassie was in it. An agitated little frog was
hopping around in my stomach, and to distract myself, I tried
to make more conversation with the Mayor.

"The Zealots want the thing. One of their holy women
told me."

"So give it to them."

"I need you to sweeten Poppa's pot first."

"I would not do that in a million years even if he promised me the Sun."

"There is room for two in this place."

"Perhaps yes but I thought it was going to be you and I."

I was going to say something in defense of myself, but a
noise went up from the crowd as they brought the final batch

of Sinners into the circle. Kassie looked strong, but this was the first time in my life that I derived no pleasure from looking at her.

I loved her, as did all who made her acquaintance. She was lively and witty and her aura radiated resplendently in a manner that seemed to soak up everything else in the air and turn it into her, and she was charming beyond reckoning; flirtatious and so free - always half-nude, unreserved, and never without an entourage of freakish faddists surrounding her. In all the years I had known her, she had been more than beautiful - she was Kassie, *my* Kassie, my Bloc-urchin sister, oh, remember how we used to steal flatbread from the Bazaar-vendors behind the night-boarding shacks? In our inseparable youth we were always together, yet even then I knew that she would get sucked into the next thing and leave me behind. She was the trendiest when it came to having opinions; she always wanted to talk about who was right and who was full-of-shit regarding what was going to happen - as if anything would happen. Nothing ever happens... or so I believed, but Kassie had to believe that things would, and whatever they happened to be, they would be just as stupendous and terrific as the latest people told us - The Sons of the Sun and the Zealots, and all the painters and writers of the Bloc, who all loved to talk about the Old Times - you couldn't be an artist if you wanted to talk about the new times, because there were no new times... save with Kassie. She was always new, and she'd make you feel new too, and excited about it. Poor girl. If she had been wrong, she would have been okay, but wouldn't you know it, she had been right all along; some things had indeed happened, and she was about to become new, that's for damn sure.

She had a set jaw and I knew she would offer no concession to the Zealots until more of her blood was outside of her than in. I decided to fuck further with the Mayor, seeing as how that bridge was burned.

"I'll wager she doesn't scream until the tenth lash at least."

"Oh Zee you are foul yes you are far more foul than I had reckoned you to be!"

"If she screams before the tenth lash, I'll stay here in Undercamp, Zealots be damned. If she holds out until then, you play Poppa's game."

"You are a sick man!"

"She's a tough chick. You wouldn't believe the things I've seen her do."

"I believe you Zee although you are a scoundrel you are honest and that is more than I can say about Poppa who is a snake yes indeed he himself is a lizard and he shall betray me at the first presented opportunity. I shall not give him anything ever any time, and you have let me down Zee. I do not feel inclined to continue speaking with you."

They started whipping Kassie. She was far across the circle from us, and for that I was thankful. Yet even if the Mayor had taken me up on my wager, it wouldn't have mattered.

What happened next was phantasmagoric.

A roar split the air, like the earth itself breaking open, the cavernous Deep expanding to receive all things minor and greater, as Monogatari leapt over the heads of those seated before us, twenty feet high, sailing over the grandstand-railing to land with a mighty crash amongst the general Undercampers, blasting a crater and scattering them in all directions. With one look I could see plainly that he was altogether restored to his former glory: upright and huge, with those savage eyes that looked at you each time like it might be the last; a force not of this world, nor of man, but wrought of boundless and celestial nature itself - my father and elder brother and dear friend, who cut an epic, arresting figure in the torchlight as he plowed through that throng, sending bodies flying up in the air like flimsy paper moppets, until he breached the torch-circle perimeter and charged like a livid, snarling beast at the Zealots.

I watched wide-eyed and enthralled as the first whiterobe to accost him was hoisted high and thrown into an oncoming band of his companions, who scattered like the oblong pins of those Bazaar knock-down games and learned forthwith that they were now in for the fight of their lives. The whiterobes surrounded him, yet none were bold enough to take him on directly.

One of the red-and-white High Prophets passed off his

lash to a lackey, careful that the hilt not touch the ground, and pulled an antique blade from the folds of his robe, two feet long and curved, resembling something that had been smithed in a Bloc forge. This rash elder thought that he could ambush Monogatari from behind and put the saber in him, but at the instant of his advancement, Monogatari spun, seized his sword-arm and broke it clean backwards, so that the bone popped clean out of the elbow-joint, and rammed this splintered point into the Priest's own neck. There came a plentitude of blood as he did this, and the dead form of the Priest was kicked aside like dross. Monogatari then took up the blade and met the advancing wave of attackers, and commotion went up from the crowd. I, at-risk of being trampled in this new intractable upheaval, had to fight with my nails to keep a view of the scene. As I was tossed and pushed about in the rollicking mob, I could glimpse only flashes of the fight past all the heads and arms and chucked oddments.

Monogatari slaughtered a dozen whiterobes like dogs and left them with their limbs cut off and their guts spilled out. To a novice, it may have appeared that they had him when they lassoed a rope around his neck and pulled him to the dirt, but I knew this was a ruse; he had let them put him down purposefully, to draw them nearer into the vicinity where he could touch them with the blade...

I shoved my way to the forefront of the grandstand. By this point, the Undercampers had shattered the boundary of the ceremony-circle and were rioting fully, and the Zealots all bore uniform expressions of delectable shock as they sought to contend with us. I couldn't be certain, but I thought I saw one of the boys whom Kassie had gone with the previous night get punched in his mouth. How I wished I was near-enough to kick him until he shit red-and-brown all over his white vestments.

Monogatari was back on his feet and cutting down Zealots in twos-and-threes. He split asunder the head of a Vestal-Elect, and at this, a jounce of distress went through me and I craned to get a look at this freshest addition to the butchered bodies on the ground. Although her face was halved, I could tell it was not my Priestess Princess, and I exhaled in relief.

A Zealot guardsman came through the commotion with a blundergun, and the boom of the shot rang out and was accompanied by a puff of sulfur-smoke as fifty steel balls flew out of the horn. Most of them hit Monogatari. He staggered, yet didn't fall, and went about picking the pellets out of himself. The guardsman was reloading the gun, but Monogatari took ten strides and chopped off the top part of his head, just above his eyes. The cusp of his brain flew out of the crown of his skull as both arched through the air. It was a damn good strike, and I appreciated it all-the-more, as I knew it would likely be the last of its kind delivered by my friend. He was still standing tall, yet bleeding and peppered with abundant holes, some of which the light shone clear through. He flexed and steel balls fell out of him, chased by gushing streams, and the Zealots fell upon him. He stabbed one and gored two others, but they took him down and this time it was no ruse. White robes turned red. I watched all of this until it was done, and then turned back to the Mayor, discerning from his gawk that nothing such as this had ever transpired at a Festival before.

A few of the tents and vendor-carts bordering the ceremony had been set ablaze, and the most rational of the Undercampers were rushing to them with buckets of well-water. There was such an uproar in the Great Hall that I was reminded that we were, in fact, underground; confined within a finite and circumscribed space, and that the gross 'forever' feeling was merely one of the many tricks of the dark. I looked for Kassie and could not spot her. The fires made the air very bad, and we as a collective began to recover our senses. How easily we came apart... I didn't suppose there was any chance of getting any good druk at this time.

***

I fell in with the hundreds dispersing into the tree and kept my head low. Up the stairs and scaffolding and catwalks and terraces, now full of people, and I amongst them in anonymity. The chaos of the riot and the fires had been the clincher - I now fit in with those people, as I had been through what they knew; both the best and worst of it. No longer was I some alien glacial ferocious Gadabout wretch wandering awash in their world through some erroneous twist of fate. No longer was I Zee. I moved through the tree and I wasn't Zee.

I followed a good smell until I came to a cookfire in an iron cauldron, and hovering over the orange flames I spied a familiar face and called his name.

"Abraham!"

He looked up at me and looked quite like he had looked down below in the dark: scarred.

"You know what has happened? Kaide! He was a Zealot all along! I knew it, I sure did! This was always his plan, to fit in with us and find this place, because he was a Zealot back in the Bloc and heard tell of the Festival and conspired to rejoin his people here! The duplicitous bastard, I always knew it! I always said, you remember down in the sewers when I said–"

I interrupted him to ask: "What is in that can there?"

"Hmm? Beans. Pea-beans and some slop, who cares? Did you see Kaide amongst the whiterobes? Did you know? Me, I always knew, always figured something had to be way-off about those people, with their robes and the way they called out every day in the Bloc, like! I'm not an ounce wrong and you know it! It's all the fault of them! At their feet I lay the blame! Oh! Damn! Poor Kaide, the bastard, he went back to them, the two-faced-fucking-buttloving–"

"Is that coffee?"

"Hm? Oh, uh, yes. They make it in a different way here."

"Smells good."

"They roast the coffee-beans and put them in a kettle with water and put the whole thing down in the fire, see? It boils real quickfast, and then they pull it out and pour it through a strainer-mesh right into the cup, fresh out of the flames... You haven't had coffee here?"

"Not yet. Is it ready?"

An old Undercamper sitting on an upturned pail nearby stood and came over to tend the fire and the roasting joe. His skin was textured like worn leather and his nose was small in a way that made his face look like it was imploding.

"Roast for an hour, at least." He grunted.

"How long has it been?"

Abraham: "He said we need to roast the coffee-beans for an hour at least before they are ready to go in the kettle–"

"Yes, I heard. How long has it been?"

"Not long enough."

The old man shuffled back to his seat. I gestured to the metal can of pea-beans stuck halfway into the coals, steaming and bubbling in the ruddy-colored slop.

"What about the beans?"

"Well, they're simmering nicely. We want to eat them with the coffee, don't we?"

Abraham looked to the old man for affirmation and received a squinched nod.

"Sorry. The Festival left me famished."

"I could see it from the catwalks up above. I was watching. I told myself I wouldn't, but I could hear the dreadful noise, and I had to climb up to see it, if even from a distance... Was that Monogatari who went into the circle?"

"Yes. He was something, wasn't he?"

"Even from up here, I could see the red. They killed him?"

"Yes."

"That is something. He was a legend in the old Bloc. There wasn't anyone unacquainted with his reputation, I don't think. An uncompromising warfighter. Did he die well?"

"Not particularly."

"But bloody, right? Swinging as he went?"

"As one would expect."

"Well, that is okay, then."

Abraham had a lot more to say, but I didn't hear much of it. I was trying to figure how things would shake out from here. Cleopatra would be the one to find me - even with all others in disarray, she could always be counted-on to come slithering out of the rubbish, and she would act as if nothing noteworthy had happened. I thought of her son, my friend, Buddy - who remembers Buddy and his girlfriend? And their child - her grandson! All three dead, or lost hopelessly, and Cleo didn't bat an eyelash. I think I said her name out loud -

not her true name, but a Bloc-moniker given to her in the Old Tongue, poorly mispronounced.

"What was that?"

"Nothing. Is the coffee nearly ready?"

"Just a few more minutes."

A few more minutes passed, and I sat with Abraham and the old man while the three of us supped watery beans and quaffed coffee that had been prepared in the manner which Abraham had described. The coffee was thick and tasted like dirt, but it was hot, and the beans were overly-salty, but they were beans, and hot beans taste swell always and forever. We conversed intermittently as we dined. Abraham was all broken-up about Kaide, feeling altogether betrayed, and this was sad. The two of them had become such good friends down in the sewers, and it was because of that friendship that they had both made it through.

My meal was interrupted by Skudd, who bounded up to the cauldron shirtless with his sweat glistening on those black tattoos; the orbs and spirals and pools. He was very distressed, yet on his feet and speaking, which I took as a good indicator of his improving condition. He had not been at the Whipping, but Kassie had fled during Monogatari's onslaught and had come to the stall we shared, flayed near death. Skudd had found a barber, yet he didn't think highly of the man's capacity for his trade. He was quite concerned about the quality of the damn barber, and I tried to calm him down, but nothing I said seemed to help. Finally I had to tell him to fuck off and deal with the situation himself. I couldn't be of any help - Kassie would likely die, even with the best barber under the earth tending her. Skudd went off, back down the terrace-platform and across an angled footbridge. I was glad to see him walking and talking. It was good to hear his voice. Maybe he would be all right. Maybe he would be the only one of us who turned out so...

TWELVE

They always come in threes - when you're smack in the midst of an unlucky day and you think that it can't possibly get any worse, it invariably does. You may think that surely you have reached the bottom, yet you have not; one bummer may lay you low, but hell, you can deal with that - it's the second that really enervates you, and then, and only then, comes the third, when it all culminates, and you know with certitude that there is no way to salvage the day...

The specifics of these trifectas vary case-to-case. For me, they're always conversational in nature; untoward interactions with people who seek me out and thrust upon me questions or demands, like pachydermatous arrears-retrievers. Recall the day after I went with Monogatari to the Favelas and first met Skudd and the Lizard? I hardly remember myself, yet the fact remains that I went there, did those things, and the day after, how many conversations did I have?

I figured Cleo would be the first (as she usually was) but no - instead it was Poppa. I met him on the big stairs on my way up to the Palace. We had words between us, and I spoke mine snidely, because Poppa was not so intimidating any longer. In Z-Bloc, he may have been some towering authoritative figure, but now he stood in the same shadows as the rest of us.

"Your goodwill with the Mayor died in that circle tonight. You're not long for this place. The way I figure it, your only salvation would be to trade the Lizard for your life. The Zealots will be out for you, seeing how you spoiled their Festival in such a red fashion."

"I don't care how you figure it." I said.

"You got bold, boy! If I didn't know better, I'd place a wager that you grew two stones in that dinky skinsack!"

I ignored that comment, and Poppa changed the subject.

"You saw Monogatari? His last dance?"

"It would have been hard to miss. "

"It was something, eh? I always knew it would be, but he outstripped all my expectations, the good old tugger..."

"He wasn't so old - not much moreso than I."

A moment of reverence settled on us as we appreciated our fallen friend and the manner of his demise, which was befitting of both his stature and temperament. He would henceforth be emblazoned in our minds forever - we, who were lucky enough to have known him while he lived.

"My goodwill may have gone tonight, but you never had any to begin with. The Mayor will have you killed soon, so your choice is the same as mine: trade the Lizard to the Zealots. I'm going up to the Palace to try and strike a bargain for my neck and the necks of my friends. You know that your girl, that courtesan with whom you keep company, who you think you control, but in reality it is *she* who controls *you*, she will be there, maneuvering for her own designs."

"That woman is a snake."

"Like. Yet, she is your woman, and if she is a snake, so are you, and I must be stark dumb fullish for associating with the both of you... Yet you're not all wrong - my dick lays aside yours in the vice, so I will talk to the Prophets and the Mayor and see what I can fix, like? But you will surrender the Lizard, like it or not."

I kept walking, trying to convince myself that there was more to life than going up stairs and failing to come up with anything else. Poppa Daddy scuttled astride me, bargaining all-the-while. He wanted to stay in Undercamp so that he could cut the Mayor's throat and hoard it all to himself, as he had done long ago in Z-Bloc.

***

Zealot guardsmen mingled with the Mayor's soldiers at the Palace entrance, all of them hard-faced and cagey. They didn't let me through, so I sat outside the gates and waited. Then, she came - The Priestess Princess. I could tell it was her by the way she walked and how her robes moved about her.

She had apparently come straight up the hill after hell had broken loose, as there was red bespattered on her white-and-gold. I screwed up my face and asked if she was hurt; a question put forth more to demonstrate tenderness rather than stemming from any authentic concern - if she had been touched by Monogatari's saber, she would not be walking upright. It was by her word that I passed through the gates and into the courtyard, and she led me briskly into the house without speaking to me.

Inside the main sitting-room buzzed a large number of the Mayor's people, wily and all conniving ways to metamorphose the Festival tumult into an advantage to their ends, and there were many Prophets and armed guardsmen watching all angles and faces assiduously. Cleo was (of course) amongst this gathering, yet the Mayor was not, but I was told that he and the High Prophets would receive me soon enough, and that I was to wait with the others in the meantime. I became an island in that room, standing quarantined and alone. I was sometimes prone to bouts of severe anxiety in such rooms, in which everyone was talking and I was left by myself, but since coming to Undercamp and becoming the subject of continual half-concealed whispers and surreptitious conjecture, I found myself alleviated of these jitters and thought perhaps I had been cured of them permanently. Alas, this was not so. I fidgeted and feigned absorption with the task of removing grime from under my fingernails, until Cleo came to me and took me aside. For this, I was only half-glad. The heat of the torches in their holders and of the many bodies made me sweat... at least that's what I thought it was, but in all probability, it may have simply been my apprehension. Cleo was not sweating at all - she looked just as she always did; all syrupy sex and sly menace.

"What are you going to do? You had better come up with something fast - they're out for your blood."

"I will try to smooth and fix things. I mean to depart from here posthaste."

"You believe the Zealots will have a spot for you?"

"They certainly have spots open. Monogatari saw to that."

"You know that's not what I meant. Tell me your plan."

"I don't think I've ever had a plan in my life, and I don't think I will change that this late in the engagement. I know things, either instinctively or from vigilance, and from this knowing I make inelaborate deductions. See, I'll make some right now. If I was Poppa, I would have brought guns from Z and kept them outside the camp, hidden in the tunnels off-shooting from the Great Hall. The Lizard cannot be brought here, as it would be alarming and pestilential to the run-of-the-millers, and besides that, it doesn't like the light... So, likely I would post Hal outside of Undercamp with my guns and my Lizard, to await in the dark for some sort of signal. In these particulars I have enough confidence to say I know them for certain. What I don't know is why such a signal was not given during the ripening of the Festival, when the cerebral, cere-monial violence exceeded its own pomp and became grasp-able, knowable, measurable violence; just as the torchfires be-came real fires, dangerous and extirpative, like all fire truly is."

Cleo was smiling at me, satisfied, almost proud. "Smooth words."

"If I was Poppa, I would have identified tonight as the best time to signal Hal and my soldiers. If I was Poppa, only one person could have talked me down..."

"Look at you! The urchin streetrat, put through a grinder and now standing not unmarred but sharpened finer! I always looked at you, you know. I liked to look, and I like looking even more now. Your big friend is dead, your little rocket-girlie is all flogged-up, and where is Poppa? Out crying on the steps, because that's where you left him. Who sat up with the Mayor as they whipped the Sinners? You. You're a big four-star boy now, and I hope you know what to do with that. I always looked at you, yes, you were always in my eye. Please don't take that lightly. They are going to summon you in just a moment, and I think it is important that you keep in-mind the interests of all of us."

"All of us?"

"Yourself, and other people, which makes us."

Cleo laid a hand on my cheek, and as I looked into her

eyes there fluttered a cloudy and indiscriminate inkling deep down in my heart; something that perhaps I knew, but didn't want to admit or look full in the face... something I knew, yet chose not to know...

***

A bare-chested servant-boy came to fetch me and I was brought in to see the Mayor - far into the house, into a small windowless room where there were two High Prophets and that High Priestess to whom I had taken a liking. All four of them looked at me with grim faces. The seated Mayor launched into the matter at-hand without paying me a greeting.

"This is a mighty serious business Zee oh yes your friend ruined the Festival and these gentlemen and this consecrated lady hold you responsible and expect recompense."

The High Prophet with the thin shaved face and stern eyes was sitting beside the Mayor in the center of the room, perched in his chair in a manner that looked rigid and stilted, yet he did not seem like he was, nor had ever in his life been, uncomfortable.

"You will procure for us the finder-creature." He said cooly, and I didn't imagine he was capable of speaking in any other tone. He was made of stone and steel cables. There was no emotion or movement in any part of him save his lips as he continued: "You will go down to the fields and meet with our man, and you will take him to the creature and retrieve it for us. You will do whatever must be done to accomplish this. Our man will carry out to-the-letter any orders you give him. You will do this presently and return with the creature tomorrow, in time for our departing ceremonies. If you fail to do so, the Mayor will price your head and kill your friends."

The gray Prophet paused for a moment, yet didn't shift his gaze or blink. Silence settled. I wasn't sure if I was expected to answer, as there had been no question posed, but finally the silence was broken by the same man who had enacted it.

"The Mayor has told us of your desire to join our Pilgrimage. An audacious ambition, to be certain, for you who stands unclean, uninitiated, and, I daresay, with an incredulous disregard of our Most Holy Faith. Yet, you carry something... something has enabled you to come out of the sewers a leader of your fellows, a venerable herald, unlike that boisterous, clownish killer under whose reign you toiled for so much of your yet-young life. It is said that you came from Z-Bloc. If this is true, you must take care to learn. You are far from home, and you conspire to go further still. Under the High Temple of Horsche, Gordyume is God, and we are His ambassadors. You will find His Mighty Will strong and His Justice swift, and we swift in our dispensation of it. That is all. You may go."

And that was it. They sure didn't leave much room for negotiation or colloquy, so I left and went out of the house with that trio of weighty conversations tucked under my belt.

***

I found Poppa outside the gates and gave him the breaks: have Hal go get the Lizard and bring it to the outskirts of camp, or the Mayor would have his head. He was sore about it, but I made him understand. More than angry, he just seemed sad. Poppa and his breed had grown fat on the gravy of power for decades; power usurped, wrested from others whom it had made weak. Such was the ultimate nature of power, and the nature of Poppa's ilk was to seek new power, or at least seek to amplify what they had. This gormandizing rapacity was a condition from which all Gunbosses suffered, yet by which none were conserved. Power made them cowards, softened by years of comfort, and now, at the deciding moment when judgment would be furnished by an authority above-and-beyond his own, Poppa's greed would not outweigh his pusillanimity. He would elect to save his hide, even at the expense of his power, comfort, and any utterly-arbitrary moral system by which he operated. My conversation with Cleo rang in my ears. Look at me, eh? Little me, telling big Poppa Daddy what to do! I would not have to venture into the darkness of the Great Hall myself, let alone into the grime of the sewers. What I required would be delivered to me. Poppa assured me of this, although I promised him nothing in return.

I went down to the outskirts of the camp, out from under the shacktree. All the sunlamps were on, despite the wee hour. In the stamped-and-bloodied circle the Zealot Pilgrims stitched their slain back together. Amongst the Whipped Sinners, laying trampled and with dirt caked in their wounds, those who were not dead called out weakly and grasped at the passing hems of the white robes, which were expeditiously pulled away. The whole scene smelt strongly of iron and excreta. A whiterobe came to me and took me across the killing-field to a place where a Pilgrim-woman was sewing together a guardsman with a thick hooked needle. It was trying labor; eighty-some stitches in the stiffening torso to put his guts back in, and now she was working on reattaching his arm.

The whiterobe introduced me to two others; Zealots without robes. They still had white hoods, but their clothing was of heavy woolen fabric and they sported packs and pouches loaded with the trappings of the Gadabout sewer-pathfinders.

The younger man introduced himself to me as Vitti, the Headguard. I thought him to be a bit fresh-faced to hold such a rank, but then I saw the red-and-white badge fastened to his chest, and the empty space where it had been taken from the corpse we stood over. Monogatari had killed the previous Headguard, (and several lieutenants as well) so the chain-of-command had trickled down to this kid. I looked at him good and flinty. He was handsome and spruce under his clothes, yet there was nothing hard or determined in his aura. His counterpart was quite the opposite; older, grizzled, scarred, mean-faced, and he Vitti introduced as Rooth, explaining that Rooth didn't speak because he had no tongue. Rooth was to be my dog to sic on whomever I deemed fit, and he was said to be the best shot amongst the Zealot Sentinels. I appraised him assiduously and could distinguish that in his day he had slain not a notable few, but a forgettable multitude. I explained to both of these men that there was no need for any wild or dangerous undertaking to be attempted, and I instructed them to wait at the perimeter of the light for a man named Hal, who would be coming out of the dark with a creature on a chain-leash, or perhaps in a cage - I was not sure which. They both seemed relieved that they didn't have to follow me into the tunnels. With that, I left them and went back up into the tree.

In my little stall, I was alone. I figured Skudd was off with Kassie and the barber, getting her mended. I was too tired to go searching for them, so I laid on my floormat and drifted off into what would be my last sleep in Undercamp.

***

It was late into the next day when I was awoken by Skudd. I could hear the drums and the sounds of the Festival, mended and put right as it could be after the unanticipated calamity of the prior night. I asked him for some privacy as I dressed.

My smock and sole pair of britches were filthy. I washed them as best I could in the water-basin and hung them to dry, and then I took out the loose board in the wall behind which I had stashed all I had to my name in the world. Well, not *all*, but rather everything I didn't mind to lose, should someone go rummaging.

My possessions seemed undisturbed from the way I had laid them, yet I took stock on my rumpled mat regardless. There was some monies - a few nicks and dimmies - my Bloc Department Service Badge, a small dull knife, a dented can of jellied-alcohol, some old smokeplant leaves that had become wet and dry and wet again and dry again, and I added to this inventory the thing which I carried concealed on my person at all times: the Battery; that small oblong cylinder with its window half-full of raven liquid; extremely shiny vantablack that didn't flow right, that flowed only in accordance with laws of its own, and I watched it flow, transfixed, until I heard Skudd returning. I tucked the Battery away with my other things and swept the lot into a cloth which I tied up into a tote. Then we went to see Kassie.

The barber had given her opium or something of the like. She was in a bed in a dingy and low-ceilinged closet of the barbershop, and there was old blood on the tile-floor, dried and cracked under Kassie's fresh slippery blood. Kassie herself was woozy, but seemed to be as okay as could be expected under the circumstances. The slashes on her back had been padded with clean linens and bandages - cuts like those were difficult to stitch. I didn't desire for Kassie nor Skudd to accompany me on my coming journey, and I hoped to avoid the awkwardness of coming up with an excuse as to why they shouldn't. If the question arose, I would use Kassie's condition as an extenuation, as she was unfit for travel. Luckily, Skudd had already figured that I was planning to leave, and he didn't want to go anywhere without sunlamp-light ever again.

"I won't go. I *won't*. I never will..." He said.

"You don't have to. You stay here and look after her."

"Why are you going?"

"Because I've seen this place, and now I wish to see another."

"Why?"

"That's just how it is."

"Do you miss Z? I miss it... I miss it so much." Skudd's lip trembled as he said this, and tears filled his eyes. I felt a sting of emotion and pulled him into a tight hug, only for an instant, before I broke off.

"Sure. I miss it."

I leaned over and gave Kassie a gentle hug as well, wary of her injuries. I could not even bring myself to look at her. She was over-and-done; that eternal flame in her eyes was now bleary. I never saw that fire dimmed, even when she smoked mushroom-dust, yet it was dim now, and getting dimmer...

"I'll see you both around." I said, knowing that I would likely never see these two again. My kin, Bloc-born kids raised in that great tower we once called home, outside of which we had known nothing until quite recently, and for which we each yearned in our own quiet ways. I said farewell and left them both and walked down to the Festival grounds.

***

Hal had brought the Lizard out of the tunnels. It was hissing in the light, and around its cage a crowd swelled so ardently that the riot of the previous night was at-risk of repeating itself. The wailing of the loathsome monster ceased when one of the High Prophets put a black tarpaulin over the cage, and the crowd began to disperse. The dynamism and

novelty of the Festival had faded entirely, as its bloody interruption was superlative, and now most of the Undercampers
were glad to see the Zealots leave.

In all, seven from Z-Bloc were permitted to go behind the
Pilgrimage-procession with a two-wheeled wagon upholding
the Lizard in its cage. These were Poppa, Hal, Cleopatra, and
two of Poppa's gunmen from Z-Bloc - only two, as the others
had abandoned loyalty to their leader now that his power was
fully-depreciated, electing instead to stay in the Undercamp. I
wondered what kind of life they would have, and what kind
of life Skudd and Kassie would have, but I put those thoughts
out of my head as Abraham joined us, laden with an oversized
pack that tottered precariously as his steps shifted the center
of its balance. I was sure that he was only coming with us because of Kaide, (who had rejoined the Zealots) as he had no
friends in Undercamp and was too old to build a new life for
himself from naught.

Regarding the Whipped Sinners, the following was re-
ported to me by Abraham: those who had been stitched
through the ear by the Vestal-Elects (and who had managed
to survive the night) were designated 'Redeemed,' given water
and opium, and hoisted onto stretchers to be borne to the
Zealot City. Apparently the prospects offered to them therein
were quite enviable. The procurement of these unorthodox
converts was the primary purpose of the Pilgrimages, as the
Doctrines of Horsche laid out specific designs for eugenic
purity, which became jeopardized by incestual concerns as the
consanguine generations propagated. The Redeemed were a
method of counteraction to this. They were to be breeders.

The Zealots were mounting up, packing their tents and
supplies, and the guardsmen were attaching lanterns to their
rifles. Rooth came over and nodded to me, and his presence
unsettled my companions, compelling me to explain that I was
acquainted with him, and that he wouldn't introduce himself
because he couldn't. He stood aside me and communicated
wordlessly that he would be accompanying us, keeping an eye
on us. Poppa glowered at him from across the way.

I wished I had better shoes for the coming journey, as

the pair I had been gifted from an Undercamp cobbler would not count for much in the tunnels - they would wear out fast against that endless cold gray stone that was broken and smooth and jagged and solid underfoot forever.

***

The closing ceremony of the Festival consisted of the piling-up of the Sinners who had perished from the flogging, the covering of their corpses in an odorous flammable liquid, and the lighting of the heap. There was music and dancing to accompany all this, and I stood amongst it like a statue. The Pilgrims carolled, yet the Undercampers looked on deadpan and austere. The Zealots had worn-out their welcome and the jubilee was now standing on shaking, spindly legs, flea-bitten and piss-stained. Those that still revelled in the tainted celebration were all drunkards and dustsmokers, too fullish to dance well, some too fullish to walk. The smell of the bonfire was horrendous and the hymn was terrible; not in tone or delivery, but in sentiment... And yet... there was a lone tenor who sang like some angelic castrato; indescribable ornamentation to his notes, long vowels, his voice dancing up, up, up higher to where his eyes were cast: that big dark out there in the Hall. Tears formed as he sang, and his hood had fallen back, so that I could see the fire in the wetness of his eyes. His hoodlessness was permitted only because the Zealot choir was otherwise in disarray, packing up, yet this was to our advantage, because we could see him and hear his marvelous voice all-the-better. He struck an aching figure, his hands outstretched, palms up, beseeching the dark for an embrace as he sang with his whole wind and spirit, the fibers of which threatened to tear apart each time he heaved for breath between the phrases.

The Pilgrims received fresh torches from bundles of them; thin wooden rods wrapped at one end in cloth dipped into a barrel of ashwax and ignited one-at-a-time from the bonfire of the Sinners, and they fell into a straight line, marching off in single-file away from Undercamp, again forming a fissure of light in the darkness, carrying packs and rolled-up tents, their burning torches held aloft as they departed orderly and serene.

The musicians had gone, leaving the last few choir-members to carry the song acapella. The quartet soon became a trio; the tenor, a baritone, and a bass, who gave the sound a bottom, and then it became only a duet between the angel-tenor and the bass. They sang profoundly and in perfect harmony, mourning and tragic, until a Prophet brought the bass a torch and he fell into the line.

The tenor continued solo, his sound full and rich and resonant, and he himself resonant, pale and young, with features that could slice stone, his wavy feathered hair dark-yet-gleaming in the firelight as the soot of the corpses fell on his face like black snow from the abyss of heaven above, and a single tear broke from his overfull eyes and cut through the ash and ran gray down his face. He sang the hymn to completion, holding the final note to the tiniest and most abstruse part of himself, until there was nothing left, and he went silent in the manner that a dying person does when their pain is at an end.

The angel took his torch and joined the long line of light. I wanted to follow him, but Rooth stopped me and shook his head grimly, and when I looked at him, I saw that he was crying too, overcome with a zeal I was only now beginning to comprehend. Our unclean group waited for the procession to pass the outskirts of the camp and go fully into the Great Hall before we followed.

At the edge of the cropfields, I cast one final look back at the Mayor, seated high on his grandstand-platform, fat and lackadaisical, scowling at me and at all of us. Undercamp shrank as we walked, and the dirt began to slope until it gave way to stone, and the Hall loomed huge and dark and empty before us.

THIRTEEN

As the bright sunlamps of Undercamp melded together into a single diminished blob behind us, I set my sights on the line of light up ahead. I could barely make out the individual torches and their carriers, yet the line was shortening, as if the darkness was steadily healing itself from the cicatrice the Zealot procession sliced through it. The dots of the torches were disappearing, going out one-by-one soundlessly, and yet I imagined a little 'pop' as each of them vanished. They were there and then gone, descending into the maze. The line shrank until only a sole light remained; a guardsman waiting at an alcove for us and our cart of unpleasant cargo.

We walked up the curvature of the Great Hall and entered a stairwell and had to lift the Lizard's cage off the cart and carry both the cart and the cage down. It took four men to carry the latter. At one point, one of Poppa's men lost footing and pulled free the tarpaulin as he fell. The creature thrashed about and snapped at our fingers. It was so ugly; sporting toothy orifices at improper locales. We were afforded no rest after this task, as the Zealot guardsman made us rush at a brisk pace to get within sight of the procession torchlight once again.

The first day was a trudge through a single winding hallway that was wide enough for us to walk astride one-another. Hal pulled the cart. Occasionally, the Lizard would fall silent, and these instances were revitalizing, yet never lasted more than a few minutes before the skittering and yipping would recommence. We walked for a full day, following the light receding before us. Once, a guardsman fell back and reproached us for following the procession too nearly. Then, hours later, we came upon another guardsman awaiting us, who told us to pitch camp. We were given only a single tent and a cut of salt-cured meat that was not big enough for two people, let alone eight. I used my knifeblade and a stone to make a tiny fire out of paper trash. Poppa sat by and watched me do this, and Cleo sat beside him, looking bored, while Hal and the other Z-bloc gangsters erected our shelter. We also had some corn from Undercamp and a big gutjug of swill. I warmed the meat over the flames and rationed it. Poppa complained, but I simply shrugged. He looked to Hal and the other two, but neither of them cared, and he looked at Cleo, but she was already tucking into the meal. Nobody cared. Poppa sat down fuming and chewed silently. Before we bedded, Vitti came to relieve Rooth. The young Headguard seemed nervous as he informed us that he would be making camp with us, yet the night passed without incident.

***

The next day, I was reminded of the reality of the darkness - its true nature, the enigmatic ambiguity which was impossible to recall outside of one's full encapsulation within it. If one's familiarity with the dark was punctuated by light, one did not have a legitimate cognizance of true darkness, as they knew only the dark of that day, and not the dark of all time. The day-dark was dependable and transitory, whereas the forever-dark was unfathomable in its constancy.

We lit torches to keep the dark at bay and continued. Half-way through the morning, the sound of a hymn sung by a multitude of the Zealots all together echoed down the halls, distorted in a manner that made my jaw tense, as it seemed to break the natural order of this place. They sang for hours and we could hear them all-the-while, and sometimes even make out the light of their torches in the straight-shots of the tunnels. The wheels of the cart rattled over the stone, the finder-creature hissing and snarling. We went on until lunch, for which we sat on large blocks in a place where the tunnel had caved half-in, eating meat and dry cornflour bread.

When Vitti and Rooth went up a ways to speak out of ear-shot of the rest of us, I made conversation with one of Poppa's gunmen and learned an interesting actuality: although he and Poppa's others had been compelled to leave their guns in Undercamp, it made little difference, as they had no ammunition save for a few shells in Hal's pistol, the powder of which was likely spoilt. Poppa Daddy hadn't tried to overthrow the Mayor because he had no means of doing so! As I learned this, I glanced at Poppa, sitting cheerlessly on a rock, and I mused that perhaps Vitti and Rooth and the rest of the Zealot guard were enacting a similar ruse for the sake of appearance alone....

We followed the Pilgrimage through the maze for another six hours before stopping, and even after we stopped, the Zealots sang hymns long into the night, filling the seemingly-endless concrete corridors with an unnerving echo. Rooth did not like the Lizard, and began poking at it through the cage-bars with the dead end of a torch. It squealed and thrashed. Hal, who seemed to have formed some sort of perverse kinship with the creature, interrupted this by throwing Rooth to the floor, and the two scuffled until Vitti settled them. Nonetheless, that caliginous knavery of the subterranean gloom had begun to penetrate us all in ways we could not help.

The third day was almost exactly akin to its predecessor, except we ventured through much smaller confinements, through wet stretches and dry ones, rounding innumerable corners, and we camped in a claustrophobic corridor wherein we could not see the lights of the procession ahead of us. There were no hymns that night, but instead a Sermon, called loudly and coming to us foreboding and disquieting from up ahead, bouncing off the oppressive stone walls and jumping all around us before our ears took it in. I could tell from the voice that it was delivered by the gray-looking long-faced High One whom I had met twice before. He preached in the Old Tongue about repentance and judgment and death, and this exhortation spanned the duration of the night.

***

The next night was spent in an open room that had many corridors leading to-and-away from it in all directions. The ceiling was thirty feet high, the floor a flush plane of concrete spiderwebbed by cracks that grew out from columns set every hundred feet in a support-grid that canvased the space. The Zealot's torches illuminated most of the chamber by the time everyone was settled and the tents were pitched. Vitti, presumably acting on orders, refused to allow us to bring the cart or the creature into the room, so Hal and Rooth were charged with keeping watch over it, and the rest of us were permitted to join the Pilgrimage for the first time. As we came into the camp, I became hyper-aware of the tunnel-filth that I had so carelessly allowed to creep into even my every pore. Whiterobes watched us from under their hoods as we proliferated amongst them. Silence followed us like a requiem pall. Shadows danced on the white robes and white tarpaulins and in the whites of our eyes.

At the far end of the room was a wide-cased entryway to a spacious hallway almost as large as a tramway tunnel. This passage had been lined and brightened with many torches, which extemporaneously designated it as significant. As I approached it, I could see the etchings even at a distance - the walls and floor and ceilings covered by them; thousands-upon-thousands of notches carved and tinctured with black ink, together forming a rudimentary depiction of mortal acculturation: great crowds, Mountainships, Winged beasts in Skykingdom, spirals both ragged and clean and all etched optically so they fell down and up and corkscrewed sideways, and the true Sun above and the Undersun below (many depictions of these) all black as buried night, and horizon-lines hilly and mountainous, dotted with stick-people and animals I could not name, and scenes of life and domestication - nascency and childrearing and communal supping and dancing and religious rites and sex and the violence of war and hunting and sacrificial ceremonies; heads stuck atop upright poles, and the ocean and the heavens and the Sun, with its cherished lifegiving rays blazing down eternal on rolling bluffs and roily water. Any scene confederated with all the others seamlessly, commensurate-yet-distinct. One stickman grew into ten-thousand of his kind, all falling headlong into a yawning cavity in the earth, and these scenes appeared animate in the amaranthine torchlight as I neared them and gazed perplexed.

The torches were set in piles of stones on the floor, each of these slick with the black wax that dripped from the torch-heads, this resin layered over itself many times, so that the rockpiles gleamed glossily. This place was old and often-visited. I reached out and touched the painted etchings, apprehensive that they might turn to mist beneath my fingers. I thought of the hands that must have made them... so long ago... did they too live in the dark? Did they know these tunnels and hold dominion over them? What wisdom did they intend to impart to us, the children of their children, now squatting in firelight holding hands two-by-two in the gloom and venturing only so far as to empty shitbuckets where their contents wouldn't be smelt?

The turbid waters of my contemplation were rippled by her. I never felt so small as I did in her presence, and feeling small had been my lot all my life - that is, until I found the Battery in that meager chamber adorned in a manner similar to this one. She startled me out of my thoughts with her head held high and her eyes cold, much meanness in her lovely countenance.

"Attend me." She commanded.

I followed her further down the corridor. Upright torches passed us on both sides until the Painted Hallway split, and we took the path leading away from the noise of the Pilgrimage to a place where the shadows settled unbroken.

"I never got a chance to—"

"Be silent, you! Lowly wretched unclean tunnel-scummer!" Her displeasure with me was such that it inhibited her speech. "You, y-you, *ugh*—" She looked mad enough to hit me, and may have brought me out of sight to do just that, yet now found herself unable to go through with it. Instead, she lashed out with her words, which stung no less. "I will have you know that I will rue your existence for all the remaining days of mine!"

"What have I done to you?"

"To me? To us all! Bringing your deranged friend to the Whipping, so that he would—"

"You promised me your god would restore him!"

"I made no such promise!"

"A strong implication, then! And a correct one, perhaps... He came alive real right before his end, did he not?"

"You unleashed an animal upon us! Sicced him doglike on Holy Brothers and Sisters of mine! Your hands are red with the chaste blood of tragedy and the stench of death trails in your wake! Your uncleanliness offends my eyes!"

"I am sorry. I will bathe. I plead innocence. I may have suspected that he would charge the ring, but I thought six or seven of your Brothers would be enough to subdue him. Had he not gotten hold of that sword–"

"Rityoro was a High Prophet! He served for decades under the Holy banner of–"

"And he passed under the same banner, like! He might've waited, and Monogatari would not have gotten the blade, and far fewer would have been killed–"

"None should have been killed!" She cried.

"I languish a thousand apologies."

"No amount could suffice! You have taken everything from me - everything! I was to be a Vestal Priestess! I was meant to join his Holiness in the High Temple! You have stripped me of my purpose with your carelessness and your hedonism and your thirst for violence!"

"I am contrite! You are the last person I wished to harm or offend in any way!"

She explained to me, with no small amount of angry words and disparaging remarks, that none of those she had selected for Redemption had lived. She told me she had pierced Kassie's ear and had been quite certain that Kassie would be her ticket, but alas. With this failure to show discernment in her selection, she was ineligible for the Vestal position. I asked her what did it matter? Ah yes, his Holiness Horsche, the man larger-than-life. Sure. I couldn't wait to meet him. I had met great men before - Poppa Daddy used to be great, and now he wasn't. Monogatari had been great, (in his own right) until he stopped... but then came back for a final valedictory flourish. The Mayor must have been great at one point, years ago, before he bloated and splayed out to rest upon his laurels. Our underworld was brimming with once-great men now embittered and with foul, drunk, spitting mouths. There were very few faces like hers, young and beautiful, unmarked by scars of abuse healed outside (but not within) or adorned with needleworks; tattoos like the Sons had; symbols they made up for themselves and to which they attributed their own meanings. If there was to be a Holy Vestal something-or-other, it should be her, and I told her so.

"I would not expect you to understand. You, who have lived for nothing - no cause, no purpose greater than your own immediate pleasure."

"I may yet surprise you. I have seen many things, some of great beauty."

"You know nothing of beauty."

"I have seen the lights of the Deep."

She looked at me and could tell I was telling the truth, and this seemed to both impress and discourage her. I continued: "We were down very low. Myself and my friends were swept by a current and we fell and ended up very, very low - well, who can really say, comparatively... but there was a place where our way ended and there was nothing, only the dark, save for some little lights way up above. I have since learned that those lights are a place called Hearthstone."

"The gates of the High City Under Ground - a place of light, happy under Horsche and heedful of all His Parables."

"You were born there?"

"And will likely die there, thanks be to you."

"I will make it right. I will find some way to fix it. I have a good knack for fixing things, you know. I used to work on the Hydrosystems in Z-Bloc, and a few old-timers told me I could hold me mine. I will fix it. I promise."

"You are a stupid boy."

"I am a man. I would wager I'm your elder by five years at least."

"They will leave you down here, and I will be glad of it..."

"What does that mean?"

Her eyes flitted. She had said something she was not supposed to say.

"Hey! What does that mean, they will leave us? By my stinking muddy ass they will! Tell me! You tell me right now!"

"I don't know! I don't know why I said that!"

"You meant something by it!"

"Maybe I did, but far be it from you to know. You are a lowly, vile, repulsive man—"

"Aha, so you concur! I am a man!"

"Not so much as a conniving dog. I told them so at the gathering earlier, when I pled my case. I made them hate you as I do. You and your friends will be abandoned down here with that horrid creature. None of you are even half-worthy of the splendor of the High City."

"They will bring me up." I said, and I was quite confident of it. I would fix things...

***

Back in the main room was singing and dancing; celebration galvanized by enthusiasm for the coming day. The Treacherous Ascent was supposedly the ultimate crucible by which the practitioners of this recently-ancient faith were gauged; the final trial of their Pilgrimage. Every Ascent saw deaths, yet not a man or woman amongst them seemed nervous in the slightest; each was totally certain of his-or-her own abilities. I admired them. I wanted to talk to them and share in their elation, yet I was but a worm to them. Cast out to my own scheming circle I laid down on the cold stone and felt sorry for myself. They all hoped I would die - even some of those in my own group - and we carried a thing that desired nothing more ardently than our demise. Those sounds it made became liquid in the air and we became wet and sticky with it. I forced out the noise of the Lizard and the Zealots, and sleep came after a while.

I was in the dark the next morning. In the dimness I bumped Abraham, and we both made simultaneous apologies in a dead monotone. The finder-creature had been silent for most of the night, but it made noise and rattled the cage when the cart was taken-up. We had to hurry out of that big open room and down the corridor after the fast-fading procession torchlight. My throat was chapped. I asked Rooth for his gut-jug and he, without voice, handed it over for me to take a draw.

We moved through the maze for a half-day before a long straightaway bent and dumped us back out into the Great Hall. It went unexplained, but I surmised that we were on the other side of the cave-in against which Undercamp was constructed. With this, the navigations through the lower sewers were accomplished, and everyone was much-relieved to be back out in the open, with fresher air above-and-around them.

We formed a river of firelight in the darkness, and I took notice of a draft whisking the almost-imperceptibly-thin blue smoke of the ashwax down the Hall. The air was very clean and once-again took on that quality of substantiality, so I filled my lungs and quickened my pace. Eventually, the Hall gave way to darkness in all directions forever, and a solemnness came down over the Pilgrimage, now faced with the final and most perilous leg of its journey.

Few besides Abraham and I had ever beheld the Deep before, and the sheer enormity of it fell outside of what was comprehensible, because all our lives were spent circumscribed below ceilings and between walls, with our faith predicated on the existence of something beyond these, that neither we nor our fathers had ever seen, but someone must have seen these things, right? Those myths came from the sky, not the earth... and yet, the idea that there must be something out there came into stark contrast with the sight and soundlessness of the Deep - that cavern beyond reckoning or estimation, a silence cold, air stirred not by any specific movement; only a general restlessness, hopelessness made physical, darkness tangible, touchable, even, that you could feel it on your hide. Dry lips, dry eyes, dry dicks; that was all we were in the unfathomable face of it...

It was early after lunchtime, but camp was made nonetheless, with the tents of the High Prophets pitched thirty-or-so feet back from where the pipeline ended in a jagged break and the darkness extended. I settled down and had a meal; the last of the corncobs, which had since lost all freshness and juice, and then I walked to the edge of the cavern to join the many others at the precipice of infinity. I was ragged and filthy amongst the whiterobes, yet we all stood aside one-another to gaze out. Above us was the top of the tube, and beyond that, the Lights of Hearthstone; brilliant white and bright, yet still quite small. It would be a long climb up to them. The Prophets called a Sermon, encouraging steadfastness and resolve.

Those who Monogatari had slain had been stitched together and embalmed in ashwax back in Undercamp. The wax had been slow-heated in iron woks and poured over the bodies to harden into smooth cocoons. These were borne on stretchers alongside the Redeemed Sinners, and they did not stink even days after death. Now, in ceremony, the smooth oblong forms were set alight and committed to the Deep. They fell forever and burned to specks, each one flashing out in an unreal instant, one after the next. There was no singing or drums or speech during this. The Redeemed who had perished between here and Undercamp were also tossed off the edge, although without the fire-sheaths. The darkness ate them as they went - there was no way of knowing if they had even fallen or not - they might have floated out horizontally, away from us. All that we could know for certain was that they did not go upwards into the lights above, because those did not blink. Watching the conflagrant mummies fall brought me a shuddersome discomfort. I decided to return to the cart, to the creature, to my people, and search for sleep. The open air made it easier to find.

***

I had come to acquire an adequate understanding of the Holy Hierarchy of Horsche, and the decrees thereby established, to which absolute adherence was expected of all Zealots. This knowledge was gained in-part through observance, and supplemented by my recent travels with the sect. Back in Z, entire floors were controlled by the faith and run in undeviating conformance to these sacred doctrines, which were liturgically conveyed from the senior Priests. Occasionally, exclusive Sermons and ceremonial proceedings were held, during which access to those levels was completely restricted. This, of course, resulted in no small amount of suspicion and distrust for the whiterobes amongst the rest of us. New converts to the faith would often be granted living accommodations on the Zealot floors, where they ate food prepared in the old ways and drank only water, foregoing the pleasures of druk and swill and dustsmoke, and they were forbidden to fuck or fraternize with the uninitiated. Punishment for disobedience was invariably harsh.

Zealot neophytes were required to serve in The Shadows of Those Blessed By His Holy and Eternal Light for a period of five years. In this time, they scrubbed shitpans and washed feet, and were not permitted to wear shoes, and the hems of their robes were to be kept soiled. After this trial-epoch, they were anointed Blameless, Reborn In His Saintly Wisdom, and were given white slippers, their robe-hems to be kept unbesmirched thenceforth. If, in the enactment of their virtuous duties, their robes were dirtied, they must be bleached anew before the wearer could again be seen amongst the ranks of the Holy Brethren. The whiterobes that desired to rise within the tiers of the religion and commit themselves fully to The Unremitting Righteousness of His Sovereign Holiness could submit an application for Pilgrimage Permission to the Holy Eldership. Concession was granted with consideration given to a number of factors, of which youth, beauty, and fertility were always the foremost. The selected Pilgrims would then embark on a journey, typically six weeks long all-told, carrying provisions between the Blocs and collecting more of themselves, until the march to Undercamp, the Festival of the Whipping, and the final trek through the sewers to the Treacherous Ascent.

Over the course of many years and various peregrinations, the Zealot cartographers had compiled an ever-evolving book of maps and diagrams detailing routes of safe passage between the Blocs. Amongst the many purposes served by these expeditions, updating these logs was key, as tunnels would often collapse, flood, or became otherwise-unsuitable for traversal. A secondary (yet still-significant) purpose of the

Pilgrimages was to expand the faith through the upkeep of inter-Bloc supply-lines. If the Zealots had food, cloth, and ammunition, they would steadily and inevitably attract new members. The results of this practice had established the faith as the oldest and farthest-spread faction in our world, and the only one with influence across all surviving megastructures.

It had been nearly thirty years since a Pilgrimage had come to Z-Bloc, which explained why I had never seen High Prophets garbed in the red-and-white, as such vestments were only granted to those who had previously led Pilgrimages to fruition. Each Pilgrimage was headed by twelve High Prophets; four to oversee headcounting, four keeping supply-inventory, and four cartographers responsible for the revision of the maps. The only known route to Z-Bloc had been obstructed years ago, before my birth, and the surrounding tunnels were said to be exceptionally treacherous...

***

These were the things I knew with certitude, yet I would come to learn a great deal more before I took my leave from this strange and polysemous confederacy. Of course, that time was not yet at-hand. While the Zealots prized pacifism and elevated tranquility and nonbelligerent discourse to the topmost height of their standards, the predisposition for bloodlust remains an inextricable concomitant in the heart and mind of every man. This I had come to understand as a child, and never in all my days since had I beheld any evidence contradictory to the fact.

FOURTEEN

The camp was stirred by chaotic noise; raised voices and footsteps overlapping. The majority of the torches were extinguished, but those still-lit were moving fast in the hands of
runners, the flames blurring as they dragged against the head-
winds of panicked flight. I got up fast as gunshots rang loud
and pronounced down the Great Hall towards me. In the failing glow of a cookfire I found our cart and the creature; our
things kicked-over and sewn about. The black tarp had been
flung loose from the cage and Hal was working the lock with
a steelfile, as the key was kept by one of the High Prophets.
I interrupted his efforts and demanded to be told what was
happening, but he said he did not know. I then asked him for
his pistol, a rust-greened hogleg, and to my surprise he surrendered it to me without objection, and I went with celerity
towards the sound of the shots and the tents amongst which
the whiterobes rushed in all ways indiscriminately

My speculation was that Poppa had gone and done it.
Perhaps he had been compelled by the end of the Hall, by
the sight of the Deep, that alveolate abyss. Whatever his rea-
soning, I had no doubt that he was the cause of the gunfire and chaos - he and Cleo - for if this commotion was his
brainchild, she was surely its arbiter. She probably lured one
of the whiterobes off in the dark and committed some foul
act; a soundless bloodless murder, and then donned the robes
herself and left the lifeless body bare-butted in the shadows
on the smooth rough. Thus robed, she must have slipped
between the tents, a perfect mountebank, stepping over the
sleeping bodies until she found the guardsmen and slit their
throats. Such would have caused noise, (I have heard men
screaming past slit throats and it is indeed a noise) and hearing
these ghastly whelps, men would have roused and moved for

their rifles, and Poppa's two soldiers would have been standing ready for them, so that Poppa himself could intrude into the big tent of the High Prophets. He wasn't much to look at anymore, but I had no doubt he could summon up all that meanness that made him who he was and make it get in his blood like swill and channel it to the blunt side or sharp end of something. I was sure that he went in the tent and amongst them. Had he ordered Hal to release the creature? Of this, I could not be sure. Hal seemed to have a relationship with the thing; it was apparent that he did not like keeping it caged up...

The tents had been pitched at the curved base of the tube a short distance back from the chasm and the crowd was thick around these. To be in that crowd was to be utterly human. Alabastrine fabrics whirled, the bodies within like spectre-marionettes, and all were shouting and crying - some had taken up songs or prayers and others had been shot and were wetting the dusty stone with their blood, their robes red-streaked and handprinted, yet the red looked black in the frenzied torchlight...

I found Poppa ranting and roaring as I came through the havoc. He stood over the decapitated body of that old thin-faced stern-voiced High Prophet that I knew presided over the rest of them. I could tell it was this one by the way the headless body had settled; slumped almost gracefully, yet I still looked at the head Poppa was brandishing to make myself certain.

"You all listen good now! It's big Poppa Daddy's time, and that means what's yours is mine! Big Poppa Daddy has come to town to FUCK! You all heard that I'm sure-and-certain to feel fine-and-dandy killing any one of you motherless earthworm-suckin sister-fuckin self-servin' hot holy shitters! *Argh*!"

He flung the High Prophet's head as far-and-high as he could into the crowd, and blood trailed behind it and hovered in a suspended arch before falling in droplets on white hoods.

"It's big Poppa Daddy's time! That means what's yours is mine! Anyone thinkin' of trying me will see! If ya gotta doubt, come find out!"

As he threw the head, I saw him wincing. He had a wound

in his side; his clothes were darkened by blood that made part of him shimmer...

"Yes, I kilt each one in the same manner! Go and see for yourselves! You all watched me shoot that boy at a good distance, you all saw! He tried to kill me - I even gave him the benefit of the first shot, but he couldn't make it stick! He shot me and I stood tall as a reed in water under the Sun and I shot him back and he dropped in the dirt like a Sunray! Move out the way, so that I might shoot him again!"

I didn't want it to be me, but it was just-as-well - somebody had to do it. I moved through the crowd, pistol in-hand, and stepped up to Poppa and put the gun beside his head and pulled the trigger. The rusty hunk clicked dead. I cursed myself for expecting more of it, and for going out boldly before everyone to make a heroic gesture of the attempt... Yet, my gesture must have meant something, seeing how it spurred the rest of those mouth-gaping idiots to stampede, and thank Gordyume for that - you would think these people had never seen the head cut off a man before! Poppa swung his rifle on me and I ducked and he shot someone in the crowd behind me. He tried to pull back the bolt, yet realized midway that there was no time, so he dropped the gun in favor of his knife, (which was already dripping bloody) and there-and-then he had his last fight. The whiterobes fell upon him, heated and feverish, and beat him down and killed him.

I should have focused my efforts on getting that old gun working, because in two moments after Poppa was dead, the Zealot crowd, with white robes crimson and eyes of the same shade, turned on me. I felt hands tearing at my garb and trappings and I hugged my bag the way a mother hugs her baby at the chopping-block and fought, but they dragged me towards the edge nonetheless. Oh, how I kicked and fought and shouted, but my voice could not be heard over the miscellany of theirs.

"Get him! Seize him! Take him!"

"Where are the others, and that infernal creature? I say we cast them all down into the Deep straightaway!"

"Yes! Cast them! Cast them now, and let us be done with

this terrible business!"

A familiar voice: "You are all what he said you were! You cannot do this!"

"Him! He is one of them!"

"Oh-oh-oh-oh no, I'm not! I'm a friend of you people!"

"Bring him forward and throw him off as well!"

Abraham was brought up near me. The crowd had torches and hate-faces, so I figured we might be fucked-like.

"Please! Calm down! Please! I-I-I–"

"Hit this dog! Find me a pole with which I might push him over the edge!"

"Get some tentpoles!"

"This one weeps! He knows he will fall through the ice! You shall not see the light!"

"You shall not see the light, sewer-dweller!"

"Look! He has pissed himself!"

"Throw them off!"

"And this one as well! This turncoat! He betrayed us, Brothers and Sisters! He fled and destroyed his robes, so that he might disguise himself amongst these unclean tunnelers!"

"Kaide! Kaide! Tell them!"

"Shut up, you!"

"Kaide! Oof, *spughhh*–t-tell them... tell them how I saved your life!"

"Matters not! We will throw you all over and be done with it! All of you and that creature cursed our Pilgrimage and destroyed our Holy Festival! The High Prophets brought dishonor on themselves in dealing with you, and Gordyume, in his Eternal Insight, has passed judgment on them; their dishonor turned not to the profit they sought, but to a weapon used to rend them! Let us harken at this time to the twelfth passage of The Sacred Parables of His Holiness Horsche - I speak of course of the second chapter, in which the verses tell of–"

"Let us have them over already!"

"Wait for the creature! It shall go over first! I want to hear it shrieking as it goes!"

"Where is it?"

"A few have gone for it!"

"Give me that club! I'm going to beat this one! He is still fighting!"

"Please, Kaide, do something! You must speak to these people–"

"Don't appear to be doing much speaking, do he?"

"Pull yourself together, Abraham! We might be fucked-like, here - don't depart sniveling and tearful. Stand up!"

"Listen to your friend, dog!"

"I have brought the tentpoles! Now let us find the Lashes of the High Prophets, and whip them bloody before we cast them off!"

"You shall do no such thing!"

Ah, sweet and much-needed amelioration came with her voice. I stopped fighting and fell to my knees, and from the whispers that went through the crowd I was able for the first time to glean her common-tongue name. She was Yvonessa, High Priestess and Vestal-Elect of the Council of the Temple of the High City. She spoke in a tone that commanded deference, fierce and forbidding, as she stood in glory and gold upon a stone, elevating herself above the unsettled horde.

"Hear me! You, my faithful Brothers and steadfast Sisters, you will compose yourselves! We will recall His Light and shall not succumb to the base natures and madnesses inspired by the Deep! Lift your eyes skyward, to the lights of Hearthstone, and take heart! His Lights will never falter nor lack luster! Take hold of one another, join hands, and praise Him! Praise!"

Those immediately surrounding the rock on which she stood went to their faces, and the foremost persecutors of myself and Abraham fell back sheepishly, embarrassed by the fervor by which they had been consumed only moments prior. How quickly changes the tune of any mob...

The Priestess Yvonessa stepped down to move amongst them, whispering blessings in the Old Tongue as she drove them back from us. The crowd thinned, yet didn't disperse fully, and the meanmuggers who had beaten us still stood near and looming. Behind me, the Deep yawned carnivorous, swallowing up light and sound alike...

She came to me in all her grandeur and ordered me to tell her what had transpired.

"He's a dirty lying–"

"Hold your tongue, Brother!"

The whiterobe who had punched me and kicked me in my ribs fell silent at her stern command. When she set her eyes on mine, they cut me so that I bled on the inside, from unplumbed corners of my pneuma, as she looked on and awaited my rejoinder.

"I can only speculate."

"Begin."

"It was Poppa, most-like. How do you suppose he built himself up that his birthname was forgotten and he was henceforth known as Poppa Daddy? Through diplomacy? He was always a throatcutter and a Gunboss, and he was waiting for an opportunity and he spied one tonight. He went into the big tent and cut the head off the High One and pitched it."

She turned back and could see from the faces of the others that this was true. She ordered the head fetched, and then went into the big tent alone. When she reemerged, it was with tears on her face, yet she still looked strong as steel. She quelled the dissent and made the herd busy with breaking camp and bringing ashwax with which to embalm the bodies of the High Prophets and Zealot guardsmen, all of whom had been killed. I learned that Vitti was the boy whom Poppa had bragged of shooting. He had died, and Rooth as well; stabbed to death, yet he was found with his hands fast around the neck of his assailant, one of Poppa's goons, who was also stone-dead and stiffening. The thick thread and hooked needles were brought out to repair the beheaded while Poppa and his gunmen were committed to the deep forthwith. There was no sign of Cleo, but I knew she was out there, lurking somewhere in the shadows...

The enactment of these commands gave the Zealots much-needed focus and diversion. Yvonessa proclaimed that the camp had become unclean, and that the Pilgrimage must start up the Treacherous Ascent presently, to seek the guidance of the High Council. As the whiterobes made ready for the climb, she took me aside and we stood six feet back from the precipice and had further words, the lights of Hearthstone visible past the camber-ceiling of the Great Hall.

***

They called it the Great Climb, and indeed the climb was great. It was quite eerie to walk up the curvature of the Hall until the incline became so steep that we were climbing on all fours,to a place where a staircase became visible in the torch-light. These stairs had been chiseled into the serrate surface of the rock - time-worn ledges of varying widths and breadths and heights, and there were places where the torches could be fitted into drilled apertures every fifty feet or so. Up and out of the Great Hall we cracked our little orange line...

Making that climb gave me my first empirical and intimate understanding of the faith of these people. If this emptiness was not proof of the existence of God, there could be none. As in the Old Times our ancestors had basked and lolled in Sunlight, we had this giant pit - or not even a pit at all, as the word 'pit' infers that there are sides and a bottom - no, this was not a pit; it was a whole hole, and to look down into it from the precipice of the Great Hall was infinitesimal in comparison to doing so while teetering on a tiny step, shirked back flat against the uneven stone, feeling for handholds as faraway black winds swept silently up the sheer cliff-face. I went along, watching my steps, keeping one hand always on the rock as the stairs steeped and leveled; narrow, wide, steep again, and went on...

When I first ventured out, I felt only fear; tremendous and overpowering of all my senses save for an icy ringing in my ears. I tried to count my steps, as I had on that cursed endless staircase deep deep deep below us, (that's three deeps, mind you, because that's how far we had to fucking climb) but I couldn't count, or even think, past my fear and awe. This was no petty ritual of consolatory exculpation for the elderly or guilty - no, to make this climb was to prove to God that you existed and demand his avowal of the fact. Those who chiseled these stairs stood up to Him the way an adolescent boy defies his father, saying 'I'm a man now; a big one with big bones, and I can stand up to you, like?'

Yet faith is not an act of rebellion, but one of surrender. As I made that climb, I listened to the prayers of those before-and-behind me, and repeated these in my own heart with more ardor than I had ever known myself capable of. They were not pleas; they were praises, and from hearing them and submitting my own to the Deep likewise, the nature of true faith became clear to me. While it may not fix you, it will show you how small you are, and it may not change your fate, but it will sure mark your heart. What else in this life is at once a climb and a fall, a battle and a resignation? Faith won't answer your questions, but it will lay to them to rest just the same.

How was I born? I don't know. Babies are just born. There is screaming from the barber's door and the slosh of an afterbirth-bucket being dumped down a drain. Who was responsible for my birth? A whore and a fullish dustsmoker? Why hadn't the nurse laid my head on a brick and smashed another one down upon it? (Another brick, not another head.) I thought of my nameless, faceless lifegivers, likely long-dead... yet might I meet them in the bright place towards which I was advancing? How far I had come! I also thought of Kassie, who, for all her badassery, could never have walked with these people. She might have easily killed the High Priestess in a fight, but she could not have done this...

Those in front bore torches, while those behind removed these from their apertures and passed them back up the line so that they could be affixed in slots further up, and all kept one hand perpetually on the wall, feeling for holds in the rock worn by a thousand hands before... The cuts, so individual-ly-insignificant, yet made with such meritorious aspiration, filled me with faith in the virtue of my race.

The lights of Hearthstone became brighter as we went, all with our eyes downcast. They told me not to look down, the bastards - we had to look down to see the placement of our feet! At first, it was so inky-dark that the torchlight only touched the steps and made shadow-pools in the chisel-strikes, and past that there was nothing; *true* nothing, so pure that you thought that it was something. As we climbed, we could see by the light above more of the rocky cliffside, craggy, wet in places where the light reflected against ambiguous liquids, and we could see more of that depth beneath us. The torchlight was obstructed by the opacity of our bodies, so we had to feel with tentative feet for each step, with the abyss calling to us all-the-while. I wanted it and it wanted me. The lights above grew ever-brighter, so that we could see more of nothing, and the brighter the lights became, so the larger-and-darker grew the cavern, and the smaller we shrunk. This was a place of pure and distinct apportionment; there was only the dark and the light and the stone and us - those in their white robes and me in my rags, as up from the underworld we bore ourselves; I carrying a secret sacred treasure moreover, to a holy place built at the summit of true oblivion.

The first fall was just as terrible as I imagined all of us imagined it would be; a sharp scream, an audible twang of vocal-tissue rending, and the faller simply went away. It was behind me, so I did not witness the disappearance, but the next one was up the slope a ways before me, and those of us who saw it wouldn't soon forget the sight. This one gave a quick yelp of fright as he took the misstep and plummeted, and his screaming faded fast, yet we still heard it long after it dissolved. As we came further into the light we could see the fallers for longer periods before they vanished, thrashing and turning, and each plunge imbued us with more dismay than the last. All told, there were nine.

The stairs became slick at a place where wet was dripping down the jagged cliffside. We took care, baptized now in the harsh hot white-blonde of the lights, which made the scarped face of the rockwall gleam. We were very small in a vast place, and we all felt it, and to feel such a thing was enough to make a believer out of anyone.

***

We arrived at a hollowed-out grotto shaded from the Hearthstone radiance, large enough to accommodate thirty bodies. My position near the front of the line afforded me admittance, and I seated myself as far back as I could get from the ledge. Two chains hung down from the lights; one very large, and the other much smaller. Yvonessa took hold of the smaller one and pulled it with all her strength, letting her full weight drop with the effort, and above us rang out the clear sound of a bell. This euphonious clanging echoed through the abyss, and then came a sharp staccato buzz, and the sunlamps of Hearthstone died. Darkness rushed in with hurricane spleen to surround us and remind us of our forgotten-yet-throughgoing reliance on the ashwax torches.

The final hundred feet of the ascent were to be made by climbing straight up the larger chain, the links of which were big enough for human hands and feet to utilize as a makeshift ladder. It was customary for the Pilgrims to go first, before the Prophets and guardsmen, as there was a ceremony awaiting them at Hearthstone. Yvonessa gave a brief address, after which she came and sat near me. Needing both hands free to grip the chain, the climbers could not bring their torches, so each one was cast into the Deep. The flames whooshed and the lights got smaller until they went out. The cave grew darker with each discarding and the chain swayed as the Pilgrims mounted it and went up hand-over-hand. The first of the climbers disappeared into the dark above. Silence abounded for a spell; broken by no speech or sound save for the soft clinking of the chainlinks and the whooshing of the torches as they were tossed. Finally, I asked the Priestess if there was some significance to this final leg of the journey being made in absolute darkness.

"The Hearthstone Lights would blind the climbers."

"And the Prophets and Vestals go last? After all the torches are dropped?"

"Yes."

"You climbed down that chain, and down those stairs, at the outset of the Pilgrimage?"

"Yes. That is how it begins and ends."

"The traditions of your sect strike me as excessive."

"There can be no spiritual ontogenesis without tribulation, as there can be no true courage without physical danger.

The still-living fallen become one with Gordyume."

"Is it better to be cast over dead and burning, or fall alive and screaming?"

"They are two paths to an equivalent destination. The Gospels of Horsche teach us that the Dark is the Light. The Dark was present before the Light, and is ever-present beyond it. Light is merely the tool with which we make sense of the world - we use Light to paint our lives, to cut the Dark and force it to retreat... yet it is always there, both within and without us. We sleep in darkness, think in darkness, and when we die, we ourselves become darkness. The Dark is the absolute truth. Within it, all is contained. Hearthstone was built to remind us of this."

"I always thought truth was in good swill and spiced dog-meat and the wetness between a woman's legs."

Her brows met in a humorless frown. "I believe the wisdom of our faith shall penetrate your insensate head yet."

"Haughty words. You may think you know all of life, after spending time amongst those in the Blocs and Undercamp, but there is much that you have never seen, Vestal."

"I am not a Vestal."

"Who is to say that? When we get up there, you and I will say what is what. If we do not, rumors will spread, and that will do it."

"Do it?"

"End it for us, most-like."

"Are you suggesting we lie to the Esteemed Elders of the Council?"

"Not as such. I say we simply tell the truth as we see it. In my eyes, you are a Vestal Priestess destined to serve in the High Temple. Has any Pilgrimage returned to the City as ours, with all the Prophets and all-save-one of the Vestal-Elects slain? You have endured trials and met challenges that I reckon no other Vestal ever has, and you have risen to each occasion."

As I made this statement, I tried to imbue it with gravity, nodding thoughtfully, as if I was making some grand philosophical observation. Yvonessa looked at me, her eyes glistening in the shrinking apricot flicker with something like sympathy, profound and sincere. I wanted to keep speaking with her, but I could feel that she was upset, and what I had to say only deepened her melancholy. She was very beautiful. I kept looking at her, because to look at her felt like looking at the Sun, or some other sterling royal thing that escaped my unrefined comprehension.

The Pilgrim-line kept tossing their torches and climbing into darkness until the last man. The Priestess and I were left just the two of us with the final flame. The light was very small and we were together in it, set a million miles apart from the rest of the world. We got to our feet and walked to the ledge. I was expecting her to say something before taking hold of the chain, yet she did not. Once she was eight feet up, I took hold of the cool hard metal and dropped the last torch. As it fell to infinity, the dark became complete.

BOOK IV

'The High City'

FIFTEEN

Above the lights of Hearthstone were iron-grate platforms suspended from the top of the Deep by steel cables. These also upheld the light-panels; thousands-upon-thousands of sunlamp-bulbs which together formed down-facing squares of blazing illumination that could blind a person under them, yet could hardly scratch that abyssal ocean. The Welcoming Procession awaited the ascending Pilgrims on these platforms, where a Sermon was called, and there was a relighting ceremony that I would have liked to witness, but armed Sentinels swept up Yvonessa and I immediately upon our arrival. It had taken no time for news of the Pilgrimage incidents to reach the ears of the authorities here, and the High Prophets of the Elder Council had demanded an immediate report. We were escorted down a catwalk leading away from the platforms and the ceremony, and after forty yards, this catwalk yielded to the stone floor of a tunnel that extended for a similar distance, before two large iron doors swung open to admit us into the Zealot High City.

The High City was all carved stone washed white, and it was, like the stairs leading to it, a magnificent feather in the cap of humanity. The systems under a Bloc had been mined-out; the tunnels and plumbing-complexes all rerouted and conjoined together into the grand metropolis now spread before us, partitioned down the center by a main street, with spacious garden-parks laid bountifully between the structures, all of which gleamed brilliant ivory. It was altogether a paradise. There were no huts or shanties, only carefully-calculated architecture devised of stones cut and laid together perfectly. Light touched everything, cast from large sunlamp-arrays above, (a great many of them; more than the number in Undercamp and Z-Bloc put together) and while the illumination was blinding, the warmth was a gratifying deviation from the cold of the tunnels and the Deep. The footpaths were cobbled with iron tiles polished to shine, and the domiciles were all doorless, open and inviting, boasting commodious rooms and glass windows, and there were stone flowerbeds irrigated by pipes laid beneath the streets, and blue water sparkled in fountains and spouted from drinking-podiums in neat unbroken streams that arched perfectly into drains without splattering. Here there was no visible filth or garbage whatsoever, nor any stench of sewage nor smoke. This City and its people breathed as one, taking for-granted prosperous unity, homogeneity, and the resulting sense of community bestowed by these. The general impression given was akin to the experience of attending the wedding-reception of a handsome groom to his treasured and eternally-beautiful bride, wherein all attendees ardently affirmed the good fortune of both parties while the eldership traded guileful jests about how pleasurable the consummation of the union would doubtlessly prove to be.

Most residential structures stood double-storied, and the temples and meetinghouses were built higher still; some four or five floors, topped with steepled belfries below which green grew healthily and people walked freely, all in spotless white linen, and prayers and hymns and music imbued the whole scene with buoyancy. Even in dreamscapes, I had never beheld such a vision; each edge and angle adhered to a uniform system of design, and every measurement was impeccable. To walk through that place made me shudder at the existence of anything besides it.

We were led up a staircase that was less of a staircase and more a series of long-and-wide landings, then to the irontile mainstreet, golden under the sunlamps, with pagoda apartments on either side and flat-topped buildings with rooftop patios and balconies that overlooked all.

My clothes were ragged and my skin was wan and pale under the grime, crisscrossed with the healed-over scars that designated the places where bad things had happened to me as a child in the Bazaar - that same child I still was; still frayed and rent and scared and standing with balled fists. As I strode,

Zealot crowds gathered to gawk at me, as I was entirely alien to them, heaving, filthy, with starving eyes compunctious of my philistine deportment meeting theirs ashamedly and flitting fast away, unlike the Priestess, who walked at my side with her chin uplifted proudly.

The mainstreet came to an end at a large three-tiered fountain, circular, laid in the center of an open square floored with flagstones painted a thick untarnishable white. On the far side of this square was the Low Temple of Horsche; the largest building in the High City. All the ingenuity of the prized Zealot architects had been utilized in the design of its arches, minarets, and the trio of spires atop it, which seemed to have been made by pouring liquid gold over stones cut into cones. These spires reached almost to the top of the cavern, (which was made nearly-invisible by the sunlamp-clusters) and I looked at them in awe as we came into their shadows. The entire City had a feeling of openness; dissimilar to the foreboding oppugnancy of the openness of the Great Hall, but rather a soaring sense of emancipation - like how I imagined our forefathers felt under the true blue sky.

We were taken into the Low Temple nave, which was sectioned with clerestory windows between which the walls were adorned with varicolored paintings like those in the tunnels: inked etchings depicting stickmen-crowds under the Sun, the fabled celestial spheres all surrounded with great patches of dark color and writings in the Old Tongue. The Sentinels left us in that auditorium; its arches meeting above my head in support of the groin-vaulted ceiling, yellow cutting the room in slates of light and shadow that fell on the ground in bright rectangles, dim between the slates, bright within them. We walked through these slates and broke them, moving towards the transept and the High Pulpit of the High - which was indeed high, and made of wrought and gaudily-ornamented steel. Beside the Pulpit stood two red-and-white-robed High Prophets, who took down their hoods and descended the stairs to meet us. All our footsteps echoed in the otherwise-vacant room.

***

I still had it. I had never let it loose since I found it. I felt its weight in the pocket of my shitmud-ruined britches and suppressed an inclination to touch it, as such would have been too obvious - the approaching High Prophets might suspect I had something; a small and dirty secret, something valuable or forbidden, or perhaps even cursed...

***

Yvonessa knew both of the Prophets and they knew her. Both were old and bearded. One was my height, skinny, long-limbed, and the other was short and squat with a neatly-trimmed beard. I later learned that this Prophet was named Quabba. He had a longstanding familiarity with the Priestess, judging from the manner in which the two of them embraced, and Yvonessa wasted no time in summarizing most-all of the tragedies that had befallen the Pilgrimage while Quabba eyed me from behind lids that rested at uneven, half-closed degrees. Although she did me no favors, she auspiciously neglected to mention the fact that it was I who had brought Monogatari to the Whipping Ceremony... Then, Quabba used the back of a limp hand to move her out of his way, so that he could face me fully. He told me to kneel. I felt compelled to, so I obeyed.

"On both knees."

"Alright..."

He reached out and laid a hand on my forehead, gently palming my skull. I kept my eyes open, looking up at him. He kept his hand on my head for a long time and remained silent. This continued until someone else (a whiterobe) entered from a sidedoor and called out to Quabba and the other High Prophet, who had said nothing thus-far and had simply been observing. Quabba withdrew his hand and told me to stand, which I did, and then he took my hand and raised it softly to his lips. I glanced at Yvonessa, who deliberately avoided my eyes, and then we all followed the whiterobe down a corridor, the walls of which displayed murals of stickmen in the throes of worship and war.

We came into an apse, dim save for an incandescent ring of dappled chromaticity cutting down from a stained-glass dome directly above. I harked back to a conversation with the Mayor of Undercamp, in which he informed me that the window in his Palace foyer was a gift from the Zealots; a token of their uncustomary alliance.

The walls were bare, yet fixed into them were twelve sizable slabs of cracked concrete bearing ancient carvings identical in technique and style to those I had seen far below. I thought of the dusty remains of the man and his children... These slabs must have been brought up from very deep, and I wondered how. Stairs wrapped around the semicircular chamber and went up to the High Places of the High Council of the Twelve High Prophets Under Horsche; a dias-platform narrow and elevated, with red tapestries unfurled down its front. Behind the precariously-low railing sat twelve thrones, high-backed and red-upholstered.

The Council of the High Twelve assembled, appearing from a set of double-doors under the platform and making their way up the stairs until they found their seats fifteen feet above us. Quabba and the other High Prophet joined them. All wore red-and-white, and while they were a mix of shapes and heights, they were all old men, and the sneering dubiety in their faces was uniform. As our hearing began, I marked that one of the dozen seats remained empty...

The Prophet that did most of the speaking had a ringing voice, intense and distinct. His skin was a shade of flushed pink and he had straight white hair that fell about his shoulders and seemed to mold to his form. He was tall - about the same height as Monogatari, I reckoned, and well-built and broad-chested, despite his age. He recited a litany in the Old Tongue, each syllable laden with allusive connotation, and then he dropped his eyes to us, scrutinizing every cell that comprised our makeups and appearing to read plainly every thought that flashed through our minds.

"Sister Yvonessa, Vestal-Elect and Pious Priestess Under Horsche... rumors have reached this Most High and Holy Council that the Sacred Pilgrimage entrusted-to and chaperoned by you has returned fragmentary and stricken with scandalous accounts of bloodshed and dishonor, and now, with mine own eyes I behold a wretched infidel standing black-clad and heathenish in our most esteemed sunlit gallery, throwing his greedy gaze all over the treasures of our faith! Pray explain, Sister, why this nonbeliever has been brought here without first being Cleansed and Redeemed at the Ceremony of the Whipping?"

Yvonessa took three strides forward, floating soundlessly and gracefully as she did so, her robes swaying like liquid controlled through preternatural means. She removed her hood, letting her hair fall, and knelt on both knees, her hands folded before her, becoming entirely saintlike in that circle of light and color. I looked on and tried to crystallize the sight into a memory that would endure forever. When she spoke, she did not look up at those she was addressing.

"Oh High One, dearest and most revered Brother Gongaphah of the High Council, One Bedight and Bathed in His Holy Light, I humble myself in your prestigious presence, so that I might beseech you and the Council to hear me with the patience and consideration you would grant yourselves before passing most Righteous Judgment. It is true that He, in His Infinite Wisdom, deemed it fit to vituperate our Pilgrimage with many tragedies and tribulations, and while the cost has been great, I make the claim before you that the Brothers and Sisters brought to this most Sacred City are devoted all-the-more-so, having beheld not only the beauty of the Deep, but the myriad horrors of which their kin are capable, and perhaps even fain-to and inclined-towards. I shall tell you of all that befell us, so that you might sort out the veracity from the prevarication, and I yield myself eagerly and entirely to whatever fate or castigation you prescribe."

"Who is the infidel?"

She said my name without looking back at me.

"Tell him to step forward, alongside you!"

I didn't need to be told. I did, and I knelt beside her, perspiring in the bright color and feeling acutely-aware of it. The big High One, Gongaphah, ordered in his knifelike voice for Yvonessa to commence with the recounting, and the happenings of the Pilgrimage were narrated in-detail. The Priestess gave approximate headcounts, distances, and cartographical estimations in regards to the first few weeks of the journey. It was when she came to the Undercamp Festival (and to me) that the first interruption came.

"Z-Bloc? Nay! Preposterous! He must be a tunneler!"

"What proof does he carry of his claim?!"

"What proof would you have him carry? We have but his word!"

Quabba spoke, with a touch more compassion than the others: "I would like to hear from his own lips a description of Z-Bloc, so that I might reconcile it against the testimonies in the existing annals—"

"Yes, yes, but at another time. Tonight our City must welcome fresh faces, who indeed must be presented with only the utmost hospitality we can offer, after what they have endured. Continue, Vestal-Elect, as we have yet to hear of the slayings of our brethren!"

Yvonessa recounted the massacre at Undercamp and the insurrection of Poppa Daddy at the base of the Treacherous Ascent. She told them who Poppa was, and of his dealings with the Pilgrimage Prophets concerning the Lizard.

"Surely you did not bring this mongrel up from the depths, did you?"

"Of course not. It was left at the base of the Ascent, guarded by two of its keepers."

"And what assurance do we have that these two, left to their own devices, will not run off with it, be it as valuable a prize as you claim?"

"Where might they go? They have few provisions and little water - I left them only with assurances of forthcoming rescue from above."

"And what of the creature itself? How can we be certain that indeed it can do the things you claim it to be capable of? Will the infidel-scoundrel also regale us with tales regarding that?"

At this point, there was disagreement between the Council Prophets. It seemed that half of them were willing to give Yvonessa the benefit of the doubt, yet the other half wanted some punitive measures to be taken. Counterpoints were made against one-another until the argument had to be tabled in the interest of time. Before this interim conclusion was reached, however, a redrobe who had remained mute up until this point put forth an accusation to the Vestal-Elect.

"You claim this brute, this 'poppa-dandy' or whoever, aided by his lethal cohort, forced entry into the tent of the High Prophets and killed them... including, it seems, your Sister-Elects. This bodes noticeably-convenient for you, does it not? Why were you absent from the tent on the night before the Ascent?"

"I had gone off to the edge, to pray."

"By yourself?"

"Yes. I was apprehensive of the coming climb. I wished to make my peace with the Deep, lest Gordyume called me home still-living."

"We will hear a great deal more on this matter at another time - now we must digress, and make ready to receive our new Brothers and Sisters. Yvonessa shall attend us tonight, in lieu of a proper Vestal, and the infidel shall be jailed to await our final decision."

"If I may—" Quabba cut in eagerly, "I would like to take possession of this purported Z-Blocker. It seems to me that we should decide straightaway if he is lying, as a great deal hinges on the validity of his testimony. If he is true, such could spell a new era in the exploration of—"

"He will be confined in the cells below, and there he will stay, until what to do with him is decided and agreed-upon."

Quabba frowned, yet didn't press his point any further. With this verdict dispensed, the Council adjourned.

***

For two sleeps I was kept in a cell with three stone walls and a fourth wall of iron bars. There were other cells in the basement of the Temple, but none were occupied, and judging from the half-inch-thick layer of dust that softened the floors, they had not been in ages. I passed my time sitting in silence or else singing badly-butchered parodies of the Zealot hymns. During my incarceration, I was paid two visits.

Yvonessa was the first. She came down after the Welcoming Ceremonies above, which, judging from the noise, carried on well-into the night. The way she glanced over her shoulder as she walked down the corridor made me suspect that she wasn't supposed to be visiting me. We spoke in hushed tones. She assured me that everything was fine; that I would be okay. Gongaphah, she told me, was next in-line for ascendance to the High Temple, to join Horsche himself, and to this end he was solely motivated. Quabba was the one who would help us. He was the Keeper of the High Histories, so I was already of-interest to him, and I was told he would be petitioning for my release and would visit me personally the next morning. Despite my best efforts to continue conversing, the Priestess had to depart. I slept the night through, albeit fitfully.

Sure enough, Quabba came the next day. Unlike Yvonessa, he walked down the corridor with the confidence of a manfighter coming into the ring, looking straight into my face. What a strange-looking fellow he was, with his round chin and froglips, and those mismatched lids low over his eyes, and no length to his legs, which were short and knobby with knees bent back and bowed-out wide from his hips, and his torso fat, but only in the stomach, as if a fluid-filled sack hung beneath his sternum. All this was clearly distinguishable even past his flowing robes. He asked me in his breathy lisp to remind him what my name was, and I did so.

"You come from Z-Bloc?"

"I do."

"How can you be certain it was Z?"

"There were steel plaques affixed to the main columns, and inside the lifts, and in the Subsection courtyards."

"What do you know of the Histories?"

"The Bright Times? Sunlight? Only myths and legends. Whatever stood as true in the times before the Corporation stopped mattering after it."

"Tell me about the Corporation."

"Are you going to get me out of here? I hate this cell."

"Efforts are being made. Presently, let us converse and lay

between us the foundational bricks of friendship."

I didn't feel together. It had been longer than a week since I'd had any druk or swill, and I felt the many trodden miles in my feet and spine... Nonetheless, I talked with Quabba about my old life, all-the-while growing sour. What justification could I provide to him (or myself) for the needlessness of it all? So many opportunities for my own demise had been passed-up for want of further suffrage. I was a fool with a gluttonous appetite for my own self-immortalization via the endurance of adversity. We talked for a while, until I was bored with my own voice. Somehow, all the things I had to say seemed far-removed and abstract. The faces of those with whom I had once broken bread now seemed less clear in my memory than the meals themselves. I thought of the many deaths I had witnessed, of those nine who had fallen during the Treacherous Ascent...

***

The next day, the captain of the Zealot Guard came to unlock my cell-door and escort me back upstairs and into that sunlit color-swatch under the eyes of the High Elders. Few details were given to me - only that I was to be released and granted temporary quarters in the High City, and that I was to make daily reports to Quabba and his cabinet, and slake any interrogations they put to me. I was also informed that the Lizard would indeed be brought up from the Deep, to stand under the judgment of the Council. Although I didn't voice the misgiving, I failed to see how such a creature could be expected to stand under the judgment of even God himself.

The Temple guardsmen led me past the fountain, out into the mainstreet, and turned me over to the custody of two whiterobes; a man and a woman, both with youthful faces, yet erudite eyes. They led me to my quarters; two footpaths off from the mainstreet, where townhomes stood high on both sides of the way. Stone balconies with iron railings hung over the street, providing shade from the sunlamps, and there were woven baskets of greenery and fruitplants strung-up from these railings, through which the light broke down verdant.

My allocated unit was on the second floor, beyond a pleasant lobby and up a half-turn staircase. I had three rooms; a washroom with a stone basin of clean water, a spacious main room with mats and cushions around a low table (and a doorway that opened to a balcony that faced in the direction of Hearthstone) and a sleeping-room, wherein a fabric mattress sat atop an iron-legged frame. Everything was freshly-painted ivory, and the air carried aromatic hints of floral incense. Save for those set in Hearthstone and the Low Temple, (and obviously the iron bars of the cell in which I was kept previously) there were no doors in the High City, as there was no distrust amongst the residents here, nor any shame or wariness between neighbors. This shamelessness of the High City Zealots was fully-impressed upon me when the whiterobes asked me if I would like assistance disrobing. I told them I was okay. They informed me that I must cleanse myself before I could walk freely in their streets, and they gave me a towel whitened many times over with lye soap. I stripped naked before them, feeling extremely self-conscious - suddenly my own body revolted me; the film of grime, the scars, the starved boniness... I quickly covered myself with the towel as my clothes were pilfered from me to be burned. Then I was led out of the apartment and through the High City like some unclean animal, until we came to the bathhouse.

This large circular building had a domed roof slotted intermittently, so that steam could escape it. The interior was humid and every surface was mosaiced with thousands of stone tiles fitted together and painted shades of blue and white. In the center of the bathhouse was a multi-layered construct of oval pools, the water overflowing from the shallow ones at the top to the deeper ones at the bottom. The sound of the water was loud and the floor was very warm, presumably kept-so by ashwax coals bellowed perpetually beneath us. The pools were filled with naked forms all gleaming and slick, and past the haze I could see bodies, some youthfully fetching and others wrinkled by age, jiggling with their steps or flexing as they raised or lowered themselves into or out-of the water.

I was led past these main communal baths to smaller

chambers utterly beclouded by hot steam, where a stone lip formed a bench along one wall. There were spouting showers in the wall opposite this, and I was directed to rinse off under these. My towel was taken from me and I was left alone, as the few other occupants of the room departed upon my arrival, not wanting to look upon me even in the obscurity of the fog. I stood under a showerhead and watched the water at my feet turn black and race for the drain...

SIXTEEN

Life in the High City was a monotonous series of placid delights. I often woke early, before the sunlamps came on, and went out onto my balcony to stretch and enjoy the cool dark, and then I would go down to the lobby drinking-fountain, usually a full hour before the daybreak-bell beckoned those multitudes in white hoods (and their children without hoods) to emerge into the fresh morn.

We ate only fruits and vegetables and roots here, although they were prepared in a greater variety of methods than those to which I was accustomed. Mealtimes were always communal, shared with several-hundred others sitting at the long tables in the dining-gardens. Salads were prepared from greens fresh-cut out of the planters and washed right near us, and we ate under the pleasant shade of white tarpaulins pulled taut by cords at their corners tied to high posts. The Zealots all spoke the Old Tongue in a dialect I was unfamiliar with. I felt stupid amongst them. They would look ponderously into one-another's eyes and would take great care with even the smallest of banal pleasantries. There was an overabundance of love and total freedom with regards to the expression of it. These people all kissed often on the lips and cheeks, walked arm-in-arm or side-hugging, and their children, in their short white hoodless smocks, clambered over the adults indiscriminately and hooted as they were piggybacked. Strangers would embrace me and eagerly introduce me to their friends, neighbors, and even their offspring, withholding no clemency.

There were multiple temples dedicated to different facets of the faith, and a great amount of music made with both drums and stringed instruments, usually accompanied by the singing of hymns. Entire groups would break spontaneously into song; joyful, praising, hands outstretched, eyes closed, faces teary and earnest and beautiful. These people were all beautiful; well-tanned from lifetimes spent under the lights, kept fit from clean diets and sex aplenty. When the Zealots made love, it was good and righteous to them; a physical manifestation of the love they had, not only for each other, but for their food and their home. Everywhere I looked, I saw the happiness and contentment that made these people of one body and voice - save for me, alas - I was stuck quite out-of-place, gloomy and verminous, come to tread dirt on these clean tile floors and molt the manicured crops by my presence alone.

Here there were no bum-broke beggars nor urchin-children, no germsick or druksick or smoked-out dust-fucked-like. No Unregisturds; only architects, stonecutters, mathematicians; no johnnies or Cowboys or whores; only painters, writers, sculptors, historians, and musicians. I had no people here, and thus became a novelty. I ate and drank and bathed with them, yet I was not one of them. I sat in their temples and admired their stonework, reclined in the light-lines made by their slit-windows, and I watched their women walk in the streets and imagined the faces they made as they fucked, set far apart, and as such, I was cloaked in ever-shifting rumors and was the subject of much hearsay. None understood the true reason for my presence, yet all knew that I was the first infidel to walk Unwhipped amidst the High City, bathed in Holy Light Eternal. Enigmatic and mystical I moved through this herd with inscrutable intentions... Yet, in my own time, I came to understand that they (yes, even they, who lived so happily in such blest abundance and security) still yearned for a groundswell - albeit a subliminal yearning. They wanted action; the Opening of the Great Gates, the shooting-down of Lawmaker, the Burning of the Bazaar, Monogatari's whetted blade swooshing through them at Undercamp... I would tell them stories, but none seemed to care about what had happened, and just like in Z, only speculations about the future held any colloquial merit.

Only one Zealot amongst the five-some-odd-thousand cared, and indeed had a boundless well of enthusiasm for my anecdotes of the Bloc and my old life as one of its residents. This was Quabba, to whom I paid daily visits at the Hall of Histories; the second-largest building in the High City, and every bit as ornate as all the rest.

The slanted roof was paneled with glass that reflected the light that, from certain angles, was too bright to look at. Inside was huge and open, the entire hall standing as a single long main room, with tables and sitting-places amongst rows of shelves piled high and packed past-capacity with scrolls and bound books, and, in some cases, stone tablets. The hall interior was overlooked on all sides by the upper-level mezzanines. On the second level were more shelves with more documents, and then a third level with more still, although this level was restricted - accessible only to the High Prophets and their cabinet-members. Amongst the books and scrolls kept here were the oldest surviving documentations of the bygone times; all yellowed and brittled by age, dog-eared, falling apart to dust. Also on the third level was the entrance to the Learned Tower, the highest accessible point of the City, where Quabba kept his office. Up those spiral stairs I climbed each day, typically after the midday meal, to confer with the Keeper of the Histories.

Quabba's office was every bit as eccentric as the man himself. His furniture was a mix of wood and stone carved baroque with almost-audacious skill, and there was nary a clean surface; parchments and scrolls covered the tables, desks, chairtops, even the floor. There were many shelves upholding glass jars, these filled with murky liquids and containing things like petrified rat corpses or human eyeballs, and there was a big seeing-glass, and a kettle shaped like a globe, with a thin stemlike neck, that was kept whistling at a low boil by a can of jellied alcohol.

Quabba himself was always buried out-of-sight beneath his charts and parchments, and would spring forth buggish and agile when I entered, causing his eternal workload to re-arrange itself in a flutter. He would take me to the cushions by the tower-window and look out over the City as we spoke at-length; durations filled with the frantic scribbling of Quabba's quill as he filled pages with my descriptions and musings, often in his own hand, but sometimes one of his assistants would sit in with us, writing silently, taking down almost every word I uttered.

During these sessions, Quabba exhibited voracious interest in what I had to say of my travels, and particularly of my youth-years in Z-Bloc. I, on the other hand, was more engaged in what he told me. Each day, when his business would cut short our meetings, he would scribble a note for me to pass to one of the Keepers, designating a specific document for me to peruse. The quality and variety of the Zealot Archives astonished me - there were some accounts that dated back to the times before the First Uprising, translations made by Zealot Historians of official Corporation documents, essays and dissertations on past dignitaries and statesmen - such a wealth that I soon came to regard the Hall of Histories as the center of the known world.

Quabba was perhaps the wisest and most interesting man I'd ever met. He could speak for hours on any given topic, offering whys and wherefores and justifications of his explanations with that patience and placidity that classifies adept teachers. His eyes, always behind those lazy half-lids, would roll in circles as he spoke, often making rotations up into his skull as he began his sentences with Old-Tongue-exclamations, or breathy 'you sees' or 'and furthermores.' I quite enjoyed talking with him, as he, like all born pedagogues, possessed the ability to make his pupil feel smart. When his schedule allowed, I would walk home with him after my readings, feeling a mile more enlightened and an inch more at-home amongst this haughty tribe.

***

Reclined and sipping the bitter mint-tea Quabba's secretary always served us, the topic of our conversation emigrated from the distant past to the immediate present when I inquired after the wellbeing of Yvonessa, whom I hadn't seen a glimpse of in days. Quabba frowned at me.

"In a respectful tongue, you might refer to her as the

Priestess Most High, or else by her true name, and spare my ears the gutter-speak."

"Why is it that you don't require to be presented with the same respect?"

"Chiefly because my name sounds much the same in either tongue, and secondly, to make myself more personable, so that you might be more comfortable with me."

"I wish to know how she is. I haven't seen her in days."

"A result of her specific and explicit intent, no doubt."

"You don't wish to speak of her?"

Quabba exhaled weightily and lines deepened across his face. He hauled himself up to a sitting position and set aside his tea to fold his hands on his belly with his fingers interlaced.

"The Priestess is quite dear to me, and she has found herself entangled in a web of intrigue both political and sacerdotal. I fear her very life may hang in the balance. She is yet a young woman, and although she, like all chosen Vestal-Elects, is blessed with wisdom far beyond her years, no Priestess has ever stood in so instrumental and critical a position."

"I thought as much. I feel culpable, as surely the decision to bring me up is the foremost cause of this controversy?"

"Yes... but in a grander sense, it is far more intricate. You have come to us at a strange time. Likely in days long-following these, scholars like ourselves will hold discussions about you and I, and the impact of our decisions. Here exists a water-weight that has been dammed for decades, and as you may well be the crack that finally breaks the dam, you did not put the water behind it. Walk not guiltily with your head low, for indeed, we are both blessed to live in such a significant and revolutionary era!"

"She told me something of similar effect; of some argument between the Pilgrimage Prophets regarding the decision to allow myself and my people to tail the procession–"

"Yes, and furthermore–" Quabba interrupted me, as he so-often did, to hasten me along to the point towards which he was driving "–you have unwittingly brought the aggrandizement of that dispute along with you to our City; indeed to the height of our ranks! You see, you yourself, your regiment, and most-particularly that creature, have called into question a larger debate that has been long-discussed and hotly-impugned for years."

"The debate of making deeper descents into the tunnels?"

"Precisely."

I pondered for a moment, and then I asked what harm could come of it.

"Much. Regardless if we find treasure or terror, both corrupt the spirits of men. To seek in the abyss is a heretical enterprise, according to some. It is said that in striving to understand the giants who came before, we seek to align ourselves in positions of equality with them."

"Would that be so bad?"

"Ah, misunderstanding manifests naivete! I shall recommend some passages from the Holy Gospels, and of course, some supplementary texts that will illuminate–"

"Must you go so soon?"

"I? Oh no, I am quite free today, after my morning appointments. I was merely going to walk down to the fountain-baths and lay out in the light. Care to accompany me?"

"Happily."

Quabba nodded and wrote out the prescription for the new texts I was to study, and then gathered his long red-and-white robes and a bundle of scrolls to carry under his arm, and the both of us descended the stairs to walk through the open main floor of the majestic hall, past the rows of ionic columns, to the wide and doorless egress.

***

As was typical, the High City was abuzz with life. Down the neatly-cobbled streets we strolled, continuing our conversation all-the-while, save for the instances when Quabba paused to acknowledge passers that, for the most part, made small bows to him. The dignity with which he carried himself was made all-the-more impressive when one considered his stumpy stature.

"Yvonessa wishes to send expeditions into the lower sewers, does she not?" I was frowned-at for my usage of the common-tongue name, but this time remained unrebuked. "She believes that the creature may lead exploratory parties to new and fantastic discoveries."

"I wonder who would have encouraged such an idea?"

"You as much as I, surely. In mapping out the deeper levels, we might learn more of those who built them; more of the Corporation, more of our own history. Surely such an undertaking holds allure for you as well?"

"Yes, but you see, it is not so simple as that. The Holy Will of Horsche governs us all."

"What would his Holiness want with a sleazy Lizard?"

"Ah, sleazy as it may well be, it remains a very significant Lizard! It possesses the ability to navigate an untold trackless labyrinth, and that makes it a very valuable Lizard indeed! You must understand that long ago, men not entirely dissimilar to ourselves could, and indeed did know the full extent of that million miles of passages beneath our feet, and in knowing them, they held dominion over them. While it may be easy to apotheosize these men and imagine that they must have been enlightened and superlative, we must remember that, in truth, they were no better than you, and likely a great deal worse than I."

"I have suspicions."

"Regarding?"

"All of it."

"Naturally. Pray tell."

We came to a place where the streetpath sloped down past some large houses and led to the fountain-gardens; the bottommost point of the High City, arranged where the Sun-lamps shone on all sides, so that no shadows were ever cast. We walked down and came into a thin crowd of Zealots disrobed and swimming in the waters, or else lying on the sand and sunning themselves. The uniform bronze of their skin was fascinating to me and I gawked at their nudity. Quabba let down his hood in a gesture of repose as we found two folding deckchairs with canvas seatbacks at the far edge of the courtyard. There were ranks of cornstalks rising from planters behind us, so we had a degree of privacy, which made our situation desirable, yet those nearby gave us respectful space as we settled - a far-cry from the constant eavesdroppers and spies in Undercamp. As I gazed at the bodies, all tawny and tight and well-muscled, I felt myself stirring under my smock and sweating in the heat.

"You are a young man; why don't you cast off your garb and swim with them?"

"Does Yvonessa hope to deliver the Lizard to Horsche personally, as a means of gaining favor with him?"

"It is ostensible that the thought has crossed her mind. A great deal depends on Beevil."

"Beevil?"

"The Council Rector, Holy Voice of the Most High."

"The old one?"

"Boy, we're all old!" Quabba said with a hearty laugh.

"The eldest - the one who looks to have years on the rest of you—"

"No, no, you have not seen Beevil. His is the vacant seat in the Council Gallery. He is presently in the High Temple, serving his Holiness directly. Ten years have passed since his ascendance, and on his last visit, he informed us of his intention to retire after a new Vestal appointment. His forthcoming replacement was amongst those slain at the Undercamp."

"How often are new Vestals appointed?"

"Customarily, every year... yet this epoch is variable. There were two who held the position for decades, if I recall correctly."

I nodded. In the past days, I had come to understand that to be selected to serve as either Voice or Vestal was the highest honor and most salient responsibility that any Zealot could hope to attain; the absolute pinnacle of service to the faith. To be eligible for such a distinction an enumerated syllabus of prerequisites had to be attained over the course of a candidate's lifetime. It was unfortunate that the cross borne by the Vestal-Elect Yvonessa, the sole goal and aspiration of her life, stood now simultaneously within her grasp, yet imperiled by novel circumstances for which I myself was the inadvertent personification of, and scapegoat for...

Alongside this knowledge, I had also expanded my understanding of the purpose and function of each of the Twelve
Arms of Gordyume, and their heads, who filled the Council
seats. I found it amusing that the High City functioned in accordance with a system not unlike the Departmental one that
had kept Z-Bloc operative. The twelve High Prophets of the
High Council each held comprehensive managerial authority
over a specific bailiwick of societal desideratum. These were
organized into three denominations, each with four heads.
The first were the Lifegivers; responsible for the upkeep of
the plumbing, ventilation, and electrical systems - the func-
tions of which were necessary for agriculture. These were
aptly designated by Old-Tongue archaisms that roughly translated to Aquarius, (the Water-Bearer) Helios, (the Charioteer)
Aeolus, (the Hornsman) and Demeter (the Seed-Sower).

There were also four Gubernatorial Overseers. Gongaphah, the one who had so-assiduously critiqued the Priestess
and I upon our arrival, was Head of the Sentinel Guard, responsible for the security of the City and the enforcement of
its jurisprudence. Besides him was the Headcounter, (responsible for the enactment of censuses and maintaining citizen-
ship records) the Stonecutter, (head architect, whose duties re-
volved around the upkeep of the temples, houses, and streets
of this metropolis) and Beevil, whom Quabba spoke of - the
Holy Rector; intermediary between the High Temple and the
Low, the Voice of Horsche himself. As such, he was bestowed
with a measure of authority beyond that of any of the other
members of the Council.

Additionally, there were four Culturalists, one of which
was Quabba, the Keeper of the Histories. Besides him was
the Cartographer, (whose duties were similar to Quabba's, but
with a specific focus on the Pilgrimage-maps and charts of
the tunnels) the Educationalist, (who set the precedents for
the rearing and teaching of the young, and instituted curric-
ulums by which they would be indoctrinated into the faith)
and the Composer; the artist and musician in this City full
of them, an arbiter of taste, who was considered peerless in
ability and expertise.

"Do the ascended Vestals ever return to the High City?"

"As the closest and most intimate confidants of He, The Great One Singular Above The Rest, their departures from us are permanent. The magnitude of their assignment and the service required from them is so considerable that to return to the lower places after living in His Light would be akin to you or I crawling in the sewer-dirt with the worms."

"I see." I said simply, and for the first time since we sat, Quabba rolled himself halfway over and looked me in the face with a curiosity that bordered on incredulity.

"It is plain on your face that you are quite enamored with her. You poor man; you fan the flames of a vainglorious and futile fantasy. Such is common in the Whipped Sinners, and, as you are Unwhipped, this folly is all-the-less surprising."

"Let us not forget that I have climbed a great deal higher than you, or anyone else here."

I was becoming irritable. All this socialization without the behavioral lubricant of druk or swill, the constant heat of the sunlamps, the way that Quabba would bully me with his superior intellect, making his grand statements in the Old Tongue or referencing old texts or the words of long-bygone Prophets, which he spoke with that sense of finality only achievable to one who had lived his whole life in a place such as this - all of it was tiring. If he had been a Bloc resident or a Gadabout, he would have known that not all angles are so right as to form perfect corners...

***

We departed the fountain-gardens after a time, following the wet footsteps of the crowd back up the aforementioned rise, towards the temple where the Zealot matrimonial unions were consolidated: The Temple of Holy Love. Quabba insisted that we go in, saying that tonight, two Redeemed, both of striking physical beauty, would be married and breed and conceive, and he intended to witness it firsthand. He encouraged me to do the same, saying that it would fix me right up, but I was not inclined to witness such a thing in the presence of Quabba. I was polite in taking my leave of him, and walked against the oncoming crowd, which was legion.

I strode alone up a streetpath unfamiliar to me, coming to a place where ashwax torches had been set into iron holders for light in the nighttime hours, which were fast-approaching. I wandered for a while, as did my thoughts. I bent over a drinking-spout and let it run cool and refreshing against my face. Two children in their hoodless smocks rushed laughing past me, and I walked on. The sunlamps shone bright on the white stones until the Low Temple bells sounded and the great big bright above went dark with that electrical buzz, the last of it dying slowly on the red-orange coils, putting a thousand fast-fading specks on the top of the cave for a brief few seconds. Mothers called out for their children from the doorless entries of the white houses, and unshuttered windows threw candlelight into the streets alongside cordial voices which joined the hymns of the first Night Procession, making its rounds with their swinging thuribles, their white robes fringed by sweet and sticky incense-smoke.

I wandered and wondered if I would be okay. I touched it in my pocket. It was always in my pocket; I never let it go off my person for a second since I found it. Nobody else knew about it. It was my secret, and it felt good to have. I found a quiet spot on a bench beside a gurgling fountain, and I took it out and held it to the now-faroff torchlight and watched the liquid flow inside the little window, shimmering onyx behind the glass and brushed steel.

SEVENTEEN

The First Uprising was literal. The Blocs had become unsustainably overcrowded, fraught with barbarity and starvation to such degrees that people ate one-another, and from them was birthed a new generation who knew only the tunnels and nothing besides them. The Corporation decreed a culling, yet they were tardy in this declaration, for the subterranean generation was already vast in number, while Lawmaker was only one. Up they rose out of indignation and sewage, a hard people, warlike, flesh-fed, hateful, hellbent on vengeance and the bringing-about of fantastic calamity like those of yore under the True Sun in the Old Times.

This Unregisturd Army had at its prow a fearless leader; a warrior of mythical lethality and magnetic charisma who stood godlike in battle, and by his awesome presence and versant strategies myriad victories were taken - so many that his true name paled entirely in contrast to the title given to him (by both his enemies and his own men) that it was lost forever; discarded and rightly-deemed insignificant to history. He was not born as such, yet became known, through hardness-of-will, soundness-of-mind, and matchless enactments of violence, as Xirexi - the Red Prince, Butcher of the Blocs. According to the Histories, he was indeed red, both with the gore of the tens-of-thousands he slew, as well as the deep-maroon ink needled into every inch of his skin, (lips and eyelids and penis included) in testimony of his claim that in the Old Times, the Sun burned the skin of those who stood too long under its light, pigmenting them an analogous rubicund shade. It was fabled that he could fight toe-to-toe with Lawmaker himself, and did so on several occasions, although neither ever came out the undisputed victor.

The tide of war did not turn until Xirexi perished. He was

not killed in battle - the nature of his demise seems to be ambiguous; something of metaphysical means. Quabba alluded that it was his own power that overwhelmed him, in the most unvarnished sense, as if his physical body spontaneously tore apart under the strain of containing his spirit. With his death, the Unregisturd Coalition fell to pieces, driven back by what remained of the Corporation after a series of poor strategic maneuvers and the general ill-effects of the power-vacuum left by their potentate. Back down they were forced to abscond, back to the underworld from whence they came, and further still, having provoked the full wrath of their oppressors after years of unending battle. Deep they fled from the forthcoming extermination... yet, in those most desperate hours, a final plan was hatched; some deathwish-stratagem by means of which they intended to destroy Lawmaker and establish enduring freedom for themselves and their progeny.

This scheme, much like the passing of Xirexi, also had its specifics lost to history. What is known is that Lawmaker was lured deep underground, to a place where some enigmatical annihilatory force was unleashed upon him. According to the account of Quabba, this event (or the attempt of it, at least) opened the Deep and disunited the Blocs. Although the Corporation endured, it was hamstrung, merely a feeble remnant of what it once was; its labyrinth-network of tunnels made dark and dingy, now the sole commonwealth of rebels and secessionists...

Years and decades passed. Alliances formed between the governments of those Blocs that remained connected, either by tramways or Gadabout shortcuts. It became one Gunboss versus another, until again civilization fell to infighting and the indiscriminate slaughter of the innocent and guilty alike - all to no avail or purpose beyond that to which mass murder is its own. Bombs were detonated, firearm ammunition became exceedingly scarce, swords and pikes were smelted, and this Second Uprising established balkanized governments more immediate in necessity than the Corporation, which heaved its last breath and died not all at once, but in the consolidation of many varied mini-deaths, some public and pronounced, others private and diplomatic, observed only by a backroom few who happened to stand in the right places at the opportune moments, or speak the right words in the proper ears.

The Third Uprising was not one with which Quabba was familiar. After the Second, Z-Bloc was amongst the megastructures cut-off entirely from the main tunnels. It stood to reason that the collapsing of these routes was intentional, done to block supply-lines or entrap enemy divisions. It happened before my birth, its indissoluble ramifications to endure forever-and-a-day regardless.

Like Horsche himself, the Zealot faith was born in H-Bloc, and became widespread at the start of the Second Uprising. Once again forced deep under the earth by overpopulation and war, the early pioneers of the religion began mining under H to construct for themselves a Holy City. Expeditions into the tunnels brought discoveries of the Sacred Painted Places, and in these places were uncovered Holy Secrets of the Deep, which empowered their efforts. While war was waged around them, they dug and chiseled, mining sphalerite zinc-ore and oxidizing it for their white paint, and sending forth Pilgrimages to spread their influence and recruit new laborers to aid and aggrandize the spread of ideals that were proliferated not through force, but through altruism; the peaceful efforts of missionaries who journeyed through filth and darkness to far-flung Blocs... until, after many years, a countless multitude of the disciples of Gordyume walked enlightened through the heretical underworld.

***

I thought of all these things as I stood in the Council Gallery with Quabba. By my request he had brought me here, to where the carefully-broken slabs of cement were fixed into the wall with iron mounts, a two-inch gap between them and the wall itself, their etched-and-painted surfaces facing outwards, half-lit by the light that poured through the stained-glass dome above. Each stone was large enough to crush a person. By the forefathers these were cut and carried, explained Quabba, and hoisted up from the Deep with long chains in the same method that was being proposed to bring up the finder-creature. Some of them were carried for miles through the tunnels. I lingered on a particular depiction of Xirexi standing tall, his standard held high aloft, rallying his warfighter regiments. Black ink exploded out around him like flames, and before him a multitude of spears were raised. The Red Prince high on a hill... or no, Quabba corrected me, that wasn't a hill - it was a pile of corpses, all felled by his own hand...

I looked at the Sacred Stones while Quabba talked ceaselessly, expositing the intent and significance of each depiction. His voice faded to a dull hum in my ears. It could have been minutes or hours that passed - I had no way of discerning. Whatever length the period marked, I spent the entirety of it gazing at a specific trio of the pieces hung in the Gallery. Eventually, an impatience almost out-of-character for him compelled Quabba to ask me what time I would like to be going. I won a few more minutes, and lucky I did, too, because in those minutes, the High Priestess appeared, coming towards us through the multicolored dapple of light. Her hood was low, yet Quabba and I both knew it was her from the way she moved like an ethereal breeze. She approached and spoke to Quabba only, not looking in my direction.

"It is decided. They will bring it up tonight."

Quabba already knew, but it was news to me.

"Will they truly? What of Hal and Abraham?" I asked.

She ignored my question. I bit the inside of my mouth as she turned her shoulder further away from me, as if to cut me out of the conversation.

"A Holy Sacrifice is to be made to Gordyume."

This surprised Quabba. "Oh?"

"Yes, and Gongaphah has devised an insidious method of deciding who it shall be."

"I'm sure he has..."

"What is more, he has declared that if the Sacrifice fails to appease Gordyume enough that he sends us a Holy Sign of some sort, then we shall cut the chains and let the beast fall forever."

"What!" I cried out, pushing my way back into the dialogue. Quabba only sighed and selected one of his chins to stroke.

"Mmm, yes... naturally I hypothesized that Gongaphah would find some way to see the creature lost forever..."

"I fear there is nothing to be done, Quabba. You must attend tonight... and he."

She looked at me for the first time with a hint of concern buried beneath cold disdain, and I realized with a jolt that it was her assumption that I was to be the Sacrifice! Quabba picked this up as well, saying apprehensively: "Oh... oh no, no, surely not! I won't stand for that!"

"If it is not, it will be something worse. Let us not discredit Gongaphah and the capacity of his imagination for acrimony. If it seems so obvious to you and I, there is a good chance it will not be him."

She jerked her head slightly towards me as she said 'him.' Under typical circumstances, her mere acknowledgement of my existence would have been enough to send my heart soaring, but now I was worried about being Sacrificed - whatever that suggested. I resolved to arm myself before night fell, and if any other than Quabba came for me, I would do them in. Yvonessa and Quabba had a few more words before she left us, moving away through the light illuminated all prismatic and gold until she froze in shadow and was gone. I felt a hand on my shoulder and heard Quabba's voice reassuring me. He said our chief concern should be preventing the Lizard from being committed to the Deep. After that, he was at my side the remainder of the day - suspecting my intention, no doubt. I harbored a detestable impression that I would be unable to shed him come mealtime, and I was right. The High Prophets of the Council usually dined in the Temple, sequestered from the commoners, yet today he elected to accompany me down to the tables in the public gardens...

***

We found two spots on the long bench, which was fast-filling, and we were of-interest to the others; an unlikely pair, yet well-suited to one-another. The Zealots congregated at our end of the table and made incessant conversation, so that we could not speak frankly, and certainly could not discuss plans for what was to come, whilst surrounded by their eager ears.

The Temple Bells clanged out a bright blue ring that seemed to fill the cave and become too big for it. There was murmuring all around us. Eyes all looked out from under white hoods to Quabba, who split his face wide to show his teeth and spread his hands, the red folds of his amice swaying as he stepped up onto the wooden bench. Those nearest to him moved back, I as well, and we looked at him as he stood stately and magnificent in spite of himself. His delivery of the Blessing-Invocation shot like an arrow to the heart; made with scholarly eloquence cushioned by earnest passion. We all listened intently, and afterwards laughed politely at the genteel joke he cracked to alleviate the solemnity of the whole scene. The foodbowls were passed around - root-salads and string-beans and tomatoes cut thin and served with oil made from olives (a specialty of the Zealots) and leaves of chard and kale drizzled in the same. We ate with our hands and drank fresh-tasting water from tumblers. I found myself famished and supped as if it was my last meal, painfully-aware of the possibility that it might actually be so...

As I stuffed myself, I took a look around and marveled at how not a solitary one of these people were raffish in the slightest - they spoke happily and hugged, and all, without exception, had good teeth, unclouded eyes, and looked pleasant when they laughed. They were every one of them bulls and sows of the top stock, bred of a handsome hunky-dory world. For the first time, I longed to be one of them, resenting the squalor of my antecedent days which had left me scarred and so well-accustomed to the stench of shit and the sounds made by the bleeding dying doomed.

Quabba steered the conversation in which he was engaged with several of the near-sitters to the topic of the Red Prince, and I listened to tales of how spectacular he had been in combat; a purported genius, a fighter of transcendental ability, a pure and raw talent well-refined through drilling and rehearsal and bestowed with a razor-fine focus singular and undeterrable. To put him armed with strong steel alone against a hundred men would be the certain condemnation of them all to death, without them seeing so much as a pinprick of the Red One's blood. I listened (as did the rest of the crowd) while I ate, doing my best to appear unanxious.

***

After dinner, we left the dining-gardens and ascended the flower-bordered landings to the main streetpath. I came to suspect that Quabba had raised the topic of Xirexi on purpose, because he suggested that we walk to the Glass Square, so that we might contemplate the statue of the Red Prince erected atop the multilayered fountain there. I had not gandered at this sculpture since learning the history of whom it depicted, so I agreed. The hems of Quabba's robe swished over the warm irontiles as we walked.

The Square and the fountain was delimited on all sides by glass greenhouses in which the tomatoes and olives and other vegetation requiring specific humidities were cultivated, and the reflected sunlamp-light hit the bronze likeness of the Red One and made it gleam incandescent. I could not help but wonder at the selection of our locale... The Glass Square was set at the far edge of the City; a questionably-convenient proximity to Hearthstone Rock. As we stood in silence, a group of whiterobes passed by, carrying armfuls of dirty worksmocks to the bleachers. The light glancing off the greenhouses and the irontiles made everything very white; the whitest-of-white, and Quabba proffered this as the reason why the Red Prince's effigy was erected here - because none before him in all the Histories had shone so bright.

"In what manner are Sacrifices offered to Gordyume?" I asked, unable to stand the tortuous ambiguity any longer...

"It is an antiquated practice not performed in a number of years, so it is unsurprising that old Gongaphah has chosen it as the illegitimate means by which he will justify the disposal of the finder-creature... the cad! Let us recall that Horsche, the Most Holy and Highest himself, stated in his proverbs that power will corrupt the spirit of even the most devout. Gongaphah is fully-corrupted, I don't mind telling you - you have likely perceived such for yourself already. He plots to assume Beevil's spot–" and here came a breathy and indignant huff.

"I don't care about all that. Answer me what I asked."

"There is a chemical powder that, when lit, burns very hot and bright. It is used for mining, as it melts rock, steel, iron, what-have-you. A package of this powder is affixed to an iron plate and put on a person's breast - the offering - and touched with the lit end of a long torch as the body is pushed off the from the Hearthstone platforms. They burn very bright and scream very loudly as they fall."

"Well, that bodes quite fucking poorly!"

"I daresay you will be fine - I don't believe that the black-guard's eye is on you..."

"Yvonessa?"

"We mustn't speak of it further."

"I must go! I must make ready–"

"No! No, you must wait here! This is the place I told her."

My suspicions were confirmed! Part of me wanted to kill this short squabbish talker. He would lead me to my potential death and all-the-while act so casually about it? I scowled and paced restlessly and cupped my hands into the fountain for a drink. The water was warm. I spat out a dark shape on the cobbled ground and watched it dry. When the Low Temple bells chimed the end-of-day, I was glad for the absence of torches in the greenhouses, so that when the final winks of light went, and we were entrenched in hot silent murderous darkness, I could attack Quabba and take his robes... But alas, this flight-of-fancy flapped up to strike its head against the top of the cave and dropped back dead in the fountain. I didn't have it in me.

When Yvonessa came to meet us, she looked hard and cold and clear through me. It was time. I walked slowly betwixt the two of them; Quabba in his red-and-white and Yvonessa in her white-and-gold. Age and beauty. We came to the open gardens spread before Hearthstone Rock, where there stood Sentinels on either side of the open gates, holding old rifles that seemed in their hands like ugly tears in the fabric of this utopian reality. They, unlike the Pilgrimage guardsmen, wore robes indistinguishable from the rest, and stood framed by the blackness of the extending shaft behind them. The orange flicker of the nearby torches fell on their faces and cut their features with grim shadow. We crossed to them and became a quintet as we entered the tunnel. The floor fell away beneath us and the catwalk swayed gently with our steps, until we came onto the platforms hung above the Hearthstone Lights and the Deep.

***

Upon the main platform was a winchwheel and chain, (the chain up which the Pilgrims had climbed) and now I saw other chains of varying lengths and degrees-of-thickness wound on iron spools fastened to the top of the Deep, and hinged trap-doors in the iron grates through which these chains could be lowered. A certain chain had been spooled on the turncrank of the winch, which must have been accomplished through strenuous labor, as this chain, although thinner than the main anchorchain, looked to be several-thousand feet long. At its dangling end was affixed via a bolt and nug a sturdy hook. Six whiterobes stood nearby, holding iron bars that fitted into slots on the winchwheel-crank; the handles by which the ap-paratus was turned.

Ten of the High Eleven stood offside (all save Quabba) and there were an additional six Sentinel guardsmen standing beside the open trapdoor under the pulley. Everyone whose face I could see by the torchlight looked uncertain, as though they were acting on orders they didn't fully understand. I was included amongst them in this regard, yet they all looked at me like the whole thing was my contrivance. Yvonessa and Quab-ba left me standing alone as they joined the High Prophets. Everyone on the platforms stood in groups, save I, the sole loner, scared and trying hard not to show it.

There was a pause that protracted until it was broken by Gongaphah. He took slow steps across the platform, carrying an ashwax torch, and he walked further than I, or anyone, expected him to, coming all the way to me. I got a good look under his hood for the first time. He was ugly in a way that made me think he must have emerged from the womb like that, and his ugliness sneered at me, looking almost cross-eyed down the bridge of his hooked nose.

"Well?"

"Well?" I repeated. My voice had little strength.

"Will you get to it while you're still young?"

An impulsive and incredulous scoff on my end - almost a chuckle, because for a moment I truly thought it was a joke, but no, it was very serious.

"What... um, what am I... I thought—"

"You might save yourself the trouble of thinking!"

I looked about desperately, but I was condemned. The eyes of those gathered avoided mine, preferring instead the steel grate.

"What am I to do? Hang onto the chain as it's lowered?"

The look on Gongaphah's face told me that was precisely what was expected of me. He thrust the torch in my direction and I took it stupidly, amazed by the audacity of the expectation, and I stood silent for a pause, until he said: "Get on with it, or I'll have you cast off!"

With no choice left me, I crossed the platform, sweating under sidelong gazes both guilty and hatefully-amused. Beside the opening up through which I had ascended from the Deep, (and through which I would return to it presently) sat a pile of thick leather straps. These were for attaching the Lizard's cage to the hook, so that it might be reeled back up to the top. I hung them about my shoulders, using one to fasten myself to the chain, which was as thick as my wrist. It was silent as I did this, and I couldn't help but contemplate the dread magnitude of the coming undertaking as I stood at the edge of that cut-out square in the platform. Below, the Hearthstone Lights blazed down into dizzying nothingness. My positioning would allow me to slip between two of the light-panels; those giant squares each housing countless electric blooms - the nerve-endings of thousands of cables; one to each bulb, that grew like a root-system out of the backs of the panels and were bound together in places where fifty became one, and fifty became one again, until they came together in thick rubberized trunks strapped under the maintenance-catwalks. The altitude was so soaring, and the lights were so bright, and the dark so dark; barely penetrated by that yellow-white light that grew gray and softened in a gradient until eventually the abyss crept into it with tendrils that thickened and congealed until all was black. As I looked down, I felt the eyes of all the others fixed on me intently...

"Will you turn off the lights?"

"Why would that be done?"

"They could blind me!"

"Keep your eyes shut and your head turned away."

"What of the creature? I'll tell you, it is not one bit fond of light!"

"The lights stay shining." Gongaphah said, and a sadistic grin that I considered unworthy of anyone called a High One widened his purple lips. His teeth glowed wet in the torch-light, and I found courage, deciding then-and-there not to die a coward in his bullying presence. I took hold of the chain, winding it around my forearm, and held myself to it, putting one foot into the crook of the hook and stepping onto it, swinging away from the sturdy safety of the platform, dan-gling over the drop. I may have imagined it, but I thought I heard a quiet gasp tighten the chests of my audience as I did this. With one hand I adjusted my grip, improving my hold, and with the other I held the torch aloft, and I took a breath and readied myself, and when I was ready as I could be, I said: "Let's be on with it!"

There was a metallic squeal as the whiterobes threw their weight against the turning-pins, and the winch began unspool-ing, grinding as though rust needed to be worked-through, but after the first thirty feet, the drop became smooth and speedy. I shut my eyes tight and tucked my chin as I passed the panels and fell into the heat. Beyond my eyelids was all blinding white. My skin sizzled and my sweat boiled as I fell smoothly down, squinching my whole face shut until the sheer bright faded to colorful dancing spots. I could feel the wind of my controlled descent as the heat paled to a bearable temperature, though I was certain I had been scorched red and cancerous in those few moments I had been close to the sun-lamp-panels. The rattling of the winch and the buzzing of the lights faded as well, yet I kept my eyes closed until I felt steely darkness calming my being from the outside-in. As the chain unspooled, I began to sway gently to-and-fro, like a long needlelike pendulum in the inky sea...

I opened my eyes. The light was far above me, reflecting dully off my rusty lifeline, and the dark was racing up so that I was bathed in it. The further down I fell, the darker it became as I oscillated in infinity, holding fast to a chain fastened to the sunlit summit of an unimaginable height. Down I fell, into the darkness with which I amalgamated and became one... and as I was swallowed-by and became darkness, I found that, as the darkness, I could touch all things, and indeed *was* all things...

I descended; now a Holy Prophet tried-and-true, marred by trial, yet standing undefeated and therefore wise. The torch burned a fishbowl around me, and my world became only this as the Hearthstone Lights receded... solely my eyes and the orange aura in which I was cast, with nothing else to make me human save the chain to which I clung.

EIGHTEEN

I came to a sudden halt, dizzy, impossibly nauseated, and feeling so small - man was not meant to feel small in the way I did at the end of that iron line. Simply swinging in place was far worse than descending. Had they run out of length? Had I reached the appropriate depth? The chainlinks creaked with my oscillations and the disorientation brought on from this motion (and the general vacuity) gave me a migraine. I vomited liquid and red bits of tomato that fell out of my fishbowl and ceased to exist as I gagged and retched myself dry. Hot tears strung my cheeks, which were doubtlessly seared from the sunlamps, and I felt a bad cramp in my grip. At an utter loss, I started wailing like a spirit-raped thaumaturgist into the abyss... until an answer came; indistinguishable and faraway, yet seemingly-parallel with my position in that purgatorial gulf.

I shouted 'hello' and a voice not my own called back. Then came an explosion of red: a flare, held aloft by a human-esque figure standing at a distance I estimated to be two-hundred feet across from me, at the base of a shaft that extended back from the escarpment of the Deep; surely the Great Hall. The silhouette was strikingly-familiar, as I had beheld the very same sight before. It was Hal. I lurched with all my weight in one direction, and then the opposite, and back again, building momentum until I was swinging to-and-fro, nearer each time to the red of the flare and the edge of the Hall, until at the apex of a great swoop Hal caught my legs and held fast with his heels dug into the floor. He managed to reel me in, and by some miracle I maintained hold of the chain, although I dropped the torch, which clattered too near to the verge and fell, whooshing down forever.

"Woo! How is it like, Hal?"

He simply stared at me and didn't say anything. The expression on his face resembled that which Monogatari bore as he sat motionless in the darkened room of the Palace guest-house. This concerned me. It had been nearly a week since we had ascended and left him and Abraham down here to watch over the Lizard, and as I looked about for Abraham and saw no sign of him, my concern deepened. The darkness by-itself was disturbing, and spending days enveloped in it with only the creature for company, becoming increasingly-uncertain with each passing day of the prospect of rescue, was more than enough to make a man flee his mental post. With my feet now on sturdy ground, I asked him where his counterpart was. He said nothing.

"Hal? You together? Where is Abraham?"

He still said nothing.

"Did you hear me? You haven't gone mad down here, have you?"

He looked quite insane. I hoped against my instinct that it was simply a trick of the harsh red as I asked again after the whereabouts of Abraham. If something bad had happened to him, I would struggle to forgive myself...

"Look here, I'm in no mood for this! You see what I have just been through? Lowered down like they made me do? I did it for you, you know! You and him! I would not have left you stranded down here forever; I owed you rescue, as it was you who rescued us from the tunnels, and all-the-while up above I was well-aware of the debt! Now tell me where Abraham is! I must bring him up as well, because he made that journey with me through all that filth and darkness in the endless hopeless halls and he never wavered more than the rest of us, despite being older - so it wouldn't have been as much for him to resign himself to death - yet he stood tall, and not just for himself, but for the group! So to him I owe an even greater debt! Tell me where he is!"

Still without words, Hal took a few steps back and held the sizzling light-stick away from me, so that a place previously shrouded by his shadow became lit. At first I saw nothing, un-til I squinted and saw a dark patch on the slightly-sloped floor; a spot with that reflective quality of liquid, and then I saw the scattered bones; dull-white and not quite picked-clean, decaying gristle stuck on their rounded ends. I felt myself go pale. My blood surged a hundred-million gallons in my ears and I began to shake, not with the adrenaline of the descent, but with rage. Hal looked at me dully, as if he was staring through me, and he gave no indication of any emotional affectivity or sentiment whatsoever as I stuttered, stumbling through the thicket of my shock.

"Y-you... he... what the—"

Finally the fucker spoke emptily, impassive, toneless: "She was hungry."

"She? Who... y-you mean the—"

"She had to feed."

"So you... oh, no... no, no, no—"

The witless glaze over Hal's eyes faded as he focused on me more intently, yet his look did not become any less demented; it grew more-so. He said: "You will not take her up."

"It's... how do you know that it's— oh, fuck, listen, Hal; step closer to me."

He stood just a few feet out of my reach - a gap I could not close without letting go of the chain and losing it. He did not step closer. He simply stood in-place, looking at me with those soulless orbs sunken back in his oval head. I continued: "See here, we must go up! This is no life for a man - it is not even a life for a dog! Above awaits a city bright and clean and free, and this creature will help us secure a place for ourselves there!"

"They will harm her!"

"Be reasonable! Please! Hand me the light, so that—"

"You are a fluttering and frivolous breed of nothing, boy."

"I... um, what?"

"You, without any motivations of your own, just do whatever *he* needs you to do. He tells you what to do and you do it. Aimlessly you wander about as things happen to you - all of it just the veneer of a thin plot with naught to do with you - you, nameless, faceless, and the rest of us with names and faces! You don't make anything happen; you are just there as *he* makes things happen! You are a phony yellowboy fullish and empty as the words themselves!"

"Woah... okay, I think you had better not talk like that..."

"I do not care."

"Have you been speaking to that fucking monster? Did it tell you these things in some orphic snakelike tongue?!"

"It's a *she*!"

"Of course it is! Oh– oh... you haven't laid with the thing, right? Tell me not!"

"Is that meant to be funny?"

"It is no laughing matter!"

"You will not bring her up!"

In his rising anger, Hal took a few threatening steps in my direction. A dull thud rang out as I struck him in the head with the blunt back of the hook, and then a second, weightier thud followed as he went to the dust. The porous concrete drank the blood that ran from the cut above his ear as he lay motionless. I prodded him with my foot a few times and called his name until I was satisfied that he was felled, and then I put the hook of the chain under his belt, so that it would not swing out of my reach. As I did this, I checked to confirm that I had not killed him, although I didn't care much, after what he had done to Abraham. He still pulled air, albeit faintly. Then I kicked the flare further down the Hall, so that I would have light for the forthcoming task.

The cage still sat atop the cart and was covered with the thick black tarpaulin, which I lifted to confirm that the beast was indeed still housed within. It was. I pulled the cart over beside Hal's fallen form, clambered up on top, and went about fastening the hook to the cage by means of the leather straps. The fabric rippled with animalistic seething as I did this. After my work was finished, I realized that no plan had been ratified by which I might return, and from this depth, there was no way to signal those above, so I had to take it on faith that they would eventually turn the winchwheel back and see what it brought up. I sat on top of the cage, detesting being in such close proximity to the finder-creature, yet left with no other option. The prospect of trying to lug Hal along crossed my mind, but I decided against it. Let him rot down here, the bastard. Such seemed a fitting retribution for Abraham's unseemly death.

***

After maybe twenty minutes, the slack in the chain went tense and the cart and cage were pulled forth (with I still atop them) until off the edge we swung. The cart plummeted to infinity below, and the whole cage shook precariously with the Lizard's thrashing displeasure. I clung to the straps for my dear life. The tarp flapped as the chain emitted a terrible screech I could feel in my teeth, and, owing to all that weight at the end of the very long length, we spun and swiveled without settling. The ascent was far slower than the descent, but up we traveled nonetheless, one rotation of the winchcrank at a time. The Lizard was vexed by the motion, yet I knew its current indignation would pale in comparison to the enragement it would exhibit once we came directly under the Hearthstone Lights.

As those grew brighter above me, I tried to reconcile their perceived insignificance with the sight of those huge suspended panels each fed by cables-bundles four feet in circumference. The gradually-increasing light made the chain look wet as it reflected off the iron links, as there was nothing else for it to catch. My muscular tension was such that I was vibrating; my every molecule standing in place and then shifting a tiny distance to the right and then back again in an anxious cellular two-step.

Sure enough, when the lights became bright enough to show the true cavernous emptiness of the space, the beast expelled an unequaled calamitous protest - a ghastly noise like nothing I, or any man, had ever heard before; a guttural croaking yowl like discordant stradivariuses. It screamed and squirmed, swaying the cage so dangerously that I figured myself for fucked-like. The fiendish sound and lurching movement continued whilst up we went with the lights growing ever-brighter, so that soon I would have to close my eyes...

It screamed and screamed and in the screaming of that creature was contained, I think, the voice of all of us underground, who have never seen the Sun and are at-home in and at-ease with the dark and the abyss engendered by a cause that mattered not; it could have been one Uprising or another, one revolution or the next by which we were entombed eternally, left only with cognizance that in bygone times people once worked and played and loved in Holy Sunlight cutting down from a different abyss; one blue, not black, above, not below, that gave relativity to all corporeality; yet now, in darkness complete, like bugs or rats lowly we slither and with picks and chisels carve out trifling lives for ourselves, breeding and bearing children to be raised up underground without Sunlight or hope, because it simply is what it is: a dark world; a cave like the one inside our mothers, out of which we emerge into another cave, less damp, yet no less confined, wherein we, in naive infantility, covet shiny things and blood; and we love these because they reflect the light, and the light is us; we liken ourselves to the light because darkness is all, and we long for something other than that, besides it, separate from it, to realize and reassure us of our idealizations of ourselves - our light, not our shadows - and for this we live and do our earnest utmost to find faith in the dark.

The Lizard shook the cage so much that I was certain to fall, so I shouted desperately for the lights to be turned off. They were now so bright I could not face them, so I looked down and beheld what I thought to be movement below - a flutter in the gray-layer at the brink of nothing, where light gave way to the dark. I stared hard until my eyes watered... It was impossible to be certain, and the way that infernal creature was tossing itself against the bars left me little to do save cling to the leather straps and pray for forthcoming salvation. By this point, the light was all around me and white-hot. I shut my eyes and tucked my chin to my chest as it grew whiter and warmer, the heat becoming unbearable, until I felt my blood boiling under my skin and smelled the acrid stench of my hair smoldering. I longed for death and was certain it had come, yet still it illiberally desired for me to prove my worthiness through the endurance of sublime agony before it tendered me sweet alleviation...

Then, at the absolute apex of the tribulation, the suffrage

quelled and I could hear clearly the ratcheting of the winch and the footsteps of its turners against the metal grate above, and I opened my eyes and could see the pulley. Joy filled me; a good, true joy, like love or holidays. I was past the lights and almost up, moving through the square trapdoor, and my joy was so full and intense that it momentarily superseded the screaming of the Lizard.

***

Once raised parallel to the platform, I leapt off the cage and fell prostrate on the grate. I was no small mess; my vision spotty and my skin blistered. The High Prophets and the Sentinels crowded a circle around the cage. Then, from my facedown position, I beheld it again: something moving down in the deep, at the edge of the sunlamp-illumination, and this time the exclamation of a guardsman confirmed that it was no trick of the light.

"Oh-ho! Hey! I see something! Something moves below!"

The scene fell into disorganization. Shouting overlapped with those terrible yawps of the Lizard in its cage beside me as guardsmen rushed to the catwalk-railings for better sight-lines. I squinted down past the light-panels as the shapeless movement accrued form, melding itself out of shadow into the contours of immense wings, fully-extended and supinating, primary feathers five feet long and sharp as obsidian, steel scapular blades flexing, rusted talons gleaming, thick interlocking plates of armor flexing, as up from the Deep He came...

Lawmaker.

Fear seized me vicelike. I was already on my feet and running before the impact. The whole platform gave a lurch as, with a powerful thrust of his wings, Lawmaker smashed upwards through the light-panels, live wire-ends exploding and flying all around him as he landed in a shower of glass and metal and electricity on the platform. I was thrown raglike back to the iron grate and covered my head with my arms as gunshots sounded from the rank of Sentinels who stood between Lawmaker and the Prophets. He lunged forth, heedless of the bullets, and ripped them all to scarlet ribbons in a blink.

Quabba moved in a quicksilver beeline for the exit. It was Yvoness who demonstrated the wherewithal to take action - she pulled the tarp clear of the cage and yanked the bolt free and threw the door wide, and the Lizard sprung forth instantaneously and went screaming over my head, wriggling over the grate, and flung itself in an unbelievable bound over the railing. It must have flown nearly seventy feet straight out over the Deep before falling twisting and contorted downwards. Lawmaker stretched out his bladed wings, the ends of which severed many of the suspension-cables as he pushed off and took flight. One cable snapped back and hit a man and took all of him away save for his foot, which remained upright beside me, spouting blood from the stump. Another cable went in the direction of the High Prophets and cut three of them clean in half. Lawmaker crashed down through the half-destroyed panels, shattering them totally and bringing glass and sparks with him as he went into a nosedive after his prey.

The remaining cables could not uphold us. My ears were split by the squeal of sundering metal as the entire platform heaved and dropped to an alarming angle. The remaining Sentinels went plummeting - one grabbed a flailing wire cut free from the root-system, and all his skin and muscle was burned off in a bright flash, and his skeleton disassembled in midair. I moved up the platform and spied Yvonessa with her hood down, her eyes wild with terror, and I moved fleetly towards her, dodging the rolling spool of the winchcrank, which had broken loose. The extreme weight of the thing caused another cable to give, and the angle of the platform fell to forty-five degrees. I held tightly to the grate, hooking my fingers into the slots - there were four cables left, and I knew these couldn't hold at so steep an angle. Two of them tore simultaneously out of their fasteners. The entire platform dropped to hang vertically, and all except Yvonessa, Gongaphah, and myself were cast into the Deep. The metal quadrate now swung free, broken-off from the access-catwalks, and completed a gradual rotation as the remaining cables unwound. There was a horrible stomach-turning downward lurch, and the edges of the grateslots cut into my fingers as the third one broke. Below me, I heard Gongaphah screaming for help.

"Climb up higher!" I shouted - not to him, but to her. The High Priestess locked eyes with me, her comely visage cracked apart by sheer stark plumb dismay.

"Climb! Climb!"

Already at a decent position, a few brutal hand-over-head clenches-and-pulls brought me parallel with the twisted metal end of the exit-walkway. As the platform made rotations on that sole string by which it dangled, it swung me near this... Near, yet not near enough for comfort... Clinging to the platform, I waited for another rotation to complete. Above me, the noise made by the cable was so harrowing that it could not be the last noise I heard - no, I would not let it be!

I jumped! Away from the platform, through the air, over the fall, flailing and screaming, but I had judged the distance properly and caught the mangled end of the catwalk-railing with both hands! The railing dipped, yet held my weight, and I pulled the bar to my chest and crooked my arms around it and looked back. Yvonessa was climbing; she had kicked off her slippers so that her toes could fit into the slots, and I could see her and Gongaphah's outlines clearly through these as the grate turned. She was almost high enough... I shouted for her to jump, telling her it was the only way. She looked down at Gongaphah. Fuck him, I cried! It's his own doing! She looked at him, then at me, and decided I was right, yet hesitated as the platform made its final pivot...

The last cable tore and snapped against the side of the cave, making a long gash in the rockface. Yvonessa jumped at the last possible instant, pushing off from the platform as it fell, and through the belching darkness windmilling she flew as the great iron slab went down into the Deep, trailing the fluttering ends of the broken cables as it went, with Gongaphah still gripping it, howling. Yvonessa wouldn't make it; she hadn't pushed off from the platform soon enough, so I gripped the rail with my left hand and extended myself out, reaching with my right as far as I could as she flew towards me, near me, to me... *oh*! Her hand caught mine and I caught her! The weight of her popped my shoulder out of its socket, and a searing lancing sting shot through me, yet I kept my grip on the railing and she kept her grip on me - my hold was tenacious and would not give in a thousand years, but I had not the strength to pull us up even an inch, so she climbed up my body. I caterwauled as she grabbed my shoulder, but a few seconds later she had a hand on the railing, and another, and she climbed up the twisted end of the catwalk until it leveled-out and she could stand against the rail.

"Give me your hand!"

"I can't! It's pulled out-of-place!"

"Try to swing it up! You have to!"

I tried and failed and screamed and cursed and tried again. As she caught my wrist and pulled, I felt all manner of cartilage and ligaments severing within. The climb up the catwalk was short, yet it might as well have been miles to a man in my condition. Still, with her assistance, I accomplished it, and on that blessed horizontal plane I collapsed, half-delirious with pain, and cried out to Yvonessa for comfort. She took me in her arms and with my good hand I clutched limply at the folds of her robe. I could feel her tears falling on my face and pulled myself close to her, and we sat at the edge of the catwalk and both wept our tears into the abyss; hers of loss and mine of agony, and the abyss forever-indifferent to us both.

I could have (and desired to) stay that way forever, yet the world awaited, and she was compelled to attend to it, given her place of prominence and stature within it, so she helped me up and looked in my eyes with a softened and indebted countenance, for the first time regarding me compassionately, with care and concern, and, oh yes, maybe even a little bit of wanting. I felt burnt and broken and rubbed-raw. My heart came pouring out of my mouth undevised; babblings that only served to diminish the purity of the sentiments that wracked my heart.

"You are the only beautiful thing I have ever seen I have never seen you in any other than plain unflattering garb and never in airs or finary but from the sight of your face alone I tell you I drank clean water whereas before my lips tasted only fetid sludge for a lifetime—"

"Come now, we haven't time for all that!"

"You must be protected. You must. You are an artifact."

"Well, I'll tell you that I don't much like being called an artifact!" She said with a hint of her old familiar frown; that crimp in the skin between her eyes. "Let us go, we must get to the City..." and she trailed off, overwhelmed by it all.

As I looked at her, I was struck by the sudden realization that, from the moment we had met, this woman's entire life had undergone a steady domino-tumbling to pieces, and this was simply the latest-and-greatest in the series of her relentless misfortunes. I pitied her and admired her strength; the way she held her head proudly even now, and straightened her robes and adjusted her gold stole so that it fell evenly on both sides, and she looked on past her tears with those old wise eyes housed in the beauty of effervescent youth...

I loved her, yet I didn't say such aloud. Instead, I pulled myself together and walked by her side down the tunnel leading to the gates of the High City.

NINETEEN

At the entrance to the Zealot City, we came upon Quabba, who (in his eminent intelligence) had split straightaway upon the first sight of the light glancing off Lawmaker's armor, and therefore was the only one besides us who survived the on-slaught. The manner in which he looked at us let me know what the next few hours promised. When Quabba watched those who stood astride him in appointment swept in an in-stant to nothing, he perceived not a ruinous tragedy, but a golden opportunity. Removed from his path were those en-cumbrances by which he was hemmed into his position, and he now stood enabled to finally enact his ascendency beyond the Hall of Histories (and general bureaucracy) to what he saw as his rightful role of unrivaled authority - a promotion that would never have been achievable otherwise. My pity for Yvonessa deepened. As she looked teary-eyed at her mentor, I could tell she did not yet comprehend the portentous strata-gems brewing in his head. Now she would be truly alone; the last of the semi-virtuous Low Temple leadership, left to fend off Quabba without the diplomatic checks-and-safeguards of the Council. Today was a new day indeed. When the sunlamps alighted over the Zealot City in a few hours, so would dawn a new regime captained by those opportunistic enough to seize power, either via force, charm, or simply by prepossessing the amplitude to fill the newly-opened executive void.

***

I would have killed ten men for a single sip of swill as I stood in the Gallery of the High Prophets, where the etchings on the Sacred Stones looked different in the jumping flames of the ashwax torches, without sunlamp-light cutting down through the dome above us. Quabba had reaffixed my arm back into place, and it now sat limp in a sling, which he assured me would only be necessary for several days, as there were no broken bones or tendons irreparably damaged.

I could hear the commotion of the amassing crowds in the square outside the Temple. The winds of rumorous speculation had already ripped through them - tidings of death and Lawmaker repeated-and-exchanged in a thousand murmurs. Orders had been given to the night guardsmen for all to be roused and assembled in the Nave of Eternal Worship, and the Zealots were pulsing, anxious, restless, so that I could feel their energy cascading down the corridor into our privacy.

We were in the midst of discussion regarding how to approach those gathered masses. It was well-agreed that Quabba should do most of the talking; the consoling and reassuring, and then the Vestal-Elect, as a woman of the people, a symbol of tomorrow, would deliver a message of hope for the future. What was to be done with me was the sole point of dispute between us.

"If you simply slip out amongst the crowd and become one of them, you shall create for yourself a shield. There is safety in anonymity–"

"There is no anonymity to be had for me! They will tear me to pieces with their questions and curiosities! I should stand on the rostrum with the two of you!"

"You are not of our faith." Yvonessa said hesitantly. "You have not been cleansed in the Holy Light of His Wisdom–"

"Well, I've done a lot! I rode that chain right down into the Deep, you saw! Tell me, have either of you ever done a thing like that? No, nor have neither of you ever spent days in the dark, starving, thirsting so bad you'd gladly suck up puddles of what-have-you from the grimey floor! Well, I've done those things and more! I'm entitled to some measure of protection, lest the blame for what happened falls on me!"

Quabba considered me. "Perhaps he is right... he could make a statement in specific regards to the creature–"

"Oh, don't pass me the worst part of the dog! It'll be one of you that addresses the matter of the creature, thank you! I never had any interest in the damn thing!"

"He does not wear the Holy Vestments! He should not stand above the people in the Low Temple! Such would be sacrilege!"

"Dear Sister, we must keep him close. If he runs amok and spreads a narrative of his own, he could turn our people against us. They currently stand bewildered, looking for feet at which to lay the blame for this terrible thing, and we must take care that those feet are not our own!"

As the nature of the current situation became apparent to her, Yvonessa grew quite upset. As she spoke, her tone rose and her hands clenched and pulled at one-another. "Who is it with whom I am speaking, Quabba? These new thinly-veiled intentions leave me crestfallen! It seems that you aim to seize unrighteous power, and you would utilize this tunnel-dwelling scoundrel as your means of doing so!"

These words brought up anger in me. "You are fast-forgetting that I just saved your life!"

"You are a lying loud-talking smallminded scumsucker!"

Quabba's eyes went wide (as did mine) to hear this language spit by the Priestess. Indeed, she delivered the words with a fire reminiscent of Kassie, all blue heat and claws, and in spite of myself, I was reminded of the existence of that thing between my legs... Yvonessa pushed further into our stunned silence: "There was no Z-Bloc! Those in it would have starved many years ago! You are a wretched Gadabout looking for a crack to fit into, hoping it will be mine!"

"Sister, come now! Keep your voice down! We cannot give the general assemblage any sense of disharmony between us!"

"You would be so lucky as to have me in your crack!" I retorted, my anger aggrandizing by the second.

"Disgusting! Contemptible! Vile!"

"Please! We must allow cooler heads to prevail! You hear them out there? They are anxious, and—"

"I will *not* stand before my people with him at my side!"

Yvonessa had her head turned as far as it would go in the direction opposite me. Quabba threw up exasperated hands, pleading the both of us for compromise, and then his eyes went past us and his expression changed in a blink; all color flushed from his cheeks and lines of mortified surprise furrowed his forehead. Behind me, I heard an unfamiliar voice speak a greeting in the Old Tongue...

The three of us turned and beheld what was by-a-mile the most disheveled-looking Zealot Prophet I had ever seen. He wore the red-and-white of the High Ones, yet the white was gray and the red a dirty purple; the whole lot wrinkled and soiled. His hood was down, and he gave the tragic impression of a noble who had at one time emanated a transhumanistically regal aura, yet whose stately dignity had disintegrated in every possible regard. He was not naturally ugly, like Gongaphah, nor transformed to such through gluttony or violence such as the Undercamp Mayor or Poppa Daddy - he was not bulging or brutish or emblematic of any physical extremes; he stood of average height and build, yet was hunched over, bent double beneath the weight of some recondite psychic suffering beyond reckoning. His eyes were bloodshot and cloudy, and his hair (of which he had almost none save for a few thin tufts and patches) was white as the stones of the City, yet unclean and unkempt. His skin was a sickly shade of ashen yellow and it hung off his bones at the points and joints. He was old; I reckoned nearly eighty, and he sported the epidermis of an ancient mummified corpse. The semidarkness of the room had allowed him to draw quite near to us before his presence became known, and now he came nearer still.

This was Beevil.

Yvonessa looked more relieved to see him than when I caught her hand over the Deep. Quabba looked perturbed, yet he pulled together and put on a boisterous mien of cheer. There were questions thrust upon Beevil immediately, none of which he answered. Instead, he simply posed one of his own, wishing to be told what had happened.

Quabba invoked a byword in the Old Tongue that meant 'tragedy' and said: "The High One Gongaphah made a deal with this heathen infidel that stands in our most Holy Gallery. Oh Beevil, I am so thankful that this is the night you selected to make your return to us, when we are most desperately wanting for your guidance, yet I am sorrowful that you find us in the throes of grief and yoked with such burdensome responsibility. So much has transpired in your absence, I don't even know how to begin the task of catching you up to speed..."

Quabba's speech faltered as Beevil brushed past him, his eyes on me.

"This infidel?" His voice was hoarse, like a lifelong dust-smoker. It originated from way down in his stomach and had to struggle ferociously to climb out past his lips.

Yvonessa seemed happy to confirm. "Yes, Brother. He is an infidel Unwhipped, and he claims to have been born in Z-Bloc, and to have made a long journey through the under-passages, where he encountered a creature–"

"I shall speak for myself, woman!" I protested at a thundering volume, and Beevil stuck me with a closed fist; pushed his arm straight out from his chest and popped me good on the kisser. I staggered and felt pain - more surprise-pain than anything else - and looked at him with disbelief.

"You are blessed to walk in the light of the High City of Horsche - you surely must be the first infidel to set foot in the Low Temple since its construction, and you cast your unclean eyes on holy cuts of stone! Do not raise your voice in the presence of we, the Great High Ones, ever again, lest you wish for your tongue to be hotknifed!" With these words he turned away from me and did not look at me again, instead electing to address his High counterparts: "Come, my dear Brethren, ye bedight in righteousness good and pure and true, calm your spirits. Sister Yvonessa, reaffix your hair into place and adjust yourself so that you look worthy of the Vestal title bestowed upon you. We must attend to our people, as they have grown restless and faithless. Divisions will soon crack asunder the households and families of our Great White Faith and City. Come now, I shall address them with this–" and he made reference to me using an Old Tongue adage that translated roughly to 'sodomite' "–by my side. I come bearing a message from The Most High, who, in all of His divine prudence, foresaw the events of this night and sent me back to share His Eternal Wisdom with His flock, who are already gathered with their spirits ripened and their ears keen for His

Holy Guidance."

All of that was a lot for this carcass of a man to voice, yet the words climbed up his throat and jumped out strong, as if they had made the Treacherous Ascent with stone-filled rucksacks. Quabba and Yvonessa put great stock in both him and his words, and they followed him without hesitation as he hobbled across the sanctum towards the corridor that led to the cathedral nave. I lagged in their trail and he barked at me: "At my side, heathen!"

***

I stood at Beevil's elbow as we walked onto the rostrum before the crowd, tormented by the sense that I was about to be scapegoated and strung-up for events that fell far outside my sphere of influence...

To take in all-at-once the High City residents congregated in the nave was indeed a sight. The Low Temple remained illuminated at all times by candles kept lit by whiterobes who made rounds to replenish them when they burned low, and to refill the incense thuribles, so that the insomniacs of the City could venture into the Low Temple at any hour to worship at the Altar of Gordyume. Now, that vast glowing room was filled wall-to-wall with restless faces. At the foot of the steps going up to the rostrum sat dozens of children, some so young that they sucked their thumbs, and behind them, their parents and conservators formed an unsteady white sea; Zealots one-and-all, sitting, standing, circled and grouped individually, yet altogether united, robed and whispering. When our foursome walked out of the Council Apse and crossed the stage, a pall of silence settled on the buzzing crowd as all the hooded heads turned in unison to face us. I could feel the multitude of eyes examining my curvatures and edges, searching for any fault to magnify and hold up as justification for the enactment of bloody punishment upon me.

Beevil shuffled to the center of the rostrum and stood behind the lectern. He stretched his arms out wide, and the sensation of all those leering eyes shifting from my person to his was physically-palpable. There came a pause pregnant and foreboding, and then he began to speak in his gasping-yet-deliberate timbre, and the crowd leaned in to hear his words, like they were trying to bend steel collectively with their weight; perhaps that of invisible bars set before the stage, by which they were kept at-bay.

"Hear me, my Blessed and Holy Brothers and Sisters, ye of His Holy Light, Practicing of the Parables of The One Most High Above All Others, heeding of His Holy Wisdom, keeping of His Eternal Spotless Faith, appreciative of Divine Beauty and Immaculate Goodness, I say to you all, my Holy Brethren, that I have never seen His Light shine like it is shining today on the Low Temple of the White City of the Great and Eternal Horsche! Yes! Praise! Praise be to He, and love and beauty be, and all righteousness and abundance, which through Him flows! Enumerated enlightened days I have passed in the High Temple with The Highest, and ceaselessly He speaks only of ye, His Beloved, His Spotless Flock, His Virgin Bride, His loyal and triumphant Children who, in the darkness of the Deep, belaud He and He alone! Oh! Praise! Praise! To be once again in your midst, my heart soars and I am overcome with an elation only comparable to that found in His Holy and Eternal Presence! Praise be to He! Praise! Praise! Praise!"

As he spoke, Beevil's voice gained incredible resonance. His mouth stretched open wide as he white-knuckled the sides of the pulpit, shuddering, hurling forth his words with a sonorous zeal that climbed in both pitch and volume until it hit an apex of brilliant, striking intensity. A cheer was elicited from a sole voice at the back of the room; an impassioned litany of 'praise be,' which was followed at first by scattered repetitions which spread swiftly and became stentorian, nearly uncontrollable, and yet somehow Beevil continued to speak above the ripening din.

"We stand together in His Holy Light! Praise Gordyume, the God of the Dark and the Deep! Come ye to your feet, one and all! As foretold in His Most Holy Parables, in Book Nine, Passages sixteen-through-forty - I am certain none here need reminding of the words, yet I adore the very sound of them - 'And Behold, Ye True Of Mine Most Sacred Flock All White And Of Pure Soul And Mind, Steadfast Of Spirit, Take Heart In Deep Dark Days With Comfort In The Un-erring Assurance That Indeed Ye Will Live To See That Most Sacred Age Wherein One Of Gordyume's Own Shall Ascend From Your Ranks' - ah, with only this single verse, my Holy Brethren, it is made so irrefutably-knowable to us that His Will Shall Be Done, and we might celebrate joyously now, be-cause indeed His Most Divine and Holy Prophecy has come to pass before our very faithful and dauntless eyes! Oh! Oh! Praise! My Brothers, my Sisters, ye children of the Light, it is he! IT IS HE!"

Beevil sprung out, his entire body forming a rigid line from the heel of his arched foot to his revelatory fingertip, which was pointing at me! The eyes of all the thousands shift-ed back to me in this instant, and a stunned silence settled - a silence of such weight and depth that it might as well have been the Deep itself, and I might have fallen into it, if not for the lifeline of Beevil's shrieking voice, which threatened to falter with a throaty twang at any moment regardless.

"Yes! The infidel! Up from the Deep, from an untold lab-yrinth of filth and darkness, from a far-flung place - indeed perhaps the most distant place that we know to have existed once our kind found their true home - he has come to us! Hark, Brothers and Sisters: in the veins of this man courses the blood of the Red Prince! It is he! He is the Red One re-born! Praise be! Let all praise be lifted high to Horsche the Most High, and to Gordyume, our God! Praise! Yes! Oh! Oh! Praise! Praise! Praise!"

Beevil was a spectacle; his voice hairraising, his body shaking, writhing, eyes bulging, and everyone believing him, save perhaps Yvonessa and Quabba. A wave of sound kicked up from the crowd and traveled to the back of the hall - a cheer pouring like Sunlight, and when this wave hit the stage and I staggered and struggled to retain my footing. They were all looking at me, so many of them, all bright-eyed and staring out from under their hoods, all clean and all stricken manic with a euphoric fervor that bordered on derangement...

At that moment, the bells of Low Temple chimed the morning hour and the cathedral was filled suddenly with ringing loud and sharp and clear as the sunlamps came on, dumping light of those same qualities through the long clerestory windows, and the bells and the breaking of day at that exact moment sent the Zealot crowd into a frenzy which shattered the invisible barrier between them and I. They came up the rostrum-stairs at me like a flood undeterrable. Quabba, always fast in spite of his stature, always maneuvering, was at my side in a blink, urging the whiterobes and their smock-clad children to lay hands upon me.

"Yes! Yes! So speaks Horsche, in all His High and Eternal Wisdom! This boy is indeed the distant descendant of the Red One! Since I made his acquaintance I tempered my skepticism, but now I digress! Yes, come! Come hither, child, don't be frightened! Put hands upon him! Let us all lay our blessed hands upon him, for he needs our prayers! Let us call the Light of Horsche into his heart! Touch him! Touch him!"

A great many hands fell upon me and I was made quite uncomfortable. I looked for Yvonessa, thinking surely she would somehow intervene and dispel the crowd, but I couldn't see her past the many whiterobes and their hands on my shoulders and head - so many dozens of hands - and the children holding fast to my legs and grasping at the hems of my half-robe. A prayer began; a chant, in which they placed my name within the grating language of the Old Tongue. *My* name. I wondered how they knew it... As they chanted, I was drawn into the center of that multitude of interconnected bodies - a root-system like that which had fed the Hearthstone Lights, and through all of these bodies flowed an electricity overpowering and superordinary.

Beevil, Quabba, and eventually Yvonessa led the population in prayer and worship for the duration of the morning hours, until the first mealtime, and then the congregation poured out of the Low Temple, into the fountain-square and the faux sunlight and the gleaming perfect white, and marched communal and refreshed with no shortage of excitement to the community-gardens and the long wooden dining-tables. I was swept-up by them - quite literally - they carried me all the way, singing in the brightened streetpaths at the tops of their voices. I smiled and laughed, but I couldn't help but wonder if I had just been fucked...

***

If I had any measure of prominence with this crowd before, it had exploded now. I was embosomed by them and they fawned over me with utter infatuation. At the breakfast table, my sandals were removed from my feet and a scented balm was rubbed pleasantly by nimble fingers between my toes, and I was fed berries and fanned and massaged, all-the-while so unsure of what to make of things that I was actually damn affrighted.

Then I noticed a woman seated across the table from me. I noticed her because she was the only one with her hood pulled low, not looking at me. She was supple and sublime beneath her robes, yet something about her made my heart beat high in my chest, and not in a good way. No kindness extended by fate or bestowed unearned comes without a debt incurred to pain. Hurt will come as it always does - after all, what is happiness, if not only an interval between its visits? I had been perfectly content to be nobody, and I almost was again, until Beevil had made me somebody quite significant indeed. I felt the other shoe hovering, about to drop, and for some reason I suspected that it would be worn by this anonymous woman. I wished she would look at me...

Fresh commotion split the crowd. A way was made for Beevil, who appeared somehow worse-for-the-wear in the brightness of day. He came to me and told the girls to dry my feet and replace my sandals. The Hooded Woman slipped away. Beevil gave words to the crowd that the two of us must speak alone, for apparently there were things that I, this make-shift chosen one, should hear privately.

We departed the general congregation, and as we went, I came to the realization that we were retracing the route I had walked with Quabba the previous night, off the main-street, past the double-leveled houses with lush green at their tops, down the slight decline towards the City outskirts. In the Glass Square of the Red Prince, I asked Beevil if I was truly the descendant of the figure immortalized in the gleaming hammered bronze. He remained silent. I asked where we were going, despite already knowing.

We passed the shimmering glass of the greenhouses and the waters of the fountain on our way to Hearthstone Rock. The entrance was unguarded and the gates were ajar. We went through them and into the tunnel, where the air smelled wet and cool, and became cooler and fresher as we neared the Deep, until we came to the mangled and bent-down end of the catwalk. It was here we stopped. The air was open where the platforms had fallen, affording us an unobstructed view of the beckoning blackness above which the severed cables swayed gently. Across from us, the rent ends of live wires flashed intermittently, their spark-showers falling like handfuls of crushed glass into that morbid umbra. Beevil looked over the empty space and breathed heavily, and then spoke without looking at me.

"You witnessed Lawmaker come up?"

"Yeah..."

"Hm. Must have been a sight."

I asked again: "Why did you say those things about me? Is it true?"

"Boy, I will not do you the disservice of telling you it is false. Someone has to go up. It may as well be you, rather than one of those two moralistic bickerers holed up in the Temple."

"Go up?"

"Yes."

"To the High Temple?"

"Yes."

"To meet Horsche?"

"Are you slow?"

"Just surprised, is all."

Beevil made a noise that halfway-resembled a chuckle. It seemed the speech he delivered had drained from him whatever strength remained in his pulse. His skin was almost translucent, spiderwebbed with thin bluish veins, and his words crawled out of him strained and scratchy. He reached into the dirty folds of his robe and withdrew a small flat rectangle. I knew what it was at once; a Bloc keycard, and I observed from the symbols arranged beside the stripe that it was a Security-Administrator card - one that would open any door in the Bloc; a coveted possession back in Z. Men were killed over cards such as those. I took it from him and pocketed it.

"That will admit you entry. Have one of the bickerers show you the passage."

"What of you?"

"I am finished."

"Finished?"

"Yes."

There was silence. Then: "Is there anything else you wish to know?"

There were a great many things I wished to know, but in trying to select any single one out of the innumerable collection, I failed.

Beevil continued: "At the top of the High Temple, you will stand at the highest point of the earth. There exists no accessible place nearer to the Old Sun. At this pinnacle, you will be confronted with a choice that shall be yours alone. It is a great and terrible choice, and I think it best that the man who makes it should not fully grasp the ramifications it shall bring. All our fates have always rested in the hands of those recklessly courageous or cunningly yellow. So it has always been, and so it shall continue to be..."

Beevil looked hard in my face and wished me luck before he said goodbye. He did not jump, so much as he simply walked off the bent edge of the catwalk and pitched headfirst down.

TWENTY

Infernal days passed in which I had nary a moment to myself save for shitting. Owing to my not-new, yet now much-amplified celebrity, my old quarters in the mid-city townhouse became too-often visited by unsolicited callers, necessitating that I take up residence in the Low Temple, in chambers previously occupied by one of the High Prophets. These accommodations, although utilitarian, were spartan and without character of any sort. The simplicity was a comfort to me.

In the week subsequent to Beevil's return, (and almost-immediate departure) the winds of change swept through the High City and brought to it the ambition for influence and the various means-and-methods of working towards such, which was neoteric to the Zealots, yet of no real divarication from the norms to which I was accustomed. Many believed that a new High Council would be elected from the people, and campaigns sprung up like mushrooms in the dark. Camps formed and comparisons were drawn between them - who was more pietistic, more enlightened? Some of the residents began to look at me dirty as I passed them in the streets, as the news of Beevil's unceremonious and permanent exodus had fostered untamed speculation. Some believed that I had killed him, that I was a demon, or, alternatively, that I was indeed the foretold savior.

Quabba made the best ploys for control; Yvonessa nor I could hardly stand in his way. He cashed-in a thousand favors and promised a thousand more in return, and very soon had brought almost all of the City under his direct command. I saw little of him, as his days were consumed with private meetings taken in Gongaphah's old office; exchanges always made in furtive tones.

Yvonessa took the opposite approach. She held public

vigils daily for the slain, (who by this point were quite numerous indeed) and gave Sermons and conducted ceremonies which were attended by most-all of the Zealot City residents, save for those who sat snuggly in Quabba's pocket.

Even I myself had some sway, not simply because of the status Beevil's proclamation had given me, but because of that keycard by which the ascent could be made to the High Temple of Horsche. My possession of this demanded that whoever came out on top of the City would have no choice but to make an alliance with me. Via messengers, Quabba had subpoenaed me several times, but I always spurned him. I was the heir of the Red Prince - Quabba could approach me personally, or else risk losing me to his opposition.

***

I spent my hours in the only place privacy was afforded me; the Holy Gallery, gazing at the Sacred Etchings from the circle where the stained sunlight fell in swatches through the dome. The silence was broken occasionally by the comings-and-goings and murmured conversations of Quabba's affiliates, but otherwise the room remained empty and tranquil. As I considered those stones, I often pondered the nature of the Deep. How deep had we dug? To the bottom and back again? Had our forefathers made etchings on the surface of the Undersun itself, or did the Deep drop forever, a transdimensional pit, a loop, a spiral down which one falls eternally? I thought of the low room and the etchings therein, and the skeletal bodies of that man and his children, and I reached into my pocket and touched it...

It was still there. It was always there. I was so comfortable and accustomed to its size and weight that it had become a part of me, an extension of my form. It was cold and hard in my hand, and I withdrew it and held it to the colored glass and watched it drink the light through that little window. Titanium and liquid obsidian. I tilted it and the substance condensed, sticking to itself and glistening smooth-black; mesmerizing, sluicing unnaturally, like a flow of molten steel reversed, the liquid wroth, detesting to be agitated, hating its containment and forever searching for any crack or imperfection in the glass through which it might escape...

"What is that?"

I jumped, startled, as Yvonessa stepped out of the shadows behind me. With what I hoped was a clandestine bit of trickery, I swapped the Battery in my hand with the Bloc keycard.

"This? The card Beevil gave me, to go up."

"I was hoping to have words with you about that."

"I was hoping the same."

"I would like to accompany you. I think myself the worthiest to do so... and furthermore, I am of the opinion that the two of us should go alone."

"What of Quabba?"

"It would be best if he remained here, until true judgment can be passed down."

"I see."

"Do you have any objections?"

"No, I don't suppose I do."

"Splendid. I shall put myself in-order and will be ready to depart by the nightfall chimes. Tonight we shall meet here, in this very spot."

I nodded, and she departed just as soundlessly as she had arrived. I was left alone for a moment. So tonight was the night. Just as well. I had grown sick of waiting.

***

I went up to the topmost floor of the Low Temple, to the offices of the High Council. There were two Sentinel guardsmen outside the door who crossed their rifles in front of me as I tried to enter. I looked at the bigger of the two in the manner which I imagined the Red Prince might have glared across a corpse-littered battlefield, but he was much taller and stronger than I, and I could not intimidate him with the mystique of my notoriety. Nearby was a beady-eyed whiterobe; one of Quabba's dedicated subordinates, and I told him to order the guardsmen to admit me, to which I received avoidant stammering in reply: "Busy today, yes, he's very busy–"

"I won't take but a few minutes."

"Can't go in today, no, he's much too busy, far too busy–"

"Damn it, just tell him I shall await him in his old office in the Hall of Histories. Inform him that I'd like to speak with him before my departure tonight."

"D-departure? Tonight?"

I tossed another glower at the big guardsmen and ignored the simpering subservient as I went back down the spiral stairs, through the cathedral, and out into the day. As I strode through the High City, at once its messiah and pariah, I thought to myself how I had never really cared about this place. Yvonessa could have been ready to leave right at that instant and I would have followed her. In many ways, Under-camp had been more of a home to me, although my name was known to a great many more here. A heretic amongst the Zealots, a Sinner striding Unwhipped in the Low Temple. My halfrobe felt itchy and I tugged and fussed with it. My arm had healed well in the past few days - I no longer required the sling, although I still felt a stinging smart beneath the rota-tor-cuff that I suspected would never quite abate.

***

The Hall of Histories - tall stone shelves stacked with scrolls and parchments; records that were augmented daily; half of the History-Keepers dedicated to the study of old texts, the other half to the creation of new ones. Already these records were being expanded to include me. In all its banality, it was impressive. According to Quabba, they even had writings from back when the Sun still shone and we lived under it. As I walked up to Quabba's old office, needless hate went out from me and pricked the world. I felt full of aggres-sion and damn it, I wanted to be on-and-out with it all! The light and the stark white of the City made pronounced and ar-resting the smallest smudge. The Zealots and their holy words and Histories - fuck it all in the dirt. I was taken by a sudden homesickness; a yearning for my good gig in HydroElectric and my homely box, perfectly-adequate for one person, and my friends, (none of whom were too friendly) and my weekly wage to be spent at the Bronco on druk and whores to dance with when I was bored, never needing purpose beyond this, nor questioning how the dice fell.

Quabba came along eventually. I sat on a cushion by the window and he gave me an awkward nod as he entered and tried to make himself appear busy with a stack of parchments nearby, perusing them while frowning down the bridge of his nose with his uneven half-eyes, as if it wasn't solely for I that he had come. Once again I entertained the fleeting fancy of ending his life. Why shouldn't I? Xirexi would have done it in a heartbeat. Was I weak? To be certain, I had never been like Monogatari or Kassie - always ready to stick steel in somebody... yet I had made it considerably further than either of them. My insides were snakes and writhing worms, and I wondered if they were yellow. Yellow snakes... how would those look in the light?

"Well, get on with it, then." came Quabba's irate voice. "What was so damn pressing? I have business, you know. I cannot lounge about like an academic any longer, and certainly not with the likes of you."

"That's a shame. I enjoyed our sessions."

"Kindly hurry to your point, assuming you have one."

"Yvonessa and I will depart the High City tonight."

At this, Quabba could not contain his delight. He swelled and glowed and almost smiled, yet managed to restrain the corners of his lips to a taut nod. "Will you now? I had heard, but of course I put no stock in what amounted only to hearsay. That is most interesting! You shall surely be the first infidel to stand in His Holy Presence since the dawn of our faith, I do believe. Quite an honor has been bestowed upon you..."

"In our absence, will you elect a council to serve alongside you?"

"I don't see what concern that is of yours."

"I am to be the Voice of the Most High. In making my first report to His Holiness, I wish to be thorough."

"You? The Voice of the Most High?"

"Why not? Yvonessa is the Vestal, and a man customarily serves as the Voice."

"Ah, I see now why you murdered our good Brother Beevil." Quabba said with a tone of revelation, dredging up all the dramatic effect he could muster.

"I did not murder him!" I protested. "I had no cause to kill him, certainly not after he had just crowned me whatever it was he did! If you are so covetous of the position, come with us! Where is it written in the doctrine of Horsche that one is better-off the leader of the Low Temple than a servant in the High one? What grander glory exists aside serving He Higher and Holier Than All Others?"

"I am but a humble Keeper of the Histories. None of us have ever ascended to serve his Holiness directly; it is not our place. You would know, had you any understanding of those texts you are so eager to reference. I am an old man, and my place is here. This great City has suffered manifold tragedies in short succession, and it is my duty to guide them through."

"Oh yes, it is surely with only selfless intentions that you choose to remain, Quabba..."

My sarcasm was either lost or ignored. Quabba simply said it was good that I got it.

"Besides your own vainglorious cupidity, what is the reason you refuse to go? Tell me what awaits me in the High Temple!"

"I shouldn't have the faintest idea!"

"You, a lifelong Zealot and Keeper of the Histories, must have some wisdom or warning to impart - and what's more; I'm wary of your insinuations that I murdered Beevil. You don't truly believe that I did, or else you'd never sit in a room alone with me. You know he jumped of his own accord, and what's more, I think you have a damn good inkling as to why!"

"I'm certain I do not—"

"Oh, don't pander to me like I'm fullish!"

"I'll thank you not to use that gutterspeak in my presence any longer!"

"I'll use any type of speak I wish, here, or in the High Temple! I'll tell you just what kind of speak I plan to put in the holy ears of Horsche; I will poison him against the conventions now standing and convince him to appoint me a Grand

General, like the Red Prince my forefather, and I shall have him commission me a Zealot army! Oh yes, old man, the forges will burn bright once again, and the millers and croptenders shall assume the mantles of soldiers, bombmakers, blacksmiths, and stones will be ground to sand to soak up the blood shed in grueling training that will be but the gentle caress of a woman when contrasted against the hardships my troops will endure in glorious battle! And with my legions armored and marching with crimson banners all unfurled and polished iron gleaming we shall wage war on Lawmaker himself, torpedoing chains through his wings by which we will pull him down and rout him rape him tarnish and sully him until, at the end of it all, I shall stand atop him, and when I drive home my blade I shall make final-and-forever my mark on the Histories, and that mark will eclipse the whole wealth housed here within these whitewashed halls!"

As I said all this, I was possessed by the words, ascertaining their truth from the delivery alone, my tone savage and operatic and swelling with asperity until I rose to my feet, towering over Quabba, who looked up at me with no small measure of fear in his eyes. As I raised my hand to demonstrate physically the thrust with which I would carve my mark, Quabba flinched, as though I might strike him, and to behold his fear and be the cause of it filled me with a gross sense of power that I felt in my chest and genitals.

"I knew from the first day I laid eyes upon you that you would become a menace to our way of life. I saw it written plain as the Sacred Etchings! Yes, I tried my best to wisen you up, to grant you some perspective, but no, no, I should have known it was helpless from the start!"

"You'd best enjoy our absence, Quabba - it shall not be for long."

"The Priestess was right about you all along - you are a blight brought upon us as punishment for our sins."

"It is for Horsche to decide what I am."

"We shall see."

A dead silence settled in the room. The dust on the old shelves had stirred during my outburst and now danced in the cream-blonde light coming in through the window. I reseated myself on the pillows and leaned back comfortably on my elbows, gazing out at the white roofs and green gardens.

"I'm sorry." I said offhandedly after a while. "I do not wish to quarrel with you. Truth be told, I have come to consider you my friend, and I am in-need of a friend, especially a wise one. Many calamitous and violent things have transpired around me, and I'm beginning to suspect that I myself may be a calamitous and violent thing. If that be the case, I don't have an inkling as to how I might proceed. I have not felt like myself as of late."

There was more silence as Quabba considered me, still ill-at-ease and distrustful, but eventually he softened and said: "Yours is a burdensome responsibility."

"One I have not sought, nor asked for."

"Perhaps not, yet you have taken it up still-and-all the same. You might have succumbed to madness in the tunnels, or stayed at the Undercamp, or slipped on the stairs of the Treacherous Ascent... why is it that you have pushed so far, all-the-while without a true standard to fly before you? You are no leader - you are a follower who takes up a new cause at the place where the old one can go no further. You are utterly unscrupulous and unbeholden, and as such, you possess the capacity to exceed the boundaries of those who lead you... Yet, who will follow such a man? If I may leave you with only one single lesson, let it be this: faith has its foundations laid in myths and symbols, not in the personalities or fickle celebrity of its clergy."

This struck me and I dwelt on it for a long period, even after giving my response, which was naught but an ambiguous grunt. Then I gave Quabba a cordial-yet-inauspicious dismissal, saying that the hour was late and the nightfall chimes would be sounding soon.

✳✳✳

As I left the Hall of Histories and took the wide iron-cobbled streetpath back towards the Low Temple, I thought to myself how this would likely be the last time I saw the City in the light of its sunlamps. I took a roundabout route to my destination, not out of appreciation for the white bricks and terraces, but simply to take stock of them and catalog them in my memory, lest any minute details might bring me happiness when recalled nostalgically in my twilight years.

I was lost in my thoughts until I became aware of a white-robe trailing me; a woman, the face of whom I could not see. Recalling the foreboding figure from the mealtime feast days prior, I quickened my steps. My pursuer followed suit.

I decided that I would not, in my final hours in this Holy City, bring unrest to its most hallowed of places, so I stopped at the arching fountain in the Temple Square and waited. She could come up and confront me; this craven spectre who stalked me. It would be fitting that this be the final issue I laid to rest before taking my leave of this assemblage of columns and steeples. She must have seen me from around a corner and known there was nothing left to do but step out into the light and face me, and she did so with confidence. As she drew near, she let down her hood and showed me herself.

I had hoped she was dead, and I had allowed this hope to take root in my heart and make itself true. I cursed myself for this, the most common fallacy of man; the delusion that hoping for something will harden it into reality. I should have known better - known not to assume her dead, lest I touched her lifeless shape with my own hands and pitched her into the grave personally. As I had done neither of these things, I therefore should have held surety in the absolute fact that she was indeed still alive, and would come stealing out of some unseemly shadowed corner at the moment least-convenient for me. As she approached, I addressed her by the foremost of the many names by which she had been commonly known. *Cleopatra.* It sounded strange passing my lips in this sacred and sublime suburb. She gave me a knowing smirk.

"Surprised to see me?"

"Only momentarily."

"I've missed you."

"You killed some poor unsuspecting Pilgrim down below and donned their robe?"

"It's possible. Have you killed yet? You have a different look about you..."

"Is it possible to have such a low opinion of a person that, after a while, you actually find yourself respecting them?"

"Oh, hush. You know I get in where I fit in."

"You don't fit in here."

"Neither do you."

"I'm leaving."

"I'm not. I rather like it here. It's quite nice, isn't it? These people know how to eat and love, and they do not play in the dirt with sticks, like doltish children."

"You've answered at least one question for me..."

"Which is?"

"The state I shall find this place in, should I ever return."

"There has been a lot of talk about you. I told you, didn't I? Back in Undercamp, you remember, I told you I always saw great things in you. Only me, remember? It was nobody else who saw those things, predicted them. I always knew you'd grow up big and important, and I'm happy to be proven right."

"There are bugs on the inside of you."

"You won't know for certain unless you find out."

"I wouldn't stain these clean streets with upchuck, so I would thank you not to allude to such a vile union."

"You sure? Might be the last chance you get. You think her Highness will lay down with you? She's already got a stick up her ass bigger than any you could offer."

"I'm not concerned about it."

"Gonna rape her?"

"Be silent! Have you not a single shred of respect? She is a Holy Vestal!"

"Oh, right. I suppose the cock of a god dwarfs all competition..."

"What is it, precisely, that you want from me? Tell me, and let us be forever finished with this swinish dance! I do not wish to see you again!"

"My dear, this dance is the only thing we have that is ours. It is a cosmic intertwining of a nature older than the stones from which this city is constructed... as old as time itself! I am yours, and you are mine, and mine alone."

"What does that mean?"

"You know. Part of you has always known. Although you may very well get your wish and never lay eyes on me again, I thought it best to tell you, so that the Faceless Lady of your dreams might henceforth have a face..."

"No..."

"*Yes.*"

The nightfall chimes sounded. Their echoes filled the air where the sunlamp-light shone only an instant previously, and the darkness descended upon us hard and heavy, a numinous accentuation of Cleopatra's words, and I went cold as ice down to my core. I had never in my life comprehended why I couldn't shake her, via meanness or disinterest, or why my disparagements invariably failed to penetrate her silken skin. Beauty was never more wasted than it was on her; to look upon her made a man love whatever god had created her, yet to know her calcified that same man's heart with hatred. Yet as I stood before her, suddenly feeling naked and diminutive, I understood why, and the comprehension lanced through me like a bullet or a blade, although it caused no pain. In truth, it felt good. It felt like the sweet relief of death, and perhaps in some spiritual or esoteric way, it was...

She touched me on the arm and walked away, her final cryptic-yet-concise disclosure ringing in my ears with the bells of the Low Temple. Weak in the knees and headsick I watched her go before stumbling buffaloed through the double doors under those needlelike gold spires.

***

Yvonessa was not in the Gallery, but I had faith she would come, so I waited before those consecrated cuts of stone. What had the forefathers beheld in the depths of the earth that had inspired them to make these etchings? The shapes of flags and fires and wars and sex and birth and life and death and even themselves they depicted, yet could this space not have been used to provide clean straightforward answers? Or indeed, were these the answers in their plainest and simplest forms, and our language had since become so polluted with contradiction that our very thoughts and collective consciousness was disheveled to such a degree that we could no longer recognize the truest of lessons, warnings, proverbs unmistakable and elementary, so instead we warped these into obscure myths to fit the designs of our misguided dogmas?

I waited for ten minutes before Yvonessa arrived and led me to a place in the corner of the room. Here, in this doorless city, a door had been hidden in the bricks of the wall. She pushed against one of the stones and it slid back, revealing an old Bloc keycard-reader. I laid the card against the reader, and it beeped, and a rectangular section of the wall receded on rails to expose a staircase descending into darkness. I took a torch from a nearby holder and offered my hand to the Priestess, and to my surprise, she took it.

BOOK V

'Lawmaker'

TWENTY-ONE

The stairs descended, becoming narrower and more uneven until we came to a hole with a rusted iron ladder coming up from it, leant against the edge. I held the torch over the hole and observed that it wasn't so deep - a mere dozen-or-so feet. We climbed down, me first, making a long step past the distance of a missing rung and then helping Yvonessa do the same, and then both of us looked off down a square-walled corridor exactly alike the thousands that I had previously traversed. The one end was a few feet to our backs, yet the other stretched straight off into blackness beyond what we could see by the torchlight. As we set off, part of me felt happy to be back home in the underworld, and another part of me hated that first part, and a third part felt nothing at all. Although I was surely wrong, I felt that the torch could have burned out right then and I would not have cared. The darkness was a ubiquitous assuagement.

We walked a distance I estimated to be around a half-mile. The path remained straight until the corridor ended and the torchlight fled from us and found nothing to touch save the circle of floor around our feet, leaving us fishbowled and adrift in the dark. The air had that same odor and 'bigness' of the Great Hall, so I knew that we were once again in a very spacious place - a cavern we found to be filled with rubbish and stonepiles that formed cordilleras of varying sizes. The floor was uneven gravel, and we found bones amongst the stones as we went on, ambling aimlessly, mostly climbing; dislodging with our hands and feet rocks that clattered loudly in the dead air. This place was desolate and destroyed - cineral granite and concrete and nothing besides these.

The torchlight caught something reflective and the scintillation caught my eye, strikingly evident in the midst of the muted uniform colorlessness. I knelt beside a certain large flat block of stone and found a tarnished iron plaque, across which I moved my hand to unsettle the dust. The embossment was faded almost away, yet still legible. *G-Bloc.*

We kept moving, climbing, the alabaster of our clothing already begrimed to heather, until at the top of a large stone-pile we discovered an amalgamation of shoddily-constructed scaffolding. It went up maybe thirty feet to a ledge protruding from what was otherwise a smooth concrete face that rose up out of sight into the darkness above us. I asked Yvonessa what was with her people and the undertaking of precarious climbs, yet received no answer. Although we had only been traveling for an hour or so, we made camp on the rocks where we stood.

The Priestess spread a simple meal of dried figs and roots before us on a cloth, which we ate quietly. The jagged unevenness of our surroundings made a lot of shadowy places in our fishbowl. We shared the quaint supper inside the cold cadaver of long-gone civilization; only rubble and brittle forgotten bones. I was ready to continue upon finishing, but Yvonessa was not. She had a blanket in her pack and made herself as comfortable as could be expected, telling me almost-pleadingly that she wanted to rest before pressing on. I agreed, beholding her now in a new light; small and uncertain - of course still very beautiful, but with the deadness of this place sinking into her and inducing a discordance within and without her; purple tendrils extending hungrily from beyond our bowl to permeate her sunburst spirit and toss it about like a plaything.

There was a space to sit beside her and I took it. She didn't shy away from my proximity, which made me feel good. Her hood was low, yet I looked under it and could tell from her face that she was contemplating many inextricably-linked things in thoughts so loud and worrisome I could almost hear them. Despite her even breathing, she vibrated in that manner people do in the dark - all her molecules rearranging themselves a hairbreadth to the right-and-left alternatively. When I asked her for a drink of water, my voice rang sharp and clear in the doughy silence. She handed me a gutjug, and the water tasted like the inside of it. I replaced the cap and wiped my lips with the back of my hand, and I asked her if she was nervous.

"No."

"It's okay if you are. I am."

"Are you?"

"Yes... but not terribly. Bad things don't happen to me. It's like I've got some omnipotent presence moving the pieces around me..."

"Perhaps you do." Yvonessa said thoughtfully.

I let the silence linger a while before speaking again.

"When I fled Z-Bloc, a small group of us were lost in the tunnels for days, so long that we lost count - not that we ever bothered to keep such. We drank from dripping places or licked wet spots on the stones where we could find them, and when our last flashlight gave out, I began to believe that we had died. The deep dark is narcotically psychotomimetic like nothing else... it plays tricks on you."

"It is not the dark alone... It is said that there are places offshooting from the Deep where rifts between this world and others have been opened. These are referenced in the Histories and depicted in the Sacred Etchings."

"I may have found such a place..."

Yvonessa turned to face me, giving a nonverbal indication to continue.

"There was a place with etchings over etchings on the walls and floors and ceiling, on every inch of every surface. I saw many similar painted places below, but never so many layered and crowded together. It was a small room, and I entered it..." here I trailed off, suddenly unsure of how much of this I wanted to disclose...

"What did you find in this room?"

"Skeletons. A man and two children, long, long dead."

"Anything else?"

I shifted my back against the stone. "What do you suppose waits for us up there?" I asked, changing the subject, nodding up at the general space above us.

"We shall meet the Holy Father of our faith." she replied,

as if reciting from a book or scroll.

"He'll be aged over a century, will he not?"

Nothing.

"Think he'll have a beard?" I jested benignantly.

"I don't know."

More nothing . Silence lasted a while, and my thoughts galloped in the meadows of my head wild and desultory, until the silence started to choke me like an absence of oxygen.

"Do you... um..."

"Yes?"

"I mean, I assumed, but I don't know for certain... forgive me, umm, have you ever... " I trailed off again awkwardly.

"No."

"Right. Didn't think so. Well, do you think... I mean, I suppose it stands to reason that you and Horsche..."

"It stands to reason."

However Yvonessa felt about this, she didn't show it. I did my best to match her blank matter-of-factness, but felt myself twisting and itching as I ruminated, painfully-aware of my own transparency. I turned my head away from her. She seemed perfectly content to stop talking, but the silence un-settled me moreso, so I asked again if she was nervous.

"You asked me that afore."

"I know, but then I was speaking in a general sense. Now I mean..."

"Why would I be nervous about that?"

"I don't know. It's a thing people are sometimes nervous about doing for the first time."

"It is the most divine act of which we are capable. The pleasure we take from it is a gift to us from Gordyume him-self; a reward for the toil of conceiving life. In the Temple of Love, the young are given demonstrations by the finest stock, and at the coming of the Pairing Festival we are each prepared and eager. There is no cause to fear that which ensures the continuation of His Sacred Light."

"It was different in Z-Bloc."

"So I have observed. The Whipped Sinners always come to the High City with untoward perceptions of many things, with that always foremost amongst them."

"Your people are an eccentric lot. I have felt quite stuck-out amongst you."

"In what ways?"

"Well, your air and water is of superb quality, because you have the Deep to filter your air and into which you dump your waste. In Z-Bloc, our air stank and was smokey always, and our water was tainted and there was never enough to go around. Life was rubbing stabbing beating fucking noise and pain without a rest, always, another day older... like?"

She smiled. It was radiant and it was fire. Something I had said had made her smile.

"That's guttertalk... yet I know what you mean. The Blocs are all stricken with such things, the plagues of our basest nature."

"I often wonder if there stands a reason for all of this... wretches like me streetborn, given something clean and white to aspire-to by your people, yet once I pilgrimaged, you gave me new aspirations, and once I walked the streets of the High City, still new aspirations came, not to take the place of, but only to be heaped atop the old ones... and now, the two of us."

"The two of us?"

"Yes. We're on a path now, like? Barreling towards the grandest aspiration of all - why, it's even grander than death! We go to serve at the right hand of God himself!"

"Don't be spiteful."

"I don't mean to be."

"You know that I did not ask for this. Never once. Vestal-Elects are selected by the will of the High Council alone. It is a great honor, and I never wavered in its face, but I never had any ambition to seek it. Even now... oh, I see you looking at me like you don't understand, and how could you, you who knows naught but vinegar and misery, but please try to understand that I love Him! I have loved Him my whole life, so to lay down with Him will be the happiest thing I can imagine. You speak of our eccentric ways, but you, after a lifetime in Bloc-squallor, remain hard-boiled. You spend weeks in our City, the first Sinner Unwhipped to live amongst us, and you still don't see, do you? You cannot fathom the love I feel, the love that is felt by all of us in His Light."

Diamond tears sat fat on the brinks of her eyes. As she spoke, she reached out to take my hand and her skin felt cool and electric. She made me want to apologize, yet for what I had no clue, and I knew that such would come empty and condescending, as would any other measly comforts I might try to extend.

"I have tried to understand... I have not sought my title or position either; they simply seemed to find their ways to me. You have prepared your entire life for the duties now set before you - you have language and knowledge of the Histories, and great beauty in spades... You are prepared to be a leader, but what of I? An old man I'd never met before proclaimed me to be of royal lineage and handpicked by a god I do not worship!"

"Such is the Will and the Way of Gordyume. He chooses for greatness those of His Flock who are meek-hearted and diminutive. Reluctance to lead is the surest proof of worthiness to do so."

"I'm just having it said. Although I do not understand the task at-hand, I am worried that I shall fail. Who am I? Who will follow me? Quabba told me that I take up whatever standard have you and march behind it until its leader falls, and to the end of marching further, take up a new standard, remaining forever unbeholden."

Yvonessa considered me for a long moment, looking into my eyes as if she was untangling the knots in my thoughts. Then: "I have a request to make of you."

"Make it."

"I am concerned that you may undertake some unsavory measures in the High Temple, in the presence of His Holiness the Most High. I would like to request that you do not."

"You'll have to explain what you mean."

"Frankly, I suspect that the idea of my Vestal duties makes you angry, because you want me for yourself."

"Oh."

"Is it true? Are you scheming to usurp even He, The Most

High Above All Others?"

"It is true that I desire you, but I harbor no schemes."

"You surely see by now that you cannot have me."

"Surely, yet my desire persists."

"You cannot."

"I know."

"Then give me your word. I have never tried to thrust my faith upon you, nor make you understand. Even as you sit before me I see plainly that you don't grasp the significance of the responsibility yoked across both of our shoulders. We are both of us the New Times - in our wake will come new symbols and etchings, and yes; perhaps even new temples, cities; a great expansion of the reach and righteousness of the faith... but it could just as easily be chaos and death and suffering. I believe that *you* will play the most instrumental role, because you are not cleansed by His Holy Light and Doctrines - you are of the Undercamp and the Blocs and the tunnel-mazes, and it is *you*, not the Lizard, who will bring us into the New World... You are the Sinner Unwhipped, who has climbed the stairs of the Treacherous Ascent and looked into the Deep past the sunlights of Hearthstone, and very soon the time to choose will be upon you. Will you be a champion of my people, or will you let us succumb to the entropy from which you were birthed? You must choose, you see, and the time is fast-forthcoming. It is almost at-hand."

"I will give you my word... yet, hear this: what if that all-seeing all-knowing presence aforementioned, the one that I think moves the pieces, what if *he* is guiding me on a malicious path? What if he has sent me to kill Horsche, if indeed the man still lives?"

Yvonessa was disturbed by this. She pulled away from me, shirking back into the shadows between the stones, and said: "Please don't say such things."

***

Upon the conclusion of our discussion it was clear that neither of us would find rest that night, so Yvonessa packed up her satchel and we climbed up the scaffolding to the ledge, which was so narrow that we had to shimmy with our toes angled outwards as we faced the wall and felt for fingerholds, until we came to a crack large enough for our bodies to slip through. On the other side of this was a closed-in staircase that went for five flights and had rubble piled on the edges of the steps, so that we could only walk up the middle of them. These stairs led us to a higher level of the colossal room, and the layout confirmed my notion that we were in a gutted Bloc megastructure. Indeed, this was G - or whatever remained of it. All the levels must have collapsed; all the residences crashing down through the ground floor to bury the HydroElectric mills and basements. I made a comment on this, but Yvonessa didn't seem to care.

I cared. I felt an updraft in the winds of my soul. I was above the surface now, and on the other side of these walls shone the Sun... and then came the deeper, more arcane consideration of the Sun itself - that derelict idea passed down acroamatic through generations. What proof did I have that the Sun was truly on the other side? Like the nature of the Deep and the idea of a bottom, was there really any 'surface' at all? What if, on the other side of this calcified stone, was only more stone and dirt and segregated mineral-and-water deposits? We could be miles underground still, if there even existed any ground to be under! This question I had pondered daily since I was old enough to conceive of it, yet never had it brought me more malaise than it did then...

We came to a service liftshaft, the car and counterweights of which had fallen long-ago. We used the maintenance-access ladder to move skyward. The shaft was dark, but our path was laid plainly before us - there was simply nowhere else to go but up. The liftshaft took us to what I figured was likely the forty-seventh level. Here there was a ceiling, but the floor and all the apartments save for the ones on our side had fallen away, and a shattered concrete ledge hung sloped; twisted rebar leaping from the ends of the stone like the drooping vibrissae of some abstruse extraterrestrial behemoth. I kicked a small rock. It rolled and clattered off the edge, and the distant echo of it smashing against its fellows at the bottom rushed up the Bloc-shell and evidenced to us (as the torch could not) the finite nature of the space we occupied.

There was another closed-in staircase, and I knew that, if we were on level forty-seven, this one would go up to the top. In Z-Bloc, the penthouse floors had been bombed-out during the Second Uprising, and the explosions had collapsed the roof and rendered the topmost part of the structure uninhabitable. This being the case, I had never seen a Bloc penthouse before...

At the top of this second staircase, (which went up only a single floor; fifteen steps to a landing and then fifteen more in the opposite direction) we found ourselves in a dingy hallway that opened up into a lobby two stories high. There was rubble and stonepiles on the floor, and the walls were cracked and thinned in places so that the rebar was exposed. A dormant fountain sat in the middle of the room, and beyond it was what had surely in the light of its heyday been an ornate carpeted staircase with bronze rails and balusters, yet it was now just as drab as everything else. There were rat skeletons sewn about - I stepped on an upturned ribcage and it crunched to dust underfoot. Gloom had seeped so deep into every surface that it became them. I started to wonder if we had taken the wrong route, and I could tell Yvonessa was daunted by similar uncertainty.

We stood at the foot of the staircase, breathing the dust unsettled by our feet. The Sun seemed no closer now than it ever had. There were probably thirty steps before us, and then a landing with hallways going off sideways in either direction.

"Do we go up? The top of those stairs is likely the closest we can come to the Sun, unless you get up on my shoulders once we're up there..."

Yvonessa said nothing. We went up the stairs. At the top, I noticed fresh footprints in the grime. We looked at each other and followed the footprints down a hallway, until we were frozen by a croaking call that materialized out of the darkness.

The words themselves were impossibly strained and were followed by a gut-wrenching cough; a retching hack that hurt to hear. Yvonessa found my hand and we stood still in the torchlight and listened. The voice had come from up ahead. When the coughing subsided, the voice came again; a choked cry of hopefulness misplaced: "B-Beevil... oh, o-oh please... let that be y-you!"

More infirm and sickly-green coughing echoed down the hall, and then came a light - a single tiny flame muffled by the heat-browned glass of an oillamp chimney. As the light came towards us we saw its bearer in sharper detail. It was a woman, emaciated, and long in every sense - long limbs, a long neck, and long knobby wandlike fingers that curled around the handle of the oil-lantern far too many times. Although she was not exorbitantly elderly, she was clearly ridden lousy with a disease that made her appear quite bad. She coughed verdurous phlegm and had fresh swollen boils on her skin alongside the oozing sores where old ones had burst. Her eyesight must have been failing, because she had to draw very close to Yvonessa and I before realizing that we were not Beevil, and her wrung face contorted in terror and confusion as she shrank back from us, her body shuddering with that horrible gagging cough, as she demanded an explanation.

"Ah! *cough* Oh! Who-w-who-who are y-you?!"

Yvonessa took the torch from me and neared the woman, holding out the light, and then cried out a name in recognition: "Sister Bessie! Is it really you?!"

The ragged form looked sheepishly at the High Priestess, then, cautiously, she straightened her back and brought herself up tall to inspect us with her left eye, as a clustergrowth of boils on her brow had forced-shut the right one. Whoever 'Bessie' supposedly was, this woman answered to her name and seemed to identify Yvonessa with delight.

She invited us to trail her and welcomed us into her dismal quarters - an open room, empty save for a cot bowed a foot down in the middle and dressed with a filthy quilt and pillows thin and threadbare, attended only by a single chair. The room grew darkness from its corners, and because of the meagreness of the lantern-light, this darkness joined with itself in a vignette that encroached around the pathetic scene on all sides. As Bessie settled back into her imprint on the mattress, Yvonessa took down her hood. I could see fear plain as day in her face.

"Dear Sister, what is this place?"

"Oh, you have grown so much, my dear darling Yvonessa, I am surprised you can *gag cough* remember me *cough* you were only eight when I– *cough cough* oh– *arg ack gag cough*–"

Yvonessa looked around at the long-faded tatters of what used to be; the grimy stone up from which the carpet had been pulled, the dangling wires where light-sconces were once mounted, and lying amongst the rockpiles only dusty shattered remnants of the furnishings. She could clearly not believe the wretchedness of the whole setting, and I hardly could either.

"Is... is this the High Temple? What of His Holiness?"

"Yes *gag spit* you shall stand in His Divine Presence soon enough. First please wait with me *cough cough* it is almost mealtime *cough gag cough* and Shraine should be coming *cough cough* oh *ack gag cough cough cough*–"

I half-expected this woman to die before our eyes right at that very moment, but by the virtue of some miraculous strength she managed to continue: "Shraine will be along *cough* shortly *cough cough* in no time at all..."

Yvonessa looked at me. Oh no. Please, I didn't want to be the one to break her the news. I harbored suspicions, sure - I even had outright agnosticism this whole time, yet I possessed not even half the courage to voice such disbeliefs aloud to her.

"W-who is… Shraine?"

"He'll *cough cough* fetch us *cough* d-dinner..."

I was hungry, as the figs and roots had not filled me well, yet I was also absolutely certain that we were about to be served ratmeat, which was tough and stringy and almost always had an unpleasant flavor, lest it was expertly-seasoned by a competent chef. After a vegetarian lifetime, we would see how the Priestess liked it...

I sat in the chair and waited. Bessie didn't want to talk much, because talking made her cough. She was extremely ill. Even in the Bloc, I don't think I ever saw anyone so ill as her in all my life. Visible past her frayed robe were the nubs and points of her jutting out angrily. Yvonessa knelt by the bed and stroked her hair; a thinned gray fringe of wiry strands that seemed not to be rooted in her scalp at all, judging by how they pulled out and fell away. I had a nasty feeling flourishing that demanded manumission, so I repeated Yvonessa's inquisition as to who 'Shraine' was.

"Shh... don't make her speak, she is sick."

"You think I can't see that?"

From Bessie, weakly: "It's alright *cough* I have so few visitors *cough cough cough* when I first heard you I thought you were Beevil *ack ack gag* what *cough cough* whatever became of him, I wonder... he left, and I hadn't pegged him for a *cough ack gag* fullish y-yellow slitlicker!"

"Sister!"

"Oh *cough* I'm sorry, you must forgive me *cough* I've been alone for such a very long time *cough cough cough* ohh all alone *cough* with only Shraine for company *cough cough gag—*"

Bessie slumped back on the cot, utterly overcome with a fit. Whatever her lungs worked so unremittingly to dispel must have been infectious indeed. Green mucus seeped out of the corners of her mouth as her eyelids slipped down.

"It's okay, Sister... you mustn't speak..."

"*Cough cough* yes *cough*... I shall rest... until the *cough* ratmeat comes..."

The room went soundless, save for Bessie's sucking heaving breath and the occasional choked-out consonant. I could tell Yvonessa didn't want to look at me, yet did after a while.

"Ratmeat?"

I nodded. "Back in Z-Bloc, they'd cook it in a wok with fruitswill that they'd light on fire. The burning fruitswill gave the meat a flavored char. Catchers in the Bazaar would sell rats singular or by the dozen. Good steady money in it."

"Why are you telling me this?"

"You asked what ratmeat was, huh?"

"I know what ratmeat is. It would not escape me, so obvious a name."

"Well, if you were asking after the taste, I'll say it's generally not great. Dog is much better."

"I still have some figs..."

"Do you have water?"

She handed me the almost-empty gutjug. I drank a bit and handed it back to her and she drank a bit. Then we heard shuffling in the hallway and got to our feet as an approaching glow of lantern-light became visible beyond the doorframe. Bessie called out: "Shraine! Oh Shraine, you should know that we will have dinner-guests *cough cough cough* for the next few *cough cough* days, is that right *gag cough* Priestess? You and your companion shall stay *cough* with us *cough ack cough cough* oh *ack gag* Horsche have *cough cough* m-mercy—"

The approaching light illuminated the doorframe until it was filled by a rag-clad human form with a line of several dead rats slung over one shoulder. This was Shraine, a short man with a circular face, hooked nose, fat wet lips, and unkempt locs the gray shade of which matched that of everything else. He looked bewildered to see us, yet nonetheless confidently entered the room and plopped his haul down on the floor, nodding a stiff acknowledgement, treating our presence almost as an inconvenience as he went about skinning and gutting the rats, separating the meat from the bones and tendons, cubing it, and skewering it on thin footlong metal spikes. He then set two cinderbricks on either side of a lit can of jellied-alcohol and set the spikes longways across these, forming spits which he turned by hand. The meat was seasoned with saltdust likely harvested from the stones of the Bloc itself, and it shrank and sizzled on the skewers as it dripped fat into the flame. My mouth wetted at the redolence, as it was a scent I had not smelt in weeks.

Once the salted meat was ready and we were chewing on it, Shraine's hospitality seemed to germinate. We found him to be quite talkative, although certainly very sordid and ignoble. He had flappy ears and buckteeth with a gap betwixt the front two that could have been used to pull nails out of boards. He actually looked a lot like a rat himself, which made his vocation (in which he took much apparent pride) that much more grotesque, imbuing him with an insidious, apostate quality, as if he was more rat than human, and a traitor to his own kind to boot, who delighted in their crucifixion and butchery.

As he and I and Bessie (but not Yvonessa) gnawed the rat-meat, Shraine launched into an unprompted soliloquy, pompously delineating for us his ancestry.

TWENTY-TWO

Shraine's great-grandfather was born in the tunnels after the First Uprising; a time when inter-Bloc relations had stabilized (albeit temporarily) as humanity sought repose after those years of warfare by which no man's existence went unimpressed. G-Bloc, Shraine explained, had been an epicenter of the fighting, and its population had been decimated, opening a great number of units for new residents - migrants from below who had lived in the tunnels for the entirety of their lives. Shraine the First was amongst these, and, like most tunnel-born, he had learned from an early age how to catch rats. It was shortly after his resettlement in G, at an age Shraine estimated to be close to my own, that Shraine One, likely fullish off druk or dustsmoke, participated in a dice-game that proved to be of pivotal significance for him and his descendants. As the victor of this game, he claimed the prize of several young gotes.

At this point, Shraine (the one sat before me) had to explain to Yvonessa and I that gotes were small four-leggers, similar to dogs, but with horns and thicker hides and drinkable milk. I informed him that dogmilk was also indeed drinkable, and was considered a delicacy in Z-Bloc. Shraine said that he had never seen a dog in all his living days, and continued, telling us that his ancestor discovered that this gotesmilk could be fermented into a cheese that could be left under a sunlamp to mold. Although the odor of this molding gotesmilk-cheese was enough to turn the stomach of anyone except him, (as Shraine I had accustomed himself to the stench) it was a pre-eminently-effective form of ratbait, and it was through the invention of this novel and superior bait that Shraine I made himself an important man during the Second Uprising.

"He sold ratmeat to the warfighters?"

"Far more than that, me bully! He was charged with the catchin' n' cookin' of rats for the whole army; three legions of tunnel-warriors, all fed and kept strong by me great-grand-pap! Amassed a right respectable fortune, he did! No doubt ya heard of–" and he spoke a name in the Old Tongue that I had never heard before, that sounded like 'Zars-sharsh', who was apparently a Gunboss from G-Bloc and a general in the Second Uprising. "In the worst days of the tunnel-fighting, he was the only one 'mongst the generals with the good sense to journey to High City and cry for the aid of the Zealots. See, old Horsche had been made strong by the Red Prince - his people controlled the water and power of several Blocs, but they didn't involve themselves with the war, what with their pacifism and all–"

"I know this story–" interrupted Yvonessa, "–it was through this alliance that the High Temple was restored to its former glory."

"Yessir bully! After the Second Uprising, the remainder of Zars-sharsh's armies supplied the labor for Horsche's dream. Ya see, H-Bloc was the High One's birthplace, and he was real sentimental about it, but it was razed in the First Uprisin' and lay in ruins ever since. If a bully were to ask me, I'd also recker that Horsche knew his City would soon get overfull, and that he'd need a whole 'nother place to stow his people. Oh, once it was complete, the High Temple was the jewel of the world, that it surely was! "

Shraine went on to tell us how, after feeding Zars-sharsh's armies, the general guaranteed the now-wealthy ratcatcher a permanent seat at his table henceforth. As Horsche required a great number of laborers for the renovation of the High Temple, (an undertaking as ambitious as could be conceived-of) Zars-sharsh and his cabinet were granted permission to live in the presence of the High One as H-Bloc was polished and painted anew and made to glitter in the light - fifty glorious golden levels, all to be filled with those of the Holy Flock who had been raised up in the High City; those purest of mind and body, the most steadfast and devout.

The year before the Second Uprising concluded, Shraine

and his wife (a tunnel-born woman he had known since his youth, who had emigrated with him to G-Bloc) had a son. They named the child after his father, and all three of them were permitted to ascend with His Holiness to the High Temple after the war. As Shraine II matured, he, like all non-Zealots granted High Temple residency by means of political stature, was expected to convert. To this end, he was betrothed to a Zealot woman by whom he sired a son, who was also given the name of Shraine.

Unlike his father, Shraine III was born in the High Temple. Like his father, however, he married a Zealot woman. Although they had several daughters, Shraine III remained unsatisfied, as he desired a son to whom he could bequeath both his namesake and his generationally-accrued knowledge of the ratcatching trade (although by this point the practice of eating ratmeat was long-disbanded, as the High Temple gardens yielded 'enough green food to feed the world'). Regardless, once he got his wish, Shraine the Third would regularly bring his son on excursions into the basement levels of the Bloc, to teach him how to trap vermin with the expertise that was the appanage of his pedigree.

"See, he never quite trusted the Zealots. He may have been borned amongst 'em and may have wedded-n-bedded one of their women, but he always told me tales of grandpapa. Methinks he was tunnel-dweller at-heart, and wished he could have lived like they did back in the bloody old days. Naw, he never trusted Horsche's ilk... always figured something would snap off bad, and sure enough, he was proved real right when Lawmaker came a-calling and ravaged the whole mess–"

Yvonessa flew to her feet, her voice high and tight, and the rest of us startled by the suddenness of it. "I've heard my fill! You will take me to His Holiness at once!"

Shraine looked uncertain, glancing nervously between us. "Wellum, sure, I suppose it could be done me bully..."

"*Cough cough cough* no, no, I shall *cough cough* take her–"

"Would you mind very much, Sister? I see that you are unwell, but I am so confused, I would very much appreciate if you could make the introduction–"

"Of course *cough cough gag spit cough–*"

It took all of Bessie's strength just to sit up on the cot, and the increased light made her look starved right down to her spirit. Yvonessa had to almost-carry her out of the room. Although no invitation was extended to the ratcatcher or I, I stood and followed all the same, while Shraine stayed behind and helped himself to Yvonessa's untouched portion of meat.

***

We went further down the hallway and entered what had once been another luxury unit; the spacious shell of a livingroom that in its glory would have been carpeted lusciously and kept bright from the mini-sunlamps and the large window-screens that were now cracked black ice. Yvonessa helped the near-death hag into the bedroom, which was high-ceilinged and sizable and illuminated apricot by a rectangle of light that fell out of another door leading to a smaller room; a walk-in closet brightened resplendently with what had to be over one-thousand ashwax candles melted and dripped down into one-another to form a single solid piece of wax under the scorched-black ceiling. One could feel the heat from ten feet outside the closet.

This was the Reliquary of Horsche.

In the center of all these candles was a shabby square of carpet upon which rested twelve white rocks of varying shapes and dimensions, the smallest being about the size of a child's fist. Although they clearly bore some great significance, I could not, at first, discern what they were. Neither could Yvonessa, and this caused me concern. She looked breathless, and I could easily guess the questions she harbored and the conclusions she was drawing, and I thought back to our conversation on the rockpile some hours earlier...

Yes, I wanted her for myself, but not at the cost of her faith, because her faith was a thing pure and true - as deciding a factor to her epitomizing beauty as her physical features themselves, because this faith elevated her beauty and dressed it in modesty, making her something grander than a mere mortal. To what I supposed was the intended effect, she was herself a deistic symbol, imbued with a grace and maturity that could not have been produced by the gloam of the tunnels and Blocs... no, it could have only been forged by the creative design of some higher power; not that merciless pitiless one that seemed to drive me, but something universal and cosmic, like the ancestral echoes of old songs in bygone tongues, the laughing and crying of millions given a sole voice billeted in a vessel worthy of their timeless greatness and golden glory...

I had known not what to expect in the High Temple, but I knew from the outset that we would find no truer god in this place than her.

"Oh, ohh, *ack hack cough cough* He is divine *hack cough* He is infinite in His *ack gag* wisdom *cough cough* and *cough* eternal in His g-glory! *Ack cough* Praise! *Cough cough–*"

Sick Bessie fell on her face before the rocks in reverence. As I moved closer, I deduced that together they made up the pieces of a broken bust. I stared at them. Here, in this diminutive corner, sat all that remained of the Most Holy Godhead.

***

On our return to Bessie's chamber, I caught the eye of the Ratcatcher and tried to size up his opinion of the stones. Sick Bessie had been quite affected by them - she fully believed those few cracked rocks to be Horsche himself. Indeed, she did not even look at the rocks, but rather above them, at a spot of air that would be about head-high on a man of average height, and when she looked at this place she shrieked and covered her face with her hands, as if His glory was too brilliant for her comprehension. Between her coughs she submitted a fervent prayer to the rocks and languished a thousand blessings upon them, with Yvonessa and I both staring slack-jawed in disbelief. After a while, I started to think the whole thing was pretty damn humorous, yet I didn't dare laugh, for fear of further-upsetting the Priestess. As this crying prayer went on, standing in that room became awkward, until eventually Yvonessa helped the other woman back to her feet and assured her that yes, she was awed by the magnificence of Him. Bessie seemed disconcerted by our reactions (or lack thereof) to the shrine and stones, and in the intermittent calms afforded her by her ill health, she put to us desperate questions for which no clear answers could be given. Back in her bedchamber, the familiar voice and presence of the Ratcatcher seemed to put her at ease, and she drifted off straightaway when the High Priestess helped her back into bed.

Shraine had finished Yvonessa's allotted ratmeat, sporting an air of indignation, slighted that she had not touched what was surely his great-grandfather's recipe. As he glowered at her I thought he was about to demand an explanation or apology, but instead he simply put forth a tentative 'well?' and when it became apparent that neither of us were keen to speak, he pushed on, asking: "How's ol' Horsche doing? I think he's seen better days, meself!"

"He didn't seem very put-together." I quipped grimly.

This elicited a chuckle from the Ratcatcher, but the shadow across Yvonessa's face grew darker, compelling us to quell our mirth for her sake.

"Sorry, me bullies… Sure must be a disappointment! I figured you probably didn't know. When Beevil saw, he looked real sad deep inside. I hadn't ever thought about it before, but when he took his leave of us a few days ago, he spoke to me afore he did - didn't have the heart to say nothing to Bessie, but he spoke to me, and I thought how awful of a secret that must be to carry back to the city of his people... walkin about knowin' they're all just prayin' to a pile of dusty rocks! There were times I envied ol' Beevil, but I'll tell you, that was the last time I ever did."

A cyclone of anguish ripped through Yvonessa, and her struggle to find the words by which she might contain or expel the storm was evident on her whole exterior. At long last, the best she could come up with was: "What is this place?"

"The New House of the High Family - not that there's any of 'em left... I suppose now it's just the house of Sick Bessie and Ratcatcher Shraine, since poor Gloobie passed and Beevil went away... say, whatever became of ol' Beevil? Did he ever find his way back to the High City?"

"Gloobie?"

"Shush bully! Not so loud, or Bessie'll hear! Don't let her catch you callin' him by that name. Hates it, she does! 'Course it's not his real name, but it was something he used to say. 'Gloobie, gloobie, gloobie!' Heh... yeah, that was him. He'd blow spitbubbles on the 'B' and that seemed to amuse him greatly, so I started calling him Gloobie, and he liked that too. Just seemed silly to call him 'Your Holiness the Great One' and all that what-have-you as he was hootin' and slobberin' on hisself. All that formality made him uncomfortable - I recker he just wanted a name that suited him."

"Who? Of whom do you speak?"

Shraine went over to Bessie's cot and shuffled around underneath it, rifling through a stack of old parchments until he found the one he was looking for. He did this quietly, for fear of waking Bessie, whose sleep was fitful; every breath a fight, like climbing a rope hand-over-hand. He laid the parchment out before us on the stone ground. The writings were in the Old Tongue, but I could tell from the accompanying diagram that it was meant to be a family tree.

"Beevil was workin' on this. He went through quite a few renditions of it to settle on this one, which is likely as final an account as any that will ever stand. 'Course, Gloobie wasn't much of a conversationalist, and Bessie's memory, like the rest of her, is not what it once was. It mostly comes from meself!"

Shraine said this with pride, and did his best to give us an accounting of the document; the family history of Horsche. He claimed he could read once, yet had not kept in-practice, so Yvonessa had to help him. As was to be expected, the report was patchy, even downright inconsistent in places where Beevil had attempted to compare conflicting testimonies and provide theoretical winners between them. To my admittedly-flawed comprehension, the true history of Horsche and the Zealot theology unfolded as thus:

***

The beginnings of the faith had their roots in the First Uprising; a peacemongering reaction to the unrivaled cruelty and bloodshed of the times. Horsche was around thirty years of age. As his home, H-Bloc, was of infrastructural significance due to its central positioning within the Bloc tramway systems, it was a site of continuous hostilities. Bombings, assassinations, and firefights were accommodated into the routine of daily life. Amidst this chaos, only Horsche and his (at the time) sparse following could wield any measure of control over the Bloc at-large, and this made him a valuable ally for Xirexi, who was by-now years-deep in his conquests. H-Bloc had the strategic potential to turn the tide of the war, and indeed became the deciding factor in both the downfall of the Corporation, and the rise of the Zealots.

After the First, nearly forty years passed before widespread conflict once again became inevitable. Horsche had completed the construction of his High City only a few years earlier, and already overpopulation was threatening all that he had built. Interestingly enough, the High City was originally conceived as a means of escaping H-Bloc, and the damage wrought therein by the First Uprising, which had eradicated all remnants of civilized habitability. Horsche had all but given-up his dream of restoring his birthplace, yet at the ripe age of seventy-two, this fancy was put back within reach, and by another war, of all things. Just as the pacifist-prophet had used civil chaos to build his City, he would now do the same again to reclaim his cradle.

It was the estimation of his architects and mathematicians that the full refurbishment of H-Bloc would take twenty-five years, but once his own private chambers were completed on the upper levels, Horsche and his cabinet of confidants took permanent leave of the High City and ascended to this freshly-established earthly purgatory. Thus, the High Temple was founded, and it was in a single fell swoop that Horsche solved his growing problem of overpopulation, added a fresh echelon to his sect, and solidified himself in his twilight years as the untouchable and unrivaled steward of all humanity. It was now assured that the Zealot theology would stand for centuries, with its aging pioneer henceforth sequestered from his proselytizers and therefore immortalized. Yet one issue still remained...

(The fact may appear obvious to an outsider, as it did to me, that Horsche, although an intellectual giant who had carved an irrefragable mark on the granite tablets of posterity, was still a man - no more or less mortal than the rest of us. I myself had found incredulous the idea that he could still be alive, sitting at the top of some high tower, possibly even basking in Sunlight, until I had spent time in the High City; during-and-after which I will admit that a part of me came to half-believe it. To walk those streets and breathe that clean air, one could not help but place stock in the ideals upon which the whole arrangement was founded... Yet, where I had mere questions, Yvonessa held certainties... and questions can be resolutely answered, either in the positive or negative, whereas a certainty can only be obliterated.)

Elderly and now nearing the end of his life, Horsche was faced with the dilemma of his succession; a matter of critical importance to the continuation and conservation of the faith. He had become a god; revered and worshiped by followers more numerous than even the armies of Xirexi had been in the early days of the First Uprising, and for the faith to remain uncorrupted, his most holy seat would need to be filled by a single trusted ass. Anything less than the absolute regimentation and compartmentalization of control would result in dissent and eventual anarchy, and this Horsche knew well. He, the father of the flock, must appear to live on - if not literally, than through a son whom he could twist and mold into a close approximation of himself; a boy bred solely for sacred duty.

It was the year after his ascent that a decree came from the High Temple establishing the practice of Vestal Election. (Even from the first days of the High City, Horsche always placed a great importance on eugenics, as the practice was amongst his most effective methods of creating distinction between the Zealots and the common residents of the tunnels and Blocs, as it ensured that those born of the High City were all beautiful, and paired so that their offspring might retain the most desirable attributes of their forebears, be these strength, structure of the bones, prolific intelligence, or fertility. There were no whores made pregnant by johnnies, the children of which were invariably dysgenic, with dull minds made duller by druk and dustsmoke - no, there could be only beauty and good speech and fair hair and shapely bodies amidst the Zealot ranks.) Now, after almost eighty years of purported celibacy, Horsche had his High Prophets select for him from this supple and slender crop a single girl of superlative allure; one befitting of He the Most High (and surely Most Wrinkled, by now) to be brought to the High Temple and into his private quarters and bed. Apparently the old dog could still fuck, as the First Vestal bore him a son and two daughters. His son, obviously, was named Horsche.

Unlike the days of yore, in which the High One would feast at the head of a large table with a cabinet of his most trusted advisors; priests, Gunbosses, and warfighters-turned-holymen, now the Most High took his meals in solitude and only conferred with his intermediary, the High Voice. No longer did the great leader of these people walk amongst them. He was rarely seen, always at the topmost balcony of the Bloc, towards which his people had to crane their necks to catch a glimpse of him, forever-unable to behold his face past his low hood, until eventually he receded from the public eye entirely and spent his last years locked away on the penthouse levels, his every hour dedicated to the vigorous indoctrination of his children.

He watched with sharp eyes both of his daughters, as to make a judgment before their first bleeding which would grow to be the more beautiful of the two. Once this decision was reached, the first Holy Voice, a lifetime follower of Horsche surely elated beyond measure to receive the honor, found his elation now overshadowed by dismay when he was entrusted with the task of murdering the High One's eldest (and marginally less-attractive) daughter. It can be assumed that the First Vestal, the poor girl's mother, protested against this to such a degree that it jeopardized Horsche's unbesmirched reputation, so she had to go likewise. It is not entirely clear by whose hand these two killings were carried-out, and this is possibly by design, as the name of the First Holy Voice was lost - or, more rightly, erased - from the Histories. There also exists no record of the death of Horsche himself - not the year, nor the day, nor time...

Amongst the final decrees of the High One was the stipulation that the purity of his Holy Bloodline be protected and maintained. To this end, Horsche II impregnated his sister, who gave him a son and daughter, who would in-turn procreate with one-another when they came of age. These male heirs were cycled into the position of High One at the age of twenty-two, remaining in the godchair until the age of fifty, so as to give the holy station a quality of agelessness. When Horsche II and III reached adulthood, they were presented to the inhabitants of the High Temple with no distinction made between themselves and their fathers.

It was not until Horsche IV that complications of a genetic nature became manifest, as the generations of sibling inbreeding produced offspring plagued by deformities both physical and psychological. Horsche IV had a clubbed foot and pituitary problems, and his sister was a retard. The two of them could not conceive, owing in equal parts to the brother's inability to achieve an erection, and the tendency of the sister to go into violent fits whenever she was made to lie down for it. After years of fruitless attempts, Horsche III was advised by the Second Holy Voice to order the High City Council to elect another Vestal for the purpose of bearing his son a son. This Vestal, after three stillbirths in as many years, managed to deliver a daughter to the High One to-be, and died in the childbirth. Fast-approaching was the time for III to step down and IV to take his place on the Godseat, yet further tragedy stuck, (if indeed it can be thought-of as a tragedy, and not a harsh mercy) when one night, taken by a rare urge, Horsche IV entered his slumbering sister's bedchamber and set himself upon her. She awoke terrified, slipped into one of her fits, and slew her brother with a dinner utensil.

Horsche III was then left with no choice but to remain in the Godseat, aging, hoping the womb of his granddaughter would take his seed. Her usefulness unfulfilled, III disposed of his daughter following the killing of her brother. Unable to live with the grief of losing both her children, the sister (and wife) of III committed Sudoku. Though it would not be made final for over a decade, this was the beginning of the Fall of the High Temple.

By this point, the written accounts were so fragmentary that Shraine the Ratcatcher, fourth of his name, became the primary source of the narrative. Born in the High Temple to his ratcatcher father and Zealot mother, he was sixteen years old when Lawmaker came to H-bloc, yet he claimed he could remember the day as starkly as any in his lifetime, as it was all noise and light and flame. Fewer than two-dozen survived, their escape facilitated by Shraine, who was the only High Temple resident with knowledge of the basement tunnels. Both Shraine's father and Horsche III perished in Lawmaker's incursion, and of the Holy Priesthood, only the High Voice of the time, and the daughter of IV (now pregnant by her own grandfather) survived. The group waited for stragglers, squatting for days in the dark, yet none came. So it was that, many years after it had actually occurred, the death of Horsche was finally mourned, and lumped-in with it was the idea of the demise of the faith at-large, and all it stood for; which, even above love and peace and beauty, was ultimately a controlling interest in posterity.

The survivors of the High Temple wandered lost in the tunnels, as it had been so many years since the Voice had come from the High City that he had forgotten the route. In their starving state they welcomed the ratmeat procured for them by Shraine, and in their camps, arguments over how to best proceed broke out nightly. Fearing the end of the faith, the Holy Voice took it upon himself to ensure that news of the Fall would never reach the High City and those therein. He bore the largest (and perhaps the only) gutjug, and poisoned the water it contained, so that the next day only he, the pregnant princess, and the Ratcatcher remained - the latter only spared so that he might continue to catch rats - and this forsaken threesome found their way to G-Bloc.

As the Princess was due very soon, the Holy Voice decided (against the advisements of his companions) that this final descendant of the High One would be birthed and raised in the dead tower. If the child was male, he would be educated in the customs of his forebears until he was of-age, at which point he would be presented to the people of the High City. No explicit plan was laid-out for the possibility of the child being a member of the fairer sex, yet this proved to be of no consequence, as the child, a hideously-deformed invalid, was born with a dick and a set.

On his ratcatching jaunts, Shraine discovered a passage between G-Bloc and the High City, and although by his own admission he should have fled, he had developed a soft spot for the Princess, and thought that by remaining at her side he might position himself to become her lover. Although he had meant to keep his discovery just between them, the Voice overheard the two planning to make their escape once an opportunity presented itself. From that point forward, the Princess was kept under constant watch, and Shraine could not bring himself to abandon her. For years, the four of them led an abominable existence, lonely and altogether hopeless. As Horsche V matured and grew ever more oafish, his mother (who, at fifteen, was hardly more than a child herself) began to openly detest her wretched spawn, as well as the Voice, who kept her locked away at the summit of that ashen tower. Yet this hatred paled in comparison to that which she harbored for her own existence; and when an unsupervised opportunity came, she opened her wrists with a sharp piece of wire. Although he had not given it to her, this wire had come from one of Shraine's rattraps, and he was therefore held responsible for her passing. The Voice administered upon him a savage beating and threatened him with a hundred kinds of death, but Shraine claimed that as he endured this, he never truly feared for his life, because without him the Voice and the High Child Horsche the Fifth would starve.

The Voice made a trip to the High City (the first in over thirty years) to commission the appointment of a new Vestal. This woman, named Bessecka, was brought up to serve as both the child's mother and eventual lover. Years passed. The Voice fell gravely ill. Shraine laid the blame on the rats, claiming that in G-Bloc they were sickly and their meat didn't taste correct, because whatever they subsisted on down in the rockpiles was toxic, and whoever ate the meat for more than a few years became sick like how Bessie was. (He proclaimed that the sole reason he was so-far unaffected was because he was of a long line of strong stomachs accustomed to ratmeat of all variants and tinged with all manner of contaminants.)

As his last act before his death, the Voice installed his replacement; a High One named Beevil. Beevil and Bessie raised Horsche V, the three of them fed by Shraine, and in the gloom and neverending solitude of the gutted Bloc they wasted away their years attempting to teach the invalid how to speak and act in a manner befitting of a Prophet. When he came of-age, Bessie laid down with him every night, yet failed to conceive. With a sort of sick delectation, Shraine (unprompted) drew a comparison between a coiled rattail and two pebbles for Horsche the Fifth's (or 'Gloobie's') genitals. The prospect of educating the final descendant of Horsche and dressing him up to lead the faith was abandoned, yet the hope that Gloobie might manage to continue his lineage remained...

Other Vestals were elected and sent to bed with the mutant boy, with Bessie in attendance, often in the very bed, coaching the new girls on how to attend to the malformed Holy child, but none of these unions ever yielded results, and, as none of the new Vestals loved Gloobie like a mother, they all grew very quickly to abhor their duties. Most killed themselves, while others fell ill from the ratmeat and passed naturally. One tried to run away, but was caught by Shraine. Beevil made him break her legs. As the years dragged on, Bessie became ill, and the forthcoming arrival of a new Vestal was delayed, as her Pilgrimage was befallen by violence and tragedy... Still, the delinquency of her accession notwithstanding, Yvonessa had indeed arrived like all those before her; eager-and-willing to serve his Holiness in the holiest of ways... yet she was too late. Gloobie always had a flutter in his heartbeat, and his aorta had collapsed on itself only a month before.

With the Holy Line of Horsche ended forever, and Bessie certain to pass in the next few weeks, if not days, Beevil quietly disposed of the body and took his leave of this place. Surely ill himself and standing in the shadow of the reaper's scythe, he had decided to lay eyes on the High City, and on innocence itself, one last time before surrendering his spirit to the Deep.

***

So there it was. There was no longer a High Temple - there was only this sick woman and this obscene little man, both keeping fast the secrets that propped-up the known world. With the realization that there was none more holy than Yvonessa or more worthy than I, a dread pitiful emptiness consumed me. All this noise and pain and life; fucking life, so confined, spent in sleep and waking, walking in familiar safety or else wandering in tunnels that went nowhere, all for nothing. Could it really be so? Did any of it go anywhere? What a cruel and aimless jest...

TWENTY-THREE

We spent days in those dingy units, their silence filled only by the sound of Bessie's bad cough. Yvonessa tended to her tirelessly and the two of us hardly spoke. I worried about her. She kept her hood pulled low at all times and went off by herself in the dark while the rest of us sat around and gnawed at the poisonous yield of Shraine's labor. I kept the Ratcatcher in my sight always, because he had a hungry way about him and panted through his mouth like a dog when he looked at the High Priestess. As close an eye as I kept on him, he kept the same on me in-turn, making by-the-minute estimations of whether or not he had outlived his utility.

I often tried to pull Yvonessa aside and engage her in private conversation about what the two of us should do next, but she would shake me off without a word and take Bessie to go pray to the shattered bust - which the two of them did twice a day, each session often lasting hours. Shraine and I could hear their prayers echoing down the hall, those hellish dead walls of gray that sponged up the feeble light, as we sat in the darkness and dust, chewing the bad ratmeat, of which I tried to eat as little as possible despite my hunger. When Bessie grew too weak to stand, (even supported) I had to carry her down the hall to the reliquary. As I did so, her eyes would sometimes slide half-open, and she would whisper in a strained-yet-joyous tone: "Horsche..." and that rancid green stink would come; not wafting, but instead gusting out of her, as if her whole interior had rotted - even her soul, the reduction of which was hacked-up and excreted in jelly-splatters of the same green shade. At these instances, I turned my head away.

After several days, Bessie was no better. Yvonessa ignored Shraine's cautionary words to let her rest, yet heeded me when

I voiced agreement. Bessie slept in her fitful way for most of the day, but that night she awoke us with delirious screaming and a desperate insistence to be taken to Horsche. The trio of us labored to carry her, because we could tell from the severity of her voice that this would be her last night. Shraine and I left the women to pray and stayed awake, awaiting the inevitable, him looking at me and I at him; the both of us taking turns looking when the other wasn't. We traded no words.

***

In the late morning, Yvonessa returned to the bedchamber alone. She told us that Bessie was gone, and asked the Ratcatcher to show us the supply-stock, if there was one. It was meagre. That being the case, we had no means to give Bessie a proper funeral. Yvonessa made a strong protest against the body being wrapped in the bedclothes and thrown down the liftshaft, but there really wasn't anything else to be done - within hours the stench (already present) would fill the whole floor. Shraine and I rolled up the bony stillness in the stained bedsheets and Yvonessa used a candle from the reliquary to light the wrap. We let the flames grow for a moment before rolling dead Bessie off the edge, and I felt only relief as I put forth my foot and pushed. As the bundle tumbled, the burning sheet came unwrapped and caught the air, separating from the body, which spun into darkness and impacted on the rockpile below with a brittle crack. The sheet floated, glowing and graceful - each time I thought it would crumple and plummet, the air caught it, and it danced and burned, the flames simultaneously fighting the wind and feeding off it. It was a thing both violent and gentle.

***

Yvonessa spent the remainder of that day in the candlelit closet with the stones, lost in prayer. I left her alone for hours, yet went looking for her when the Ratcatcher went to check his traps. My eyes had adjusted to the constant dismal half-light of the oil-lanterns, so the brightness of the many candles in the shrineroom brought on a headache. Yvonessa was knelt before those pieces of rock, her chin to her chest, hands folded in her lap, docile, yet shaking subtly.

"We should speak." I said.

She said nothing and didn't even turn to me. I hadn't seen her face in days.

"There are words to be had between us. Let them be here or in the other room, it makes no difference. Shraine has gone to check his traps, and I would have us speak out of his earshot."

She stood and walked out of the closet, away from the illumination cast out of its door, to a corner of the unit where the weak light of my oil-lantern made our forms move on the walls. She turned and looked me in my face, and I saw her as if for the first time: still beautiful and with proud grace, yet as the shadows fell back from her eyes, I shuddered at the heartbreak, world-break, the furious question of why why why, and the anger at the liars long-dead and therefore unimpeachable for their sins. She, that thing made perfect by a predetermined doctrine of purity and its consequent beauty, which was not contained by a corporeal form alone, but also in a spirit empowered by faith - blind, perhaps, but no less true - oh so true; true right down to the bones of the vessel that bore it... yet faith needs an object, a symbol, ideals towards which to strive, and these coupled with the expectation of a paradisal reward that, in her case, (and perhaps in all cases) had been callously revoked; swapped instead with only a few dusty broken stones. Under her eyes were dark rings and her eyes themselves had sunk back into her head and become red. She had lost weight, which made more pronounced her cheek-and-collarbones, and gone from her hair was its shine, and the ends of it were splitting. She had not eaten or slept in days, and she exuded a tantamount personification of ropeburn. She was still beautiful, yes, but no longer a perfect thing, because her faith itself was no longer perfect, nor even fully intact. Regardless, muddied and broken as her faith now was, it was all she had, and to relinquish it would not only doom her, but all her people; those sole peasants in the history of this underworld to build for themselves a place in which to live in harmony. Truly, all the goodness and hope of humanity had come to rest upon the shoulders of this poor girl at the same moment her entire world had been Sunscorched to ash. I looked at her and felt that I had never loved her more intensely.

"What of our water?" She asked. I produced a gutjug and offered it to her. She weighed it in her hands but did not drink.

"Is this all?"

"There is a place where it leaks out of an old pipe, where the Ratcatcher has set up a filterbucket."

"You've seen this with your own eyes?"

"Yes."

"What of the oil for the lamps?"

"There is a well below, where it bubbles out of a crack."

"You know where this is?"

"Not precisely, but Shraine does."

"Find out."

"Okay."

She reached out in a sudden gesture and took my hand tightly and looked at me hard and sharp and final. "We cannot stay here, but *he* must. What he knows... what he has told us must never be recorded in the Histories. His account must die with him, in this place."

"You are requesting that I kill him?"

"I am. Do it tonight."

"I... I have never killed a person before."

"Once it is done, we shall lie down together."

"Um... w-what?"

She squeezed my hand and took a step nearer, vibrating the air with an intensity that was hard to stand in the field of...

"I shall birth your offspring to be the New Holy Bloodline and rule in the High City. Your firstborn son shall bear the name of He the Most High, and all his life he will be paid the respect that is due that name."

So there it was. I would have slaughtered a multitude had she asked me to do so; women, children, pleading innocents alike, so one half-crazy ratcatcher seemed like a small price to pay... yet I wondered if it was not already too late? I thought of the glint in Quabba's eye, and of Cleopatra in white robes, floating like an infectious pathogen among the Zealots. We are each of us capable of effecting outcomes far more significant than the sum of our actions, yet our very natures represent an inability to contain or assimilate these outcomes beyond our little ends. We are paradoxically desirous of peace and beauty, yet bringers of bile and filth of every ilk; abandoned children marooned on isles of shadow or adrift in oceans of Sunlight; people underground without the spiritual accouterments by the virtue of which we might ascend beyond ourselves...

***

Shraine carried on his person at all times a thin curved blade ideal for gutting rats. It was sheathed on the string that upheld his trousers in his waking hours and clutched in his right hand while he slept. Because of this, I knew that whatever method I selected to end his life, the result would have to be instant. We slept on floormats close together in Bessie's bedchamber, where the floor had been cleared of rubble so that none would trip in the semi-darkness. This meant that I would have to feel out into the dark, beyond the lantern-fishbowl, to find a rock large enough to crush his skull. In doing so, I might make enough noise while shuffling and rummaging to wake him. I could take along a lantern, but Shraine was a soft sleeper, and any disturbances in the light and shadow of the room might wake him as well, so I discarded the prospect of that procedure.

There was another option. His hair was all thick-knotted dreadlocks; decades-old tangled and intertwined ropes of hair into which he wove carved ratbones. To whittle these bits of bone he used a small iron pick that he stashed in his tool-bag, so that he would not dull his knife with anything other than the vital work. I selected a stone, flat on one side and of hideable size, yet big enough to fit in my hand, and I tucked it out of sight by my floormat.

I had a plan.

That night, I laid still and waited for a long time after his breathing slowed and evened before I rose and moved by the lamplight to purloin the pick from his bag, taking care that my shadow never fell upon him, moving at a rate of one inch per hour, or so it felt. My heart pounded in my throat and I felt stomach-sick all the way down to my hole as I knelt beside his sleeping form. His locs had fallen over his face in his sleep and he was skinny and ragged; resting so delicately that I was amazed he had not been roused by the sound of my blood surging through me. As I purloined the pick from his bag and positioned it above his temple, my shadow touched him and it felt like I myself was touching him, and I realized I was trembling. I could not place the tip of the pick against his skin until the last instant - the very millisecond before I drove it home...

I raised the rock high in my right hand, above my head. It seemed so heavy... how could a stone of this size feel thus? For as long as everything until this moment had taken, time now moved so fast; a hundred hours passed with every stifled breath... until I laid the point of the pick against his temple and struck it down with all my force. The strike was square on the flat part of the rock and the pick disappeared halfway into his mess of hair. He jerked in his sleep and quick-like I gave the pick another thump, and it sank deeper, protruding maybe an inch out of his skull.

He didn't die. He came awake, swinging his blade wildly in all directions and screaming at the top of his voice: "I'm blind! I'm blind! Oh! Oh, it hurts!"

I scrambled back away from him, but he heard my movement and came at me, slashing at the air. Blood ran out of his nose and one of his eyes. It was unsightly, yet I hadn't expected him to die proudly...

"Who is it! Who-who-who oh fuck it hurts, who-who oh I can hear you I know you're there oh fuck-fuck-oh-no-no I taste blood oh no what has been done to me no please I beg you please-please-no-please-no-please-no I-I can't yet no-no-no-no please not yet I ack-*abigga scub dargebeth slubba fub agaga nevhi abba* ack-*anozza gubba* no please no no *magabeka—*"

His speech slurred like how one hard off swill sounds, and he was frightened; more frightened than life should hold circumstances to allow. When I was young, Monogatari had told me that if I ever killed someone, I should do it fast and all-at-once. I had known why, but I didn't *really* know until this point, as I watched Shraine draw nearer to my position in the shadows. He would find and open me; gut me like one of his rats, and I would die squealing...

No! I rushed at him like a shot and flung him screaming to the ground, and we struggled for the knife until I got hold of it and slit his throat and saw dark red spread out on the floor. The sound of it I don't care to describe. He struggled and bled and died, and that was it.

I got up and wiped my bloody hands on my halfrobe and cast it off and stood shuddering in my long-drawers, hardly taking even a beat to steady myself before setting off dumbly down the hall, to the shrineroom where the High Priestess Vestal Yvonessa was waiting for me.

***

She looked at me worried and said: "You are hurt."

I became aware of a gash on my arm where Shraine had cut me. My blood shone black in the candlelight as it ran down my wrist and dripped off my fingertips. The Priestess bade me sit beside her on the mat laid in the light before the stones, and she ripped a strip from her robe to bandage me. The cut was deep and would not cease flowing, but after several strips, she made it. I focused intently on the pain and the hot stickiness of the blood congealing, not wanting to think about what had just transpired in the other room... though I did not pity Shraine - he had lived such a wretched life that death was surely a liberation, if not a welcome one.

I laid back on the floormat and tried to empty myself of everything and go to a blank place, yet I was confronted with grandiose ideas that didn't seem to fit in my head, that I could only consider from faraway vantages, so these thoughts could not be made out in-detail, nor could any meaningful conclusions could be reached regarding them...

Yvonessa stood to her full height and faced me. With delicate fingers she unfastened the collar of her robe and let it fall to her feet, revealing spotless flawless beauty ethereal and perfect as sculpted marble. To behold such living beauty in that dead hopeless empty place delivered me proof that I was alive, and although I had never felt so nervous in all my life, when she came to me and touched me I went very calm. She knew what to do; her capabilities as a greenhorn far exceeded mine as a veteran, and I felt her lips and the warm smoothness of her skin, and a trillion electric spots exploded in my vision, foretokening a superlative pleasure that would far-surpass any I had known before, or would ever know again...

***

In the hours of early morning we laid entangled in the arms of one-another, skin salty and slick with our sweat. I was exhausted and felt sleep coming down on me like the weight of the world. As if she could sense this, Yvonessa moved just-so in my arms, to rouse me back from the brink. There had been many words passed between us that night, all in hushed, breathy tones, and now came another whispered question that pushed slumber far away.

"Did you mean what you said to Quabba in the High City? The words of conquest, of war waged against Lawmaker?"

"Truth be told, I do not know."

She rolled to face me, her nose an inch from mine. No joy or comfort offered by heaven could possibly rival that in which I was sunk, and I knew no joy so great as this could possibly endure. I had to face death one manner or the other, either the little death that is sleep, or the larger one that is but submissive acquiescence to the unalterable way of all things.

"Upon our return to the High City, you must make haste on a Holy Pilgrimage to raise your armies. I think it best that you spend extended periods away on your campaigns, to ensure that none guess that you are the true father of the child..."

"Guesses would be made regardless, and I don't mind telling you that the prospect of denying my child for the entirety of his life makes me uneasy."

"Guesses may be made, certainly, but I will set the Elder's minds to rest that the child is the son of Horsche. There can be no question amongst them regarding the child's true parentage. Such is the only way to keep power out of the hands of those like Quabba."

"How could you possibly dispel such questions?"

"I will find the words."

"If any alive can, surely it is you. Yet... what if I do not wish to return to the High City?"

"Where would you go?"

"On."

"To where?"

"To H-Bloc, and possibly beyond."

"You doubt the Ratcatcher's testimony?"

"No, I believe it - Lawmaker surely razed the whole place."

"So what could be gained from going there? It must be like this place; only broken stones and dusty halls, if indeed it still stands at all!"

"I don't like the idea of going back. I have not turned back yet, and I don't think I would like to do so now."

"But there isn't anything beyond this place! The Ratcatcher said the way to H-Bloc had collapsed!"

"He said the way with which he was familiar collapsed. I am certain there is another way; another shaft or passage. There always is."

A silence settled. Yvonessa looked bewildered and upset.

"Is it because of my designs to use the child that you wish to leave me so soon after our union, or did I fail to meet your expectations in some other way?"

"Neither of those."

"Then what is it?"

"I am no Gunboss, Yvonessa... no cunning politician nor hardened warfighter. I have none of the education in the Histories and Zealot Customs that you have. I do not feel that I'm suited to lead an army of the Holy City, and I will not build my power upon a lie that would force me to keep my own child at a distance and see him raised up a spoilt prince with no knowledge of his true heritage... and this lie you suggest is so easily foundered, without unsurpassable measures taken to guard the secret. Beevil served your people well in that regard for years, yet who shall fill his shoes? It was meant to be I, but I don't mean to fill any shoes other than my own. Such is all a man can do in this world."

"You're shaking."

"No I'm not... am I?"

"You are."

"It's just tiredness. And passion. Kiss me. You are more than I ever dreamed of. You are Sunshine."

"Will you promise me something?"

"As best I can."

"If you go on and find nothing, will you return to me?"

"I will find something."

"How can you be so certain?"

"I always find something, eventually. Some other cause to take up... you should know this. I am the Sinner Unwhipped, and I shall find my way to something else. I don't know why I was chosen to make it this far, but my path will not end at the stones of that broken bust. There is still something grander than those. You thought Horsche to be a god, yet he was only a man - a great man, yes, but flawed as any man has ever been. I've met many great men and seen them all fall to their flaws sooner or later. Where is Gordyume? Where is Lawmaker? Who is the true God of the Sun? He must exist. He must! The ancient etchings on the cavewalls and the construction of the tunnels implies, no, *proves* the existence of something more! Because we are underground, we cannot see, but in the Old Times our forefathers saw and understood plainly the things that to us appear so incomprehensibly vast, and they tried to pass down that understanding to us, but either they or we failed, somewhere along the line..."

"If you wish to understand, cast yourself into the Deep. That is the only way."

"One must climb skyward to meet God, not fall down."

"You think Lawmaker is God?"

"He is something."

"Not a god."

"He is moreso a god than Horsche! How can you doubt such after witnessing him at Hearthstone? What other god so plainly demonstrates his force and fury? Even if Gordyume fills the whole abyss, has he ever manifested himself to come swooping out of the darkness to strike terror in the hearts of men?"

"Lawmaker was a tool of the Corporation, nothing more."

"The Corporation was broken generations ago. It stands no longer, yet Lawmaker still presides over all. What defines God, if not the tangible influence of his power?"

"Lawmaker's power is of this world, not the one beyond. In that, he is set apart from authentic godship. Horsche knew Gordyume, and his doctrines live on through his people; his loyal subjects; Beevil, Bessie, and yes, even that sloven rat-catcher kept him alive and built history around him, guarding him from that which threatened to make his death final."

"I wish to find something that stands as such without the need of propping-up."

"I would rather you come back to the City with me."

"Are you saying that to deter me from pressing on to H-Bloc, for fear of what I might discover there?"

"No. After the things we have seen and heard in this place, I simply suspect that I shall feel quite alone in the High City. I think that, without you, I shall feel very alone for the rest of my life..."

"I love you. Love was meaningless to me, naught but an empty syllable, until you entered my life and taught me its meaning. I love you above all else, Yvonessa... yet you do not love me as such. I do not demand that you try, nor do I even wish you to. It is your commitment to greater things that makes you pure, like Sunlight in our subterranean world. Only a god would be worthy of your love, and I tell you that no man has ever breathed that stands even half as worthy as you deserve - I least of all. I am low and simple, yet you smiled upon me."

"You are not low. You are of Holy and Royal Blood, and your descendant will restore the High Temple to its former glory. Already I can feel your seed growing within me. I am yours and you are mine."

"I love you."

"Then let us make more love."

"Yes."

TWENTY-FOUR

We dressed and divvied up the scant remaining supplies, and I used a straight piece of rebar and cloth from my bloodied halfrobe to make a torch. We did not make any sort of parting observance or intimation when we left the shrineroom and its attached bedchamber; we simply left it all behind.

We made our way back down the tower. At the bottom of the scaffolding, we both pushed against one of the supports until it gave and the whole thing came down in a heap. I accompanied Yvonessa down the rockpiles to the corridor that led back to the High City, and it was here that we said farewell. I watched the dot of her oil-lantern recede into the darkness until it was gone.

I explored aimlessly for a while, picking my way over the ruins and finding nothing. Eventually I stopped and set my torch upright between two stones and sat before it. I was cold and all alone and indeed felt ill after days of eating the tainted ratmeat. I put my hands out to the flames and watched the ashwax-covered cloth melt slowly and drip down the ribbed metal. The darkness was all around me. My arm ached - the cut hadn't closed properly, and the climb down the scaffolding had made it bleed past the rags that Yvonessa had dressed it with. I had bled a lot. I wondered if I would bleed to death by myself in the rubble. No... I would press on... So I tore what remained of my drawers to rags and selected from these the cleanest to redress my wound as best as could be done one-handed. The fire-warmth felt good against my nakedness. Then came a spell when the loneliness became overwhelming, and a big sadness came encroaching out of the purple dark, and I wept pitifully...

When the tears stopped, I took it out of my satchel. Yes, I still had it. I never lost it even for a second. I had not taken it out in what felt like a long time, and the shape and weight of it brought me a strange reassurance. It was so impeccably smooth... I held it to the torchlight and watched the stuff inside stick to the glass and spread out in odd patterns veinlike and hexagonal. They had made the Deep liquid and bottled it. To hold that little object felt spiritually cathartic. It was ancient and unbreakable and untarnished; a steel vial containing a demonic essence of some sort, or fuel that, when exposed to oxygen, would burn at ten-thousand degrees without ever extinguishing. I didn't know exactly what it was, but it was mine. I had borne it quietly a great distance. I didn't understand the thing, yet I knew it was capable of doing something permanent to me, and perhaps to the world. That black liquid was so black, blacker-than-black; just the tiny amount of it utterly blacked-out the torchlight, and it was only when I held it at an angle and let the liquid all flow to one end of the cylinder that I could see the flames shining through the microscopic patterns made by the stickiness of the stuff. The steel shell never warmed, no matter how tightly I enclosed it in my palm, and it would not collect dust, and it was hydrophobic to an extreme degree, and its weight was disproportionate to its size. Whatever adamantine material had been used for its construction I could not identify, nor could I recall any other steel I had ever seen that resembled it even halfway. I held it in my hand and looked at it for a while, until I fell asleep bare-assed against the cold stone.

***

I was awoken not by noise, but by pneumatic disturbance; a presence, something very near to me, watching me, active, scurrying over the stones. I snapped up and saw that the torch was almost burned-out, the flame only a tiny fluctuating bluish globe. My arm hurt like a dull needle in the dickhole, but the pain faded fast as adrenaline flooded my system. Whatever it was was inhuman. I listened hard. The miniscule noise of its feet made clear that it had four legs, if not six or eight or twelve. As I held my breath, I could make out yips and hisses in the dark...

It was the Lizard, come to find me, stalking just beyond the perimeter of the torchlight. I seized the torch and chased the noise up a nearby rockpile, and the Lizard retreated, always just out-of-sight, save for the occasional glimpses I caught of its spiny tail slithering over the blocks.

I followed the creature until it disappeared into a narrow space between two large stones. The crevice was absurdly claustrophobic, yet just large enough for me to squeeze into. Of course. I sighed and went headfirst into the shaft. The thin smoke from the torch began to water my eyes, so I stoved it out on a rock. A burst of sparks flashed and I was put into total darkness, all but trapped, following only my ears. It was narrow as mama-get-the-fuck-out and the sides scraped my elbows and forearms, yet still I crawled, hunched down on all-fours, hoping that the Lizard had not lured me here to kill me and taking morbid comfort in the fact that even if the Lizard did not kill me, and I became trapped or bled out in this space, my body would not decay slowly to dust, as that vile creature would surely feast upon my fresh flesh.

***

Back home in Z-Bloc, when confronted with emotional despondency or turmoil, my first reaction was always to get to the grindstone and pick up some extra HydroElectric shifts. There was no sense in sitting around feeling sorry for myself, no sir, and I wouldn't go to the Bronco unless I was in a good stable mood, because it was so easy to have one's mood spoiled there. Yet, the compartmentalization of these hurts left them largely ambiguous in both cause and effect, so that I couldn't tell how big they actually were, or how many things they were connected to...

I had lived a loner's life. The streetborn urchin with the good card and the good job, and this distinction mismatched me, because all the other streetrats grew up to be whores or killers. My friends just so happened to become good ones. Nobody was ever consigned to oblivion in the Bloc, because the megastructure fed off us - we were cells of its body, individual-yet-codependent, yet maybe I was the cancerous one, because precious-few of the other cells ever invited me to their private gatherings or into their beds. My life was a constant uphill climb of finding friends, or someone to fuck, and keeping them around. Perhaps they felt I didn't reach out to them in the ways that had been agreed-upon as conventional, and therefore assumed I didn't want their petty companionship or fleeting romance, but I did... I really did, but I was so worried about making them comfortable with me that I never stopped to consider if I was comfortable with them. I was often ill-at-ease. Perhaps I thought myself unworthy of a seat at the table of normalcy? I had never held confidence that those 'happy' people - blissfully-ignorant or else imbued with a power like that of Gordyume himself - would like me... or was it *me* who did not like *them*? Did I walk with a boulder-sized chip on my shoulder; the expectation that they should approach me first? Were they greater or less than I? Why should I go out of my way if none of them ever did? Did their thoughts run on a similar trajectory? Are all of us locked in this selfsame cycle, and I had to be the one with the boldness to break it? And if so, from what part of myself could I possibly summon such courage? What would I say? For all that I had seen and done and endured, I never felt as though I had much to say to another person. 'Hi, I like the way the light catches your hair. I want to be your friend, but I am fragile. I think you have a nice form; strong hands, or a fine face, but for fuck's sake I don't want to fuck you - not yet, at least - I just want to talk... Let us begin at the conversational antecedent of why you didn't approach me first...'

There were times when I thought that I wouldn't care if everyone else in Z-Bloc perished; all those strangers-but-not, those faces I grew up amongst and saw daily, few of whom had ever shown me love or sex or money... but when they did all actually die, I missed them a great deal.

It seemed like Kassie and Monogatari possessed these fantastic gifts, and I had to watch from the other side of an invisible, impenetrable fence as they got to play with them. I had thought that I loved Kassie from the day I first learned what the word meant, but I could never have her, because I was too weak, or too kind, or possibly just too *present*, and therefore I presented no risk or reward. I was always where it was easy to find me. Monogatari was uniquely-great, and not in the way that it was well-agreed-upon that he was. My relationship to him was what I imagine friendship with a genius is like - perhaps they amaze the world with their virtuosity, but you simply know them as a friend and can sit and talk with them, and when you do, you find that they don't want to talk about 'genius' things, they want to talk about druk and the times people said or did funny things while drinking it. Still, I looked up to the man - he became larger-than-life to me; perhaps the only truly great man I've ever known, which is why I regarded it as a personal betrayal when he stopped being himself. He was strong and mean and fast, yet when he came up against a power he couldn't vanquish with his fists, it broke him, because he had never known anything greater than himself, and when the Deep speaks, oh yeah doggy, we hear that soundless voice... and I guess he didn't like what he heard. It took something from him, whereas I felt like it added to the sum of all my parts. Then, like some vain theatrical fabulist, I had to start talking to those bosses; the Mayor, Poppa, and the whole mess of them in the High City, (and the High City was indeed a mess - a whole lot of knowledge about where we've been, yet precious-little about where we're going) and although I truly encountered a tranquility that cannot be flippantly dismissed as empty, I think that only ideas are pure, and once they come down to earth we muddy them up with our filth and use them as inane demonstrations of our self-attributed worth... and ideas themselves hold no quantitative equity. There is no man who can say he was the first to think of this-or-that, because there stands no way of knowing such for certain.

***

As I crawled through that constricted hole, I wondered if I was in my grave already, and I marveled at the convenience. The Lizard would make its intermittent chitters to reassure me of its presence, but I didn't consider the creature as company because, to be entirely honest, I am not certain that it actually existed - it might have been a communal hallucination; something scummy inside of us made manifest, so that we could find our way in the dark. We are driven by a compulsion to dig forever deeper, and why shouldn't we? Others did. Were they also chaperoned by creatures of unnatural birth? And what are we ourselves, if not creatures of unnatural birth? We, who worship the Sun that we have never seen and carve out places for ourselves where the machinations of our forefathers still half-function... was this the design circumscribed by whatever force, be it willful or arbitrary, that created us? Did I want anyone here with me, or did I fancy my solitude? Did I wish that I had been born in the High City and raised like Yvonessa, to be something spotless and faithful, or did I appreciate the scurrilousness of my early days with Kassie? Was it better to burn out like Monogatari, in a brilliant flame of violence, or like Gloobie; the quiet end of a royal line, the final felling of an empty ideal?

***

I crawled for a long time. Hours. The shaft seemed to be going at an upward angle. Weak and bleeding, I shimmied on my elbows until the space widened and I knew from its noises that the Lizard had halted and expected me to crawl past it. As I did, my skin rubbed against those godforsaken scales... and then the tunnel opened into a larger space in which I could stand, so I did, fatigued and nude and consumed by an empty astonishment - not hopelessness, more just a numb feeling of wow.

Everything was dim, yet not completely dark. As best as I could tell, I was standing in a linear hallway, and faroff down it was light. I walked towards this light and it didn't seem to become brighter until I came out into a vast chamber, and into the light itself, blazing in a single beam through a crack high at the top of a ruined megastructure; brilliant blinding scintillating holy yellow light beaming straight downward and hitting the wall.

It was the Sun.

It had to be. I was looking upon a fissure in our world:

the Sun beyond cutting through a break in reality and shining so bright that it made me cry. I squinted and put a hand up to block out the luminescence as I walked into the open concourse. The cleft in the top of the Bloc-shell was small, but the Sunlight poured through fulsomely nonetheless. I looked long and hard at it.

H-Bloc had been gutted in a fashion similar to G. All the floors and apartments had been torn down, so that only the outer walls remained, yet here there were no rockpiles or rubble. Every surface had been glassed and scorched black, the stones crushed to sand. My footsteps fell soft on the floor and I could see a hundred-million particles twirling in incoherent pirouettes in the Sunbeam as I walked under it, to the middle of the great room, staring up in awe at the otherworldly sheen... until it was suddenly obstructed.

The shadow of a great steel wing fell over my face.

Lawmaker stretched himself out from his adumbral perch halfway up the tower, and his wings had a dull shine in the light. He was huge and tarnished; the plates of him creaking and groaning with his movements as he turned his beakish face towards me and with a single flap of his wings soared out and settled epically before me, powderfine ash puffing up in clouds about his talons, which, although rusted, still came to razor-sharp points regardless. I was made tiny in his presence; he towered at five times my height, his wings stretched out sixty feet on each side, and all the steel pieces of him moved together as he took a step towards me, and another step, until he blotted out the Sun.

He spoke. His first words were in a garbled ringing voice of such stentorian volume and horrendous tone that I threw my hands up to cover my ears. Then came a series of rough, distorted scritching noises; a sort of harsh coughing, and then real, true speech in the Old Tongue. Despite my poor comprehension, the resonance of the words and the way they filled that empty place made their meaning as plain to me as the Daylight I had just beheld.

"*HAND ME MINE.*"

I held up the Battery, which I had carried since the tunnels without ever once letting it out of my arm's reach. It was all I had to offer, save the bloodied rags that bound my wound. It was all I had to give, and I had borne it far while maintaining its secrecy, never letting on that I had possession of it. Lawmaker bent low and put an eye near me; a giant bulbish steel mesh, and then came more hissing and a repetition of those guttural words from the squawkbox in his neckplate.

"*HAND ME MINE.*"

I clutched the Battery to my chest with a closed fist. I didn't want to give it to him... He held out a grasping claw and beckoned me closer, and I took a tentative step as he drew himself up tall, his wings bent behind-and-above him, rusted and creaking, yet still magnificent with the blazing halo of Sunlight behind him... and then he moved down towards me. I stumbled back in fear as he knelt slowly, dropping one knee to the ash floor, and then the other, and then crouching facedown, his back arched in a curve, arms past his head in a prostrate pose. His wings went up high above me and I could see the Sunlight shining between the feather-blades. He was breathing slowly and did not budge an inch. Then became audible the rattling of his internal machinery, which culminated in a pronounced clank at which I jumped in surprise. The noise came from the back of his head, at the base of his neck, as two steel plates shifted outwards from an interlocked position to reveal a third narrow piece of metal that, unlike the rest of him, was brushed clean and shone without any trace of rust. This strip of armor slid upwards with a metallic siss.

I forced myself forward, between his outstretched talons, close enough to touch him, yet even from this position I could not see into the opening in his armor. I moved closer, now inches away from the slow-breathing steel giant. My heart was pounding as I placed a clammy hand on his shoulder-joint. He did not stir. The Sun above was warm, but he was icy-cold. I gripped his shoulder-plate and pulled myself up to peer into the back of his skull. Inside was a compartment that housed a small steel cylinder - a Battery exactly like the one I clasped...

All this time it had been clear to me that the Lizard had put me on a path to Lawmaker, and now I gleaned certainty of the purpose for which it had done so. Lawmaker's seeking of the creature served as proof of its novelty and importance; a beast with the ability to live beyond the eye of God; perhaps the first thing to exist in our world with such a privilege, yet it could not stand directly against him. It must have been aware that I had the Battery, as if it could smell it, or, if not the Battery itself, perhaps my innermost reasons for harboring it, which were unclear even to me... or maybe it could sense the liquid; that stuff which had surely destroyed lives, perhaps even entire civilizations... Although it was miniscule in volume, I knew that whatever that black liquid was, it was corrosive, devastative, the essence of bombs and plagues... and if the creature could process such a sentiment as hope, it hoped that I would now banish Lawmaker, and his influence, from this earth forever...

I reached into the compartment and seized the Battery and twisted it clockwise. It turned a full rotation smoothly and clicked and came free. The gigantic form of Lawmaker gave a sharp twitch as I pulled it out of him. There was a groan from deep inside his hulking metal body and his wings jerked. For an instant, I was assured of immediately-forthcoming death, yet the wings grinded against their rust and folded to settle dormant. Lawmaker fell asleep, or possibly he died. Had I killed him?

The instant I had removed this second Battery from the valve, the end of it clicked shut in a blink and sealed itself in such a way that it now fully resembled mine, yet with one substantive distinction: as I held it up to the light and peered into the little glass window, I found that, in this cylinder, there was no black liquid. I shook it good and peered again and still none appeared. It was empty. Spent.

The one I carried was nearly three-quarters full.

The stuff that powered Lawmaker, the awesome enforcer of Corporation Authority. In my generation, there were those who didn't even know that the Corporation had once ruled, yet we all knew Lawmaker - there was not a soul under earth who didn't tremble in the shadow of his wings and tell stories of him to frighten children. We were his subjects, unloved and sometimes victimized, yet never quite abandoned. He had killed more of us than any Uprising, and had long-outlived his creators, yet still upheld their cause, the utter irrelevance of which was lost on him. He was merciless, yet had never been known to be cruel, and he alone was revered as a God by all, because unlike all the other gods that were peddled like wares and trinkets in the Blocs, he left us no choice but to fear him, and to fear him from your first day was something each of us knew intrinsically and never needed to be taught...

I held in my hand the power to set free generations from fear, but what was kept at bay by that fear? What unimaginable evil lurked down in the Deep, down from whence the Lizard came crawling? With Lawmaker dead, would we uncover creatures more malevolent and bloodthirsty than could be dreamt-up by our wildest unbridled imaginations? We are underground and cannot fly the Deep, and therefore we have no way of knowing what we are sheltered from by he whose name we curse. Our world had never known itself without Lawmaker, so who is to say if it would be better or worse?

Had Lawmaker breached the wall of the Bloc so that he could enjoy the Sunlight? I lifted my eyes skyward. It was bright - so bright that it hurt to look at, and it speckled my vision when I turned away and shut my eyes. I held the Battery to the crack, thinking that the inky blackness in that little window surely could not hold back the Sun itself, yet as I framed the fissure in that window and shut one eye and once again tilted the Battery to such an angle that the liquid flowed to obstruct the light, no trace of illumination broke through...

The Lizard hated the light and could not speak. Lawmaker wanted to kill the Lizard, and I suppose the adverse applied, and it was (for the time) accomplished... Yet, with a simple motion of my hand, I could bring him back newer and more powerful than before, perhaps replenished to strike terror in the hearts of my child's children. Would he remember me if I resurrected him? Or would he awake just as icy and expressionless as he was dead, and with unfeeling eyes look upon me heartlessly before cutting me down?

Horsche had risen as the Corporation fell, yet had either

done us any good? Would the Lizard eat us, or would we tame it and breed it with some other hideous supernatural varmint and rear its wicked offspring to further our ambitions?

Would the world be better without Lawmaker?

Did the Lizard mean to devour us all?

By killing the Ratcatcher, I had ensured the survival of an ancient and fading faith, and had restored a long-dead god from the shame and disrepair of the grave, ensuring that he would live on unblemished by his tenure there...

I had resurrected one God. Did I owe the world another?

I had saved God and killed Lawmaker.

I looked up at the Sun streaming through the rift in the stone. The angle of it was shifting, moving downward at an almost-imperceptibly slow rate. It was coming towards me.

I had saved God and killed Lawmaker, but I could reverse these...

If I wanted to...

Should I?

THE END.

www.ingramcontent.com/pod-product-compliance
Lightning Source LLC
Chambersburg PA
CBHW070919260626
47162CB00007B/2724